For Don and Pam Cryan, my legal friends,
and Tim Rice, my musical friend, in gratitude

1

There was, he decided, something peculiarly comforting about cornflakes with hot milk and tried to remember the last time he had eaten them. In his junior houseman days, was it? When he would fall out of bed, aching for more sleep, to sit over the breakfast table, bleary-eyed and half paralysed with fatigue, trying to work up enough energy to get himself through the long frantic day that lay ahead? Certainly he had eaten huge breakfasts in those days when he had been thin as well as over-worked. Now black coffee and wholemeal toast were all he allowed himself, and the bare minimum of that. At almost fifty a man had to be careful if he wasn't to flood his heart with fatty acids and his arteries with atheroma.

He chased the last spoonful of soggy cornflakes round his plate and ate them, trying to concentrate on the here and now, the taste of the food, the smell of the little café, the sight of the curly edged posters of over-developed females grinning inanely over their top-heavy breasts, even the bleat of Radio One, grinding out its eternity of pop.

But it didn't work. The cornflakes weren't comforting after all, reminding him as they did of other times, the smell of sour, elderly coffee was nauseating, and no matter how he concentrated on the messages being delivered to his brain by his senses, thoughts of the day ahead pushed at his awareness with an insistence that was almost physical in its intensity.

The man behind the counter was involved in an acrimonious argument with the only other customer about the relative merits of Queen's Park Rangers and Arsenal and barely looked at him as he took his money; for a moment he wanted to lean over the counter and shake him, to make him pay attention to him, treat him as though he were a real person, to say, 'I am Professor Sampson Stermont, and how dare you ignore me?' And grimaced a little at his own foolishness and escaped to the street outside.

The clock over the jeweller's on the other side of the street stood at nine-fifteen; he sighed and thrust his hands deeply into his overcoat pockets. He had not meant to get here so early. He had promised himself he would arrive at the court late, would slip in quietly after it had all started so that no one would notice he was there. But he had woken at half past six and been totally unable to stay in bed, and even more unable, after the years of living his life against the clock, to linger over bathing and shaving. Even when he had found himself on the road before eight o'clock, he had hurried; to dawdle in the slow lane, to fail to overtake other traffic at every opportunity, was quite beyond him. Which meant he had now been in Fleet Street for over an hour and still had even more time to kill before half past ten and the start of the judicial process.

The street was bustling now. Vans and cars, taxis and lorries clogged up the turnings into Chancery Lane and Fetter Lane, the lumbering red buses dropped their clusters of secretaries and shop girls – too early yet for journalists – and the first of the tourists were wandering purposefully, looking for the Cheshire Cheese and Dr Johnson's house. He stared at it all, letting the hurrying passers-by eddy round him, trying to see it through a tourist's eyes. It was supposed to be glamorous, a street of drama and excitement, but all it offered him was grime and noise and the stink of diesel. Except for a moment, when he was briefly a child again, standing staring up a great black glass building, hearing his father telling him portentously, 'The hand-maiden of capitalism lives in there, my boy. The bastard daughter of the gift of tongues, the yellow journalism that rots the workers' wills and poisons their minds, that's who lives in there –' Dad, with his fancy words and rolling phrases; he hadn't thought of him for years.

A gust of wind blew rubbish round his ankles and he shivered and turned up his coat collar. He certainly couldn't stand here until the court was in session. A walk; that was all he could do. And it would perhaps burn off some of the rubbish food he'd eaten in that foul café.

Across the road, past Bouverie Street where the first of the great paper lorries was filling the narrow entry, past the Printer's Pie, the ice-cream shop, El Vino's. Ahead of him the street curved and opened out and he could see the bulk of the Law Courts rising white and blank in the thin March sunshine. Too early, too early; and he turned sharply left, under the over-hanging buildings, into Middle Temple Lane.

For the first time since opening his eyes in bed at half past six he felt comfortable. The peace of the Temple slid over him as he walked down past the old buildings into the tree-filled quietness. The church, stolid and grey, seemed to welcome him; he went in and slipped into a pew and stretched his legs under the one in front, a little amused at his choice of resting-place. He, a lapsed Jew, in a church! But it was tolerant of his presence, so he would sit here and think and perhaps doze a bit; he would think of his patients, of the problem of who was to be appointed to the registrarship of the country branch hospital, and whether young Agnahotri's undoubted brilliance would get him over the patients' deep-dyed loathing of bleedin' Pakis, and whether he really wanted to accept the offer of the Oxford job. Lots to think about, all of which would keep his mind off the day that stretched ahead, full of threat and yet so empty of landmarks to which he could pin himself. If only he knew what would be likely to happen. If only he knew how the thing would be done. But he knew nothing of the law and its processes. Only what he had seen in films, long ago in the days when he would go to the Roxy or the Royalty or the Regal and sneak in through the push-bar-to-open doors, so that he could save his money to buy an ice cream for whichever of them had come with him. And films didn't teach you much. Not really –

NOVEMBER 1942

'*When you wish upon a star,*
Makes no difference who you are,
When you wish upon a star,
Your dreams come true . . . .'

'You don't know anything,' she said disgustedly. 'Just sitting there like that! You don't know *anything*.'

'I know as much as you do! Just try me. Go on, ask me questions –'

'Oh, you're soft, you know that? Of course you can answer questions! Anyone, even you, can answer *questions*. The bloody Memory Man can answer questions. It's not that I'm talking about.'

He looked at her sideways, trying not to show how shocked he was by her easy way with swear words. He'd never even heard his father say that word and Hetty was only twelve and she said it as though it didn't matter. She was sitting with her arms folded staring out over the seats with her chin held high and her nose wrinkled in what was clearly meant to be disdain.

'Well, what are you talking about, then?' He leaned back in his seat trying to pretend to be as disdainful as she was, the way he'd seen some of the older boys behave. He wasn't very good at it, and looked at her profile again, and caught her looking at him slyly, and she giggled and nudged him with her shoulder.

'I think you're pretending. That's what I think. I mean, you asked me to come to the pictures with you, didn't you?'

'Er – yes. Yes; of course I did.' He tried to remember, and couldn't quite. They'd been in the school playground, the one the boys and girls had shared ever since the other one had been bombed, and anyway, with so many kids evacuated there was lots of room for them all in the old infants' playground. He'd been sorting out old cigarette cards his father had given him, with an audience of three other admiring boys, and she'd come and joined in, and he wasn't quite sure how it had happened but there had been a bit of talking and nudging and then the other boys had gone off and he'd ended up giving her half the cigarette cards and promising to meet her outside the Roxy at half past one on Saturday. 'Yes,' he said again, 'of course I did.'

'Well, then!' she said triumphantly. 'You must've known something about it, or you wouldn't't've asked.'

The lights began to go down again as the curtains opened on to *Movietone News* and she wriggled in her seat so that her bare leg was against his; he could feel her sock rubbing against the part of his shin where his own socks ought to be, and weren't, since he'd lost his garters and you couldn't get elastic for new ones in wartime, and at once he knew and felt his face go crimson in the darkness. And also felt a sensation in his belly that he usually only got at night when he was almost asleep and thinking of things he shouldn't.

Experimentally he moved his hand until it rested against her leg, and at once her fingers were there, warm and a little sticky from the acid drops he'd given her, entwining themselves in his and holding on hard. Once more he looked sideways at her and

10

it was as though he wasn't there. She was sitting bolt upright staring at the screen, her face absorbed, just as though she didn't know what her fingers were doing and how he kept getting that same wicked feeling. But of course she did know. He was certain of that, or at least he thought he was. As certain as he'd been of anything since he'd first met her, and that wasn't much.

The news passed, with soldiers making thumbs-up signs at them and the sing-song voice going on about how British Guts Will Show the Hun, and there were some cartoons which he liked a lot, even though he could never understand what Donald Duck was saying, and then the big film started, and his attention snapped back to his fingers, still held tightly in Hetty's grip. He frowned at the screen, trying to get involved with it the way he usually did, but it was dull. A soppy man everyone was trying to cheat out of some money was in court and lawyers were jumping up and down and asking questions. A silly film. He didn't know why she'd wanted to see it.

Again he looked sideways at her, and now he realized that she was no longer sitting bolt upright but had swayed a little so that she was sitting very close to him, her cheek so near he could feel its warmth. She was still staring at the screen in apparent absorption, but he knew now what was expected of him, and moving as carefully as he could untwined his fingers and then slid his arm behind her and round her waist.

That had been the first time. The first time he had sat in the half darkness filled with sensations he could hardly contain with her bony body pressed hard against his and the arm of the cinema seat pressing painfully against his ribs. The first time, and in lots of ways the best time, even though later on she'd give him other surprises and other sensations.

When the film was over she made him go out of the exit by the lavatories, and he was genuinely mystified.

'What for?' he demanded. 'It's easier to go out to the front, and you can look at the pictures of what's coming next week.'

'You can look at them any time, without paying. You do what I say, and you won't have to pay ever again. Come *on*.'

He'd followed her, just managing to keep her blue coat in view, and then they were in the dim corridor that led to the exit doors, with its thick smell of lavatory and Jeyes Fluid.

'See?' she said. 'Next time you want to go to the pictures here, all you have to do is wait outside till someone comes out of this door and nip in under their arm.'

'That's stealing!' he said after a moment. 'That's not honest.'

She stood there in the dimness as the last few people pushed past them on their way out, grinning at him. Her hair was tied in tight ugly little bunches that stuck out over her ears, and her eyes were almost like slits because her grin was so wide. Her teeth looked big and very white in the darkness and it was as though they were jeering at him too, and he felt a surge of anger, suddenly. 'It *is* stealing. I wouldn't do no such thing, I wouldn't. That's the sort of thing real guttersnipes does, my dad says –'

'Your dad? Your dad's a conshie, so what does he know about what's honest? He says it's against his conscience to go killing people in the army, so he stays at home all safe while others gets killed for him. I don't reckon he's much of a one to talk about being honest.'

At once the sick rage began to rise in him. Was there to be no end to it? After three years of it from the kids in the parks and at school, after the way the neighbours ostentatiously spat on the ground when any of the family went by, after the countless fights he'd had, was she going to start it all over again?

'He's a Communist an' all, 'nt he? I know all about him – so don't you go telling me what's honest and what – no, don't get mad –'

Her hand shot out and seized him above the elbow as he turned to go and her fingers were as sharp as a cat's claws; he tried to pull away, but her grip only tightened.

'I didn't mean to make you mad,' she said and there was a conciliatory note in her voice now. 'Honest, I didn't. I think your dad's got twice the sense of anyone round here, and that's the truth of it. Honest! Any bloody fool can get himself killed. Your dad won't. I bet he's a smashing dad to have.'

He stopped pulling away. It hurt too much. 'Better'n yours, that's for sure. He wouldn't let me act like a guttersnipe.'

'He's got to be better'n mine.' she said and let go his arm. 'Mine's dead.' She turned and pushed the bar on the big exit doors and a little shaft of light sprang across the dusty floor. 'Him and my mother. Both dead. I'm an *orphan*.'

She looked back at him over her shoulder and there must have been an expression in his face that spoke to her because she pulled the door shut again and came and stood very close in front of him. 'Thank you for bringing me to the pictures, Sammy,' she said softly. 'It was smashing.'

'That's all right. It was – it was a good film.'

'It wasn't. But it was nice being with you.'

He blinked, trying to work out what he was supposed to do or say next. She was too fast for him. The rage she had conjured up had been doused by horrified pity and now both of those feelings were being swamped again.

'You can kiss me if you like.'

He took hold of the last shreds of his self-respect. 'I'll let you know when that is.'

'Eh?'

'When I feel like it. I'm goin' home. You'd better go home an' all. Your – they'll be worried –' He pushed the door open firmly and walked out, blinking, into the dwindling afternoon. 'It's nearly blackout time.'

'No one'll be *worried*,' she said, and kicked the door closed behind her, and stood beside him on the pavement with her hands in her pockets and staring at him from under her eyebrows. He noticed for the first time how straight they were, almost as if they'd been drawn with a ruler, and he kept his gaze fixed on them. That was easier than looking her in the eye.

'Someone'll wonder where you are, though, won't they? Everyone's got to be in by blackout time.'

She laughed suddenly, and it sounded like a grown-up, he thought, and let his eyes meet her gaze for a moment before they slid away. 'My sisters'll wonder, I dare say, but they won't *worry.*'

He lingered, much as he wanted to be away, running down Mare Street to Morning Lane, and home to the warmth of mum and dad and the cluttered kitchen. 'Why won't they worry?'

She shrugged. 'Sisters don't.'

'Are they older than you? Do they look after you? Now you're – since your –' He swallowed. 'You know.'

She shook her head and laughed again, that thin adult sound that seemed so strange and yet so interesting. 'They're younger'n me. I'm the oldest. I'm the one who leads them. If

13

they're late, or playing up, then *I* might worry. Because I'm the eldest.'

'Are they at our school?'

She nodded.

'Whose class?'

'You're very nosy, aren't you? I thought it was me you took to the pictures, not my bloody sisters.'

He flinched a little at that word again. 'Don't talk like that. It's common.'

She tilted her head to one side and stared at him.

'Common?'

He flushed. 'Well, you know – not the right way to talk. The guttersnipes talk like that. Not decent people.'

'What sort of behaviour is that for a nice Yiddisher girl?' she said in a savage little mockery of an adult voice and he smiled then.

'Well, I know. They do go on a bit. But all the same – swearing – it's like going into pubs. Common.'

'What do you know about it?'

He lifted his chin. 'My mum. She's not from round here. She *knows*. Her family won't have nothing to do with her because she married my dad. They met in Russia.'

She was fascinated now. 'In Russia?'

'There was fighting there. Long time ago – Communists and that. They was both there. He was a fighter, dad was. That's why he's a conshie and a Communist now. Because of what happened in Russia. She was a fighter too, I think, but then she got ill and had to come back, and now she's – well, they got married after Russia and then I was born.' He shrugged. 'That's all really. But she knows about what's right behaviour and what isn't, and she doesn't use words like that.'

'Then I won't,' Hetty said and moved a little closer. 'Will we go to the pictures again?'

'Only if we pay.' He was in the ascendant again, and it felt good. 'None of your sneaking in.'

'Not if you don't want to,' she said and smiled up at him, and he could just see her teeth flashing, for the day had disappeared into darkness and the blackout around them was almost complete.

'Have you got far to go home?' he said then, and tried to take

14

a deep breath. It was hard to breathe properly for a moment.

'Not far. Down Cassland Road. When will we go to the pictures again? Tomorrow?'

He shook his head, even though she couldn't really see him. 'No. You get bored with pictures.' And he had no money to support his high ideals of paying his way.

'Down the park, then? Meet you by the swings?'

He hesitated a moment, thinking of the way his parents liked him to stay with them on Sunday afternoons to help when the visitors came. There were always visitors, talking interminable politics, drinking interminable cups of tea which he helped make for them. 'All right. About two o'clock. Just till half past three, though. I'm busy after that.'

'All right,' she said, and in the darkness put her hands up and linked them behind his neck and kissed him. 'Two o'clock, round by the swings. Don't forget.' She was away from him and almost out of earshot when he said suddenly, 'Who does look after you, then? You and your sisters?'

'Auntie Fido,' she called back, and he heard her footsteps diminishing into the distance.

2

Bonnie Maddern parked her car in the Brewer Street garage and set out to walk to the Law Courts. It was early yet and she needed the exercise and the time to herself. She'd missed her meditation this morning, because Warren had woken early and been noisily sick in the children's bathroom, and she'd had to go and hold his head, and then Stanley's Auntie Rae had phoned, full of misery because she'd had a bad night, and one way and another she just hadn't had the chance to sit armfolded and remote on the *chaise longue* in her bedroom silently reciting her mantra and concentrating.

It ought to be possible, really, to meditate while you were walking, leaving it to your lower functions to make sure you didn't walk under a bus or something, but the question was, had anyone ever tried it? She'd ask at the next group meeting. If she could manage to get to it. With the children home for the Easter holidays next week and Stanley involved in the end of the financial year it was all getting very difficult.

'Don't push yourself,' he'd said at breakfast. 'I'll get there as soon as I can and I want to be the one they call first, so don't push yourself forward. Keep back, out of sight –'

'It won't make any difference,' she'd said mildly. 'They plan it their own way, I imagine, and take it for granted the people they want will be there when they want them. It won't make any difference whether they notice me or not.'

'All the same, keep out of the way. Why you've got to get there before me anyway I don't know – I'll be finished with the tax office by twelve, no later, and you could meet me at Joe's and we could go together. You don't have to be there at the kick-off.'

But for once she'd been firm, pretending not to notice the petulant note in his voice. 'I'd rather be there from the start. Hear everything they say. And anyway, it'll help you, won't it? To know what happens? I'll take notes.'

'You're stupid! Witnesses aren't allowed in court until after they've given their evidence,' Sharon said, not lifting her head from the paper. While everyone else read the *Daily Mail* or the *Express* she read *The Times* with some ostentation.

'Then you're the stupid one,' Daniel said. 'This isn't a criminal action. It's the High Court – different. From where should you know?'

'Shut up and mind your own business, the pair of you!' Stanley said loudly, 'and for Christ's sake, Sharon, do you have to wear that stinking stuff at breakfast? It's like a brothel in here –'

'And from where should *you* know?' Sharon folded her paper with even greater ostentation. 'Are you coming? I'm going to be late.'

'Then go by train, already, and leave me alone,' Stanley said. 'I've got enough to put up with without you sitting moaning all the way. If you want to come with me, take that bloody scent off, and sit shtoom. Otherwise you can bloody well walk.'

'Stan – Sharon –' Bonnie murmured. 'Don't start arguing so early – you'll upset yourselves.'

'They're upsetting me,' Warren said loudly. 'Why does this house have to be like a menagerie all the time? Everyone snarling and snapping –'

'You shouldn't drink so much,' Sharon said, and smiled at him with great sweetness. 'That's what's upsetting you. And it makes you upsetting to be with. As for a menagerie – the way you smell it's no wonder civilized people need to protect themselves with a *pleasant* odour.'

'Oh, fuck off,' Warren said. 'Listen, Mum, can you let me have a few quid? Just till – oh, don't look at me like that! So I swore! So what? She's bloody lucky she only gets sworn at, the bitch. Listen, Mum –'

'I'm going. I'll see you at the court. Twelve o'clock – quarter past. Keep out of it, till I come, you hear me? Keep out of it.'

With Stanley and Sharon gone, and Warren sent off with a fiver – it was easier to let him have it than be a Good Mother and make him go without – she'd had time to get Tracy out of bed and she and Daniel on their way to school. It ought to get easier as they get older, she thought. Babies and toddlers were bad enough but these are hell. O-levels and A-levels and degrees, and Warren isn't going to get much of a degree if at all and there'll be hell to pay over that, too. Stanley had said from the start that the best thing for him was the business, that furniture was a good business and people always had to have beds and tables, and sending him to LSE was lunacy, sheer lunacy. And it was looking more and more likely that he was right. Warren was bored and drinking and that was why.

That was why. She stood in the kitchen staring out at the garden, while the au pair moved noisily about clearing the breakfast table and loading the dishwasher. 'Always think of why people behave as they do, and how it makes you feel, Bonnie,' Mr Hermann said. 'Always work out the whys and when you get the answer to the first question why, then ask it again. That's the core of analysis, Bonnie. Till you get all the ultimate answers, you can't understand yourself. Till you understand yourself, you can't understand anyone else.'

All right then, why does Warren drink too much? Because he's bored. Why is he bored? Because he's doing the wrong sort of thing. He's not really interested in studying philosophy and politics. Then why is he studying it? Because I wanted him to. Why did I want him to? Because I want him to be better than other people's kids. Why? What's wrong with other people's kids? Why should he be better? Because they're grabby and glossy and *empty*. Because they're all like St –

She shook her head sharply and turned away from the window, and began to tell the au pair in slow careful English how to wash salad and get the steaks ready to grill for when everyone got home tonight. Analysis was all very well, but there were times when it made it impossible to go on living your life properly. Why do you feel like that? Because the life I'm living isn't living life properly –

'And ice cream,' she said loudly. 'The strawberry ice cream in the freezer; and don't forget the laundry man comes today. I leave money, all right? I leave money.'

She was ready to leave the house at a quarter to nine exactly, the way she'd planned. Being organized was important; doing what you'd said you do, when you'd said you'd do it – it made life possible. Structured and possible. Why does it have to be structured? Because –

'Because nothing,' she said out loud to the mirror. 'Because I like it that way.'

She studied her appearance carefully. A Hildegarde suit, but not an obvious Hildegarde suit. That would be asking for trou-

18

ble. But this one with its quiet good looks would be right. Beige was a difficult colour, but on her it looked – suitable. The brown scarf, the heavy leather bag, the Gucci shoes; all understated, but right. No need to cause trouble wearing the wrong things. Hester would notice of course, and so would the others, probably, but she'd thought carefully about it, and decided she'd do it. As for Stanley – he'd never give it another thought. Unless someone else mentioned it.

Her mind began to slide away, the way it so often did, creating scenes. All of them standing outside the court – in the street? In a corridor? That part was hazy, but anyway, outside the courtroom. Stanley, glaring at the others. Them glaring too. Shouting? Not really. They did a lot of shouting, all of them; it was part of the way they were. But not usually in public, where others could see and gawp. Like her own children, squabbling and bickering and nagging at each other till she thought she'd go out of her mind and start shouting herself, but outside the house, always perfect ladies and gentlemen. It was the way they were. So there wouldn't be any shouting.

But maybe there would? After all, who would have thought they'd ever get involved in a court case? If you'd asked her last year if such a thing were possible, she'd have laughed. *Hester* parading such a thing? Hester who cared so much about appearances and knew all about what publicity was and what it could do? Never.

But then, a year ago, she couldn't have imagined herself doing what she was doing. Meditating and being in analysis with Mr Hermann and the psychology lectures at the City Lit. She'd never even heard of the City Lit. a year ago, and now, here she was, on her way to a diploma. Who'd have thought it?

She took a last look round her bedroom at the peach mirrors and the deep pile carpet and the round bed with its fur headboard, and wondered whether it would after all be such a mistake to bring some of them home for a coffee meeting some time. On a Thursday, Stanley's Masonic night. She could put them in the little sitting room, where the TV was and which had last year's black leather furniture and wasn't as – well – as obvious as the lounge. Stanley was delighted with the way the lounge looked now, with its smoked glass tables and its cream suede sofas and tiffany lamps, and she'd liked it too, at first.

Until she'd gone with them all after a lecture to have a drink at Fran's flat and they'd all talked about kitsch, and she'd discovered that her entire house was kitsch, down to the gold taps in their *en suite* bathroom. No, she couldn't bring them here. Edgware was a long way out anyway. She had a good excuse.

All the way up to town, driving carefully in the slow lane, concentrating on the traffic, she was able to keep her mind clear, but once she started walking she couldn't. Then the weight of the day pressed down on her, together with the weight of all the days that had gone before. No amount of asking why helped at all.

AUGUST 1945

'... *A face in the misty night,*
Footsteps that you hear down the hall,
A voice that drifts on the summer breeze,
That you can never quite recall . . . .'

The water was rising, cold and thick and steady. She felt it covering her knees and then her thighs, creeping up her bottom, and she wanted to start screaming, but she knew she couldn't because first the gas had to come, twisting and turning in great wreaths and tendrils. She sat there and waited and at last it started and she heard the thin plopping as the gas came out and the steady hiss as it built up and at last she could start screaming.

So she did, pushing the sound out as hard as she could but all that came out, of course, was the little whining wail that was no louder than the hissing of the gas. It was the same, it was always the same, and she began to move about, rocking from side to side to see if that would change it, make it happen differently, but it didn't. Still the water crept up and the gas crept down and still the sound wouldn't come out of her throat, however hard she pushed. Please, let it be over soon, let it be over soon –

And then it was. Hilda was kicking her and Hetty was shaking her and she came up and up, out of the water, through the gas, and she was in bed with her eyes wet and her throat all sore and tight and Hilda was sitting up at the foot of the bed, her feet rhythmically thumping her.

20

'Shut up, you soppy thing, you'll have her in here moaning. Do shut *up*.' Hetty was saying, and Bertha gasped and said breathlessly, 'Sorry – all right – sorry.'

After a while Hilda stopped kicking, and Bertha could sit up, and she pushed her pillow behind her head against the iron railings of the bedhead and tucked her hands under her arms. It always took a while to get over it, when it happened, and trying to go back to sleep too soon made it worse. She was learning that.

The room was bright because of the street light outside, and she stared at the shape of the window, enjoying it. All those long black nights when the window was covered in black cloth to make the darkness in their room so complete it was like a solid wall you could touch; they had gone on for so long that even though it was nearly a year now since they'd stopped putting it up it was still a joy to be able to see. And since VE day, when they'd put the street lights on again, it had been even better.

She looked round the room, counting the shapes. The big bed they shared, with its iron rails and the brass balls on the corners, in which they had been used to sleep in a row until Hilda started falling out and Hetty had made her sleep at the bottom; the tallboy with its six drawers, two for each of them; the table in the corner with the glass ink-well where they were supposed to do homework, but never did – it was comforting in its familiarity. All her life she had been here sleeping in this bed. All her life that she could remember.

'Bertha,' Hilda said softly. 'Bertha, tell me about –'

'Bonnie.' Hetty's voice came out of her pillow, quiet but very firm. 'She's *Bonnie*, Hildegarde.'

'Bertha,' Bertha said. 'That's my name. Bertha.'

'Bertha, Bertha, Bertha!' Hetty sang it sneeringly. 'Silly old fat woman with warts on her chin and hairs coming out of her nose, that's what a Bertha is. You'll never be anything if you're called Bertha. I keep telling you.''

'Bonnie,' Hilda said. 'Tell me about –'

'I'm not telling you anything till you call me by my name. Ask Hetty. She'll tell you.'

'Hester. I'm Hester. Hetty's skinny and got a big nose and squints. I'm not a Hetty, I'm a Hester.'

'What's a Hester like?' Hilda said and turned over in the dimness, so that she could stare across the humped bedclothes at her oldest sister. 'What's a Hester like?'

Hetty sat up and leaned back against the bed head, beside Bertha, her arms hooked round her knees. 'Hester is tall and slim, lovely as the dawn. Hester is sophisticated and witty, and makes people swoon at her feet. Hester is –'

'Tell me what Hildegarde is,' Hilda said, and Bertha could see her eyes glinting, wide open, in the dim light. 'Hilda's short and fat and silly but Hildegarde's different. Tell me what Hildegarde is –'

'Hildegarde's fat and silly too. Shut up,' Hester said. 'I'll kick you if you don't shut up –'

'I'll tell everyone you're really Hetty if you don't tell me what Hildegarde is,' Hilda said. 'All the people down at the Settlement you're always swanning round with! I'll tell them you're Hetty with a squint –'

'If you do, I'll wait for you when you come out of school and cut you up with a breadknife. And then I'll come home and no one will know it was me. Shut up.'

'Tell me about Hildegarde.' Hilda was beginning to whine and Hetty took a sharp impatient breath.

'Oh, Hildegarde – she's pretty and good and does as she's told and people say, "Isn't she sweet" all the time. That's Hildegarde.'

'I'll stay Hilda,' Hilda said. 'It isn't short and fat. It's wise and intelligent. Hilda's wise – Bonnie –Bertha, tell me.'

'Tell you what?' Bertha was getting sleepy now, safely sleepy. If she could drop off now the dream wouldn't happen again and she'd be all right. She tried to hold on to the rags of sleep which were drifting around her, sliding down into the bedclothes and pushing her head into the pillow. 'Don't know about anything –'

Hilda's voice came muffled, and she tried to shut it out. But she couldn't.

'Tell me what happened when *it* happened. Tell me about your dream and how you keep having it and what it feels like. Tell me how they –'

'She doesn't know,' Hetty said, cold and sharp on the other side of Bertha's pillow. 'I'm the only one who can remember. I'm the one you have to ask because I'm the only one who knows. I can remember them. Really remember them. You can't. Bonnie can't –'

'Bertha,' Bertha said into her pillow, trying to stay half asleep. But it was too late. Hetty's voice had cut away the sleep the way Auntie Fido's knife cut away the crusts on the bread when she made sandwiches for her visitors. Sharp and edged, her voice sliced into Bertha, and made her mind slip in half, to let the words get in.

'Tell me,' Hilda said, and she sounded sleepy. 'Talk me to sleep, Hetty – Hester. Tell me about it all, Hester, every single bit – where were we?'

'We were at the seaside,' Hetty said, and her voice was softer now, but just as clear. It was her special voice, the one she used to tell stories with, deeper and with a bubble in it at the back of her throat. It was as though she were on the wireless, because her words changed too. She sounded smart, and la-di-da and not a bit like Millfields Road School. Bertha didn't want to listen, but of course she did. She always listened.

'It was summer time. Summer, nineteen forty. Not as beautiful a summer as it had been the year before, but the skies were blue and the air was balmy. The three little girls, aged ten and almost nine and six, were sent by their loving mother and father away from the heat of Coronation Buildings in bustling Stoke Newington to visit their aunt –'

Hilda giggled softly. 'Auntie Fido, Auntie Fido,' she chanted. 'Soppy, skinny Auntie Fido –'

'Shut up,' Hetty said. 'Or I won't tell you –'

'You shut up, Hetty,' Bertha said and pushed her head deeper into her pillow. 'I don't want to know. I want to forget all about it.'

'You can't forget what you can't remember,' Hetty said sharply. 'So you listen and I'll tell you because I'm the only one who remembers and you ought to as well. They went to visit their auntie at the seaside. It was wartime of course so they couldn't go on the sands, because the government wouldn't let them. It wasn't like it used to be at Thorpe Bay before the war, when they sold comics and ice creams and buckets and spades and there was *Snow White* on at the pictures to go to on the day it rained. But it was sunny and they could walk in the fields and have tea in a little house where the lady called the oldest little girl Miss – "Will you have some more jam, Miss?" That was what she said. And the little girl was very happy –'

'Tell it properly. Not a story. Tell it properly,' Hilda said, fretful suddenly.

'I'll tell it my way or not at all,' Hetty said and suddenly yawned. 'Anyway, they were at the seaside with the aunt. And then it happened –'

'No,' Bertha said, but Hetty wasn't listening to her. She was listening to herself. 'The night came, the fateful night came when the joy swept out of the lives of the little girls for ever. Aeroplanes over the great metropolis, bearing their evil harvest of death and disaster. Below them, deep in the basement of Coronation Buildings, were the mother and father, happy to know their beloved little girls were safe and sound in far off Essex. Soon they would be home again, but tonight they were safe. And then, it happened –'

I hate you, Bertha thought. I hate you, I hate you, you're going to make it all happen again.

'Then it came, whistling furiously out of the silken summer darkness,' Hetty said and the relish in her voice made Hilda wriggle with delight. 'The bomb. The bomb with their names on. Down, down, turning and twisting in the darkness, deceptively lazy –'

'That's a new bit,' Hilda said. 'You never said it like that last time.'

'That's the way I'm saying it this time. Shut up. Twisting and turning in the darkness it came, and then – *crump*! It struck –'

'And the water main burst and the gas main burst and the people in the basement all got drowned or gassed or both,' Bertha gabbled loudly, so that she could stop Hetty's voice. 'And they died, and that was the end of it. Now go to sleep, Hilda. It's school in the morning, go to sleep –'

Hilda began to whimper. 'You spoiled it. You spoiled it all, finishing it like that – you're a pig, Bertha –'

The knocking on the wall came sharply and suddenly and Bertha lay down again, gratefully.

'Be quiet, you three! It's gone midnight – be quiet at *once*. Do you hear me? Or I'll be in there with a strap.'

'Good night, Auntie Fido,' Hilda called out sugar-sweet, and giggled softly. 'Soppy Fido. Down, boy!'

24

Hetty kicked her, and burrowed down into the bedclothes again. 'You don't deserve to have parents killed like that. I remember what it was like, and you don't. I shan't tell you again.'

I hate you, Bertha thought. I'll have to stay awake now, think of different things. I daren't go to sleep now, not for a long time. I hate you.

3

'Which court?' The doorman squinted at the piece of paper he held in his hand. 'Let's see now – ah, yes, sir. Court thirty-six. Through the main hall, stairs to the left, follow the signs, can't miss it –'

'I probably will,' David said gloomily. 'Place looks like a barn –' and he squinted over the doorman's shoulder at the huge echoing expanse of terrazzo flooring and pillars and high skylights.

The doorman laughed indulgently. 'They all say that, sir, but it's surprising how easy it is to find your way about, once you knows, like. There's another chap up at the far end you can ask again, if you're worried. Straight through the hall, sir.'

He took his time walking, looking about him, hoping to see a familiar face. Hers maybe? He tried to imagine how it would be, actually seeing her face to face instead of just on the small screen. Would he be able to say all the things he'd imagined saying over the years? Would he be able to bring out the scalding words, the vituperation he had so often planned? Or would he just stand there and then sweep on, his expression unchanging, ignoring her?

Somewhere at the back of his mind he knew the likelihood was that he'd just grin and say inanely, 'Do you remember me? Spero – David Spero? It's over twenty-five years ago, now, of course, so you mightn't. Mind you, you haven't changed a bit. I like your programme – never miss it, really – you must come and have dinner some time. Meet my wife – the children –'

His step became more rapid. He wouldn't do that, would he? He'd have the courage to tell her what a bitch she'd been, how she'd ruined his whole life? His eyes moistened; they so easily did as he contemplated the wreck of his life. Plenty of money, of course. That had never been in question; even in the last few years when most people in the property business had found it tough and even gone down, Spero Estates had done well enough, and were picking up nicely now. No, it was happiness of which she'd robbed him. The joy of life with the one and only

26

woman with whom a man could be happy, the joy of having that woman bear his children. The satisfaction of life with the perfect partner –

Not that he could actually remember his perfect partner's face now, if the truth were told. It was easy to remember how Hester looked. She was there in front of him every Tuesday night, and on the Sunday afternoon repeats. So it was no shame that Bonnie's face had become misted in the wreaths of time. No shame at all.

JUNE 1951

'I've got a feeling called the blues,
Lovesick 'cos my baby said goodbye . . . .'

'Oooh!' they went, and then, 'Aaah!' and picked up their children to hold them high over everyone's heads so that they could see the Guinness clock go through its paces, and he had to duck his head to see under the arms of the man in front of him who was holding up a particularly large and vociferous child.

Not that he was interested in the Guinness clock – but she was. And he'd been watching her and following her ever since he'd first spotted her walking ahead of him in the tree walk, along the shaky pathways built from branch to branch right up the side of the funfair. He'd hardly been able to see her face, what with the darkness and the sharp swinging shadows cast by the lights from the fair, but her shape had beguiled him at once. A small waist and tight round buttocks and breasts to match, a curving full-bodied girl, just the sort he'd liked to get hold of. She'd pushed herself into a pointed bra, of course, like all the girls did, but under her thin tightly-fitting dress it cut into her so that each bouncing breast came welling up over the edge of its confinement to give her an undulating, almost four-breasted look. He could imagine all too easily how she'd be with no clothes on, and the mere act of imagining made his body stir with excitement.

Now, standing in the crowd round this silly clock he could see her face, and his excitement rose. That body and a smashing face as well. Dark eyes. Lustrous was the word, he told himself, because they looked moist and swimmy and the lashes were long and thick. A button of a mouth, very curved and cupid-bowed. A rather heavy nose that some people would sneer at but which warmed him, because it made her look undoubtedly suitable to talk to. A nice Jewish girl, and just his type.

He'd known tonight his luck would be in. He'd come to the Battersea funfair because he was bored, because all the others had gone out to London Airport – where was the fun in eating kippers there more than twice in one week? – and he needed a new girl. That bitch Corinne had turned her back on him for some bloody dentist and had sneered because he wasn't a professional man. A professional man, for God's sake – some stinking shlapper who spent all his time digging around in people's filthy mouths: that was a professional man? To hell with it. He'd rather be a business man any day. And this girl looked the sort that would prefer a businessman. Sensible as well as sexy.

He used the trick he'd used lots of times before. It always worked because it wasn't like an ordinary pick-up. He made his way through the crowd till he was standing in front of her and then just as she began to move away turned his ankle so that he lurched and had to reach out to grab someone or something to prevent himself falling. And managed to grab her. The ensuing apologies and sympathy and rubbing of ankles led naturally to the suggestion of cups of frothy coffee in the open-air expresso bar by the open-air dance floor – everything was very Continental in London this Festival of Britain Year – and from then on it was easy. Lovely and easy.

Not that *she* was easy. Far from it. It had taken ages to get anywhere. She'd been impressed by his car that first night, amazed that he had a radio in it – real luxury, that was – and appreciated his offer of a lift home. But she wouldn't accept it, not until she'd had six dates with him. Six meetings at the bus stop on the bridge, or at Waterloo. Six visits to the Battersea funfair and the South Bank exhibition because she said she liked them, and it was better to be out of doors even in poor weather than cooped up in West End cinemas and restaurants. He'd realized then that she had very few clothes, and none of them really right for wearing to restaurants, and had been even more smitten with her. Such a nice girl, and so poor. No risk of this one ever turning up her nose at him.

So, for six evenings, meeting twice a week, they strolled around the South Bank, and ate ices and danced on the open-air floor and talked, and she laughed at all his jokes. He looked at the Skylon, standing pencil-slim above the Dome of Discovery and told her in his best Noël Coward voice that it was 'that permanent erection on the South Bank' and bless her, she smiled and didn't understand the joke. A lovely girl, naïve and teachable.

But not cheap, not Bonnie. When he'd put his arm round her waist, she'd frozen. But by the sixth date he was able to hold her hand as they walked along, and dance very close to 'Some Enchanted Evening', and could sit knee to knee when they drank their coffee, and he talked knowledgeably about Burgess and Maclean going to Russia, and she didn't know he knew damn all about it and listened with total absorption.

She'd allowed him to drive her home that night and he had been a bit taken aback to find where she lived. Hackney. He'd known she was poor, and he'd found that touching, but Hackney wasn't touching at all. Drab and old, almost a slum when you compared it with Willesden. And the house – a narrow terraced house in grey stucco with a front door trimmed with coloured glass, as vulgar as you like, and smelling of fried fish when the door was opened. Not a bit like his parents' four-bedroomed red-brick detached in Sidmouth Road, where they had a downstairs toilet which smelled of lavender air freshener. But she'd invited him in so he had to go, and then it had been different. The aunt – a stupid name they called her, but families were like that – and the sisters.

He'd sat there that first night after the aunt had gone to bed and left them all there in the frowsy over-furnished front room, almost swamped by them. Hilda, sparkling and seventeen, chattered and glittered at him and he'd almost fallen for it, very taken by her curly fair hair and wide green eyes, but then he'd looked across at Bonnie, quiet and still on the sofa and been glad she wasn't like that. Hilda was good for a laugh, obviously, but she could be uncomfortably sharp, and when Bonnie said something about the Festival and the South Bank she murmured the Noël Coward joke about the Skylon and looked at him so knowingly that he blushed, and was glad that Bonnie hadn't heard her.

Hester, on the other hand, he found quite resistible from the start. As straight and as dull in shape as her sister was curvaceous, he'd almost been sorry for her with her thick straight eyebrows, and her harsh way of talking, but then she'd talked more and his pity had melted very abruptly.

'What do you do for a living?'

'I beg your pardon?' Trying to be dignified. People shouldn't ask such direct questions. Not at all the thing.

'Better to sell matches than beg,' she'd retorted. 'Ashamed of it, are you?'

'Hester, do be quiet,' Bonnie had said mildly. 'Take no notice, David. She's in one of her moods tonight. She gets like this sometimes.'

'How do you mean, mood? So I'm taking an interest in your friends! Since when was that being moody?'

'It's being nosy,' Hilda said and smiled at him with great sweetness. 'I'm nosy too. Tell *me*, David. What do you do?'

'I work with my people. They're in property.'

Hester looked at him, her head on one side and her boot button eyes gleaming. 'We have a friend who says that people who deal in property, buying and selling the homes of the poor, are little more than robbers and predators. What'd you say to that?'

'I'd say he was a Communist,' David said after a moment, red-faced and feeling his muscles tense up. He'd got into arguments like this before with some of that crowd Corinne hung about with. Medical students, law students, thought they knew it all because they were going into professions. Twisting everything a man said till he didn't know which way was up, and all because they were jealous because he had a bob or two. 'That's what I'd say. A Communist. One of these Burgess and Maclean types –'

Hilda crowed with laughter and clapped her hands. 'You're clever, David, you really are! He *is* a Communist, and lovely with it, isn't he, Hester? One minute he's all on about the poor common people and the next he's telling you off for saying lav instead of toilet. Isn't David clever?'

Hester grinned, twisting her legs even more tightly under her on the sofa, if that were possible. 'Quite clever. Do you ever think about why you're in property? I mean do you work in it because Daddy told you to, or because you have a burning desire to do it?'

He frowned at her. 'I don't see that it's any business of yours,' he said stiffly.

'Then you don't like it. So why do it?'

'Because it's a family business! Because I like my comforts! And because – because –'

She smiled then, her eyes seeming to disappear into slits and suddenly he thought, 'She's got a marvellous face,' but the moment of approval passed as rapidly as it had come.

'Because you never had the chance to choose anything for yourself. That's what comes of being rich. It's only the poor, like us, can choose what we want to do, isn't it, Hilda?'

Hilda stretched and grinned at him, once more sparkling and glittering. 'So you say, my duck, so you say.'

'What do *you* do, then?' he said sharply and suddenly realized he didn't know what Bonnie did all day, let alone her sisters. He'd told her all about him, but she'd said hardly anything about herself. 'Work in an office, I suppose?'

Hester's eyes narrowed as she looked back at him, and then said very coolly, 'There's offices and offices.'

'Hester works for a record company,' Bonnie said, defensive suddenly. 'It's temporary. Till she gets a part. She's an actress, you know. But a record company office is good while she's looking for a part because it's all show business –'

'You don't have to explain anything,' Hester said loudly. '*Qui s'excuse, s'accuse*.'

'I wasn't,' Bonnie said. 'Just saying –'

'I'm at art school,' Hilda said. 'I'm studying line and form and colour values. At Chelsea.'

He looked at her, impressed. Art school sounded raffish and exciting. He began to understand how it was she talked about erections on the South Bank so easily, at only seventeen. 'Then what, when you've finished?'

'Oh, I'll be like you,' she said and grinned again. 'Go where the money is. And make no mistake about it – so will she.' She looked across at Hester. 'Won't you, my duck? You like the stuff as much as anyone.'

'Indeed I do,' Hester said calmly and got to her feet. 'Only I won't go where the money is. I'll make it come to where I am.

Well, are you going now? It's getting late.'

'Oh Hester –' Bonnie said, and smiled at him. 'Take no notice, David. She's playing a strong part this week. She's in a play, you know. At the Settlement. She's ever so good.'

'Buy a ticket?' Hester said, and stood there staring at him, her hands balled into fists on her hips and suddenly he laughed.

'Do you act all the time? Or is this just for me because I'm here for the first time?'

Again Hilda produced that crowing laugh of hers, and Hester shifted her eyes to stare at her for a brief moment and then looked back at him.

'Are you buying a ticket?' she demanded. 'Five bob, half a crown and a shilling at the back. Cheap at the price. You'll be able to boast you saw me way back when, one of these days.'

He grinned, amiable now and very comfortable. He had her measure. 'I'll take six at five bob,' he said easily, and reached in his pocket for his wallet and peeled a pound note and a ten-shilling note off the thick wad, aware of Hilda's wide-eyed gaze on his hands. 'I dare say I'll find some people who'll come out here and take a look.'

'Nice of you,' she said coolly, and took the notes. 'I'll get the address from Bonnie and send the tickets on. You'd better get out now. Auntie Fido'll start bashing on the ceiling any moment now.'

'I'll tell her – it's all right,' Bonnie said and reddened a little as Hilda stood up and said with great exaggeration, 'Well, if I go too, now, you two can be *quiet* together. Fido won't bash then. She'll be too busy sitting up there with her ear to the floor trying to hear what's going on and imagining what it's all like. If the light begins to swing, you'll know why, David. She has her problems, has Auntie Fido.'

He was crimson too, and trying not to look at Bonnie. 'Odd name for you to call her,' he said, desperately trying to be ordinary. 'Fido. Nickname, is it?'

Hilda giggled. 'Hester called her that when we'd been living with her less than a month. It's because she keeps on saying it.'

He looked at Hester who was by the door now, and she turned and stared at him and then suddenly folded her arms over her thin chest and let her shoulders sag, and it was as though a different person stood there.

32

'Oh, my dear,' she said, and her voice was thin and querulous. 'My dear, 'f I'd 'a had my chances, what I couldn't've done! Never think no man's ever wanted to marry me – I've turned them away, I have, turned 'em away. 'f I'd 'a been free, of course, it would've been different. But with my only brother's three orphans to take care of, what could I do? I ask you, could I put myself first, when these three girls needed me so? 'f I'd 'a done that, I'd not've been able to live with myself. But I tell you, when I think sometimes how things would be 'f I'd 'a had my chances –'

She grimaced and was suddenly herself again. 'Auntie Fido,' she said. 'You see? Good night. See you around.'

He saw her around, indeed. As the weeks passed he became more and more involved with Bonnie, with her quietness and her eagerness to please and her shrinking reaction to his attempts to make love to her. He thought a lot about sex, enjoyed reading a dirty book with the best of them, but got a bit nervous when he was involved with the real thing. And a girl like Bonnie who looked so good and so luscious but was so hard to get was the ideal for him.

One of the problems with Corinne, he had to admit, had been that she was a lot more forthcoming than he was. One of the reasons she liked medical students and dentists, he thought sourly, was that they knew all about it. But as he'd told her, he couldn't imagine any girl with any real refinement liking to have someone use on her knowledge he'd picked up from cutting up dead bodies and working in maternity wards. Horrible idea.

But he didn't have to worry with Bonnie. She was different. She held hands with him and they did a bit of cuddling in cinemas, now that she agreed to go to them with him, with his arm round her and his hand as close to that billowing breast as she'd let him, and sat kissing and cuddling afterwards for an hour or two in the steamed-up car, parked in quiet side streets round Hackney. She never let him go further than paddling a bit in her bra however, firmly refusing to unhook it, and certainly never made any attempt to touch him where she shouldn't. Altogether it was very satisfactory for him, and he enjoyed the long hours of arousal in her company even though it meant that sometimes his control faltered and there were mishaps. But it didn't worry him unduly to sit there damply beside her – and it

33

was agreeable to start all over again, anyway.

Being involved with Bonnie of course meant being involved with Hilda and Hester. They were close, the three of them, and as he found out more of their history, he understood it. To be orphaned the way they were; the mere thought of it sent a *frisson* through him. And the information had come in very useful when his mother had asked him fretfully who this new girl was he went out with so often. Was there something in it? Because if so, who was she, where did she come from? What sort of people?

She had been all set for one of her nagging sessions, but when he'd told her how Bonnie's parents had died and the three sisters had been thrown on the mercy of an aunt, she had softened at once. 'Poor girl,' she had crooned, and, 'Bring her often' and had found clothes she no longer needed to offer to Bonnie, none of which suited her but which she accepted as smilingly as she accepted most things that happened.

All of which had made Hester and Hilda easier to get on with. Not that he told either of them of his mother's early suspicions; not only was it none of their business, but he could all too easily imagine how sarcastic Hester would be about it.

Hester. He was exasperated by Hester. Sometimes they would all go out, six of them; Hester and Hilda with whatever boy they happened to choose to bring along. Sometimes art students, when it was taken for granted that David would foot the bill for all of them, sometimes members of Hester's drama group, when he would at least share some of the burden of payment, since they usually had jobs of one sort or another and therefore some money. Once it had been just one other man, a quiet, almost sullen chap, tall and solid, with dark eyes and a long straight mouth and heavy eyebrows that met in the middle. He'd been introduced as Sammy, and then Hilda, her eyes bright with malice, said, 'He used to be called Sammy Sternberg. Now he's Sampson Stermont. Hester thinks it suits him better. What do you think?'

David had shrugged. 'People change their names all the time. Why not? It's useful, sometimes, in business.'

'Business.' Sammy had looked at him under those heavy brows. 'Do I look like a *business*man? That's a sickening thought.'

'He's a medical student,' Hester said, and shot David a malicious look. 'And our friend the Communist.'

'Shut up,' Sammy said equably. 'You know nothing about it.'

'His parents are Communists too. Card-carriers.'

'Card-carriers?' David said and tried not to look blank. 'Really?'

'Really,' Sammy said sourly. 'Isn't that something? If you've nothing better to talk about than me, Hilda, I'm going home. I get bored easily.'

'Depends on what you're doing,' Hilda said softly and Sammy's heavy face became even heavier and for the first time David noticed that Hilda had one hand under the tablecloth and he looked away quickly. Hilda was a bit too Corinne-ish for comfort.

They were sitting in a Chinese restaurant overlooking Glasshouse Street. Everyone who was anyone was eating Chinese now, Hester had pronounced, so that was where they went when they went out in a big group. Sometimes he wanted to rebel at her *diktats*; but he didn't; any more than her sisters or the dim men they brought along ever did. Hester was Hester, and what she said went. And it suited him well enough. She didn't interfere with him and his Bonnie, though she watched them sometimes, he realized, as he caught her sharp glance on them as he sat and whispered in Bonnie's ear. But leaving it all to her was easy. And interesting too.

He would sit and watch her, manipulating chopsticks as though she were born to them, pushing bean sprouts and noodles greedily into her mouth, and wonder what made her as she was. So different from her sisters, even though they shared some superficial likenesses. She had the same dark eyes that Bonnie did, the same dark brows, and the same curly hair, though it was darker, that Hilda had. But she was very much herself, exotic and frightening and always horribly knowing.

It wasn't till the night of her play that he discovered just how frightening and knowing she could be.

4

Counsel were beginning to gather. Sammy leaned against the pillar nearest the entrance to the staircase that led to the court and watched them go, their black gowns billowing importantly behind them, white bands fluttering at their necks and wigs perched absurdly over their noses. They're in it for the dressing-up, he thought, and was amused at the idea. He knew surgeons who were in it for the dressing-up, who would paddle self-importantly along the hospital corridors in their heavy white wellington boots, masks around their necks and hair curling boyishly under their white caps, tickled to death with themselves, Kildares to a man, liking nothing better than to have visitors press themselves respectfully against the walls as they went by. These lawyers were the same; actors every one of them.

The hall was beginning to fill. On benches along the sides under the handsome portraits clusters of people sat and talked; clients and solicitors, occasionally counsel, worried faces, urgent mutterings. The whole place seemed to reek of anxiety and he stirred restlessly against his pillar and moved his overcoat from one arm to the other. Was the anxiety in the place infecting him or had he brought it in with him? A bit of each, he decided, just as the hospital which was home to him and breathed into his nostrils nothing but security and comfort filled strangers with the ache of dread, so this place inevitably reacted on the strangers who passed its huge gates. But his own anxiety simmered away under the surface, and mattered most.

He saw them almost at the same time; the old woman, ostentatiously leaning on a stick but to his professional eye a good deal more spry than she was prepared to admit, with a thin-faced, worried-looking woman also supporting her; and, across the far side of the great expanse of terrazzo, Bonnie.

She looks marvellous, he thought; whoever would have thought that homely girl could ever have turned out so well? When they had been young she had almost disappeared beside her sisters. Now, looking at her as a person standing alone, she

36

was splendid. Always on the plump side, now she had a firmness about her that made her look very young. She must be – he worked it out quickly – she must be all of forty-seven. But at this distance certainly she didn't look it. Her hair was thick and glossy, her eyes as lustrous as ever – perhaps even more so because she'd become rather heavy-lidded over the years – and her body; he smiled a little as he thought of her body. Rich, that was the word for it. Sumptuous. He almost said it aloud, watching her. Sump-tu-ous.

She didn't see him. She was walking fairly slowly, her head up, her leather bag over her shoulder and staring straight ahead. Would she see the old woman? And if she did, would she acknowledge her? It was the other two who had been most vociferous in their rage and rejection. Bonnie had said little, but then Bonnie never did say much that was positive. But would Bonnie be positive now if she caught sight of the two women making their slow way in the same direction as she was?

He stepped back a little, moving further round the pillar. He didn't want to be seen by anyone. Yet. He went on watching, the old woman this time. She was wearing a straight cloth coat with a heavy fox fur round the neck, a fashion that had been old forty years ago; though the girls had always been embarrassed by the way she clung to ancient styles, now it looked good. On her gaunt body, over that ebony stick, it gave her authority, an air of the *grande dame*; and he grinned at that thought. Auntie Fido, a *grande dame*? A pantomime dame she'd been, a pantomime dame.

CHRISTMAS 1942

*'May your days be merry and bright, and may all your
Christmasses be white . . . .'*

'Such a thing!' Fido said. 'Such a thing! Your poor father must be turning in his grave!' and she looked at the little tree in the window with mock dismay and shook her head so that her earrings tinkled.

'No, he wouldn't,' Hetty said. 'He'd have had a bigger and better one. There was nothing mean about *him*. Best of everything, that's what he believed in, best of everything and all he could get of it.'

'Not Christmas trees,' Auntie Fido said, and patted her tightly-waved yellow hair, watching herself carefully in the mirror over the fireplace as she talked, watching her own lips move, turning her head from side to side to observe the play of expression over her narrow cheeks. Sammy looked at her and was embarrassed. She didn't know how silly she was, didn't know other people watched her watching herself. Didn't see Hetty's sardonic face as she stared at her. Poor Auntie Fido.

She turned and gave him a brilliant smile, showing her top and bottom teeth, and he tried not to look. The line of pink gum that showed beneath her upper lip repelled him and he couldn't trust himself not to show it. 'I'm sure your dear mother and father don't have such a thing in their house, do they, Sammy? I'm sure I don't know what they'll say if they hear your little friend is allowed to have such things. But what can I do with her? You know her too, my dear boy, don't you? How wilful she is?' And she looked at Hetty, her smile there on her face, meant to be rueful, the expression of a gentle, loving woman faced with a rebellious little orphan she was trying so hard to bring up. But she looked only watchful, unsure, and underneath that, frightened.

'Oh, we've got one too,' Sammy said quickly. 'My father says trees have nothing to do with religion. Not Christian at all. Ancient tree worship, fertility rites and so on – all because of Prince Albert –' His voice trailed away and he looked appealingly at Hetty but she only grinned at him. She knew perfectly well there was no Christmas tree at the Sternbergs. 'That's what he says,' he said and Hetty said loudly, 'Does he? How *sensible* of him. And how *generous*. I hate meanness, don't you, Sammy?'

'There's cake,' Auntie Fido said, suddenly bright. 'I managed a cake. Go and get tea ready, Hetty dear, and then we can all have it together, cosy and happy by the fireside.'

'I'm busy,' Hetty said savagely, and sat down heavily on the sofa, her feet under her, and staring at Auntie Fido with such an obvious sneer on her face that Sammy reddened with embarrassment.

'I'll do it,' Bertha said, and got up from the rug. She'd been sitting there in front of the fender with Hilda, helping her colour in her painting book. In fact her helping had been restricted to holding the crayons ready for when Hilda wanted them; any attempt by Bertha to choose a colour for her made Hilda's face tighten and her mouth open ready to shriek. So Bertha gave in.

Sammy was beginning to know this about Bertha, although he had seen little of her since he had started being Hetty's friend six weeks ago. Hetty had kept her sisters well at arms' length; until now, when she'd told him he was to come to tea on Christmas Day, at her command. And though he'd tried to refuse, tried to demonstrate his own willpower against her, he'd agreed, if only because Christmas with his parents was so awful. They always pretended it wasn't happening.

'I'll help you,' he said. 'I like making tea.'

And Auntie Fido beamed at him, almost coquettish. 'A boy, making tea? My dear, how very nice! You must be a great joy to your dear mother.'

'Er – yes –' he said, and followed Bertha out of the living room into the kitchen. He caught a glimpse of Hetty glaring at him furiously from the sofa and that pleased him. He'd show her.

Bertha prepared the tea tray with smooth deft movements and for a while he tried to help, dabbling ineffectually at drawers, trying to find things, but she smiled at him and said kindly, 'It doesn't matter. It was nice of you to come but I can manage, honestly. You make the tea when the kettle boils.'

He stood by the gas stove and waited for the big kettle to boil, looking round him. His own kitchen was different; cluttered, probably dirty in corners, but comfortable enough with a rag rug his mother had hooked herself, out of an old sack and cut-up pieces of his old clothes and a couple of her dresses, a bentwood rocking chair, and a big clothes horse in front of the old black-leaded range that was always festooned with damp washing. The big wooden table in the middle was usually pleasantly littered with this and that – half-eaten loaves and heels of cheese; a big brown teapot; comfortable, easy things.

But this kitchen was not at all comfortable. Shiny lino in red and yellow squares on the floor, a small table with matching American cloth on it naked of any ornament, very spick and span, a gas stove that was the latest thing in enamel and curling legs, and above all, the Easiwerk.

He knew about Easiwerks. His mother sometimes said helplessly that they could be tidier if they had one. He looked at this one with admiration as Bertha took things out of it and piled them on the tray; it was red and yellow like the lino, and had drawers and shelves and pull-out bits, and let-down bits; a miracle of space-saving design.

And the things she was taking out; cups and saucers with flowers on them. He thought of his mother's heavy white chipped things and said abruptly, 'They're pretty.'

'Auntie Fido likes pretty things,' Bertha said, and began to cut bread to make sandwiches. Grateful for something to do he took the knife from her, and carefully sliced the bread and she spread it with margarine and fishpaste.

'Hetty doesn't like her, does she?'

Bertha looked troubled and he glanced at her and felt a surge of agreeable feeling. Such a *nice* face. Chipmunk cheeks and a splodgy nose. So unlike Hetty's sharpness. Not as exciting, but very nice all the same. 'Does she?' he said again.

'She sort of does.' Bertha struggled to be loyal. You shouldn't talk about family things to strangers. The Family was everything.

She looked up at him and then away, shy suddenly. He was very nice; it has been amazing that Hetty should ever bring anyone so nice to tea. And a boy too. He was big and had a deep voice for a boy, she thought, and she could see a shadow of hair on his upper lip. A big boy.

'She says she's mean,' Sammy said.

'Oh, dear,' Bertha said, and put the sandwiches, neatly cut into triangles, on a plate to match the cups and saucers. 'Well, she's careful – she has to be with three of us to feed and clothe and –'

'Hetty says she's got lots of money for that. That you were left enough by your – when you were left alone, you know?' His curiosity was leaping up now. He'd been eaten with it ever since he'd met Hetty, but you couldn't quiz her. She told you what she wanted to and no more. But this one was different. She was soft. No, not soft. That sounded as though she were soppy. Just *nice*.

40

'Hetty says all sorts of things,' Bertha said unhappily. 'It's hard to know – she's the only one who remembers, really. I've forgotten such a lot.' She wrinkled her eyes. 'I was nine. Older than what Hilda is now. But I can't remember them at all.'

She looked up at him with her eyes wide and shiny damp. 'Isn't that awful? Not to remember them? That makes me cry sometimes. Not because of *them*, you know. Because I've forgotten.'

A door opened on the other side of the closed kitchen door, and they could hear Hetty's voice, loud and strident, shouting at Hilda, and Hilda was crying, a high whining sound, and Auntie Fido's voice bleated over the top.

'Will you come for a walk with me?' Sammy said urgently, his voice low. 'In the park?'

She looked at him, pink and dubious.

'Please. Not for anything special. Just friendly. Meet you at the swings, tomorrow. After dinner.'

Hetty was at the door. 'What are you two doing? Milking the cow? Or growing the corn for the bread?'

'The kettle's just boiling,' Bertha said, and began to make the tea, warming the pot, spooning in the leaves with punctilious care. 'What's Hilda shouting about?'

'Oh, silly bitch – always wants her own way, that one.'

'You shouldn't call her that,' Sammy said.

Hetty stared at him and picked up a sandwich and shoved it into her mouth. 'Common, is it?'

'Yes. So's talking with your mouth full.'

'Who told you you could tell me what to do?'

'You did. Said you wanted to know. Said you couldn't get it all from books.'

'Get what?' Bertha was standing by the table, carefully putting the cake, a small greyish-coloured fruit cake on a plate with a paper doily, beside the milk jug.

'Things,' Hetty said. 'Just things.' And smiled at Sammy, her eyes slitting. 'Are you having a *lovely* time, Sammy? A lovely, lovely time with us? Or would you rather be somewhere else? Shall we go for a walk after tea? In the park?'

Sammy took the tray from Bertha, and his hand touched hers. It felt good. 'No,' he said. 'It's not polite to rush off too soon after eating.' But he didn't look at her.

Bonnie moved out of his line of vision, disappeared into the stairwell, and he looked again at the two women moving towards him. They had seen her. The old woman was standing with her head up, her chin jutting forwards and peering, and they were close enough now for him to see her eyes. White rims round the pallid blue, the lashes stringy and almost gone, and he felt a stab of pity for her. A silly, posturing woman, full of giggles and exclamations, sudden bursts of ridiculous anger when she would make empty threats; but a pitiful one for all that. All those years when the three girls had circled round her and she round them; what had they given her? What was she left with? Alone and friendless.

He looked then at the other woman, trying to place her. He'd seen her before, he knew. There was a familiarity about her that ran so deep that he couldn't get hold of it; but he knew she was part of all this. She had as much reason to be here in court today as anyone. He felt that. But who the hell *was* she?

Thinking about who she was would keep him occupied a little longer, he told himself, and watched them move slowly out of sight, after Bonnie, towards Court thirty-six.

APRIL 1947

'*Do you love me, do you love me, do you love me, do you love me, tell me, do you,*
Do I really mean the whole world to you?'

'Why *should* she be here?' Hester said and poured another bottle of cider into the big glass bowl. 'That should pep it up a bit.'

'Well, I don't know – she's your aunt after all. Looks after you, I mean. It's not as though you haven't got any other old people here.' Sammy looked across the crowded little room at Sylvia Justin, lean and elegant in a long brown dress and with a Spanish shawl draped oh-so-negligently over her shoulders. 'What's she doing here, f'r example?'

Hester shot a look at her, her lip a little lifted. 'Isn't she a guy? What a way to dress! And her hair –'

'Oh, I dunno – interesting. She looks like those old magazine pictures. I like it. And people have had hair like that for – oh, ages. It's classical. Why is she here?'

'Classical,' said Hester witheringly and touched her own hair, cut into a fashionable Rita Hayworth ripple but not quite making it. 'She's nothing to do with me. Hilda said she wanted her. She's her art teacher.'

He looked at Hilda, sitting cross-legged on the floor between two girls and giggling, her curly fair hair springing about her head in a startled way. She could never look classical. 'She's getting very grown up,' he said.

'Very grown up,' mimicked Hester and giggled. 'Honestly, you're too much, sometimes, you really are. You've still got wet ears – who are you to say who's grown up?'

He grinned, slowly, looking at her with a direct gaze, and she stared back, her face very straight. 'You should know,' he said softly. 'You should know.'

She giggled again, and moved closer to him. 'I know.' Her voice was low with a thrill in it and he was chilled for a moment. He liked sharing these moments of intimacy with her, liked reminding her in noisy public places of what they did together in his room at home or sometimes here, in hers, behind the locked doors. They'd been doing it properly for over two months now, and he felt good about it. The first time hadn't been easy; it had hurt him like hell and she'd been so eager she hadn't given him time to ease it and the result had been a fiasco. He'd even bled a little. But now it was getting better all the time; he could even ask for the necessary in barbers' shops without blushing. But she shouldn't respond with that special voice; it was one she used to indicate deep feeling, or her version of passion. But it always had the effect of making him feel pushed away, instead of closer. So now he stopped smiling and looked again at Hilda.

'Why should she bring her art teacher to your birthday party?'

She shrugged, looking at him, trying to work out what had gone wrong. Every time she thought she had him, there he was again, gone. She liked that thought; there he was again, gone. That was what made him so interesting.

She looked round the room briefly, at the fluffed-up girls in their tightly-waisted cheap imitations of Dior New Look dresses, and felt a sudden surge of exultation. They thought they knew it all, but she had done things none of them would dare, for all their pretensions to be up to date; she had actually *done* it. She hadn't enjoyed it much but she'd done it. She wished she could tell them all. Stand on a chair and tell them all.

'It seems such a funny thing to do. When even your Auntie Fido isn't here.'

'Oh, shut up,' she said and turned away to pick up a cup and fill it with punch. 'You're getting boring. On and on – ask her if you're so interested.'

Sylvia Justin was a little surprised when he came and sat beside her, pushing his way through the crowd jigging up and down to the scratchy gramophone.

'Hello,' he said, and she smiled at him, putting up both hands to smooth the wings of hair on each side of her face. Someone had told her, when she was a student, that she looked like Virginia Woolf, so she'd looked like her ever since. He was a very good-looking young man, and she knew his face from somewhere.

'Hello,' she said, and smiled. 'I'm afraid you'll have to remind me. I meet so many of you all and I can never remember names. Shame-making, isn't it?'

'Not at all,' he said, very courteously. 'No reason why you should. You don't know me anyway. I'm a – well, a friend of the family.'

'Oh! Weren't you at Millfields Road school then, like the others?'

He looked briefly around at the sleek-headed boys trying to dance like Fred Astaire on a piece of floor as big as a minute and grimaced. 'Well, yes. Till I was thirteen. But then I went somewhere else. City of London School.'

'I knew I'd seen you!' she said triumphantly and smoothed her hair again, comfortably this time. Placing him as an ex-pupil made it all right, good looking though he was. Now she could be the indulgent on-looking adult again. I've been teaching there since – oh, thirty-seven it was. I must have seen you then.'

'I didn't take art,' he said absently. He was watching Hilda who was dancing with a very tall, very shiny young man, and moving with a grace and rhythm that was most beguiling. 'Woodwork.'

'Oh, dear, yes, they will separate you all so!' Sylvia said and sighed. 'So much talent lost! But I must have seen you about. Where are you at school now?'

44

He was still watching Hilda, a little startled. For a girl of fourteen she moved in a way that was remarkable. He couldn't believe she knew the effects of that sort of moving. 'Where are you now?' Sylvia said again, more insistently.

'Eh? Oh, I beg your pardon. It's the music. Noisy. Where now? I'm –' He reddened. 'I go to medical school in September. I'm working in the market at present. Ridley Road. To make some pocket money, you know.'

Her eyes had widened. '*Medical* school? My dear boy, you must have had very good School Cert. results. What did you say your name was?'

'They weren't bad. Er – I'm Sam –' He stopped. Getting used to the new name wasn't easy. Hester had had to force it on him in the first place, and then when his father had amazingly agreed that it wouldn't be a bad thing to do – people didn't like foreign names, and he cared nothing for his origins anyway, so why be burdened with a name like Sternberg? – he'd given in. 'Sampson Stermont,' he said self-consciously. 'Everyone calls me Sammy.'

She smiled. 'I used to be Jorowski, when I was a child. It's better the way it is now.'

Hilda was sitting down again. 'I was surprised to see you here,' he said after a moment. 'I mean – all these kids –' He looked round with a faint lift of one eyebrow. Apart from Sylvia Justin, he was the oldest person there, he decided. By at least two years. 'I certainly find it a bit childish.'

She tried not to be flattered and once more smoothed her hair, briskly this time. At thirty-two it was agreeable to have a boy of nineteen treat you as a contemporary. 'Hilda,' she said after a moment. 'She asked me to come and I have to coax her, so I said I would.'

He stared at her. 'Coax? How do you mean?'

'You say you're a friend of the family?' she said after a moment.

'Yes. For years – ages.' Five years is ages, when it's Hetty and Bertha and Hilda.

'Then you know about Hilda.'

'I know she can be very spoiled sometimes.' He looked at Hilda again and she caught his eye this time and he went pink. 'But she seems to be improving a bit.'

'Well – children,' Sylvia said. 'But Hilda – she's different. I've always been interested in her. Ever since I heard how her parents were killed. Dreadful affair that. Dreadful.'

'Yes, it was. Bertha has nightmares about it. All the time.'

'Bertha? Who? Oh yes, there's the other sister, isn't there? I'm afraid I tend to forget that. I know Hester, of course –' she shrugged. 'Well, Hilda is very gifted.'

He raised his eyebrows at that. 'Really? What in? Laughing her head off?'

She smiled. 'She does giggle a lot, I know. No, she's an artist. Inside, she's an artist. She has in her – oh, it's hard to explain.' Her shoulders lifted and she became a great deal more animated. 'Line and colour. She's really a very clever little girl. An – an exciting artistic personality. I – I recognized her talent some time ago, and started to give her special teaching. She comes to me every week. I –' Her voice dropped. 'I'm going to get her into Chelsea if it's the last thing I do.'

He shook his head, amused. 'And you have to *coax* her to come to your lessons? Never! Not the Hilda I know! That one'll go anywhere for someone to fuss over her!'

She smiled again, a little thinly. 'Well, of course, she *does* like attention – but don't we all? And she likes having tea with me.' She looked at him consideringly and then risked it. 'The aunt's a bit – well, times are hard. And Hilda gets very hungry, poor child.'

He laughed aloud then. 'Hilda, hungry? I'll say! Never stops, she doesn't. She's the greediest –'

Someone changed the record on the gramophone and then there were giggles as someone else put the light out, leaving the room illuminated only by the small lamp on the floor by the door, and the firelight. The new music was soft and slow and Sammy felt a hand on his arm, pulling him up.

'Dance with me,' Hilda's voice came commandingly. 'Sammy, dance with me. Teach me some new steps,' and then he was on his feet and her arms were round his neck and she had pulled him into the knot of swaying bodies in the middle of the room.

'You were talking about me,' she said in his ear, her chin pressed hard against his cheek. 'Weren't you?'

'Swankpot,' he said, trying to sound as reproving as he could. 'Why should we waste time talking about you?'

'I'm all the silly creature ever talks about, that's why. She thinks she's discovered me. She thinks I'm going to be a great artist. She *adores* me –'

'Swankpot,' he said again, uneasily. She was pressing her body close to his, and he could feel her small breasts against his shirt, hard and yet yielding. The way she was moving he couldn't help but feel them, as she made them shift and rub against him.

'No,' she said, 'I'm telling you! I'm very remarkable, she says. Loves me like a mother, she says, stupid object! Do you love me like a brother, Sammy?'

'Eh?'

'Well, you could, couldn't you? You've been around long enough.'

'Of course not.'

'You're sure?'

'Of course I am.'

'I'm glad,' she whispered, as the record moved into a noisier phase, violins wailing high pulsating notes that went through him sharply. 'Because I don't love you like a sister.' And she lifted her face and kissed him, finding his mouth unerringly, in spite of the dimness.

But what surprised him most was the way her tongue slid between his lips, and made his grip around her tighten, even though he hadn't intended to do anything of the kind.

5

There was a small flurry of excitement outside and David looked back, his chest lurching unpleasantly. Should he walk back and be near the entrance when she arrived – and who else but she could create this sort of response? – and let her see him there or wait and just sit in court for a while and catch her eye then? In the middle of a crowd it would be all too easy to be missed; better to wait in court.

A wise decision; but for all that he turned and went back to the entrance.

Outside in the thin March sunshine there was a little knot of people, men with cameras and women in heavy coats with shopping bags on their arms, clustered near a Rover 3.5. He looked at the car and its number 'HM 37' and thought, 'There's a few thousand there,' and tried not to be impressed. Most people in her situation would have a Rolls, but not her. Or would they? He frowned, trying to work it out; wasn't all this about money really, this whole case? How could she have such a car?

The crowd surged and thickened, people seeming to come from nowhere as another car pulled up behind the shining expanse of cellulose that was the Rover; a long rakish car, dirty yellow, with its windows tinted darkly, and people tried to push forwards and peeped in and with the prescience of a London crowd began to shout at the occupant, 'Hey JJ – come on out! JJ – come on out!'

David too moved forward, his eyes fixed on the yellow car. Above the crowd he saw the passenger door open, saw a man's head as someone got out, and then the car's engine roared and it shot out into the traffic going down to Fleet Street so sharply that a van had to swerve and the driver stood on his brakes till they shrieked; all of which distracted the crowd for a moment so that they let the man through.

He went past David with a long loping walk that was very fast, so close that his coat brushed against him, and he could hear himself telling Sandra, 'I was as close to him as I am to you. He's a lot older looking when you get close up. But a lot shorter, too. I'd imagined him quite tall, you know, but he's a real shrimp. Five foot six at the most – a real shrimp.'

But fast as the man moved, he was not fast enough to dodge the crowd altogether. They eddied, turned, re-formed and came after him, a little wave of people with their faces absorbed and their eyes staring. The men with cameras were fiddling with their equipment and there was a desultory popping of flash bulbs, and then, as David tried to get out of the way, suddenly frightened by the purposeful movements of the people bearing down on him, they shifted and eddied again as the Rover moved away, sedate and sleek.

She was left standing by the kerb with a fat man beside her, talking brightly, her face cheerful, smiling comfortably. She seemed as unconcerned and relaxed as though this were just an ordinary day and he looked at her and his throat tightened. He'd thought her ugly then, he really had, with her thin body and her sharp face, but looking at her now, he couldn't imagine why. She was everything the magazines were full of; spare and lean – lissome, he thought, really lissome, and wasn't sure he'd got it right – her face bony and cool. No wonder she's done so well, he thought, and moved further forwards, tweaking at his tie self-consciously, lifting his chin to improve the way his jaw-line looked. She seemed ageless, but he looked what he was, and he knew it. Nearly fifty and it showed in lots of ways. But he was well dressed, a smart man, and they all said women preferred maturity. That had been what had gone wrong before. He'd been immature. Young and raw, no wonder it had all been such a –

She was moving towards him, still talking animatedly to the man beside her who was bending his fat jowls and shining bald head courteously towards her, moving with a smooth swaying sort of step that made her back arch and her legs look particularly long and thin.

'I've told him I'll meet him at Joe Allen's at one. I don't give a damn whether they've adjourned by then or not. They can't keep me there if I've decided to leave, can they? I mean, Jesus Christ, man, it's not some sort of criminal action, is it? – you can tell 'em from me –'

The fat man murmured something into her ear and she frowned for a moment and opened her mouth to speak, but the fat man went on a little more urgently and David moved forwards further still. They were almost level with him now and she was listening to the fat man with her eyes narrowed, and he panicked a little, for the crowd was now surging back towards them as the short man disappeared at the far side of the huge hallway. He stepped right in front of her, and smiled, settling his features into as relaxed and welcoming an expression as he could.

'My dear!' he said. 'Hester, good to see you –'

She looked at him blankly, clearly not hearing him and he stared back into the black shining eyes that once had reminded him of little boot buttons but now seemed rich, deep and exciting. Without a flicker of recognition, she turned sharply to the fat man beside her.

'I don't bloody well agree to it, and that's all about it!' she said and moved sideways so as to pass David, and he stepped in the same direction, trying to stop her. 'Hester,' he said again, but his voice caught in his throat and came out huskily and he coughed, and again she stared at him in that blank unseeing way.

'You tell them – I'm not going to be pushed around, whatever they think. No way! Jesus God, man, who do they think they are?'

The fat man shook his head. 'We can't talk here, Miss Morrissey, really we can't. Your fans, you know –' and he giggled, a silly high-pitched giggle to come from so fat a body. 'It'll be much easier in court. Now, please, sir, make way for Miss Morrissey – if you please.' His voice had lifted, become officious and shrill; he pushed David to one side with his shoulder, and as the crowd surged round them turned his head and called to the doorman at the entrance, 'Hey – come and help here, will you? This is really too much –'

And then the doorman was there, and David was pushed further back, though he tried to tell them he wasn't one of this stupid gawping mob, but David Spero. He had a right to be here, damn it all, a right to be here. He *knew* her. He used to know her very well.

'They tried to tell us we're too young,
Too young to really fall in love ....'

Plays weren't really his thing. He liked musical shows, and went to them whenever they opened in the big theatres, but plays were something else. Corinne had been used to going to plays, droning on and on about Shakespeare and Laurence Olivier, very boring. But he preferred a film any day. *Call Me Madam*, now there was a film he'd liked, and Betty Grable and Humphrey Bogart, they were actors he liked. But plays with people he'd never heard of, in a draughty Settlement hall with hard seats, that was something else again.

He sat gloomily thinking of how much he'd paid to be there. Six seats at five bob each, and he hadn't been able to give them away, let alone get any of them to pay for one. Allowing for taking Bonnie, this evening had cost him fifteen shillings a head; he'd need a lot of comforting to get over *that*.

He twisted in his seat, staring back at the entrance. The hall was only half full, though it was ten to eight and the thing was supposed to be starting at eight o'clock, and there was still no Bonnie. The girl at the door, taking the money and the tickets importantly, fussing over a seating plan, was chattering animatedly to a middle-aged man in dirty white trousers and a heavy grey sweater with a turtle neck. His dark hair was quite long, almost over his ears, and David looked at him with distaste; the sort of clothes some people wore! He twitched at his own neat trousers with some complacency. A snappy dresser, he was, and knew good stuff when he saw it. A man's character showed in his clothes, he'd always said that.

Where the hell was Bonnie? For two pins he'd get up and walk out. Why should he sit here in this damned cold uncomfortable place waiting to see a play he wasn't interested in if she couldn't be bothered to get there in time? He sat and contemplated his loneliness, aggrieved.

'Mr – ah – Spero?'

The man in the turtle neck sweater was beside him, his head on one side. 'Are you Mr Spero?'

'Eh? Oh, yes. Were you looking for me?'

51

'You weren't hard to find,' the man said, and looked over his shoulder at the sparse audience. 'We don't get that many strangers here. Most of 'em are either shop-keepers who show our posters or relatives of the cast. There aren't many who buy six expensive tickets and then come on their own.'

'No,' David said feelingly. 'I suppose not.'

'Hester sent me round.'

'Oh! Well, yes – hello.'

'My name's Myton. Harold Myton. Most of my friends call me Hal.' He thrust one hand forward with a forceful gesture and David took it, and was startled at the strong warm grip he was given, a little lingering. 'I'm the producer of this shower of erks who call themselves actors. The only one with any real talent is Hester, of course. Marvellous little performer, marvellous.'

'Er – yes,' David said, and was oddly uncomfortable. The man was looking at him with such a direct gaze, staring him in the eye, and he wasn't used to it. Most people let their eyes slide away, didn't give you this direct manly gaze – he must be an actor too, he thought.

'Thing is, poor old aunt's ill – the one Hester lives with, you know?'

'Oh?' David was nonplussed. 'Er – I'm sorry to hear it –'

'Oh, I doubt you are really!' Hal said and winked, wrinkling his eyes charmingly at him. 'Frightful old bird she is from all accounts. Rabidly boring, you must admit. Anyway, ill she is – so poor old you, Bonnie won't be here.'

'Oh!' It made sense at last. 'She's looking after her, you mean?'

'That's about the shape of it! Poor Bonnie! Nice girl, I'm told, though I can't say I've seen much of her – Hester's the one we know best, of course – here we go! Would you believe it! Curtain ready to go up only five minutes late!'

Someone was peering round the side of the shabby red curtain hissing at him, and Hal grinned back with rueful boyishness at David. 'No peace for the wicked! Well, I'll go back and do my bit – don't like to stay behind too much during a performance – not professional, you know, not at all professional. But they like to see me – have conniption fits if I don't go and wish them luck and so forth. I'll be back if I may – use Bonnie's seat, perhaps?'

'Yes – of course,' David said, and Hal put a hand on his

shoulder, warm and heavy, and once more gave him a wrinkle-eyed boyish grin and went off to the side of the stage as a rather scratchy record of the New World Symphony hissed the sparse audience into silence.

It took him a while to understand what was going on. He was irritated at first and then sorry for them; you'd think a play would have decent scenery, but the most this lot could run to was a couple of ladders and a few battered chairs. To take money from people to watch such sorry stuff – it was a bit much.

But after a while he began to quite like what he was watching. There was a man who told the audience what it was about, which was something, at least. And he settled down to listen to the story of a small American town half a century ago, trying not to notice how cold his feet were and how the draughts from the back of the hall whistled down his neck.

Hester came on after a while, dressed in white muslin, and he wanted to laugh suddenly. She was supposed to be a pretty young girl, he could tell that, but she was anything but pretty, there was no question about that. Her bony shoulders looked scrawnier than ever, poking up out of the white muslin, and her legs were stick-like. But she moved well, not awkwardly like the others, and she certainly sounded young, which was more than the rest of them did. They seemed to move about the stage lumpishly, even to his uninformed eye, and whatever age the words they said made them out to be, they all seemed to be about the same, somewhere around the twenties. There were people who were meant to be old; you could tell that from the white beards and moustaches they had, or the lines drawn on their faces (from his front row seat, he could see the lines very clearly) and there were people who were meant to be children. But they all sounded much the same.

Except Hester. He watched her with a grudging approval. She really sounded American, not half and half like the others. She was really sad sometimes, and sometimes quite funny, the way she was supposed to be, and made the play which was in truth deadly dull seem quite interesting. She was still Hester though, still the sharp-tongued edgy girl he was beginning to know so well.

After a while Hal came and slipped into the seat beside him, and smiled at him in the darkness.

'Okay? Good. Terrible light cues, tonight. The usual sparks is off sick, boring old shit. Honestly, how anyone can produce anything *approaching* theatre in these circumstances is beyond me – but dear old Thornton Wilder can take a lot of bashing –'

Someone behind them hissed, 'Shh' and Hal winked at David in a conspiratorial way and turned to watch the stage, his hands resting lightly on his knees, his head on one side.

After a while David became uncomfortably aware that Hal's hand was almost on his own thigh, and he looked down, surprised. And then remembered the guffawing tales some of the other blokes had told him about what went on with actors, and at once coughed loudly and crossed his legs with some ostentation, so that his leg was taken well away from the errant hand.

Hal seemed quite unaware, but after a moment he folded his arms and sat watching with a frown of concentration on his face, and David breathed again. He might be one of *them* but at least he could pick up a message.

He thought a little more about it as the play ground boringly on, and by the time the interval came he was feeling quite good-humoured, in spite of Bonnie's absence. He'd had a pass made at him by a theatrical producer; it would make a good story at the office tomorrow and they needn't know what sort of producer the chap was, or where his play was showing. His father mustn't hear about it – he was likely to get very boring about the sort of people he went around with – but the other fellers, they'd enjoy it.

In the interval, as soon as the lights had gone up again, Hal smiled at him briefly and remotely and disappeared back stage to come back only after the lights had gone down again, and this time he said nothing as he took his seat again, offering only the briefest of nods, and the play ground on to its end at last, leaving David feeling oddly deflated. He'd enjoyed that moment of peculiar behaviour earlier; it would have been a laugh to lead him on, let him make a fool of himself and then kick him in the balls, he thought. It would have been better than listening to all this rubbish about dead people going on and on about their town.

'Not too bad, I hope?' Hal said, as the audience trickled lethargically out of the hall. 'Can't pretend they're exactly the

Old Vic, but there's a bit of talent sparking here and there, you know, quite a bit.'

'Very nice, really,' David said, and pushed his hands into his pockets. 'I – er – Hester's all right, isn't she?'

'Much more than all right!' Hal said, suddenly bright. 'Very much so! Got the real thing in her, has our Hester. With the right training she could go far.'

'Yes. I'm sure.'

There was a silence for a moment, and then the red curtain, which had closed shakily on the last act opened again and someone began to tidy up the stage. There were voices and shouting and more people came on stage, and Hal sighed sharply and clapped his hands together with a large gesture.

'My dear chaps and chapesses, do *please* try to conduct yourselves with a modicum of decorum! All this din! You'll have the neighbours in complaining again if you don't watch it – Jenny *darling*, *don't* try to shift that thing on your own. You'll do yourself a personal! My God, that'll come down like a hernia if you don't fix it properly to the cleat, you idiot – Peter, do you hear me? Fix it properly!'

Scolding and chattering busily, he went to the foot of the stage and jumped up with rather obviously lithe movements, and began to haul on a piece of furniture.

'Oh, David, my dear chap,' he looked over his shoulder into the hall. 'I forgot to say – Hester says do come round and see her. You'll have to wait till the crowd gets out of course – no star dressing rooms here! But you'll be able to get there in fifteen minutes or so –'

He sat there watching them, and they played up to their audience of one, talking loudly and with a great deal of stagy slang. One girl, very large and wearing a sort of tent, was smoking a pipe and he tried not to stare at her. It would be as embarrassing as staring at a cripple.

They went after a while, with much shouting about which pub they would favour tonight with their presence and whose turn it was to stay and lock up, and he heard someone shouting backstage about it, and a muffled reply.

'Hester says she will,' the girl called Jenny announced. 'She's got to come in first tomorrow night anyway. Are you fit, you lot?'

They all went at once, leaving him alone, and he got up a little uncertainly and after poking about awkwardly among the bunched curtains at the side of the stage found a place where he could climb up a step ladder to get to it. Not for him the leaping muscularity displayed by Hal.

He found her in a big room at the back of the stage. It smelled, a mixture of scent and sweat and grease paint and old rubber shoes and he made a face. She was sitting in a corner staring at herself in a mirror and she turned her head as he came in and looked at him and smiled.

He stood in the doorway and stared back and for a moment he was confused. On stage she'd looked painted and like an actress, obviously pretending to be young and pretty and doing it quite well, except for being pretty. But here, with the ring of lights that was round her mirror throwing their radiance on her she seemed to be softer and shinier and much more like Bonnie than she'd ever been. There was a gentle haziness around her that seemed to plump up her cheeks, and her eyes were wide and though as dark as ever, not nearly so hard.

He smiled and she leaned back in her chair and smiled too.

'Hello, David Spero! Well, was it as awful as you thought it'd be?'

'Not quite,' he said and felt pleased with himself. That had sounded quite sophisticated.

'Kind of you!' she said, drawling a little, and turned back to the mirror and began to rub at her cheeks with a piece of cotton wool, watching his reflection all the time. 'At least you were honest. Much better than that awful, "You were *mahvellous*, darling," they all go in for.'

'Do they? Really?'

She grimaced. 'No they don't. Not really. Not round here, anyway. They're awful here. Really shitty.'

He blinked at that and she laughed, the familiar sardonic note sliding back into her voice. 'Oh, lor', you goody good! Don't tell me you're going to be like Sammy and go on at me all the time about my language! He goes on and *on* about it – but he wouldn't know real class if it sat up and begged him for a biscuit.'

She turned in her chair and with very deliberate movements began to pull her stockings over her bare legs and he watched,

56

fascinated, as she stood up and without a hint of self-consciousness hitched up her dress so that she could fasten the suspenders. Her legs weren't at all the voluptuous sort he liked. but to see a girl's legs so far up at all in such circumstances was exciting in itself, and he took his hands out of his pockets and buttoned up his jacket, in case she had noticed the way his body had responded.

She smiled at him, her chin down and peeping up under her lashes so that she looked almost seductive.

'Come and do up my dress at the back, David, there's a love,' she murmured. 'I always get the hooks all wrong.'

Awkwardly he came across the clutter towards her, suddenly very aware of the emptiness of the room all round them, and of the greater emptiness of the hall and stage beyond. His fingers were clumsy, and it was difficult anyway because she was swaying back against him as he fumbled, trying to find the eyelets.

He looked over her shoulder at the mirror in front of them, and caught her eyes and stood there staring at her, feeling almost like a mesmerized rabbit, and she smiled slowly, and still the illusion of prettiness remained. Her eyes sparkled in the lights, her skin seemed translucent and her half open mouth soft and inviting.

Moving slowly and quite deliberately, she put one hand behind her and took hold of his, and pulled it round in front of her and held it to her chest on the skin revealed by the V neck, and he let her, and stood there still staring at her in the mirror, very aware of the discomfort his underpants were now causing him.

She moved her shoulders then, hunching them forwards a little and her still-unhooked dress gaped at the back and at the front too, and she pushed gently on his hand and it slid into the neck of her dress as naturally and as easily as if he'd done it himself. He couldn't tell whether or not he had, in fact; all he knew was that he could feel the curve of her breast under his hand, and her nipple, surprisingly large for so small a breast, erect and hot under his fingers.

She was still smiling at him in the mirror, still holding his gaze, and now she began to move her hips, very gently, arching her back so that her buttocks were rubbing against him and the sensation was exquisite, hurting and exciting him in equal measure.

'Don't,' he said huskily and swallowed and licked his lips, not because he was dry but to control the moistness; she was making him dribble, the thought, like a baby. Bonnie doesn't make me dribble.

The thought of Bonnie eased itself awkwardly further into his mind, and he frowned and looked away from the mirror for a moment and she sensed at once that she had lost his concentration and slid round in the circle of his arm, pressing herself against him.

'Kiss me,' she said, very softly, and put her mouth on his, pushing his lips open with a sharply pointed tongue and at the same time putting one hand up behind his head to play with the hair at the nape of his neck.

But it was her other hand of which he was most intensely aware. As easily as she had made his fingers slide under her dress, her own were manipulating the buttons on his flies, and the pain he was in and the excitement he was feeling made him straddle his legs a little wider to make it easier for her, until with an experienced flick of her wrist at last the discomfort had gone; and he pulled her closer and kissed her hard, beginning to enjoy himself consciously instead of just letting it happen to him.

They stood there, pressed together as tightly as they could and as her fingers moved across his neck as well as inside his pants he thought confusedly – wait. Not too much, oh, not too much –

But it didn't help. It was uncontrollable and he closed his eyes and threw his head back and let the sensation wash over him, feeling his pulse speed up and his lungs suck in air as greedily as his body was pumping out his excitement.

'Oh, for Christ's sake!' she said, disgustedly, and pulled away from him, staring down at her hand with her upper lip twisted in distaste. 'For Christ's sake!' and she ran away across the room to the wash basin in the corner and started to scrub at her hands almost viciously, leaving him standing there breathing deeply and feeling very shaky.

'I'm sorry,' he said after a moment, and she looked at him over her shoulder and grinned. But it wasn't a pretty grin any more, and she wasn't soft and hazy and seductive any more. She was her sharp-edged self again, and he looked at her miserably and then bent his head and turning round did what he could to tidy himself up, being as unobtrusive with a handkerchief as he could, knowing perfectly well that she was watching him and laughing.

'A fat lot of good you are!' she said. 'Honestly, a fat lot of good! You're as pretty as they come, and much good you are! You ought to have gone off with Hal, for all the use you are to anyone! Any woman, that is!'

He went white and turned on her, his teeth showing. 'Don't you ever say – how dare you – you bitch, you rotten stinking –'

She laughed aloud at that, standing leaning back against the wash basin and drying her hands.

'Oh, got you there, have I? The gentleman doth protest too much! Oh, do me a favour, sad sack! Go home to bed and play with yourself! You need practice, you do!'

He left her, almost running out of the hall; driving as fast as he dared he got to the house in Hackney at least half an hour before she could be expected to get there by bus.

Bonnie was sitting alone by the dying fire in the small sitting room, Auntie Fido being asleep and Hilda out somewhere on her own affairs. He wasted as little time as he could, being almost perfunctory about it; and by the time Hester's key was turning in the door, he'd proposed and she, blinking a little and seeming slightly startled, had accepted him. They were engaged. There was only his family to be told now.

6

'Bugger me!' Hildegarde said. 'You'd think they could do better than this!'

'Later, dear, later,' Mel murmured and slid his eyes sideways to look at her, waiting for applause for his wit.

But she'd heard the joke before and ignored him, standing there on the kerb as the taxi rolled away and looking about her with her head up and her mouth set in a tight line.

She was wearing hand-knitted cashmere trousers, very full and gathered at the knee, over high-heeled boots dyed to an exactly matching rusty colour and a tunic in deep brown over a leather waistcoat and yellow silk shirt. Her hair was, as ever, a great curly aureole of streaks running from the ashiest blonde to the most auburny red, her make up was an amalgam of yellow eyeshadow, brown lipstick and almost white cheeks, and altogether she looked startling and at first sight repelling.

But only at first sight; people who glanced and sniggered stopped and looked again, especially the women, and after a few moments her stillness as well as her clothes had the effect she wanted. People stopped and clustered, stared and whispered and a small crowd collected, and she smiled and then began to move forwards with what seemed an easy relaxed stride but which was in fact a very slow walk. It gave more people more time to see her, and by the time she had passed the doorman and was in the great hallway of the Law Courts, the crowd was sizeable. The photographers loitering at the far end of the hallway near the stairs that led to Court thirty-six picked up the vibrations somehow and turned and came hurrying back.

'That's better!' she murmured and grinned sharply at Mel walking beside her with his thumbs hooked into the belt that held his jeans precariously to his hips. 'Whose bloody case is it, damn it all?'

'Well, you could say theirs,' Mel said and moved closer to her as the photographers began to point cameras in their direction. 'They're the ones defending the action, after all.'

Hildegarde changed the angle of her strolling walk, widening the space between them fractionally but just enough, and smiled brilliantly at the only photographer who was quick enough off the mark to get her on a solo shot. 'Like bloody hell!' she said. 'I'm the one who started it, aren't I? She's the one in trouble, not me. And don't you fucking well forget it, my friend, don't you forget it!'

'Who's forgetting anything?' He put one arm across her shoulders negligently and nuzzled into her ear. 'If I forget you, oh Hildegarde, let my right hand forget her cunning.'

'Very funny – hello, Ken me old darlin'! And what are *you* doing in this pisshole on such a bright and lovely morning?'

The man who had come swiftly towards her, his heels clacking noisily on the terrazzo floor, threw his arms wide. 'My angel, my heart, loveliest thing I've seen since I got out of bed this morning, what should I be doing here but looking for you? Ready for the fray, are you?'

'Ready? I'm looking forward to it! I'm going to have a bloody marvellous time, watching 'em fall flat on their faces so hard you won't be able to see 'em for dust. How's that for a quotable quote?'

'Lovely – leave it for the camera. We've got a set-up in a corner over there. Talk to me?'

'Try and stop her,' Mel said and hugged her closer, and she shoved an elbow into his ribs so sharply that he gasped.

'For you, Ken darling, anything –' She slid her arm about Ken's waist and together they went across the hallway back towards the courtyard in front of the steps talking brightly and busily for the benefit of the gawpers and Mel followed them, walking easily and comfortably but with the line around his smiling mouth that showed his rage. Stinking bitch; one of these days she was going to come out with too much, just that little bit too much, and then she'd know what was what. He'd show her. He wasn't here just to make up the number, and the sooner she got that clear in her scheming head the better for her.

'Okay, darling, just a few words for level –' Ken was fussing over her, standing her against the steps, jerking his head at the bored lighting man, making sure he looked as good as she did, that he wasn't shut out of the pool of light that fell on her from the hand-held lamp. 'Tilt your chin a little, darling, look *up* to me – makes you look that little bit defenceless, you know? Clever girl – just a few words then –'

'And it makes you look that little bit more sexy, eh, Ken? Nothing beats having us itsy-bitsy females look up to you, unless it's having us flat on our backs –'

'Charming as ever – dear little soul,' Ken said. 'Okay, Peter? Let's get on with it then –' His voice sharpened and he tilted the microphone in his hand towards his own chin. 'Take one. Ken Adams interviewing Hildegarde Maurice at the Law Courts in the Strand, 14th March. Miss Maurice, how do you feel this case is likely to turn out? Have you any fears or doubts that – ah –'

'That justice will prevail?' Hildegarde said, and smiled a gentle sweet smile. 'None at all. How could I, standing here in this building?' She turned her head gesturing to take in the vast echoing expanse behind the cameraman. 'The place positively *breathes* security and – and – fairness, you know?' She smiled up at him, her teeth showing softly behind her parted lips.

'But it must be a painful time for you, Miss Maurice, to be involved in such a case brought by –'

'It makes no difference,' Hildegarde said, and now her face was very straight and serious again. 'Justice is justice, no matter who is involved. That was why I brought my action in the first place. But are we supposed to be talking about the case at all at this moment in time? My legal advisers –'

'Well, I dare say they're right, Miss Maurice. So let's talk about a much more interesting subject for our lady viewers – your clothes. How would you describe the outfit you're wearing now?'

The man with the camera on his shoulder began to move slowly backwards, lengthening the shot as Hildegarde launched herself into a spirited description of her clothes, turning a little from time to time, showing herself to advantage.

Watching her, Mel had to admit she looked good. For a woman of her age she was well preserved. They all three were – it was something in their blood, he imagined. I wonder what their mother would have looked like? he thought suddenly, and was a little surprised at himself. Why the hell should it matter?

Because everything about Hildegarde matters, he told himself and scowled again. He'd never meant to get like this about her; all these years and he'd used her and enjoyed her, and though he'd tried to marry her admittedly, that had been entirely for practical reasons, which seemed in some ways to be more pressing than ever now. But all the same he'd never given a damn one way or the other about how she felt, or about his own feelings. People who had feelings were bloody boring; he'd never believed in feelings, himself. And now here he was watching her and not just leching. That would be normal, but this was different. This was wanting and hurting with it. Christ, but he'd be glad to get this case over and done with. She thought it was all going to go her way, but he'd been around long enough himself to know better. Anything could happen to swing it, anything at all. This sort of case was a bastard to predict, no one could. Juries never reacted as you expected anyway.

But she was sure, the way she always was, the way she had been the day he'd first met her.

NOVEMBER 1952

'Don't laugh at me, 'cos I'm a fool,
Don't laugh at me 'cos I'm a clown....'

Cold, foggy, raw in his throat, the winter evening should have filled him with depression. He hated to be cold. But tonight he wasn't depressed. Tonight he felt good, full of excitement so solid it was as though he'd eaten a huge meal. Yet he'd had nothing but coffee all day, quantities of *cappucino* in glass cups, sitting in the Coffee House in Northumberland Avenue, waiting for the results. The others had hung around college, but not him; he wouldn't let them know he cared.

But he cared all right and when he'd gone strolling back to look at the notice board and seen his name up there high on the list it took all the control he had to prevent himself from behaving like the others, jumping about, banging each other on the back.

'Not bad,' he'd drawled, and lit another cigarette, casual, very relaxed, turning away from the notice board with never a backward look, though he wanted to look again to reassure himself just as much as anyone else.

But it was all right. He'd made it. From here on in there was to be no stopping him. The others could go get themselves dug into safe partnerships in dingy practices, all set to spend the rest of their lives conveyancing dingy houses for dingy couples who might, if they were lucky, come back to get themselves even dingier divorces. None of that would do for Melvin Bremner. He had ideas beyond that. Ideas that tinkled with money, rang with fame, rippled with power. He'd show 'em.

He ran up the steps two at a time, into the echoing green-painted corridors and wrinkled his nose at the smell of it; disinfectant and dust, old shoes and sour people. His own college smelt too, but this place was dirtier, somehow, and he looked at a couple of students clattering past him on the way out, dirty trousers, stained old duffle coats, half shaved, and could see why. No style at all.

He reached the central hall and stopped in the doorway. There were people moving about arranging paintings on tall screens and he gave them a perfunctory look. Odd stuff, all lines and swirls and nothing you could recognize. But Birgitta had laughed at him when he'd said as much, the only time she'd done anything so positive, so now he kept his mouth shut. If it was art, all right; he'd take their word for it. But from where he was standing it still looked like a lot of rubbish.

He hovered in the doorway until someone he knew vaguely saw him and called out, 'She said to tell you she's down in room twenty-six. Go and get her there –' and he nodded his thanks and went swinging down the corridor. He'd buy her a meal tonight. He didn't have to; she'd let him anyway, would lie there and let him get on with it and never object – be the ideal partner short of actually doing anything active herself, but what the hell – she'd get round to it one of these days. But he'd buy her a meal all the same, because he was hungry now, after all, and he was feeling benevolent.

The door was closed and he pushed it open, not bothering to knock, and stood at the doorway staring in. Birgitta was sitting on the teacher's desk at the front of the classroom, her head a little forwards so that the great sheet of flat yellow hair was over her face, with one arm around the shoulders of a much smaller girl. She was also fair haired, but hers was fuzzily curly and sat on her head like a knitted cap, and she was small and rounded where Birgitta was large and angled.

The younger girl had been sitting with her head on Birgitta's shoulder and she looked up as the door opened and smiled lazily at the sight of him, but Birgitta turned her head and stared at the door, her face set and tight. She looked – he couldn't say how she looked at first, for he had never before seen any real expression on her face at all; even when they were poking she was blank and blue eyed, her face broad and bovine beneath his own.

Yet now that flat face was twisted and emotional and even as it smoothed out at the sight of him and became the familiar blank again, he recognized the look. She was angry and frustrated. The only other time he'd seen anyone look quite like that was when he'd walked in on old Donald and he'd got a girl on the floor and was almost there –

Birgitta, moving awkwardly, scrambled off the desk and then stood with her hands hanging loosely at her sides and nodded solemnly at him.

'Melvin, it is you. Good evening. You are early. The news of the examination, it is good?'

'It is good,' he said, but didn't look at her. He was looking at the other girl, who had drawn her legs up and was sitting on the desk like an elf, curled up, her chin resting on her knees.

'This is Melvin,' Birgitta said after a moment and turned to the desk, still moving stiffly. 'The man I have spoken of to you, Melvin Bremner.'

'The one who buys you dinners when you're broke,' the other girl said, and she stared at Mel with her eyebrows a little arched, almost scornfully.

'Among other things,' Melvin said easily and came into the room and closed the door behind him. 'Hope I haven't interrupted anything important?'

'Not at all!' the smaller girl said and stretched and then slid off the desk. 'We were just talking about getting ready for the exhibition next week. It's the diploma show.'

'It is the one which gives us our diplomas,' Birgitta said and her sing-song accent irritated him even more than it usually did.

'I imagined as much. I'm really quite bright, sometimes.'

'Oooh, sarky, too.' The other girl tilted her head and stared at him more coolly than ever. 'Know any more clever things to say?'

'I didn't catch your name,' Mel said after a moment.

'I didn't throw it,' the girl said airily and then giggled. 'I thought you said he was all right, Gitta? He looks stuffed to me.'

'This is Hilda Morris, Mel. She is making the jokes. Always she is making the jokes,' Birgitta said woodenly, and turned back to the desk and began to pick up some papers and pieces of fabric that were piled on it.

'Really? I would never have know if you hadn't told me. Are you ready?'

'Where're you going then?' Hilda said. She was leaning against the desk with her arms folded, staring at him, and he ignored her, concentrating on Birgitta, who was taking a maddeningly long time to fold the papers, tucking them into a case. 'Straight to her room, I suppose? Get your leg over and then hop it? A great way to spend the evening –'

'Look, lady, I don't know you, never set eyes on you before tonight, and as far as I'm concerned if I never do again it'll be too soon. Who the bloody hell do you think you are to –'

'Oh, he *has* got some blood in him then, Gitta!' Hilda crowed and clapped her hands. 'See? I told you! If you tell him where he gets off, he might even get off! You don't have to put up with it! You're just being a mug, that's what you're being.' She turned and stared at him again, her eyebrows raised. 'Gitta's my friend, you know? F-R-I-E-N-D. Have you heard about friends? They look after each other. She may be a long way from the snows of home and all that, but she's got a friend. And she's told me about you, and do you know what I think?'

'It would amaze me to know you could think at all.'

'Baby face! Baby talk! I think you're a pig! You get hold of a girl who's alone and living on tuppence ha'penny and you think that for the price of a few meals you can use her as a regular mattress! Well, she's not all alone, see? I won't *let* her put up with you any more –'

He stood and stared at her and then looked at Birgitta and the words that were waiting to come out stopped in his throat. She was staring at Hilda, her mouth open and moist, her eyes shining and her face, usually so pale, mottled with pink patches.

He looked back at Hilda, embarrassed, and she winked at him suddenly and then laughed. 'Just thought I'd mention it!'

66

He shook his head, bewildered, and looked at Birgitta again. She had turned back to the desk and was bending her head over the papers once more, the sheet of yellow hair covering her face.

'I'll have to work this one out,' he said after a moment. 'I mean – who's mixed up with who around here? Are you two dykes?'

Birgitta looked up. 'Dyke? What is dyke?'

'If you don't know, then I'm not here to tell you. But you know –' He was staring at her, all the anger that this sudden argument had created in him dissolving away. Was this the reason for the way she seemed so unconcerned when they were poking? Was this what lay behind that blank face, the stillness of the pale blue eyes when he looked into them?

He turned his head, flicking his eyes back to Hilda and she laughed suddenly, lifting her chin and opening her mouth wide so that her teeth showed.

'I know!' she crowed. 'I think you're a hoot, honestly I do! Why can't a couple of girls be friends, for God's sake?'

'I don't know,' he said, and sat down on one of the desks, stretching his legs out in front of him. 'Why can't they? I've been told they can't.'

'Not like blokes, of course!' Hilda said. 'They can hang round each other's necks all day, and that's just loyalty, isn't it? When women do it, it's different –'

'Hilda, please, shall I come to your house tomorrow then, to fix the dress?' Birgitta had packed her case at last and was standing with it under her arm, pulling on a pair of knitted gloves. 'And I can then show you the way the sketch should go for next week. Shall it be the time you said?'

'It shall be the time I said,' Hilda said, her voice taking on a faint mocking sing-song note of its own, and she winked again at Mel and almost against his will he grinned back. She was the oddest girl he'd come across in months, he was thinking. Very much the oddest.

She was looking at him, too, and after a moment she said, 'Gitta, my love, do me a favour, will you? I left my coat and my case down in the east cloakroom, and my feet are killing me. If you get them, I'll talk Loverboy here into making sure you get a real tuck-in tonight – as well as him –'

'The east cloakroom. The case and red coat,' Birgitta said carefully and at once went, closing the door tidily behind her, leaving them looking at each other.

There was a small silence and then she said conversationally, 'I'm not a dyke, you know. Can't be bothered with it. The girls at school used to do it, swooning over each other like fairy queens. Not my style at all.'

'Really? You could have fooled me.'

'She is, of course.'

'What?'

'Gitta is.' She sounded impatient. 'She thinks the sun shines out of my bottom.'

He was embarrassed suddenly. 'I thought you said you were friends?'

'Well, so we are!'

'With friends like you, who needs enemies?'

'Oh, don't be so *silly*. Friends take each other as they are. That's what it's all about! *She* couldn't, of course. I've got to be the best, the sweetest, the cleverest, the kindest –' She giggled again, a sound that was becoming familiar to him. 'So, of course, I am.'

'You're a nutcase, you know that? A real nutcase.'

'Not really. Just got my eyes open. I look at people, see what they want from me and give it to them if it suits me. Is that so nutty?'

He shook his head slowly. 'No, maybe not.'

'Don't you?' She was sitting on the desk again, her arms round her knees and her chin resting on them, staring at him from beneath her raised brows.

'Don't I what?'

'Give 'em what they're looking for? No more, but no less?'

He laughed then. 'You know, I think maybe I do, at that. Can't be doing with waste –'

'Nor can I. Make the best of everything, right?'

'Right.'

There was a little silence and then she said, 'You're a lawyer, aren't you? Wigs and gowns in court and all that?'

'No. I'm a solicitor.'

'Same thing, isn't it? A lawyer.'

'Lawyer isn't a word that really means anything. A solicitor deals with clients, sorts out cases – barristers go into courts. In wigs and gowns.'

'Oh. So, you're in an office?'

'Not yet. I only qualified – well, today, actually.'

'Oh, yes, I'd forgotten. Exams and that – so now what?'

He grinned and stood up, stretching a little. 'Now, I'm going to make some money.'

'Buy Birgitta some real meals then?'

'To hell with Birgitta. What's it got to do with you?'

'A lot. She's helping me.'

He quirked his head at that. 'Helping you? How?'

'Like I said, you make the best of what you can – she's very good at the technical bits. Me, I'm good at colour and line – but she's the technical lady. So she's doing my diploma bits for me.'

He stared at her. 'Can you get away with that?'

'You watch me! Of course I can. Gitta won't say anything. She'd die before she did anything to upset me. I told you, sun rises and sets in me. It's exhausting.'

'Not as much as doing your own diploma bits, though.'

She laughed. 'Now you're beginning to get an inkling. So, like I said, are you going to start treating her right? She only lets you do it for what you give her, you know. She told me – she hates the things men do. She lies there and thinks of me – it's the only way she can stand it. Says you make her smell all fishy.'

He was red now, and he didn't look at her. 'Does she tell you – what else does she tell you?'

'Oh, everything there is to tell!' Her voice sounded cool and mocking and he felt the redness on his face deepen. 'I tell you what –'

He looked up then, as she stopped and she was looking at him, her eyes wide and seeming to be much softer.

'What?'

'I like the sound of it. I'm not like her, you see. I'm not a *bit* like her –'

He stared at her, trying to work it out and then the door behind them opened and Birgitta came in, the case under one arm, the coat over the other.

'You shall go the back way, I think, Hilda. I saw Miss Justin. She is waiting at the bottom of the stairs. She has the look that she waits for you.'

'Bloody woman,' Hilda said, and began to pull on her coat. 'She's getting boring. Now I'm here, what more does she want? "I'll get you to art school," she said. So, I'm at art school! What more does she want?'

'Who's Miss Justin?' Mel said, not wanting her to go. The crimson coat with black velvet sewn on to the revers had looked cheap and a bit vulgar, he'd thought, as she first put it on, but now he could see it suited her, making her vivid and more exciting.

'Miss Justin?' She giggled again, the fat sensual giggle he was learning to like. 'She's another of my – *friends*, you know? Call it my fatal fascination –' She pulled the door open.

'Tomorrow,' Birgitta said urgently at the same time as Mel said, 'I'll see you again some time –'

She looked back at them standing there side by side, flicking her eyes from one to another. And then she said, 'Okay. Tomorrow. Bring him with you, Gitta.'

7

Bonnie settled herself as comfortably as she could. The place was beginning to fill up, men and women in black gowns and wigs milling about at the front of the court, and others in ordinary clothes filing into the benches where she was sitting. She tried to concentrate on the place, so that she could describe it to Mr Hermann together with the way she felt about it. The wooden benches and the panelled walls in pale yellowish wood. The high gothic windows. The blue velvet curtains – they looked like velvet from here – above the judges' bench. Well, she assumed it was the judges' bench. It was high and looked important.

But none of it would stick in her mind, any more than she could pin down the feelings she was having. She was there; there were people; and that was all she could cope with.

Someone moved in beside her and automatically she slid along, still staring ahead at the judges' bench. Why should I feel nothing? I don't know. You've got to know. How can you analyse without answers? Why don't you know?

'Bonnie.'

She turned her head, startled, and for a mad moment didn't know who it was. She knew his face as well as she knew her own, it was part of her life and had been for years and years and she couldn't say who it was. 'Oh my God,' she thought. 'Oh my God, I'm going mad. Why am I going mad?'

'Sammy? What on earth – they haven't asked *you* to come, have they?'

'Am I a witness, you mean? No.'

'Then how come? What are you doing here? I would have thought –'

He smiled then, so that his face twisted slightly. 'After all this time, all the years, you can ask what I'm doing here? I thought better of you, Bonnie, I really did. You of all of you –'

'I'm sorry. I – yes – I see what you mean. It's kind of you.'

He shrugged. 'Kind? I don't know. I just thought, when I

heard – I'd better come. Are you involved? Directly – legally, I mean?'

She stared forwards at the judges' bench again, not wanting to look at his pleasant face, lined and untidy and concerned.

'Stanley is.'

'Oh.'

'Yes, *oh*,' she snapped and, at once contrite, turned back to him, putting her hand on his arm. 'Oh, damn! I didn't mean that. Sorry.'

'That's all right.'

They sat watching the people moving about. It all seemed aimless, as though they were just there killing time, and then suddenly things began to happen. The gowned figures at the front moved, re-formed and settled into groups, one at the front of the court on the right, one on the left. People were filing into the long pair of benches on the left-hand side of the court as she stared down at it, and she thought – that must be the jury. It's odd, they look so ordinary. They ought to look different from the rest of us, really. But they don't.

And then she saw them coming in, one at a time, not paying any attention to each other, both looking extraordinarily different somehow and she shut her eyes tightly, not wanting to have them look at her, not wanting to see them.

His hand closed over hers, on the bench between them, and gratefully she turned her wrist so that she could take hold of his fingers and held on tightly.

NOVEMBER 1948

'My heart dies for you, sighs for you, cries for you,
My heart cries for you, please come back to me . . . .'

'And then what?' Bonnie said breathlessly, holding on to his arm and peering up into his face with her eyes wide.

'And then,' he said carefully, flicking over the pages of *Gray's Anatomy* in his head, 'the bile goes from the gall bladder down the duct to the duodenum –'

They were walking through the thin smoky fog towards the turn-round point at Manor House, to catch the last tram to Clapton Common. They'd have to walk home from there and probably wouldn't get to Bonnie's front door till past midnight, and he'd be that much later, now that he lived in digs in Homerton.

Bonnie wasn't quite sure which she found most impressive; his growing knowledge and the easy way in which he could reel it all out in long elegant words, or the fact that he didn't live with his parents any more, but talked airily of his land-lady and had to worry about paying his rent. Whatever it was, being with Sammy was becoming more and more important.

He was still talking about bile and the duodenum, and she let his words roll over her, very conscious of the warmth of his arm under her hand, and the way he smelled. It was an odd smell, thin and acrid, and though she had never asked him she guessed it had something to do with the work he did each day in the basement of the hospital. She had been a bit upset at first, listening to him answer Hilda's nagging questions about cutting up dead bodies; imagining it all too easily. But she knew better than to let Hilda, or worse still, Hester, know she was squeamish; they'd never let her have any peace if they found out. And in controlling it, she'd discovered it didn't matter any more. She could imagine him with a knife in his hands, slicing up liver the way they did in butchers' shops, and not be a bit bothered that it was people's liver.

They walked on, down Lordship Lane, through the ghostly patches of light thrown by the lamps, hearing their own footsteps muffled in the fogginess and he said suddenly, 'That was a stupid lot of people!'

'Who were?'

'That lot. Weren't they? Talking a lot of rubbish. The new scheme's the best thing that's ever happened to medicine, the best possible. Bevan's marvellous, that's what he is. *Marvellous*! We'll all be better doctors because of it, people'll live longer, be healthier and happier, and all that lot can do is moan about their own money. Didn't they make you sick?'

'Oh yes,' she said fervently and tried to remember what they had talked about. Five medical students, one of them a girl, two nurses and her – the only one there who wasn't medical. She'd sat in a lumpy armchair in the little sitting room, a spam sandwich on her lap and a tin mug of tea on the floor beside her, and felt very daring and special to be among such people. They'd

73

argued about Bevan, and much she'd cared. Politics wasn't really interesting – but being there with Sammy, that was interesting.

She wrinkled her forehead in the darkness, walking beside him. She'd better remember, or maybe Sammy would get bored and be sorry he'd taken her to his friend's party instead of one of the others. And if that happened he'd make sure he didn't ever take her anywhere again.

'I thought perhaps it was because of their parents they were worried,' she said carefully after a moment. 'I mean, it costs a lot to be a doctor, doesn't it? And they want to be able to make a lot of money after they've finished to pay them back –'

He snorted. 'Parents! The hell with parents! Children don't owe their parents a damned thing – not gratitude or money or anything else. Parents are the ones who carry the whole burden of duty – they create the child, indulge their sexual drives to create a child, and from then on it is the child who deserves all their care and concern. No one has to sell his damned soul for money for *parents*.'

She smiled in the darkness at that. He'd talked like that at the party, lecturing them in that special voice that came out whenever he talked about politics and she'd felt the way they'd all responded. They all had nice homes and nice parents – she could tell that by the way the girls had clean, shining hair, and the men's shirts had been so well ironed – and they'd found Sammy with his scorn and his anger and his advanced ideas rather shocking. She'd enjoyed that. Especially because she knew how careful he was about his own parents. They'd told him when he was seventeen that he had to manage on his own, because that was the way it had to be in the new world, that the young had to be free. So he'd been free, and got night jobs and week-end jobs and holiday jobs to make his scholarship money at the hospital stretch far enough and still visited his parents every week, still made sure he was there to help with the tea on Sunday afternoons, however much studying he had to do. Sammy was lovely, she told herself again, and held his arm more tightly than ever. Sammy was very lovely.

'It was worth going,' she said trying to comfort him. 'The food was nice.'

He laughed then. 'Practical Bonnie! Always the practical one!

It wasn't bad, was it? Considering.'

'Have you got enough for breakfast tomorrow?' she said, emboldened by his laughter, and at once regretted it. His arm tightened under her grasp and she said hurriedly, 'I mean – land-ladies, I've heard about land-ladies. Maybe she takes some of your stuff. They do, you know –'

'She doesn't,' he said shortly. 'And if she did it'd be because she couldn't help it. She wouldn't take it if she had enough for herself. She's a good woman, my father's known her for years. A good woman. Property's theft, anyway –' But he didn't sound convinced, and Bonnie looked up at him again in the darkness and held on tightly.

'Well, I know. Anyway, there's some fish at home. I got it today. I fried it too, before I went out, so it's all right to take some home for tomorrow.'

'You don't have to worry about me,' he said stiffly. 'I don't need charity, you know. I manage fine –'

'I know you do. And it isn't charity,' Bonnie said, and then, inspired, 'Property's theft. I don't *own* the fish, do I? So I can't give it to you. It's there, and no one's eating it, so you have it. For tomorrow.'

They reached the trams, looming over them in a glow of soft light, and he grunted and stood to one side so that she could get on first, holding her elbow to help her up the steps in a way that made her shiver. Lovely Sammy.

And when he sat down beside her at the front of the tram, where the glass curved outwards and they could see the man in the driving cab turn the great brass handles this way and that, he said no more about the fish, so she knew it was all right. He'd take it, if she wrapped it carefully. He usually did.

And while he talked about next week when he'd be starting his clinicals – and she wouldn't ask him what they were; why display her ignorance? – she worked out in her head how much money she could manage to extract from her pay packet this week and what she might be able to make for him out of it. A pie? Auntie Fido'd never let her have anything from the fat ration for the crust. Well, a potato-topped pie then. She could maybe get some liver and kidney off the ration and turn that into a pie with some onions and carrots – there were plenty of those in the shops at least – and a bread pudding. There were apples around too, she'd seen some. A bread pudding with apples in it. He'd like that.

They got home at the same time as Hilda, and Bonnie felt her lips tighten in the darkness as she saw her there at the gate, talking to someone she couldn't quite see. Hilda might think she was grown up, but she wouldn't be fifteen for a couple of months yet and to wander around in the streets like this was appalling. What was Auntie Fido thinking of to let her get away with it?

Her anger simmered, making her face feel hot, and they walked up the street towards the gate-way where they stood, Hilda and whoever it was, and she knew it was really because a bit of her, deep down, had hoped that this time, maybe, Sammy would kiss her goodnight the way she'd seen him kiss Hester goodnight once, his arm close around her, crushing her to his chest, just like a film. And with Hilda there, how could he?

'It's Hilda,' she said sharply, her voice as thin and cold as the foggy night air. 'Honestly, it's *Hilda* – that girl – and who's she with? She'll get herself talked about and then what?'

'It's all right,' Sammy said. 'It's that teacher of hers.' His voice sounded wooden and she looked at him, surprised, but his face was shaded as they went past the high privet hedge of the house next door but one and she couldn't see his expression.

'Oh.' With the chance of venting any anger on Hilda blown away she felt the heavy dullness of disappointment slide over her: oh, Sammy, Sammy, why don't you want to kiss me goodnight, and stand here in the darkness and wait till they've gone?

'Hello, Miss Justin!' he called and his voice seemed to Bonnie to be full of a sudden sparkle. 'Late tonight, aren't we?'

'It's Friday!' Hilda said and her eyes gleamed a little in the darkness as she looked from one to the other of them. 'Had a lovely time, have you?'

'I'm sure you have,' Sylvia Justin said heartily. 'So late as you are! Been to a cinema?'

'No, to a party,' Bonnie said, trying to sound casual, and began to dig in her bag for her front-door key. 'It was lovely.'

'I bet,' Hilda said jeeringly. 'I know those parties of old Sammy's. Bunch of old dismals sitting round talking their heads off, organizing the world, doing nothing. That's why I wouldn't go –'

76

Bonnie looked sharply at Sammy but still his face was in shadow and she looked then at Hilda, who was much more visible right under the street light as she was. Had he asked her? Surely not! Not silly little girl Hilda, not fifteen till January. He couldn't have, could he? And then she caught sight of Sylvia Justin's face, flat and dull in the fuzzy light, and was embarrassed. She was staring at Hilda with her eyes very wide and Bonnie knew exactly how she was feeling, and knew it was all wrong for Sylvia Justin to feel so about Hilda. It was all right for Bonnie to feel like that about Sammy, but Sylvia Justin and Hilda – that was awful.

'We've had a lovely time,' Sylvia said brightly. 'We went to an exhibition, didn't we, Hilda? Lovely work, really lovely. New, you know, definitely *avant garde*, but quite, quite, lovely. And then we had a little snack –'

'Cakes and lemonade,' Hilda said greedily, and was suddenly a little girl again, and Bonnie felt better. 'Miss Justin makes wizard cakes, don't you, Miss Justin? With jam and cream, made out of butter –'

'It's very easy, really. You just make sure the butter's not salty, and then there's this little machine, and you mix it with the milk – the butter, I mean – and shake it up and then you can whip it and it's just like pre-war cream. I'm glad you liked it, Hilda –'

'Are you coming in, Sammy?' Hilda said. 'Auntie Fido'll have gone to bed, and Bonnie can make some tea, can't you, Bonnie?'

'All right,' Sammy said after a moment.

There was a little pause and then Sylvia said brightly, 'Well, I'll be going then, Hilda. We'll talk more about the exhibition on Monday, at school, shall we? I'd better be going now.' But she lingered, standing there in the lamplight and staring at Hilda with a faintly doggish look about her.

'Oh, all right,' Hilda said, and hardly looked at her, turning and tucking her hand into Sammy's elbow. 'See you Monday. Ta for the cake and that. Sammy, let's go up West tomorrow. I haven't been up West for ages, and I want to look at the clothes in Selfridges and down Bond Street. I've got some money and we could go early and get the cheap fares –'

Bonnie made the tea out on her own in the kitchen with its

shabby red and yellow prettiness and the Easiwerk and the flowered cups and saucers, deliberately taking her time, waiting to see if he'd come out and offer to help her, the way he usually did.

But he didn't, and she could hear the buzz of their voices in the sitting room, his low and heavy, hers high and giggly, and she let her misery fill her, not even trying to be sensible.

She wrapped the fish carefully, a piece of cod, a piece of haddock and, very aware of her sacrifice, a piece of halibut. There were only four little pieces of that, and she'd queued a long time for it, but still she gave him her piece, setting it neatly in the middle of the square of greaseproof paper, slipping it carefully into the paper bag saved from last week's shopping. He ought to know how hard it was to get paper bags, and be grateful, as he carried it all home to his land-lady in Homerton.

She left the fish parcel in the kitchen when she took the tea in, and sat there pouring it, willing Hilda to go to bed, but having more sense than to tell her to go, older sister though she was. If only Hester was here, she thought, watching Hilda sparkling away at Sammy, seeing how Sammy sat there with his legs outstretched, comfortable and easy as he listened to her, a smile on his face. *She'd* send her packing!

And then stay here herself, she thought dismally, and sighed and collected the tea things and piled the tray.

'I think it's getting late, Sammy,' she said. 'You've got a long way to go home. You'll be ever so tired.'

He blinked up at her, almost as though he were surprised to see her there. The'd been talking, he and Hilda, about colours, laughing and then being serious and laughing again. Why was red the favourite colour of Communists? Why did they talk about true blues and sneer at them? Blue was a clever colour, much cleverer than red, which was obvious and easy to play around with – so Hilda had chattered, smiling up at him from her place on the floor where she sat with her arms around her knees, her chin tucked in, looking up at him with that look in her eyes. 'I hate her, I hate her, I hate her,' Bonnie thought and then felt the shame fill her. Only a little girl, only Hilda. She doesn't understand anything, won't be fifteen till January.

'Stay here!' Hilda said imperiously. 'Then we can go up West in the morning early and no problems.'

Bonnie stared at her, and opened her mouth to protest. Stay here? Where? Was she mad? Auntie Fido, what'd Auntie Fido say? What'd *Hester* say?

He was on his feet, shaking his head. 'Nice of you, but of course I couldn't –'

'Why not? You could sleep down here, on the sofa. It's not that uncomfortable. I do sometimes when I'm fed up with sharing with the others.'

It was as though Bonnie wasn't there and she rattled the tray sharply as she turned to the door.

'You're only a child, Hilda,' she said loudly. 'Small. Sammy's a grown man and he'd not get a wink on that thing. Sammy, I've got that – what I said. It's ready.'

'Yes. Thanks. I'd better be going.' He was pulling on his coat, and Hilda was sitting there staring up at him, her eyes bright.

'You'll take me up West, Sammy? Just to look at the dresses and that? I can't buy any, of course. But I could get some ideas. You'll take me?'

'Don't be silly! I've got work to do tomorrow.' He sounded relaxed and avuncular, and Bonnie, kicking the door behind her as she went out to the kitchen, felt better. She was a fool, she really was. As if Hilda – it was ridiculous. Please, Sammy, come out to the kitchen, come and get your fish. Kiss me goodnight, darling Sammy, tuck me in my little wooden bed – she shook her head, exasperated at her own silliness. She must be tired, and tomorrow was Saturday and the shop would be busy, probably. It was time he went, time she was in bed.

When she came out of the kitchen with the parcel of fish carefully held in both hands they were there in the narrow hallway, standing close together near the front door. Hilda was looking up at him, making him seem to be very tall. Well, he was tall, Bonnie thought, quite tall, but not as tall as she makes him look.

I'm imagining it. As if he'd kiss her that way. Of course he wouldn't. It was silly. Fifteen next January!

He looked up saw her and waved one hand. 'I must be going!' he said and his voice sounded gay and much more alive than it had been all evening. ' 'Night, Bonnie – see you soon –'

Hilda stood at the front door and watched him go down the path and then looked up and yawning hugely, like a cat, went upstairs. 'Wake me when you get up, will you?' she said. 'I'm going up West. Early.'

Bonnie unwrapped the fish and put it back in the safe, outside the back door in the little yard, where it was cool. There'd be enough for supper tomorrow night and probably for Sunday as well.

8

The jury had just been sworn in when it happened. The dull buzz of voices and the desultory moving-about sharpened, and there was a focussing of attention on the door to the court. Bonnie turned to look too, and could see the usher with his hands up and shaking his head from side to side with monotonous regularity.

'No,' he was saying in a kind of subdued roar. 'I've told yer – the place is as full as it can be an' there's no way you lot's gettin' in 'ere, not if you pushes till Kingdom come – now be told, will yer! Get off – go on – gerroff –'

The judge leaned forwards, muttered something to one of the people in front of him, who made his way through the crowded court to the door, spoke to the usher, went back to the judge. Bonnie watched, absorbed. Anything was better than having to force herself not to look at the others, sitting there on opposite sides of the court. Still the noise went on, and someone else came and leaned on the door beside the usher, and then there was banging, as though someone outside were rapping to be let in.

'What is happening? Will somebody explain what is happening?' The judge's voice came sharply and the usher, now rather breathless, called out something incomprehensible and suddenly, as though from nowhere, two uniformed policemen appeared, shouldering aside the usher, going out of the door.

'I would be *grateful*,' the judge said, his voice edged with cold, 'if someone would explain to me why the decorum of my court is being shattered in this fashion. *What* is the noise, who is making it, and what is being done to put an end to it and prevent any recurrence? I do not expect such a display at any time, least of all for such a case as that before me today –'

A man in a gown and with an armful of papers came hurrying down the court from the door. 'Very sorry, m'lord,' he muttered to the judge, flustered and yet somehow pleased with himself. His words could be clearly heard, though he made a pretence of keeping his voice low. 'It's the – er – there are people in court today, m'lord, that are very well known, popular you might say. I gather these are their fans, m'lord, demanding an entry. They've been told, m'lord, that there is no further accommodation –'

Bonnie couldn't help it; she had to look then.

Hester was sitting leaning back in her place, a fat man beside her talking busily into her ear, but she was ignoring him, her face set in a smile and her eyes wide as she looked at the judge sitting above her. On the other side of her on the bench behind sat J. J. Gerrard. It was odd how recognizable he looked. If I'd thought about it, Bonnie told herself, I'd have known I'd be able to recognize him, but it wasn't something you ever thought about. There were these people, actors and talkers and performers of one kind or another with faces that were on the screen all the time, and you knew they were real faces and yet you were equally certain that they were not. So that when you saw one of them in reality it was as though it was yourself that was unreal, not them.

'Who, then,' said the judge in awful tones, 'is the object of all this noise? Do they have a reason to be in court?'

One of the counsel behind Hester stood up. 'I think, m'lord, that it is my client, Miss Hester Morrissey, who is the focus of the attention, for which she of course apologizes, but reminds the court that she cannot be held responsible for the actions of others –'

Hester leaned back and whispered something, and the bewigged head tried to argue, was interrupted by Hester, listened and straightened up. 'Er – m'lord, my client asks me to withdraw the apology, since she is not at *all* responsible for the behaviour of these – er – admirers, and cannot therefore apologize for them. However, I regret, as I am sure does my client, any disturbance suffered by the court –'

The judge peered down at Hester, who smiled sweetly at him, and he frowned, looking away from her at the counsel behind. 'And why should these people appear here making this unconscionable din?' – it was indeed increasing – 'Can anybody explain this?'

'I'm popular!' Hester said loudly and clearly, her voice cutting easily above the noise coming from outside. 'It's an occupational hazard in my life.'

'And mine.' J. J. Gerrard stood up, and bowed to the judge with a slightly theatrical flourish. 'Those of us, m'lud, who, like yourself, live their working lives in the public eye –'

The counsel behind him looked scandalized, and leaned forwards, trying to hush him. To directly address a judge so, in his own court? their backs seemed to cry. Shocking! But Hester and JJ seemed unaware of their breach of protocol, looking jauntily pleased with themselves.

'Like m'self?' The judge almost spluttered it, and Sammy sitting quietly beside Bonnie laughed softly and said in her ear, 'He's like some damned caricature – straight out of *Punch* for nineteen ten. You listen – any moment now he'll ask them why they're so popular and what their occupations are – there? What did I tell you?' as the question was put, and a ripple of laughter filled the courtroom, almost as loud as the din from outside.

'It's marvellous,' Hester was thinking. 'Bloody marvellous. In this day and age, who'd've thought it? It's better than I'd hoped. If this doesn't turn out to be the best show I've ever done, I don't know what will –'

'She's doing it again,' J. J. Gerrard was thinking. 'Damn the bitch, she's doing it again. Well, she'll clobber herself this time, by Christ she will. I've had enough of it, more than enough of it. No way she can get away with it here, no way –'

She had before, though.

MAY 1956

'Well, it's one for the money, two for the show,
Three to get ready and go man go . . . .'

She went out to Wembley on the Metropolitan line, sitting in a corner seat and staring out at the rows of little houses, tight-packed and ugly at Kilburn, opening out to stuffy suburban respectability at Neasden, and finally bursting into the full Wembley glory of lilac-bedecked gardens, black-and-white pseudo-Tudor house-fronts, and housewives in their tight skirted copies of Paris originals pushing high-sprung prams from shop to shop along the local parades. Just think, she told herself, just look and think what it would have been like if you'd listened to him. He'd have had you there wrapped in a bloody pinny, cooking his meals, dusting his tables, hating your own guts as much as his. Christ, but you're lucky. Christ, but you're clever!

The studios were cluttered uncomfortably, looking as though they had been built out of rubbish picked up on bomb sites, but that was exciting. It proved the place was real, that the work they were doing was too hectic, too important to allow anyone time to think of such mundane things as supplying enough lavatory paper.

She tidied herself, peering carefully into the mirror above the unwashed basin in the ladies' loo, patching in the heavy pancake make-up, redrawing the eyeline. Not the ideal look for someone with her sort of face, and she knew it, but it looked good on camera, or would if she could get it past the make-up girls, cocky know-all bitches.

Outside, she looked the other talent over, her eyebrows raised with a faintly supercilious air, very aware that they were all prettier than she was. Five of them, all very curly, rosy, round cheeked. Younger, too. At twenty-six, just turned, she wasn't exactly old, but three of these girls at least weren't twenty yet, and the others weren't much more than a couple of years older. It would have to be cleverness; that was what she would have to rely on, and she smiled at them, sitting there in Reception, and began to chat.

They softened, relaxed, allowed the tension to show in their eyes, fluffing out their dresses and turning to her like flowers turning sunwards on a bright day, and the receptionist watched with a sardonic grin and thought – that's the one. She'll get it.

By the time they were called to the studio, 'Mr Greenock is ready for you now,' she was in command. They knew of her experience, of the influential friends she'd made, the knowledge she had of the medium, above all the easy way she used the first names of so many of the famous ones, and as they walked beside her in their freshly-starched cotton dresses they seemed to crumple, lose their bounce. And Hester walked cheerfully on, her legs long and startling in tight red trousers, a heavy yellow sweater over the top, her hair sleek against her face, knowing she could do it.

In the gallery J. J. Gerrard leaned over Dave's shoulder and stared down on the studio. 'Christ, what's that?'

'Punch up Three,' Dave said, and she shot into close-up on one of the screens. The others were sitting awkwardly on the chairs that had been set for them, ankles crossed, hands moving nervously. One of them, a little sharper than the others, had crossed her knees and was carefully showing a good deal of thigh, even a shadow of stocking top. But it was Hester who pulled their eyes. She'd turned her chair round so that she could perch on the back of it, her legs thrust out in front of her. Her buttocks, meagre though they were, swelled out on each side against the metal chair back and looked curiously voluptuous, but not unpleasantly so. Not like the curliest of the others whose round cheeks looked in the picture thrown on to the monitor by Camera Two to be flaccid and tired, like a wax doll left out in the sun too long.

'Clever,' Dave said. 'Knows the camera. Look at that make-up, will you, for God's sake?'

JJ looked and laughed. 'She's a right mess –'

'Oh, I dunno. Could be interesting. I like the shadows. Kookie, y'know? Could get 'em.'

'Does she know about the music, though? What she looks like is one thing – it's what she knows that matters. Not that it's any concern of mine, of course –'

Down on the floor Hester sat perched on the back of her chair, her chin up to show her face to best advantage to Camera Three, making sure she kept the other cameras in view. If the red light changed, showed a different camera was in action, she'd stroll over to whichever girl it was on, get her talking, make her show herself. They seemed unaware of the way they were all being watched, didn't seem to know there was a gallery up there somewhere where they were being studied. Oh, young and pretty they may be, but I'll show 'em –

The floor manager lifted his head, put his hand to his ear and nodded and across the floor the musicians muttered, grouped themselves and began, the sound coming sharp and sudden, making the other girls jump. But Hester had been aware of them and was ready. As the music began she shifted her weight from her behind to her feet in one smooth movement, was up and then dancing, moving with all the skill she had.

She loathed the noise, hated rock and roll, thought it all discordant and repellent. But she knew what they wanted, and gave it to them, deliberately turning her back to the camera, rotating her hips lewdly, using her legs as though they were unjointed. She lifted her chin, caught sight of one of the riggers standing and watching her, a gawky kid in heavy shoes and draped suit and with a jerk of her head she called him, and glory, glory, he obeyed.

They danced, giving it all they could as the music thumped and shouted and out of the corner of her eye she saw the camera move, saw it follow her movements, and knew she had the job. The other girls sat there, shocked, clumsy, still.

They went through the motions, got each girl to speak to the camera, gave them a number to introduce, make them walk into and out of shot, but it was a foregone conclusion. Hester Morrissey was City Television's new Show Band Popsie, with a contract for three months and a six-month option thereafter. Revolutionary, the management men told each other. Pos-it-ively revolutionary, but what could you do? The kids were where it was at, and the advertisers knew it, and were already sitting up and taking notice of the new pop scene.

JJ watched her afterwards as the publicity people moved in on her. They used the big board room. It was one of the few rooms in the place apart from Reception that ever looked clean, and it made a good impression on the journalists, so it was worth the effort of getting it all set up. The place was full this afternoon, with half the top brass there as well as a fair sprinkling from Fleet Street. He looked at Mack Gander from the *Chronicle* over the edge of his glass and wondered. If Mack Gander had bothered to turn out, it was for real. Maybe he'd pick the girl up at that, oddball though she unquestionably was.

He moved across the room, standing easily beside her as she chattered to the man from the *Evening News*. He knew she was aware of him as soon as he was there. Her speech seemed the same, her attention, fixed on the scribbling reporter, seemed not to waver, but he knew, felt her reaching out, exploring him with invisible fingers, watching, listening, smelling him.

The man went away and JJ raised his glass at her.

'Hi there.'

'Hi there. It's taken you long enough.'

'It has?'

'Another ten minutes and I'd have had to come and talk to you. And that ain't my style.'

'What is?'

'I'm still working on it.'

He grinned then. 'They tell me you were short-listed out of seventeen. Were they all pretty pretties like this morning?'

'They were. Real chocolate boxes. Came out of the same mould. Jellied, you know?'

He shook his head, the corners of his mouth turned down, never letting his eyes leave her face.

'So tell me, how come you made it? Whatever it is you've got, it sure ain't jelly out of a mould.'

'*Gott sei dank*! How? Would you believe me if I said I slept with the producer?'

He shook his head. 'Not if you said that you got the job that way. That you'd slept with him, sure. He screws everything that isn't pinned down under someone else. But he doesn't cast that way. That's why he's got this show. It's City's big one.'

'Then put it down to natural charm and talent. Is that so difficult?'

'Very. Yours isn't the kind that shows the first time you look.'

She opened her eyes wide. 'You mean at last, I've made my impact? That you looked the second time and *noticed*?'

'It took three looks, and I'm still looking. But I'm beginning to see. Just beginning. What'll you drink?'

'Daiquiri.'

He shook his head gently. 'No, dear. You've missed there. That's gone right out. We're all soaking up Italian wine now. Make it Chianti.'

She stared at him for a long moment and then nodded, very seriously. 'I'll make it Chianti.'

They had dinner together that night, and he went to a lot of trouble to get it right. He took her to Romano Santi in Greek Street, where everyone was going this spring, and she ate spaghetti with an experienced twirl of her fork, and didn't flinch when he ordered garlic-stuffed chicken breasts. He liked that. A girl who can eat garlic, he told himself, when she knows damned well she's going to be in bed with the man who bought it for her before the night's out, has got to be interesting. If she can be as abandoned then as she is now, she'll be a bit of all right.

Which was the first surprise. She smiled sweetly at him when he took her back to the car and said briefly, 'My place or yours?' and said, 'Mine first, and yours ten minutes later – or however long it takes you to get there.'

He stared at her, his hand still on the ignition key. 'Ye gods, are you trying to come the –'

'I'm not coming anything, so save the insults. I'm not interested right now.'

'What do you mean, not interested?' He was flabbergasted. 'Are you trying to tell me that I've been –'

She shook her head, genuinely irritated. 'Oh, you're all the damned same. You think women are like bloody clockwork dolls. Wind us up with a bit of nosh, pour in the liquor and hey presto. Well, surprise, surprise, ducky, I've got feelings. Sometimes I'm in the mood for it, sometimes I'm not. Tonight I'm not. I've had a long hard day, and I'm bushed. Another day when I've got myself together, great. I'll play games. But tonight I'm not interested, that's all! Nothing personal.'

'And what am I supposed to do?'

'Poor fella!' she said and laughed. 'Are you so worked up by passion for gorgeous me that you'll explode if you don't get your chance to nibble? You'd quite enjoy a bit with me – but it's not the end of the world if you have to wait for it. If you're desperate, I'll take the tube and you can pick yourself a girl right here –'

She looked out of the car window at the girls leaning against the restaurant doorways, parading the pavements.

'There's quite a nice jellied-looking one there, see? With the Rita Hayworth curls? Very luscious. Probably got leather knickers on, if that's your fancy.'

He took the ignition key out of the lock and leaned back in his seat, staring at her. Her profile was outlined against the yellow neon of the strip joint across the street, and he studied it. Hard lines, a straight nose that lifted just enough at the nostrils to save it from being a beak, thin hollow cheeks, a sharp jutting chin. An ugly face, but the more he looked at it the more he liked it.

'You're weird,' he said.

She grinned and turned to look at him. 'I know. I found that out a long time ago. I looked in a mirror and I said, "You're a weird-looking female, Hester," I said. "So act weird to match, it'll take you where you want to go." And it will. Jelly moulds come ten a penny. I don't. Listen, I told you – I've had a long day. Are you taking me home, or shall I take a tube and leave you to pick up what you fancy?'

It was a genuine question, without any malice or guile behind it, and he laughed and put the ignition key back in the lock.

'Home,' he said. 'When shall I see you again?'

'I'll call you,' she said. And she did. Two days later.

She wouldn't move in with him, wouldn't let him move in with her, and that hurt him more than he would have been willing to admit. She was good in bed, when she wanted to be, but never put herself out so much as an inch to please him. Which, though it seemed odd at first – for ever since he'd left newspapers for TV he'd had the pick of any girl he'd wanted, and they had all been worried about doing it wrong, humbly grateful to be taught how to please him – became very gratifying. He had to work to get what he wanted, and it meant he enjoyed it more; and that was funny, because wasn't that what all the old biddies and moralists said? 'Effort and value go hand in hand.' Only they had been talking about money. But it was true for sex too; the harder he had to try to please her the more he got out of it, and when he did torment her enough to make her wriggle and even, sometimes, cry out aloud, he felt good.

But she wouldn't move in with him.

As the weeks pleated themselves into months and her programme crept up the popularity charts, he watched her with increasing uneasiness. He wasn't doing badly himself, heaven knew. His *Spectrum* magazine programme mightn't be in the top ten for viewing figures but the critics thought well of it. City were happy too, because it was the respectable front that gave them a licence to fill the rest of their screen hours with cheap American comedy shows and Westerns, and for himself – well, it was reasonably interesting to do. A bit thin perhaps, because City weren't about to spend the money he really needed to make in-depth investigations, but not bad.

But it wasn't the *Show Band Pops* and he wasn't the Show Band Popsie. When they went out together it was her they clustered round for autographs, even pushing past him to get at

89

her. It was her the taxi-drivers joked with, her the paper-sellers called after in the streets. And though of course he wasn't interested in that sort of cheap publicity, he couldn't help being sour and short with her when it happened.

But still they went out and about, and sometimes he wondered gloomily why she bothered. She was In now, high fashion. They were all after her, the greasy young photographers, the new wave of musicians, even the old-fashioned aristos, the debs' delights who spent their nights and their incomes in the gambling clubs. She had her pick of the lot, and she took it.

But still came back to him. His phone would ring and she'd say, 'Interested?' and at once he would be. He'd tried not to be, God knew. To be at one woman's beck and call like this was damned humiliating, but it never failed. The directness of her invitation, the lack of any finesse in itself was very exciting and the sound of her cool voice on the phone was enough to create an immediate physical reaction in him. So he'd grunt and hang up the phone and drive over to her glossy new flat in Chelsea. And leave at about three in the morning because not only did she refuse to live with him; she wouldn't even let him sleep the night.

He'd tried to say no, once or twice. He'd stood there with the phone in his hand and, savagely pushing his desires aside, had said baldly, 'No!' to her 'Interested?' And all that had happened was that she'd said calmly, 'Fine! See you around.' And called him again a week or two later in just the same old way.

He had to admit it. She was using him the way he'd been using women all his adult life, and shaming though it was to face the fact, he liked it. He'd never been as randy with anyone as he was with her. Clever bitch, hateful bitch, he needed her. He was tied to her by so many complex strands of feeling that sometimes when he was maudlin with a few drinks he would tell her she was a spider. And she would laugh and agree with him and tell him that was just the way it ought to be.

And then, *Pendulum* magazine, the New Reading for the New Generation, was launched. With a lead interview with the Show Band Popsie. One way and another, he'd never forgive her for that.

9

The noise had diminished, almost gone away, and the court was settling down once more when there was again a raised voice outside and the judge looked up, his face thunderous under its heavy wig. The usher, moving fast, shot across the court to the door but he was too late; it opened and there was a man there, tall and heavy in a cream safari suit, carefully casual, his hair sleek above heavy jowls.

There was a whispered colloquy and the usher looked over his shoulder at the full benches; almost without thinking, Bonnie moved along, releasing a few inches of space between herself and Sammy. The rest of the bench's occupants obeyed her lead and they all shuffled enough to make the space needed for one more person. The man in the safari suit nodded gratefully and slid into place, pushing them all even closer together. He was big, almost fat, and looking along the line at him Bonnie could see his trousers bulging above the zip-fastened flies, and looked away, embarrassed.

After a moment Sammy leaned closer and whispered in her ear, 'You know who it is?' She looked up, puzzled, and Sammy jerked his head slightly to the other side and she looked again at the man sitting there, his arms folded.

He was staring down the court at Hester. His forehead shone a little, as though he'd been sprayed with grease, and there were traces of talcum powder on his jowls. Even from here she could smell his aftershave; waves of Brut washed over her every time he took a breath. She stared at the profile and then again at Sammy, puzzled. There was something about the newcomer that was familiar, but she wasn't sure what. He was a type, of course; the sort of comfortable businessman you could see any morning walking along leafy Edgware roads on the way to the station, or piling themselves and their school-going children into expensive cars. Probably an accountant, or maybe a coat manufacturer. Jowly, dark, shiny. Why should she recognize him?

Somewhere deep in her mind memory stirred and she pushed it away. 'No,' she hissed at Sammy and turned her attention back to the court. The counsel behind Hildegarde was on his feet, muttering. She could hardly hear him and she looked at Hester, trying to concentrate on her. It was important now to pay attention to both of them, Hildegarde and Hester, just as important to look as it had been important not to, earlier. That would help her keep away the memory involving the man at the end of the bench.

But it was no good. It clamoured, pushed, and burst out. Oh God, she thought, I haven't given him a thought in years. Why does he have to be here? What has it got to do with him, for God's sake? It never had anything to do with him. Not really.

FEBRUARY 1952

'When your sweetheart sends a letter of goodbye,
It's no secret you'll feel better if you cry . . . .'

'Listen, doll,' Mr Spero said, looking at her sternly. 'I'm not rich enough to have a small party, you understand me? In my line of business a man has to do it right. If I was Bernard Docker already I could be a schnorrer, a pastry, a cup of tea – but I'm no Docker. Not yet! So, it's the works, the whole works.'

'You really shouldn't have,' she said again, and tugged at her dress. Hilda had fixed it, told her it was all the rage, but it looked wrong on her, and she knew it. Tight blue tulle, strapless, held up by a cruel bra with wires that cut into her, a frothy skirt that made her feel all hips, it didn't suit her and she hated it.

She caught Mrs Spero's eyes on her across the expanse of parquet floor and smiled unhappily and the older woman bent her head in acknowledgement; but her face remained the same still mask it always was when she looked at Bonnie.

She could see David on the far side of the big hall, talking to the band-leader. He looked good in a dinner jacket, very rich and sure of himself, and she looked down again at her blue tulle and moved her shoulders awkwardly. She could feel the red weal that was forming under her breasts; the wire was tight, she was too heavy –

92

'It's not a bad spread, eh, Bonnie?' Mr Spero said, and for the tenth time he relit his cigar.

'It's lovely,' she said, looked at the long table stretching down one side of the room, and felt faintly sick. It was covered in an aggressively white cloth with strands of smilax looping from one end to the other in front of it, and trays and plates and heaps of food filled up every inch of the surface. There were curled up sandwiches of smoked salmon, pieces of pickled herrings on fingers of toast, anchovies and eggs and radishes and tomatoes cut into jagged shapes and olives and pickled cucumbers and cream cheese and fish balls and pastries and cake and more fish balls, more anchovies, more olives.

'It's really too much,' she said again, and this time he looked faintly annoyed.

'I've told you,' he said, and chewed his cigar. 'I've told you, for my boy nothing but the best. For my boy and his girl, only the best. All I ask is you should make him happy, be a good wife to him. He's a good boy, hard working, sensible, he deserves the best. Be a good wife to him, you'll have nothing to complain of, from him, from us –'

She looked across at Mrs Spero again, ferocious in dark green bugle beads and turquoise slipper satin, talking to the caterer, depressed in a rusty tail coat.

'Lissen,' Mr Spero said. 'Lissen, it's natural she should be a bit – you know. He's her only boy, her boobalah, what d'you expect? She should jump at you? Believe me, doll, she'll come round. As soon as the babies come, she'll be there. And you'll be glad, a girl with no mother, how can you not be glad?'

'I've got my sisters,' Bonnie said.

'Yes. Of course. Nice girls, I'm sure. Hilda, a lovely girl. Friendly, got a lovely way with her, Hilda.'

'Yes,' Bonnie said, and tweaked again at her tulle. 'When – what time is it?'

'Half past six. In fifteen minutes they'll be starting to get here.' He pulled his shoulders back, importantly. 'Believe me, Bonnie, you'll be impressed. They're good people, all of them, friends, business colleagues, family of course. You know Wolfie Laurence accepted? Best band-leader on the circuit, Wolfie. We were boys together. And my wife's cousin's girl, Judy Hersh, also coming. A lovely actress, lovely. Makes a lot of money, they tell me. I tell you it'll be a nice affair. None of your rubbish.'

'I'm sure,' Bonnie said politely and looked at David. He was talking to his mother now. She had her hand on his arm, standing very close and looking up at him, and Bonnie thought again, Oh God, what am I doing? I must be mad, stark raving mad. How can I be getting engaged? It's crazy. How can I be standing here with all these olives and cucumbers and be getting engaged? And what will getting married be like? A bigger room, more parquet, more olives?

Mrs Spero was coming towards her and she composed her face. To please David, she told herself. To please David and everyone else, be nice, be nice. Be *nice*.

'So, Bonnie? And where are your family? You'd think they'd be on time for so important an occasion? The first to get engaged, after all –' She looked round the ball-room with some complacency. 'I'm sure they'll agree we're doing our best by you.'

'Oh, I'm sure they will. They won't be long, I'm sure – my Aunt, you know – she's had some rheumatism lately – oh, there's Sammy!' Her heart lifted with relief as she saw him hovering there by the door. He looked awkward, big and clumsy with the sleeves of his dinner-jacket rather short over his bony wrists, but he looked good. 'He's our oldest friend,' she said and looked sideways at Mrs Spero. 'Our very oldest friend. He's a doctor, you know. A house physician. A very important post –'

'Very nice.' Mrs Spero looked at Sammy who had seen them and was coming across the acreage of polished floor, moving a little heavily. 'He's married?'

'No,' Bonnie said and smiled at Sammy. He looked marvellous, she thought, marvellous. So comfortable among all these strangers. Her eyes flicked to David for a moment, and then away. He wasn't really a stranger, of course. Not really.

'Good evening!' Mrs Spero said, her voice rich and round, and held out her hand. 'I've heard all about you – you're Bonnie's old friend, Sammy, aren't you? A brilliant doctor, they tell me. Oh, I've heard *all* about you – I'm Bonnie's soon-to-be mother-in-law!' And she put one hand heavily on Bonnie's bare shoulder.

They talked, Mrs Spero gushing, Sammy looking and sounding a little abstracted, and then the toast-master came bustling across the floor, urgent in red barathea, scooped them up, told them that people were arriving and they must make their reception line.

'Bonnie,' Sammy said. 'Could I have just a word –'

'Now, my dears, no time for any chatter!' Mrs Spero said brightly. 'These two love birds have to be ready to receive their guests –'

'And the presents,' Mr Spero said, and winked fatly at Sammy. 'The presents, eh? Got to start 'em off right, that's for sure!'

'Just a word,' Sammy said again, but Mrs Spero had her hand on Bonnie's arm, taking her away, and she looked back over her shoulder, making a little face.

'Later,' she called and found herself there at the door, with Mr Spero firm on one side of her, David on the other.

Auntie Fido and Hilda arrived in the first wave, Hilda demure in yellow, Auntie Fido fussy in navy blue with pink trimmings. Mrs Spero looked at her, smiled sympathetically and was very gracious.

'You must be tired, my dear,' she cooed. 'We'll arrange a chair for you – no, I won't take no for an answer – can't have you worn out, can we –'

With Auntie Fido sitting glumly in a chair and looking half as old again as Mrs Spero – although in fact they had been born in the same year – Bonnie felt the gloom lift. Her soon-to-be mother-in-law – oh, God, soon-to-be mother-in-law! – sparkled and twinkled, moving with little skips and jumps, laughing girlishly as she greeted her guests, kissing the air as she clashed cheeks with the women, looking into the men's eyes as she held their hands lingeringly after each handshake.

Auntie Fido tried, getting to her feet from time to time, trying to fluff out her navy blue skirts and the pink stole, but Mrs Spero would have none of it, re-settling her with little cries of concern, patting her shoulder sympathetically, quite over-riding Auntie Fido's occasional squeaks and giggles.

Bonnie shook hands till her thumb ached with the pressure, smiled at face after face, tried to remember names. Sadie and Sid, Bessie from Leeds, came down specially, David's favourite aunt, don't tell Rae but that's the truth of it, Uncle Lou and

Uncle Percy and Uncle everything else. Cousins and in-laws, friends and colleagues, they paraded in front of her, pushed little envelopes into David's hands – never into hers – and she smiled and blinked and smiled again.

Hilda was there somewhere, she remembered, and lifted her chin to look for her, and saw her standing with three curly-headed young men, chattering and happy. She looked young and pretty and very girlish, and comfortable too. Her dress wasn't painfully strapless tulle like her own, and like almost everyone else's under the age of thirty; she had swathed herself in yellow artificial silk, wrapping it round and round her so that the lines of her legs and hips showed through clearly. An odd dress, but it looked right and Bonnie thought, that's one of that Birgitta's – it's just the sort of thing she would do –

But no Hester. Bonnie shook hands and smiled and shook hands again and wondered about Hester. Across the room, now crowded with people and roaring with voices and the clatter of champagne glasses, she looked for Sammy. He was with Hilda too, and she stopped smiling for a moment. She really shouldn't look at him like that, it was only showing off, she never did it unless there were people around to see.

The handshaking faltered, stopped. They were all there, all the guests, and still no Hester. Bonnie let them lead her to a table, sat down, accepted champagne and allowed David to put his arm proprietorially round her shoulders and leave it there, though it was heavy and his cuff links scratched her skin.

They served food, a bevy of waitresses in frilled white aprons setting quantities of sandwiches, cream cakes, tea, in front of her, and she wished she could eat it. It was the most luxurious spread she could ever remember seeing, and she wasn't hungry. And where was Hester?

The speeches were happening when she arrived. Someone had talked at length about what marvellous parents the Speros were, about Mr Spero's business acumen, Mrs Spero's good-heartedness, the total worthiness of the entire Spero family. And then Mr Spero had talked, painting a sad picture of the struggles he'd been through and all for his own dear Jessie and son David, a lovely boy. He talked too of dear Bonnie, their soon-to-be daughter, and how lovely she was, how she had suffered, too, a poor little orphan, but with her dear aunt, quite

96

worn out with all the years of care – Auntie Fido bobbed her head and looked a little worried for a moment as the import of his words sank in and then decided to take it as a compliment and smiled bravely – but now with the Speros to love her and care for her.

And then Hester arrived. The door opened, swung back and then opened again and she came in and Bonnie stared at her and wanted to giggle. It was as though she were playing two parts at once. She was dressed like that character in *No Room at the Inn* that the Settlement Players had done last year. A too-tight green skirt with half the hem down, an even tighter jacket with red braid on it, a hat covered in veiling and bobbing cherries and flowers. And over it all that long red feather boa they'd all laughed at and which Birgitta had made for the play.

She stood there, staring at them all, and the sound of chatter faltered and then stopped, and people turned and looked.

And then she started the other role. She came across the floor towards the tables, walking sideways like a crab and then straightening up, her heels scrabbling on the polish and the feather boa bobbing. She was being the tipsy woman in *Fallen Angels*, the one she'd been in two years ago, the one the *Hackney Gazette* had said such good things about.

'Bonnie,' she shrilled. 'Hello, Bonnie, darlin' little Bonnie – sorry I'm late – had to see a man 'bout a – something can't tell little sisters about –' and she leered and came pushing her way past the tables to throw her arms round Bonnie and kiss her.

'Hester – are you mad?' Bonnie said and stared at her, and Hester grinned at her and winked and went reeling past her, her arms out towards Mrs Spero.

'You're David's mother, David's lovely mother – lucky Bonnie, gettin' a mother. We lost ours, di'n't we –' and she began to weep, loudly and stridently.

It was Sammy who showed the fastest reaction. He hurried across to the band and they suddenly started to play, swinging perkily into a selection from *Oklahoma*, 'Oh what a beautiful mornin', oh what a beautiful day', and the talk started again, loud and nervous, as Hester went reeling from table to table, talking, giggling, touching people so that they reared back and tried to pretend she wasn't there.

Bonnie started to laugh, a soft laugh at first and then louder as David tried to stop her and Mrs Spero stood staring at Hester with her face set, and the laughing got louder and then Sammy was there, leading her away as she hiccupped and cried into his ill-fitting dinner-jacket.

'You silly bitch, I did it *for* you –' Hester said again. 'If you haven't got the sense to see it's the best thing that could have happened, then you don't deserve the trouble I took!'

Auntie Fido was weeping softly, sitting in the corner of the sofa with her blue skirt crumpled round her bony knees, her pink stole in a heap on her lap. 'It was so shameful,' she was saying. 'So shameful! All that lovely food, so shameful –'

'Oh, Auntie Fido, do stop crying,' Hilda said sharply and put her hand on her shoulder and gave her a little shake. 'It's nothing to go on so about.'

'Nothing to go on about?' Auntie Fido glared at her, and Bonnie wanted to laugh again, for her mascara had smudged on her cheeks and the blue eyeshadow she had put on so carefully had slipped sideways, giving her an odd, glaring expression. But she didn't dare giggle, for fear of losing control again. Her ribs still ached from the way she had laughed there at the Empire Rooms, the way she had cried all the way home to Hackney in the taxi.

'Nothing to go on about? When it was all done so tasteful, all the food and the band, all the people dressed like that, and Hester does that silly joke? I tell you, I'll never be able to hold my head up again with the Speros, never, and they're such nice people, so refined –'

'You won't have to,' Hester said harshly. 'Will she, Bonnie? Tell her.'

'Tell her what?' Auntie Fido looked at Bonnie, and Bonnie turned her head away. She looked awful. Even more embarrassing than Hester had been at the Empire Rooms, and here there were only themselves. And Sammy, silent in the corner, staring down at his crossed ankles.

'You won't have to see them again,' Bonnie said drearily. 'It's off. It's all off.'

'Off? What's off?' Auntie Fido said in a high-pitched whine, and then began to rock from side to side. 'Oh, Bonnie, he hasn't – your lovely ring – he hasn't –'

Bonnie held out her bare left hand. 'I gave it back to him.'

'Oh, no, such a thing, she gave it back to him – it wasn't your fault, you should've told him, it wasn't your fault – it was Hester, being silly. Hester – you should've told them. I'd 'a told them, 'f I'd 'a known, I'd 'a told them, gone down on my bended knees I would sue for your happiness, Bonnie, by my life I would –'

'I did,' Hester said loudly and laughed. 'Didn't I, Bonnie? Only I did it better. Made sure of it for you.'

'It was one hell of a way to do it,' Sammy said harshly and they all turned to look at him and Hester shrugged and turned away ostentatiously. 'Not quaite naice, Sammy deah? Not quaite naice? Of course it bloody wasn't! They're not quaite naice either. Oh, I'm learning. I'm learning. I used to go along with all that stuff you filled me with. All that stuff about what was common and what wasn't – I know better now –'

'Who was it changed our names because they weren't classy enough? You're a fine one to talk!' Hilda said and looked at Sammy for approval but he ignored her, staring at Hester.

'Yes, *Hester*. What about that? You're the one who changed our names, Bertha and Hetty weren't good enough for you –'

'Of course they weren't, you great shmok!' Hester shrieked, and Auntie Fido winced and put her hands over her ears. 'Can't you see the difference between real class and this stupid fancy-shmancy stuff the stinking Speros go in for? I did what I did to prove it to you all. Bonnie'd have had a hell of a life with him, a hell of a life – he couldn't break it off fast enough, could he, Bonnie?'

She whirled, leaned over Bonnie and grabbed her shoulder and began to shake her. 'Isn't that the truth? Before all the people had gone they'd made him tell you it was all off, made him grab his stinking ring back, am I right? Am I right?'

'Yes,' Bonnie said heavily and stood up. 'I'm going to bed. I'm tired.'

'Bonnie, you did see why, didn't you? Why it had to be? Why I had to show you? There wasn't any other way to make you stop it. You'd have had a rotten time married to him. Believe me.'

Bonnie looked at her, standing there with her head thrust forwards, staring at her urgently and with her arms crossed over her chest and her hands holding on to her upper arms with a sort of desperation. 'You understand, Bonnie, don't you?'

'I would have done it if you'd told me,' Bonnie said after a moment. 'I mean, you never said to me, "Don't marry him, he won't be right for you. That family'll make you miserable." Did you? Why didn't you say that? It would have been better than all this fuss tonight.'

Hester unfolded her arms and sat down heavily. 'Would you have listened to me?'

'Probably. We usually do, all of us, don't we? You changed my name when I was seven. You could have made me change my mind over David just as easily. You didn't have to do it this way.'

Hester looked up and her mouth moved awkwardly, and she grinned, a hard, tight little grin. 'It was better this way. Made them look the fools they are.' She laughed then. 'I tell you, they won't live that down in a hurry. Nor will that David. Oh, did you see his face? Did you *see* his face?'

But Auntie Fido just went on snivelling, sitting in the corner of the sofa and twisting her pink stole in her hands, and Hilda laughed again and went over to Bonnie and thumped her on the back.

'She's right, you know, Bonnie. This time she's right. They were stinking with money, I'll grant you, but they wouldn't have given you any of it. That David – he wouldn't give you the drippings of his nose –'

'Hilda!' Sammy said, and then reddened as Hester looked at him, her eyebrows up.

'I'm going to bed,' Bonnie said again, and went to the door. 'Good night, Auntie Fido. Good night Sammy, everyone –'

'You'll see, Bonnie – you'll say to me one day thanks for everything. You will!' Hester went after her, talking all the time that Bonnie climbed the stairs. 'You will!'

'I'm already glad,' Bonnie said. 'Honestly. Good night.'

10

The morning wore on, slowly and heavily, and Sammy moved awkwardly in his seat. His behind was numb, and he visualized his ischial tuberosities pressing down on the muscles and the nerves twisting their way in between, and murmured the names of the muscles softly under his breath; *gluteus medius, gluteus maximus, gracilis, adductor magnus* – and then smiled a little. Odd how the smell of a place could affect your thinking. This place smelled very like the examination halls.

They'd opened the plaintiff's case to the jury and it was almost impossible to sort out just what it was all about, what with dates, and references to the plaintiff and defendants and mention of uncontentious points of law, and the monotonous voice of the reader going through fat bundles of correspondence. It seemed to have no impact on any of them in the court; Hester sat and listened to the fat man indefatigably whispering; Hildegarde and Mel sat with bored expressions on their faces staring into the middle distance. And Bonnie sat beside him, her face smooth and expressionless as she gazed straight ahead.

Sammy looked at her, and wondered. Why had it happened so? In lots of ways she was the pick of them, the one with the best in her. Heart, that was what Bonnie had. Compassion and concern, all the things he most valued now, all the things he sought for in the people with whom he worked, and never – or hardly ever – found. Yet Bonnie had had it all the time, and what had he done about it?

NOVEMBER 1950

'I can see,
No matter how near you be,
You'll never belong to me
But I can dream, can't I? . . .'

'So, tell me, Sammy, how does it feel to be a doctor? A real live doctor?' Auntie Fido said archly and twinkled up at him.

'Tiring,' he said, and then smiled. 'Sorry. I didn't mean that. It feels great. Really great.'

'No more studying!' Hilda said and giggled and moved up close to him and tucked her hand into his elbow, peeping up at him under her curly fringe. She'd grown up a lot this year; her baby face had lost its soft peachy roundness and there was an edge to her that he found disturbing. When she'd started her games, trying out her new-found sexuality on him like a child throwing a rubber ball against a wall to see how hard it would bounce back, he'd been amused. Or so he'd told himself. Hester was his girl friend, dammit; how could he think otherwise, considering what they did?

He moved away, lightly, going over to the tables where he'd arranged the bottles of British sherry and sausage rolls. 'Come on, now!' he said with heavy joviality. 'Party time! Someone's got to tuck into all this –'

He began to dispense the sherry and the others moved over, the men from his year and their girls firmly upholstered in paper taffeta, their faces painted a careful pink and white and their eyes doe-like with flicked-up lines at the corners. They smiled and murmured, holding their cigarettes very correctly in net gloved hands. His eyes slid across to Hilda again, now leaning against the wall and staring at him sulkily. She looked absurd, quite absurd, and he blushed a little as he caught John Spiedel's girl friend looking at her, her black-painted eyebrows arched. Why did Hilda have to get herself up in that rig? Why didn't Hester tell her? Though he had to admit it suited her somehow, outlandish though it was to wear such tight trousers, and so thick a sweater. It looked like a man's sweater, chunky and solid. It made her seem fragile and interesting. Underneath it all she must be very soft and yielding –

'Well, Stermont, have you told the unlucky contestants for your favours that they'll have to survive without you, yet? Or are you keeping a few of 'em as aces in the hole, just in case?' Spiedel said loudly and Sammy laughed. There was envy in the man's voice, but no real malice.

'I was bloody lucky, and well you know it,' he said easily. 'And of course I've told 'em all. I don't want to make life difficult for anyone else.'

'Oh, perish the thought – now you've got the best job of the lot!' Daniels said from the other side of the room and laughed rather too loudly. 'Honestly, Hester, how does he do it? Spent as much time as any of us dealing with the *practical* aspects of anatomy –' the other girls sniggered and fluttered, sipped their sherry and drew on their cigarettes '– and still managed to top the lists in every damned subject. King Surgeon, King Physician, King bloody everything. Tell us, Hester, what was his secret?'

'Maybe his practical anatomy lessons were easier for him than for you others,' Hester said, and leaned back luxuriously on the sofa, grinning sideways at Sammy. 'I mean, when a man has an enthusiastic demonstrator to help him, maybe it's less time-consuming, you know? More – ah – rewarding –'

The other girls stilled and there were no giggles as they stared at her with hard eyes and then looked away, embarrassed. It was shocking, disgusting, really it was, to flaunt it like that. The men had told them all that Hester actually did it with Sammy, had done for ages, tried to persuade them to be the same, because it was absurd in the second half of the twentieth century to be so prudish, and what were they saving it for anyway? They turned away and began to talk to each other, animated and busy, and Hester looked at Sammy and winked and held out her glass for more.

'What sort of job is it they're talking about, Sammy? You'll have to explain to silly little me, you know! I don't understand all these ins and outs. Now you're a doctor properly I'd'a thought you could do what you liked anywhere –' Auntie Fido sounded very bright, almost feverish, trying to keep up with them all. Such a very sophisticated party!

'Being qualified is only the beginning,' Sammy said kindly, and passed her the plate of sausage rolls. 'Now I really have to get the right experience behind me. We all do – so, while we're waiting for the results of the finals, we all apply for the jobs that'll give the best experience. Six or seven jobs usually. And I've been lucky. I got the one everyone hoped to have. Very lucky –'

'You'll still be around though,' Hilda said sharply and Hester looked across the room at her and then at Sammy, her eyes opaque.

'Oh, of course. That's the point. I got the job at my own

103

hospital, you see. Daniel's got one in Reading, and Spiedel's going to Swindon, and Howell's –'

'That's all right then,' Hilda said with huge satisfaction. 'Then we'll still go on seeing you a lot, won't we?'

'He's still going to be very busy,' Bonnie said, and he turned and looked at her almost for the first time this evening. She was sitting on a chair on the far side of the sofa, her knees demurely together and her hands folded on her handbag in her lap. She looked very proper and charming and he warmed to her. Why on earth had he asked all of them to come? If he'd only asked Bonnie – and of course Hester – then he wouldn't have had to have the boredom of poor old Fido and Hilda around. He tried to imagine his qualification party without Hilda in her crazy clothes, and found it suddenly very dull. Though she was only a child after all.

'And your dear Mother and Daddy, Sammy, are they pleased?' Auntie Fido said, and then reddened. Maybe there was a special reason they weren't here.

'Yes,' Sammy said easily. 'They're delighted. They'd have been here tonight, of course. But there's a meeting, you know, and Dad had to go. Never misses his meetings –'

And his mother. He didn't want to think about her. The oddness and the messiness that had been so ordinary when he was young had assumed different proportions now. She would sit in the cluttered smelly kitchen of the house in Morning Lane and stare at the wall and talk, mumbling and rhyming, her voice rising and falling monotonously. His father paid no attention at all, pretended it wasn't happening, clearing up occasionally, shopping and cooking meals, going out to work and to his meetings just as though his wife was the way she ought to be.

He'd tried to tell him. He'd sat down with the old man one winter afternoon while his mother sat there in her usual place beside the gas cooker and said gently, 'She's ill, you know, Dad. She's really very ill. We ought to do something about it.'

He'd looked up at Sammy with his eyes round and dark as pebbles. 'How do you mean, ill? Suddenly you're the know-all? Suddenly you can diagnose disease just by looking at someone? So what can you see? Cancer? TB? What can you see?'

'You know what I mean, Dad,' Sammy had said, trying to be gentle, trying so hard to be gentle. 'I think it could be schizophrenia –'

'Rubbish!' his father had shouted. 'Crazy rubbish! You've got to put labels to everyone, you so called bloody scientists, you intellectual fools – you can't let a person be her own self, do as she wishes, she's got to have a label? Schizophrenia. Schizophrenia, is it? And what's *my* illness? Am I in the grip of a raging paranoia because I know of the evil of the world and seek ways to uproot it, because I've dedicated my life to fighting the inequalities and injustices that are rife? Am I mad because I will not sit down and bow my head to the capitalist pigs who call themselves my betters? Schizophrenia – you dare say such a thing! She's a genius, your mother, she always was – a genius – give me no more of this –this mad crazy rubbish, you hear me?'

And Sammy had heard, and said no more, but in the darker stretches of the night would wonder if perhaps it was a *folie à deux*, whether perhaps his father had spoken more wisely than he knew. A schizophrenic mother, a paranoid father, a great heritage.

He looked at Bonnie now and smiled and held his hand out to her. Someone had put on a gramophone record and people had started to dance, moving through the cramped space in the middle of his room as though it were the dance floor at the Savoy Grill, and the girls' skirts whispered as their taffeta folds rubbed together. Thinking of his parents made him feel good about Bonnie.

She smiled and stood up and looked for a moment at Hester, but she seemed content enough. She was talking to Howell, their heads close together, his girl sitting a little disconsolately beside him. One thing about Hester; she never showed any concern about who he talked to, who he danced with.

'I should have said, Bonnie,' he said after a moment or two as they shuffled with the others. 'It's very good of you.'

'What is?'

'Now, you know perfectly well,' he said. 'I appreciate it. I think she does.'

'It's my pleasure,' Bonnie said. 'Honestly.'

It was. Going over to the house in Morning Lane, spending a

whole Sunday there cleaning and sweeping and cooking, while the unkempt old woman sat and whispered away beside the stove, had been marvellous. She'd been able to pretend it was her house, hers and his, and that they were married and she was getting ready for him to come home. It would have been nicer if it had been a nicer house, of course. Nice like Auntie Fido's red-and-white Easiwerk kitchen. But even in this place it was good. So she scrubbed and rubbed and remembered how he had let her hold his head against her shoulder when she had found him sitting at the foot of the stairs at home, his forehead resting on his knees.

She'd come in late from work. They'd been stocktaking and afterwards they'd sent out for fish and chips and it had been quite good fun. Overtime and an evening used up. And there he'd been, sitting at the foot of the stairs, his forehead on his knees.

He'd looked up at her with his eyes blank and miserable and she'd cried out and dropped her bag and sat down beside him and said breathlessly, 'Whatever's the matter? Sammy, whatever is it?'

He'd looked at her and thought for a moment, shall I tell her? Tell her what it was like to be laughed at? To be stared at with scorn and *laughed* at? But he couldn't do that. So he just shook his head and tried to smooth his face.

But she would not be put off. 'Where is everyone? Have you hurt yourself? What is it, Sammy? Do tell me – so's I can help –'

He shook his head and said huskily, 'It's all right – really. Your aunt's out somewhere and Hilda's at a late class and –' He swallowed. 'Hester's gone out.'

'So, are you hurt?' she persisted, her eyes wide and damp with concern and suddenly irritated he said loudly, 'No, I'm all right. Just worried. It's my mother. She's not well. I can't get them to see sense – she ought to see a doctor.'

'Oh, my dear, dear Sammy!' Bonnie said, and put her arms round him, with sympathy and love and so much assorted feeling filling her she thought she'd burst. And he, tired and ashamed and trying to control the anger that was rising in him, let her push his head against her shoulder and sit there and croon to him.

The anger subsided, leaving him feeling flat and empty and as gently as he could, for it was no fault of hers, he pushed her away and stood up.

'I must go. I'm sorry. I didn't mean to bother you.'

'It's no bother,' she said earnestly. 'Honestly. I'll go over tomorrow and see what I can do to help. She'll need some work done about the house if she's feeling poorly, and it's Sunday –'

He looked at her dubiously and a new kind of shame filled him. She was so damned usable it made him feel almost ill.

But he smiled at her, a little shakily still. He'd taken a harder beating from Hester than he'd realized, had found it agonizing to sit there on her bed watching her get ready to go out with someone else, possibly getting ready to go to bed with someone else. Because she'd made no bones about it, been very cool.

'It wouldn't worry me,' she'd said, and straightened her stocking seams, licking her thumb and fingers so that she could pinch up the nylon more easily and move it against her leg. 'He's quite fun and he's in an interesting line of business. Got plans for the movies, you know?'

'You're talking like a bad film,' he'd said, cold and lofty. 'As though real people got real jobs sleeping with people – it's bloody rubbish.'

'Is it? We'll find out,' she'd said sweetly. 'Stay here if you like, Sammy. I don't mind and Fido won't even notice, I dare say. It's up to you.' And she'd gone clattering down the stairs and out, and he'd sat on the bottom step and wept. The special, unique thing they did, and she was going to do it with someone else that she didn't even particularly like. Oh, God!

'Thanks, Bonnie,' he said now. 'Thanks a lot. It's awful there to tell the truth – really awful. She's – it's all in her head, you know. She has a – it's a psychiatric illness.' That didn't sound so bad.

She nodded, solemn and important. 'I can manage,' she said. 'I can manage most things, given the chance. Don't you worry, Sammy. You study tomorrow, and I'll manage.'

He pulled her a little closer now as they danced at his qualification party and felt the gratitude bubble up in him. She'd managed marvellously, going there, week in and week out for the past three months. A marvellous girl, so kind. As he felt her first stiffen and then relax against him he thought again. So kind. So dull –

' "How happy could I be with either, were t'other dear charmer away!" ' Howell sang in his ear as he danced past, and Sammy turned his head, pretending not to hear. But Howell had been to two other qualification parties already tonight and was well away. If he recognized the signals Sammy was throwing out he showed no sign of it. 'What do y'do, Sammy, boy? Line 'em up, bang, bang, bang, you're done? Or do you run 'em on a rota? If this is Sunday it must be Hester? Way hay, boyos, way hay! Sammy the Potentate! – "Three little girls who all unwary –" '

'Oh, honestly, Matt, you do talk a lot of nonsense,' his girl said uneasily, and tried to manoeuvre him deeper into the dancing couples. 'Take no notice, Sammy. He's had a few, I'm afraid.'

'Had a few, had a few, had a few!' carolled Howell. 'So, I'm not afraid to talk, 'fraid to talk, 'fraid to talk! Sammy's got a harem, lucky old Sammy. Sammy's got the best job and a harem to choose for his use, choose for his use, choose for his use –'

'Howell, you are not nice to be near, hear me?' Spiedel called from the other side of the room. 'You're making yourself embarrassing. Shut your north and south, put a muff in your cake-hole and generally stow it!'

Howell stopped dancing as the gramophone hissed into silence, and stood swaying in the middle of the room, his face flushed and his eyes bright. There seemed to be no more in him than silliness, no real anger or resentment, but Sammy felt the tension rising around him, and smiled down at Bonnie and began to move away. Bonnie's face was very pink and she was looking down at her feet as she moved.

'I'm sorry, Bonnie,' he murmured. 'Silly chap – no harm in him really –'

'All the jobs, all the girls, Jews' luck,' Howell said, and now there was a sharp silence and Sammy turned and looked at him very directly.

'That'll do, Matt. Really, that'll do. It's time you took Mary home, isn't it? She's got to work tomorrow, I dare say.'

'Yes,' Mary said, and began to look about her with an air of bustle. 'My bag, Matt, and my coat, can you see them? I really must be going – last train and all that –'

108

'Jews' luck,' Howell said again and this time Spiedel, a thin man with thick glasses perched on his nose, came pushing through the others and took him by the shoulders.

'Come out with that once more, and I'll throw you downstairs,' he said heavily and Howell peered up at him and blinked and said experimentally, 'Jews' luck —'

Bonnie managed not to scream. She stood there with her hands over her ears as the clumsy fighting moved awkwardly from the middle of the room to the doorway, with Sammy trying to keep Spiedel and Howell apart, and Daniels showing signs of coming in on Spiedel's side, and the other girls shrieking and shouting incomprehensibly.

The party was over. Auntie Fido stood fluttering at the door, pulling her gloves on and off and blinking rapidly and Hilda stood beside her, saying nothing, but grinning, seeming pleased at her secret thoughts. Hester was still sitting on the sofa, leaning back and looking sardonic as Sammy came back up the stairs from the front door.

'God, I'm sorry!' he said. 'That stupid man — honestly, I never had the least idea he was anti-semitic. If I'd ever thought such a thing, believe me, I'd never have invited him here, never. I mean, I know it still happens, in spite of the war and Belsen and all that, but when it's people you *work* with and they use language like that, honestly, it makes me sick. You shouldn't have had to put up with it. I'm truly sorry. Miss Morris, you'll forgive me? I wouldn't have embarrassed you for the world —'

He rattled on, helping them on with their coats, seeing them all down the stairs in a troupe, worrying away at Howell's anti-semitism like a dog with a burr in its paw.

Bonnie lingered on the doorstep as the others went down the steps to the pavement.

'I'll see your mother Sunday as usual, Sammy?' she said in a swift whisper and he looked at her and then over her head at Hester and Hilda, standing at the end of the path and looking back.

'It's kind of you, but as a matter of fact, she won't be there — er, I mean, I'm making arrangements. Other arrangements. It's been marvellous of you, honestly, but I'm making arrangements. Goodnight, all of you. And I'm sorry about Howell and his remarks. I'll see to it he apologizes —'

109

Bonnie stood and looked at the closed door, hearing him go running away upstairs on the other side and felt very low. What on earth would she do with her Sundays, now?

11

'I am not quite clear in my own mind where this line of questioning is leading, Mr Jordan-Andrews,' the judge said fretfully, as the defence counsel stood there swaying a little and looking rather smug. 'Mr Wooderson's complaint seems to have some justification in it.'

'I am trying to establish, m'lord, to the satisfaction of the jury, the status of the plaintiff in her work. The evidence will make it abundantly clear that the remarks and actions complained of were particularly offensive –'

'Hmph! Well, if that is where the questioning is leading, I will allow it. But I do not wish to see the time of the court wasted on too much delving into long ago events which have only the smallest relevance to the matter before the court. I shall be listening very carefully, Mr Jordan-Andrews. I reject your submission, Mr Wooderson. The witness may answer Counsel's question.'

The defence counsel sat down in a little flurry of silk, looking put upon and indignant. He had been thoroughly magnanimous in agreeing to Jordan-Andrews's request to interpose this witness before calling Hildegarde Maurice. Jordan-Andrews had made great play of the fact that the woman was one of Her Majesty's school examiners with rooms full of eager young pupils waiting to dive head first into their art exams, and Wooderson had smiled emolliently and said that he quite understood that the cause of education must be served; and now, to have Jordan-Andrews behaving so – it was too much! He glared at Sylvia Justin, who opened her mouth and closed it and then opened it again and shook her head.

'I shall repeat the question, Miss Justin,' Jordan-Andrews said with ponderous kindness, tucking his chin into his bands and peering up at her on the witness box. 'As her first teacher, did you find Miss Hildegarde Maurice to be – ah – a gifted person?'

'Oh – yes. Yes indeed. Only of course she wasn't Hildegarde Maurice then. She was Hilda Morris –'

111

There was a soft giggle in the court, a movement of laughter like wind bending a field of grass and the judge peered up and sniffed and Sylvia went on hurriedly. 'I mean, she was a very straightforward girl, always was. Very gifted. Her colour sense – unique, really. I did all I could to encourage her, got her to go to art school. I was always very proud of her.'

Hildegarde looked up then and smiled at her, and Sylvia reddened, looked away. 'Mind you,' she said suddenly, as Jordan-Andrews opened his mouth to ask his next question, 'I never thought she'd go into fashion. I mean, it was fine art I thought would be her – it was that friend she made. Birgitta. She was the one I knew was interested in fashion –'

Again there was a rustle in court, but this time it was not laughter. Heads lifted, turned, and people stared at Hildegarde, but she sat there looking as she had all the time; cool, relaxed, a little amused, seeming unaware of any tension anywhere.

'Yes,' Mr Jordan-Andrews said quickly. 'Yes – but of course you are talking of the very early days when she was just a child. And as m'lord said, we must not waste the court's time – Let us now move on to the later days. The very first fashion sale. You were there, I believe –'

Sylvia Justin nodded. 'Oh, yes, I was there. Very interesting it was.'

JANUARY 1953

'Don't let the stars get in your eyes,
Don't let the moon break your heart
You're the only one I'll ever love . . . .'

'Well, I must say, Hilda, dear, it all looks very interesting.'

She stood at the door staring around and twisting her bag between her fingers. Lately she'd tried to dress better; Hilda had looked at her sometimes in a way she found painful, and it had to be her clothes. So the classical look was gone; anyway, near as she was getting to forty, it was a bit ageing. So it was curls and full-skirted dresses and loose duster coats and soft pouchy handbags now. But it didn't seem to make much difference. Hilda still looked at her hurtfully sometimes and she didn't really feel comfortable in such clothes. But never mind,

112

the harder Hilda was to mother, the more mothering she needed.

Sylvia told herself often that that was what it was all about: mothering. It was a need to look after this fragile, gifted child that so absorbed her that sometimes she couldn't get the child's face out of her mind for one whole day together.

She looked at her now, and wanted to reach out and touch her, to stroke her curly fair hair and run her fingers along the line of her eyebrow, lifting its arch above those wide blue eyes. But she controlled it. Hilda could be particularly fractious about what she called mauling. It was all right if she was in the mood for it, all right if she was tired enough to lean back in the curve of a motherly arm and have her ear played with in a sweetly babyish way. But this was definitely not an all right time. So Sylvia looked round again and said brightly, 'Interesting!'

'Hardly,' Hilda said. 'Nothing's happened yet. But it's going to – just you wait and see.' She turned her head and saw Melvin at the far side of the room and shouted suddenly, 'No, you bloody idiot – keep your hands off that, you hear me?' and went running across the parquet so fast that her skirt belled and lifted, showing her knickers. Sylvia felt her throat thicken at the sight of those bare rounded thighs and the curve of the buttocks and thought hurriedly, 'Dear child. Nineteen, but still, dear child.'

'Jesus Christ!' Hilda was bawling at Melvin. 'Are you out of your tiny mind?' I spent bloody hours getting that right – give it to me!'

Mel laughed. 'So what have I done that's so terrible? I bumped into it – everything fell off so I was trying to put it back again! But if your high and mightiness wants to do it on her own, so be it!' He stood there watching her pinning the underwear back on the screen. 'It looks good,' he said after a moment. 'Sexy, but not smutty. Who did 'em?'

'A kid in the first year,' Hilda said through a mouthful of pins. 'I told her to try her hand – I thought she'd be good.'

'Mad colours,' Mel said. 'Who'd 'a thought dark brown for bras? But it's interesting.'

'Of course it is. That's why I did it,' Hilda said, and stood back to look at the clothes pinned up on the tall screen. 'I'm sick of white, white, white. Or pink, pink, pink. I'm wearing scarlet.'

'Really?' he said and leered. 'Sexiest of the lot, that.'

'Oh, I don't know.' Quite without any self-consciousness or guile she lifted her skirt in both hands and peered down. 'Could be. I chose 'em mainly for shock effect – I'll be up and down that catwalk myself, and I thought – give 'em something to gasp at.'

'They will,' Mel said, and tried to slip an arm round her. She was looking delicious, he thought. A huge circular skirt made of black felt that hung in heavy folds over her hips, a tight polo neck sweater, also black, and tied casually round her throat a scarlet scarf, its ends pointing jauntily north and south. She had big round scarlet stud ear-rings peering out beneath her fair fluffed-out curls, and her lipstick matched them exactly. Delicious.

'Oh, go and count the seats, for God's sake,' she said. 'And keep your mauling hands for counting the money. And watch it, I'll know to a penny what'll be due.'

'All right, all right, keep your wig on!' he said huffily and straightened his tie. He'd made a considerable effort to look right for tonight; his good Edwardian-style suit, his whitest shirt and silkiest tie. But she had only flicked a look at him and said nothing. Still, if he hadn't looked right she'd have been very noisy, he thought, and went over to the door and sat down behind the table that stood there ready, a book of tickets and a cash-book set neatly in the middle.

'How can you be so sure anyone'll come?' he called across to Hilda. She was prowling now, walking along the catwalk they'd rigged up in the middle of the long church hall, looking from side to side at the tall screens that stood behind the rows of chairs, at the clothes arranged on hangers on rails, at the sheets of multi-coloured crepe paper hanging on the walls.

'They'll come,' she said confidently. 'There's not one girl for miles around here who won't know she'll be right out on a limb by herself if she doesn't come tonight *and* make sure she spends –'

He watched her as she re-arranged one of the screens and Sylvia Justin, sitting alone in the front row at the far end of the catwalk, also watched. Her confidence came out of her like an almost visible thing, and infected them too.

She'd told Melvin she could make some money for him. All she needed was a float of thirty pounds and three months, and she could turn it into a hundred and fifty for herself, and a ten-pound profit for him.

He'd laughed at her at first but she'd lost her temper, made him listen, so he'd listened. Sceptic at first and then, convinced, he'd found the money, borrowing it himself. And Christ, but she'd worked. Found the church hall in Finchley – 'Pick your district right, that's the first thing,' she'd said. 'We need girls with money, lots of 'em. And it's got to be well away from the college. I don't want any fuss from the people I get stuff from' – organized the publicity, bought in everything.

He'd been amused at first and then amazed as it all started to come in. She'd had no more than drawings from the students at art school, a few addresses of outworkers, and she'd done the rest. Bought the cloth, yards and yards of cheap vividly-coloured felts and hessians, extraordinary material to be made into clothes. But there they were, and bloody good they looked, he thought, staring at the long rails and the display screens.

Half past seven. Sylvia looked uneasily at her watch. Wasn't this starting time? Hilda, seeing her face, laughed. 'Don't worry, my duck, don't you worry! Keep 'em waiting for a while. Nothing works as well as queueing! Look – you'll feel better!'

Sylvia, still uneasy, but obedient, got to her feet, and following the jerk of Hilda's chin went to the main door and peered out of the side window that showed the street outside.

'Well!' she said, and there was awe in her voice. 'You're right! There's hordes of them waiting.'

'I knew there would be,' Hilda said calmly and came and looked over her shoulder. 'Give 'em another ten minutes. The girls are ready at the back – but they'll be glad of a bit of extra time. And we want a rush when it starts. They've got to be panicked a bit to start 'em buying. Then they all catch it and we'll be off.'

'You're really sure, aren't you?' Mel said, leaning back in his chair and staring at her.

'Of course I am! Why shouldn't I be?'

He shook his head. 'Anyone else'd be in a flat spin right now, I mean, you owe me thirty quid, and all those people you've got stuff from on tick, and the hire of the hall, and the models and all –'

115

'Listen, you'll get your thirty quid *and* the tenner on the top interest you were promised. And you'll go a long way to get thirty-three-and-a-third per cent on your money anywhere else. I'll make my hundred and fifty and everyone'll be paid. So what are you worried about?'

'Only that you aren't.'

'Oh, you make me puke,' she said, and laughed as Sylvia winced a little. 'Well, honestly, if a job's done properly, then there's nothing to get into a state about. This'll work, you'll see. I intend it to.'

'Where's Birgitta?' he said after a moment and Hilda stood peering out of the window at the crowd outside and seemed not to have heard him.

'Birgitta,' he said louder. 'Where is she?'

'Eh? Oh –' She looked at him, her head on one side, considering. And then grinned. 'She'll probably be here next week.'

'Next week? Why?'

She giggled, the little girl giggle that Sylvia so loved to hear. 'Because I got the date wrong, didn't I? Told her it was next Thursday night, not this Thursday, didn't I? Well, anyone can make a mistake –'

After a moment he said, 'You bitch,' very softly and she nodded brightly at him.

'That's right. What are you going to do about it?'

He grinned. 'Me? Why should I do anything?'

'You talk sense,' she said and bobbed her head at him. 'I've got a lot going for me, you'll see. I'll let 'em in, now. Get yourself together. Sylvia! Tell them at the back we're starting and then come and help Mel with the cash. I'll settle them in their places –'

Sylvia obeyed her imperious summons, almost pathetically glad to be given something to do and Mel couldn't look at her. Poor cow, he thought. Poor stupid cow. He gave her the ticket book, kept the cash box firmly on his side and settled down to take money.

He took it. The doors opened with a little thud, and the girls came in, twittering, staring around, bright eyed and eager, gazing at the huge poster on the door that shrieked in phosphorescent orange and yellow paint: 'Fashion Show! Fashion Show! Fashion Show! The Newest Ideas. The Newest Styles. The Lat-

116

est Paris Models! From Manufacturers Direct to You – Save £s and £s and £s and £s –'

They paid their half crowns ('enough to make it worth while, not cheapskate, not so expensive it'll keep 'em out,' Hilda had said) and settled in the seats, letting Hilda arrange them as she wanted. The place filled with anticipation and Hilda slipped behind the heavy dark curtain of the church hall stage and after a moment music started; bouncy, melodic, unmemorable.

And then the lights changed. The overheads went out and spots came on, illuminating the catwalk and the front of the stage. Mel stared, as open-eyed as any of them, but stayed put; they were still coming, young, chattering, breathless girls, giggling and shrieking softly, and he took their half crowns, counted out change, issued tickets almost feverishly.

Hilda's timing was superb. The last half dozen were in, standing at the back of the seats and there were clearly few more likely to arrive, for it was now almost half an hour past the advertised starting time, and they were beginning to get just a shade restless; and the music changed, became a trumpet fanfare, and Hilda stepped out in front of the curtain.

She seemed to merge with it, in her black clothes, only her pale face with its aureole of fair curls and the splashes of scarlet that were her mouth and scarf and ear-rings really being visible, with her legs, pale in their bareness, dwindling away beneath the spotlight.

'Hi, everyone!' she called loudly. 'Hi, and hi and hi!'

One or two bolder spirits called, 'Hi' back and she lifted her hands above her head, and they too looked disembodied and exciting.

'Let's hear it again for me!' she cried. 'Hi and hi and hi!'

Obediently they cried it back, 'Hi and hi and hi!'

'Great,' she almost purred it. '*Great* to meet you. I'm Hildegarde, Hi to my friends! And tonight *you're* my friends. I'm bringing you the newest, most exciting and above all cheapest fashion you've seen since you got out of school. That's a promise, and to show I tell no more than the truth, let's get going – the only look that anyone will want to wear this Coronation Year!'

By eleven they'd gone, all of them. The models, the customers,

117

the church-hall caretaker, content, with his huge tip of a pound, to leave them half an hour longer than they'd booked the hall for, sitting staring at each other.

'Christ, but I'm hungry!' Hilda said suddenly. 'I want food, food, food! If this was New York we'd send out, wouldn't we? Like they do in the movies? Hamburgers – like Popeye. Why don't they start places where people could buy hamburgers when they're hungry?'

Mel laughed and stretched. 'Yeah. Just for you. All round Finchley I can hear 'em screaming – give us Hollywood hamburgers! I bet they don't even buy fish and chips round here! Too shprauncy.'

'Not too shprauncy to spend,' Hilda said cheerfully. 'What'd I tell you?'

'What's shprauncy?' Sylvia said suddenly and Hilda, expansive and happy, smiled kindly at her and her ears went pink. 'Fancy types. Think themselves high class. Fancy-shmancy-shprauncy. New word. Like it?'

'Here, Hilda – we've taken bloody nearly three hundred pounds!' Melvin said. He'd been counting the notes, making lists of figures, his pencil scurrying up and down the columns like a busy mouse. 'I wouldn't have thought –'

'What do you mean, *we've* taken?' Hilda said sharply, and suddenly she was fully alive again, no longer relaxed and luxurious. 'I'll have it, if you don't mind. Give me the ticket book – and my stock lists. That's right. My stock lists. I want to check.'

She checked, as the other two sat and watched her in a heavy silence. Her eyes never left her hands as she counted, the notes slipping between her fingers with the soft rustle of autumn leaves, and then she started on the silver and copper, sliding the coins from table to hand with a crisp rattle.

And then it was her pencil's turn to hurry up and down columns of figures, comparing the list of money taken with the list of goods for sale and the number of tickets sold. At last she leaned back and nodded, her face expressionless.

'Right. There's a quid short, and that was the one you gave the caretaker. I told you – write it all down.'

'So, I forgot a pound! Terrible thing!' Mel said.

'This time a pound, next time a hundred,' she said, and peeled ten one-pound notes from the pile in front of her. 'Here's your

118

profit. Do you want to leave your float in on the same basis?'

He stared at her and then shook his head.

'I borrowed it,' he said. 'I'll have to have it back. But if you're doing it again I'll come in bigger.'

'If you're asked,' she said coolly. 'Maybe I don't want you any bigger. Not at thirty-three-and-a-third, for Christ's sake.'

His eyes narrowed. 'So what about the work I do? Isn't that part of the deal?'

She was silent, staring at him, the tip of her tongue showing between her lips, and then she nodded.

'Okay. Next time – it'll be late May, just before the Coronation – you can come in at double the stake, double the take, But you work for it, you hear me? I want no sleeping partners.'

'What about the others?' Sylvia said and Hilda turned and stared at her as though she'd forgotten she were there at all. 'What about who? What others?'

'The students,' Sylvia said, and bobbed her head at the screens. 'The ones whose designs they were.'

'What designs? All they were, my duck, was scribbles on bits of paper. Silly scribbles. Like your Great Paintings. Just a lot of paint on canvas, they are. It's turning 'em into real somethings that's important, for Christ's sake. Not the scribbles. They had the pleasure of having me take their stuff, didn't they? I might give 'em some of the left-overs –' She turned her head to look at the depleted rails. 'At cost plus a small margin, maybe.'

Mel laughed, throwing his head back, displaying his teeth. 'Some giving!'

'Well, what'd you expect? Who got the ideas? Who saw the potential? Who chose the colours, the fabrics, got the manufacturers, made the bloody stuff *work*? I did. Not the scribblers with their pencils and fancy papers and silly prissy drawings. *I* did! And if you don't like it you can do the other thing. I don't need you any more, my dear Mr Solicitor Bremner! I've got my float, got what I need, I don't need *anyone* else.'

'Who said anything about not liking?' Mel said lazily. 'It was your friend Sylvia here who was asking.'

Hilda got up, and swept the money and the stock lists and the remainder of the tickets into the cash box and locked it. 'You go home, Sylvia,' she said. 'It's late and you're tired. I'll finish here.'

'I'll help,' Sylvia said. 'Glad to. Then we could pop back to my place and get something to eat, maybe? I've got some eggs –'

'Not tonight. Too late. Go home.' Hilda said, and moved across the floor and began to fold the remaining clothes, packing them meticulously into the big boxes she'd brought them in.

There was a little silence, and Mel sat and looked at Sylvia, and she stared back. But he won and she got to her feet and holding her pouch bag in front of her said awkwardly, 'Well, I'll say good night, then.'

'Good night,' Hilda said, and she didn't look round.

12

They were all coming out into the terrazzo-floored corridors, moving a little stiffly, not looking at each other.

Hildegarde came out before Hester, Mel a few steps behind her, his hands tucked inside his belt with his thumbs sticking aggressively over the top, grinning a little inanely. His effort to look insouciant was clearly a strain, and compared to Hildegarde, who seemed genuinely relaxed, he was as taut as a piano wire.

Hester too was relaxed. She seemed to show no signs of awareness of Hildegarde as she went past her, listening once more to the fat man at her ear, nor did she seem to be lingering deliberately; yet by the time she came out of the court, the others had gone, their counsel around them with their gowns belling out like ships' sails as they went hurrying along the corridors.

Bonnie lingered for a moment in the shadows, not knowing what to do. Should she follow Hilda, talk to her? Stay where she was and talk to Hester? Oh, God, decisions, why was it so hard to make decisions? And Stanley – where was he? He'd said twelve or a quarter past, here, and it was one o'clock and no sign of him, and she'd taken no notes though she'd promised to. A fat lot of help she was. Why had she forgotten to take notes? That was an important question. Why, Mr Hermann would ask, why, Bonnie, why, why, why?

'Don't look so responsible, Bonnie,' Sammy said, and slid his hand into the crook of her elbow and she turned to him gratefully.

'Responsible?'

'You're standing there looking as though all this –' he waved his hand comprehensively '– the very building and all the courts, apart from the case you're actually here for, are part of your burden. Believe me, in this you're just an on-looker.'

'Not really,' she said, and tried to make her face smooth. 'How can I be? I'm married to Stanley. He said he'd be here. I can't think why –'

'He's a big boy now. He'll find his own way.' Sammy changed things round, taking her hand and making an elbow for her. He began to urge her forwards. 'It'll be hell finding anywhere to get lunch. Everyone and his wife are here, and they'll fill every restaurant for miles around. How hungry are you?'

'Not very.'

'No. Nor me. Tell you what – I'll pick up sandwiches and rubbish, and we'll sit in Temple Gardens, eat there. What about it?'

'I would, Sammy, honestly. But there's Stanley. I said we'd meet – I can't –' She felt the anxiety begin to bubble in her, breathed deeply the way they'd shown her at meditation classes, pushed it back down again. And smiled at Sammy as brightly as she could. 'Truly, I'd love it, but Stanley's so efficient – he's probably booked a table somewhere. Forgive me?'

He seemed a little remote now, and she tightened her grip on his arm, wanting to placate him. It mattered suddenly that he should be happy, almost as much as it had used to matter all those years ago. It hadn't mattered, of course, for ages. Stanley and the children and asking why, that was what mattered now. But he looked bleak and lonely and it saddened her.

'Sammy?' she said again.

'There's Stanley,' he said, and straightened his arm so that his elbow flattened out and she had to let go.

They had reached the huge central hall, where she felt shrunken and ordinary again; it was a comforting feeling and it helped her to smile at Stanley.

'Stanley! I was just getting worried! You remember Sammy, of course –'

Stanley looked at him, flicking his eyes stonily across his face. 'Stermont. Of course. Hello,' he said and then looked at Bonnie. 'Twelve, I said, remember? Twelve. So where were you?'

'In court!' She was puzzled. 'Where else?'

'Down here to meet me would have been nice, seeing you must have known what was going on,' he said savagely. 'God Almighty, Bonnie, what sort of fool d'you take me for? They closed the court, packed full it was, they said, and though I told 'em I might be called as a witness – told 'em I was involved, the bastards wouldn't let me through. So, I said to 'em, all right. My wife's in there. Take her a message, she'll come out, let me in.

122

But the bastards wouldn't do that either. So I wait, like some great shlemiel, and out you come, strolling like it was a party! What do you take me for?'

'I'm sorry, Stanley,' she began. 'So sorry – I had no idea, I never thought –'

'No,' he said, his voice loud. 'No, you didn't, did you?'

'It'll be better this afternoon,' Sammy said, and his voice was calm and conversational. He was proud of the way it sounded. He'd disliked this man as long as he had known him, and listening to him now he could have hit him, quite easily could have lifted his hand and hit him. Pacific gentle Sampson Stermont, democratic-rights-for-everyone Sampson Stermont could have hit him. 'There are some people here just for curiosity. They won't rush back. So we'll go get a little refreshment, go back early. Then others'll be shut out. No hassle, really –'

Stanley was turning to go. 'Who's got time for lunch? I've wasted enough time already for one day. I'll be back at quarter to two, Bonnie. They said the court was starting again at two. So, a quarter to two, right here, understand? I'll see you –'

'Where are you going?' she said, and smiled, bright, friendly. People were looking at them, she knew it, could feel it. 'Can I come along? Then there's no risk we'll miss each other –'

'Listen, doll, you may have nothing to do and all day to do it in – me, I've got your living to earn, remember? So I've got phone calls to make, business to arrange. I'll be back here at one-forty-five sharp. I'll see you then.'

He went, his coat swinging out behind him, and they stood there and after a moment Sammy said lightly, 'Lunch?'

'What?' She looked at him, then at her watch. 'Is there time? I must be here at quarter to two. Honestly, he's right. I should have realized. I was in a real dream up there, I think – it was all so hot and stuffy and I kept thinking of things I'd thought I'd forgotten. Odd – no. Thanks, Sammy, but I won't.'

'You'll feel a damned sight odder when you go back if you've had no lunch,' he said. 'Look, go and find the loo, tidy yourself up, have a wash. I'll be back – that bench there, you see? I'll be back with some lunch, and we'll eat it here. You've plenty of time for food and for Stanley, I promise you.'

She looked up at him and then smiled and swallowed and nodded all at once, and he felt it again, the twist of regret.

Always the kindest, the most easily upset, the best of the lot. Oh, God, why did this place feel so dead, now that both Hildegarde and Hester had gone?

'You're right. Thanks, Sammy. You really are right. I – I'll be five minutes, then. You'll be longer, I know, but don't worry, don't break your neck rushing back –'

'I won't. I never do.'

He turned and then stopped and looked back at her.

'Bonnie, I never did know. Why did you marry him? Stanley?'

She stood there in her good Hildegarde suit, her heavy leather bag clutched in both hands, her feet in their Gucci shoes neatly side by side like a child at school prayers, and thought about it, the skin under her eyes creasing a little.

'I'm not sure,' she said at length. 'I suppose there didn't really seem to be any reason not to. You know?'

'Yes,' he said. 'I know. D'you like cherry yoghurt?'

'I'll leave it to you,' she said. 'Honestly.'

He took a sharp little irritated breath suddenly. 'All right. I won't be long. Go on – go and pee. You'll feel better.'

NOVEMBER 1955

'Love is a many-splendoured thing,
It's the April rose that only grows in the early Spring.
Love is nature's way of giving,
A reason to be living . . . .'

It was the smell of the place she liked best of all, Bonnie decided. Hot tea and cream cakes and face powder and scent and floor polish, and over all that cigars and Turkish cigarettes. It added up to excitement and now-ness and made her feel that she was really alive.

They were sitting at a table Stanley particularly liked, in the second row back from the dance floor to one side of a pillar but with a good view of the foyer and the big revolving doors.

'Here you get to see everyone who comes in,' he'd explained to Bonnie. 'And then if you want them to see you, you move your chair a little sideways, this way, they can't miss you. You don't want to see them, it's just as easy, you move your chair a

124

little bit this way, your back's to 'em, the real cold shoulder.' And he'd laughed heartily at his joke and leaned over and pinched her cheek.

Tonight he looked relaxed and expansive, leaning back against the little gilt chair, with his cigar in his mouth and his elbow on the pink tablecloth. His shirt cuffs looked big and very white, and the heavy garnet cuff links winked redly in the light from the huge chandeliers overhead. Around them the tinkle of teacups and glasses and music and the shrill chatter of voices sounded comfortable and saved them the trouble of talking. It really was all very nice, she told herself again, and sipped some more tea.

'Go on, spoil yourself,' he said and grinned at her, his teeth very white and even, gleaming a little. 'Have a gin and tonic.' He picked up his own glass of whisky and soda, drank and waved it at her.

'No, thanks, Stanley,' she said and smiled. 'Really, I'd rather not.'

'You know something, doll? I'm glad you don't like drink. Not because I'm mean, I don't have to tell you that – no one can call Stanley Maddern mean – or because I grudge you, because I tell you, I grudge you nothing, but because I *like* a girl who doesn't drink. You understand me? I got nothing against a woman having an occasional cherry brandy, a little advocaat maybe, but spirits – it's better she shouldn't. Ruins her complexion, eh? And does other things to her, I'm told. Not nice, when it comes to having babies, eh? So, another cake? No – don't stint yourself. We'll have more –'

He waved, clicking his fingers at the same time and the bored-looking waiter came over, his step faster than it usually was. Maddern was an *habitué* of the Cumberland Hotel who tipped heavily, and the staff knew it. They also knew he could make a very nasty scene if he was kept waiting for a second. Not that he was all that different from the other regular Sunday evening crowd. Young Edgware, Finchley and Maida Vale turned out in force every week-end, and they all expected to be treated to perfect service. But none quite so aggressively as Stanley Maddern.

Bonnie didn't bother to argue. She didn't want another of the rich and heavy cream cakes, but there was no chance of refusing. Once Stanley had decided she was to have something that was all there was to it. She could play with it, pretend to eat.

They danced a little, talked a little, stared at the other people a lot. A normal Sunday evening, and she sat and wondered when he was going to bring it up again. She'd have to if he didn't and she'd really much rather not.

But he did.

'So, Bonnie, doll. Have you talked to your family?'

She folded her hands over her bag on her lap under the table. 'Yes – well, in a way.'

'How do you mean, in a way? Either you told them or you didn't! Don't give me the run-around, Bonnie. I can't stand people who try to give me the run-around.'

'I'm not. It's just – oh, they're a funny lot, really, Stanley.' She reddened, hating the note of disloyalty in her voice. 'I don't mean really *funny* – my sisters are lovely people, honestly, and my Auntie Fido does the best she can, always has. It's just, well – my sister Hester, you know? She has – different ideas to other people –' Her voice dwindled away.

He leaned forwards and put one hand on the table, heavily grinding out the remaining half of his cigar with the other. 'You're worrying about what happened with the Speros?'

Her face went scarlet and he laughed indulgently and patted her arm. 'Listen, Bonnie, you don't think people haven't talked to me about that? You don't think people forget?' He lifted his head and looked round the big lounge, at its pink-clothed tables with their individual tulip-shaped lights and the chattering expensively-dressed people round them and laughed again. 'All of 'em, even the ones I don't know, they went out of their way to warn me, tip me off as soon as I started taking you out. Didn't want to make trouble, they said, but there was something they thought I should know. So I know all about what happened at the Speros' engagement party.'

He paused, looking at her very directly, his square handsome face solemn. 'And shall I tell you something, Bonnie? I never enjoyed anything so much in my life. I know the Speros. I wish I'd been there, seen the old man's face. It must have been rich! Best laugh I ever had!' And now he laughed again, throwing his head back and producing such hearty sounds that other people

126

at nearby tables turned round and looked and grinned in sympathy.

She sat there and stared at him, nonplussed. All these weeks while she'd let him take her here there and everywhere, all those weeks when she knew he was working up to ask her to marry him, and she'd been so worried – and all he could do was laugh?

Her spirits lifted. The thing that had worried her most was not so much how he would react to her family – or even more how they would react to him – but the niggling doubt about whether she really cared as much for him as she should.

He was handsome, very protective in a way that made her feel marvellously comfortable, and when he kissed her and held her close could make her feel quite excited, which was nice. She'd never felt excited that way with David. But there had never been anything to really laugh at together and that worried her. Everyone – at work, in the magazines, the girls she knew – said that a sense of humour was vital in a marriage. That after security and reliability a sense of humour was the most important. And she'd wondered, sometimes, whether Stanley had enough sense of humour.

But now her doubts shivered and broke into tiny shards and disappeared. Laughing the way he was, how could she worry?

'I'm glad you know,' she said when he stopped laughing. 'It's been worrying me – not being honest. I told the girls I was going out with someone, of course – but not any more than that, I mean, nothing about – well,' she shrugged.

'Nothing about what?' he said and put his other hand on the table, beckoning so that she had to lift her own hands from her lap and put them in his grasp.

'You know what.'

'Go on, say it. Say it in words.'

'Say what?'

'Bonnie, no run-around! Remember? Say it!'

'Oh – well, then, nothing about maybe getting – well, serious.'

'Getting serious? *Getting* serious? Listen doll, I'm always serious.'

She looked up at him and he looked very nice. His dark chin, square and neat over his white collar with its dark tie, the brown eyes, so wide open and yet concentrated in their gaze. He really looked very nice and she felt the need for someone to lean on, someone to trust, come bubbling up in her and she said, 'Oh, Stanley, it's so good to be with you! You make me feel like – all right, you know? As though no one could ever hurt me or be nasty while you were here.'

'Are you kidding? Would I let anyone hurt my little Bonnie? No one hurts what belongs to Stanley Maddern, believe me. Just let me know if anyone hurts you, and I'll be there. I've been serious about you ever since I first saw you –' and his voice thickened the way it always did when he was talking about himself and the future. 'So say it to me in words, Bonnie. Tell me what you want.'

'I want –' She stopped. 'I can't.'

'You can. Say you love me. Say you want me to look after you always, want to be married to me, have my children, look after my home.'

She looked at him, still feeling the deep undertow of doubt. But didn't everyone feel that? Didn't every girl there ever was feel unsure, shy, frightened? The people at work, the magazines, the girls she knew, they all said so. This was the natural way to feel when someone asked you to marry them. He was a marvellous person to marry, he really was. Sensible and strong and with a sense of humour, and making up his mind so firmly, no confusion, no unsureness.

'I do want to care for you,' she said and smiled, and he held her hands even more tightly, and then pulled her to her feet, and led her to the dance floor.

They danced, very close, his body pressed against hers, their cheeks stuck together with the moistness of their skins and she closed her eyes and thought, I'm going to get married, I really am. Hester won't stop this one. She'll like this one. She was right before, but this one she'll like –

He kissed her, right there in the middle of the dance floor, and some of the other dancers clapped their hands and one or two people slapped Stanley on the back and he grinned, pushed them aside, led her back to their table and ordered a bottle of Asti Spumante.

'We'll celebrate! We're engaged. You love me – it's marvellous,' he said, and they clinked glasses and danced again. It was all very romantic.

'I'll tell them, then?' Bonnie said after a while, and he nodded. 'I've already told my own family, naturally. No engagement party, of course.' His teeth gleamed again for a moment. 'Who needs it? We'll lose out on some presents of course, but my relations, bless 'em, are no schnorrers. We'll announce it in the *JC*, they'll send presents. My mother says already she'll make the wedding. She likes you, she'll help you with your sister Hester. You'll have no problems.'

'Hester won't make any problems, honestly, Stanley. Not this time. She didn't before, not really. I was upset at the time, but she was right. He wasn't for me. It'd never have worked. And she knew.'

'I'm glad she knew,' Stanley said vibrantly. 'Because if she hadn't there wouldn't be us. Listen, doll, next week bring them here, eh? Your sisters? I don't want we should embarrass anyone. There's no crime in your people not being so well off – so bring 'em here, we'll have a nice evening – I'll pick up the bill – they'll see it's all okay. What do you say?'

'Yes, Stanley. If I can I'll bring them. And my aunt –'

'Well, for her, another time. Next week, it's just us young ones, eh? Now, we'll dance a little, go home – park the car a little –'

It wasn't till she was almost asleep that she thought, 'I told him I cared. But what did he say?'

And she couldn't remember.

13

'Mr Wooderson, you seem to be missing my point,
I'm afraid,' the fat man said. 'Far be it from me to tell so noted a
Silk how to conduct a case, but it worries me, it worries me a lot,
that the plaintiff is using this ploy. If they go on and on calling
evidence to attest to her skill, to her history of success and a'l
the rest of it to prop up their case, then we should surely make
as much effort to display Miss Morrissey's integrity. If the jury
are going to be told how wonderful Hildegarde is, then it's
surely vital they know as much about Hester here –'

'Oh, Willy, do shut up,' Hester said and grinned at Wooderson. 'He does go on, doesn't he, Mr Wooderson? I know you
mean well, Willy, but leave it alone! I mean, how are we supposed to display my integrity, anyway? Get people up there to
say, "Oh yes, she's got integrity, dripping with it"? The whole
damned business is dripping with integrity, for Christ's sake!
You can get it plain or fancy, trimmed in colours or wrapped in
tinsel. I just don't see any point in digging up a lot of past
history. I tell you, Hilda's going to be in dead shtooch if she lets
her lot go on and on about it. Someone'll come up with something she'd rather not get talked about. You saw what happened
this morning when that bloody fool Sylvia dropped that bit
about her name –'

'You must remember, Miss Morrissey, that I have not yet
cross-examined Miss Justin.' Wooderson's voice was as emol-
lient and as well modulated out here in the corridor as it ever
was in court. Hester liked that; people who kept their performance up even when it wasn't really necessary were real pros.
They made it work better than anyone. 'I have questions of my
own to put to Miss Justin about Miss Maurice's past history. I
have the distinct impression that there may be a number of
useful skeletons yet to be exhumed from her cupboards.'

Hester laughed. 'You're not kidding! The poor old dyke. She
doesn't know which way is up! And I can tell you that what
Hilda did to her wasn't pretty – it wasn't pretty at all.'

130

'Really?' Mr Wooderson said, and moved closer. 'Do tell me. It might be useful.'

'We're all going on a summer holiday.
No more working for a week or two....'

'To Florence?' Sylvia said. 'Me? *With you?* Oh, Hilda, d'you mean it?'

'*Hildegarde*,' Hildegarde said. 'For God's sake, get it in your head, will you? Of course I mean it. I wouldn't have said it otherwise.'

'Oh, Hilda-garde, oh, how *marvellous!*' Sylvia knew she was twittering, and knew that it drove Hilda mad when she did, but she couldn't help it. It was all so sudden.

She'd been sitting there in her small room, beavering away on the sketches and feeling quite low really. She used to laugh about it sometimes, when she talked to Fido. 'I feel low at the very top of the house,' she'd say, and Fido would laugh, and that would make her feel better, so both of them got benefit from it. But it didn't alter the fact that being so far away from all the interesting things that went on did sometimes depress her.

It had been so exciting when Hildegarde had first asked her to give up teaching, to come and work with her. She'd offered her the job of overseeing the drawings, of making sure the sketches were right for the pattern-cutters, and there had been enough of art in that to make Sylvia think it was worth giving it all up, her secure job, her pension, all of it, to work for Hilda. And to work for Hilda, anyway, would be heaven.

But it hadn't quite worked out that way. Her job, she'd soon realized, was an odd one. What Hilda wanted was not checking the sketches, but total re-drawing, with tiny modifications of the original sketch which would change it slightly, but not really affect the line; a button here, a seam there, a dart somewhere else. She would give her sketches in all sorts of different styles, some very amateurishly drawn on scraps of tatty paper, some very skilful and finished with lots of professional gloss, but all exciting and outrageous designs in some way. Where Hilda got them from, Sylvia didn't ask. She had a shrewd idea though and

131

sometimes felt a bit sick as she looked at a piece of work from some young hand that in her teaching days would have filled her with the excitement of discovering a new talent. But now it was her job to re-draw it, to give it the Hildegarde look. So she did.

And when she'd finished, after the long laborious hours there at the top of the house in Buckingham Gate, Hilda would come and look and sometimes throw them back and make her do them again, or make her change something, but mostly she'd sign them with her big flowing scrawl, 'Hildegarde.' The mark that made her clothes special, unique, wherever the original sketches had come from, however long Sylvia had spent on the re-drawing, it was the signature that mattered. Big, confident, as outrageous as the designs. 'Hildegarde.'

But she never let Sylvia come down to the sewing rooms, or to the show rooms even further below where the carpets lay thick and the mirrors shone and the chandeliers dripped their prisms in an abandonment of light. 'You belong here,' she'd say when sometimes Sylvia said she was lonely on her own. 'You're an artist, for God's sake, Sylvia. How can you imagine wasting your time with those dolts in the sewing room? They're all half-witted Greeks who sew like angels, I grant you, but company? For you? Never! As for the show room – listen, Sylvia, those girls down there are tarts, plain tarts. Clothes horses, nothing else. They're fit to show the clothes, and after that they ought to be locked up in boxes, brought out and dusted next time I need 'em. No, Sylvia, you stay here in peace and be glad you don't have to put up with what I do!'

Until today, when she had come up and said it so casually. Florence. For two weeks. To look at – oh, everything and anything.

'So, you'll come?'

'Oh, yes,' Sylvia said. 'I can't imagine anything I'd like better – Florence! And with you – oh, my dear, dear child, you can't imagine how –'

'Some child,' Hildegarde said dryly. 'I'll be thirty in six months' time. Jesus Christ, some child!'

'You'll always be a little girl to me,' Sylvia said and held her hands close together on her lap, to stop herself from reaching out to touch her. 'A wide-eyed little scrap of a thing in a blue dress that was a bit too big for her, and sitting there in the very front of the class and asking me to give her some crayons to take home.' Her eyes moistened and she looked away, trying not to embarrass herself by letting Hilda see. 'And then, the way you learned, oh, you were such a lovely –'

'Yes – well, great. Lovely to hear it all. Again. About Florence –' Hildegarde lingered at the door. 'It's a bit of a problem.'

'What is?'

'The costings.'

'Oh. The costings.' Sylvia's belly lurched and tightened. For one sick moment she thought she was going to change her mind, to tell her it was all off. But if it was only costings –'

'I'll pay my own way, of course,' she said hastily. 'I mean, I didn't expect it to be otherwise. This house and the business to keep up – it can't be easy – of course I'll cover my own expenses.'

Hilda smiled then widely and charmingly, and it was just like it had been in the old days, loving and happy, and she wanted to laugh aloud. But she just smiled back and for a moment a bubble of happiness hung in the little room.

'You're a poppet – and listen, there's another little thing. These bloody currency restrictions. I'm going to need cash out there to do business with. But they know me, I'm in and out of the airport like a yo-yo. They look all the time at my luggage and knowing them I couldn't get so much as a threepenny bit past 'em. But you could – so, I'm going to ask you to do something for me. You've got some cash in the bank?'

Sylvia thought of her dwindling resources. Teaching hadn't paid much but it had been better than this, and since she'd moved in with Fido, for company, somehow her expenses had gone up and up. But there was something there. And for Hilda –

'Some,' she said. 'What do you need?'

'Could you take out three hundred, in fivers? It'll be easier for you to carry it than for me. I'd give you the cash but you know what they're like, the tax people. I daren't take a risk – I'm so vulnerable. They'll watch my book-keeping like – you know how it is. But if you do – no problem. I'll pay you back the minute we're back in England, honestly. Will you do it for me?'

'Of course,' Sylvia said after a moment. Smuggling money. Well, everyone was doing it, weren't they? Everyone who ever travelled abroad that she'd ever talked to. There were more and more people doing it now. Going to places like Majorca and Rimini and Benidorm, and they all had illicit pound notes with them. You couldn't do otherwise with the Government being so stupid and mean about it. And there was something dashing and rather fine about it, really. Ordinary people lived ordinary humdrum lives. Interesting people went to Florence and smuggled money. So Sylvia told herself.

And went on telling herself over and over again during the next three weeks. She did as Hilda asked, drew out the money in three stages each week, telling the bank manager she was interested in a little short-term investment, and he tutted, but that was all. She booked her holiday herself as well. Hilda told her it would be easier. They were going to the same hotel, travelling by the same flight, of course they were. It would just make the book-keeping easier if Sylvia did all her own arranging and Hilda paid her back.

'Which I will as soon as we're back. It wouldn't do to reflate your bank account beforehand, would it?'

'Why not?' Sylvia asked. It was getting easier to talk to Hilda these days. For a long time now their conversations had been almost monosyllabic and many nights had Sylvia lain awake and worried and fretted and wondered what was wrong, and long were the talks with dear old Fido, trying to work it out. But she hadn't been able to. Until now, suddenly, it was like the good old days again, talking, planning, being friends.

'Because –' Hilda looked at her sideways and then shook her head. 'Oh, Sylvia, honestly! People like you shouldn't be allowed. Not when there are people like me around.'

'I don't – what d'you mean?' Again that wash of chill. Was she wrong? Was it just as bad as ever? But it wasn't because Hilda just laughed and leaned over and patted her cheek, really affectionately.

'Oh, you're too bloody good! You'd do anything for me, wouldn't you? Any bloody thing I asked! If I said to you, "Put your arm in the fire, I need a burned bone," you'd do it. It's bad for me, that is. Bad for me.'

'Love can't be bad for anyone,' Sylvia said, her voice a little thick. All the years of love and needing and fearing seemed to crystallize in this moment. All that she had ever wanted to give this child, this beautiful beloved creature who had obsessed her for so long, had been worth it. To have her speak so was more than balm to the soul, Sylvia told herself. It was manna from heaven. Oh, Hilda, I do love you so!

'It's bad, believe me. And I love it. Listen. You'll do it all right, then? You'll sort out all the details?'

Every one of them, Sylvia promised. And she did.

The airport felt lovely, bristling with excitement and drama and real people. In the cab on the way she'd sat on the dusty plastic of the back seat and stared out at the suburban shoppers of Hayes and Yeading, and pitied them because they were so dull and weren't going to Florence, and here in the big echoing concourse she pitied the people who were obviously not travellers but who had come to watch the travellers; the mothers with little children looking for the viewing platforms, the teenagers coming out for a Saturday afternoon loiter around the coffee shops and souvenir kiosks. Poor them, they weren't going to Florence.

She enjoyed every moment of it. Having coffee and Danish pastry, because of course she was much too early, and Hilda wouldn't be here for an hour yet, buying *Peyton Place* from the bookstall, selecting chocolates and boiled sweets to stow in the new shoulder bag.

When it was twenty minutes to checking-in time, she began to get nervous, sitting very upright on a bench and staring at the big doors, looking from one to the other in an agony of tension, afraid she would miss her.

People began to check in at the desk, chattering, counting luggage, getting excited and nervous and it communicated itself to her, and she had to join them, carrying her big case carefully, her shoulder bag clutched under her arm. They took her ticket and marked her off on the seating plan and she wanted to tell them to be sure she was next to Miss Hildegarde Maurice but before she could the sleek, polished girl in the tight uniform had given her her boarding ticket, murmured, 'Have a good flight,' and was already dealing with the next passenger, and her big case was disappearing terrifyingly on the conveyor belt beyond.

Uneasily she clutched her shoulder bag more tightly still and followed the rest of the people to the departure lounge, still looking over her shoulder for Hilda. Surely, surely she wasn't going to miss the plane! Not Hilda, always so efficient, so organized. She couldn't miss it. It was now only forty-five minutes to departure time, and there was no sign of her. Oh, Hilda, Hilda, where are you?

The departure lounge buzzed with talk as duty-free shoppers compared perfumes and loaded themselves with whisky and cartons of cigarettes, and she sat there, still trying to watch for Hilda, but it wasn't easy, with so many people bustling about. And then they called the flight and she felt sick. Oh, God, she was going to miss it. She was going to be late, she was going to miss it.

People were moving, gathering up their bags and chattering on their way to passport and currency control and she went with them. She could think of nothing else to do. To sit here and miss the plane as well was unthinkable, but wasn't going without Hilda more unthinkable still? She was numb with anxiety.

The queue shuffled through passport control slowly, and she kept staring back at the departure lounge, watching, almost praying, but then she was there and the man was holding out his hand, and she fumbled for her passport in her shoulder bag, her fingers stiff and awkward.

She shook her head dumbly when the man in uniform asked her, 'Any currency, madam?' turning her head nervously to stare back over her shoulder and the man beckoned and said smoothly, 'If I might just check your hand luggage, madam?'

She tried to tell him the reason she was nervous was that Hilda hadn't arrived but it came out in a gabble and she held on to her bag tightly, still trying to explain but the man courteously but firmly removed it from her grasp and led her to a table at one side of the desk and began to empty it. And then she remembered.

Oh, God, she should have remembered sooner. She'd meant to be so relaxed, so ordinary and if Hilda had been there she would have managed it, but because she wasn't there, she'd forgotten.

She watched him dully, beyond feeling anything. The chocolate and sweets came out, made a greedy-looking pile, and then her diary and her copy of *Peyton Place* and the magazines and the little towel with a piece of soap rolled in it because you never knew, did you, when you mightn't be glad of your own nice things. Her purse then and the man looked at her and she stared blankly and he opened it, and counted the money in it very slowly and carefully and put it down next to the chocolate and then put his hand in the shoulder bag again and came out with her handkerchief sachet.

She looked at it and could have cried. It was one Hilda had made when she first came into her class at Millfields Road school. Criss-crossed red and blue stitches on binca, sewn together with sprawling childish stitches, folded back at one corner with a big satin bow sewn in place by her own small hands. It had seemed the right place to put it, and she put her hand out and tried to take it from the man, tried to say, 'It's only my hankies,' but he shook his head almost regretfully and put his hand in and took out the handkerchiefs and then the wad of notes and began to count them.

'Oh, dear, madam, we have been silly, haven't we?' he said mournfully and looked at her, and she stared back and was suddenly very aware of the people in the line up behind her craning their necks, trying to see what was happening, whispering to each other.

They took her off to an office, read things to her, made her sign things, and after an eternity of time, gave her back her things, with only the handkerchiefs in the binca sachet with its red-and-blue cross-stich embroidery, and sent her back to the main concourse. They were sorry, they said, that she'd missed her plane. Not their fault, was it? If people would persist in breaking currency regulations you couldn't expect airlines to hold planes for them.

She went to the airline desk, as the uniformed man had advised her; he seemed almost sorry for her, was quite avuncular. The girl at the desk wasn't nearly so kind. She just shook her head as Sylvia explained as coherently as she could what had happened, that she'd missed her plane, an oversight about money, she was sorry, could she find out if Miss Hildegarde Maurice had caught the plane, could she arrange for her, Miss Sylvia Justin, J-U-S-T-I-N – that's right, Justin, to go on another plane?

'No,' the girl said shortly, sorry but she couldn't help. The Florence flight had been a charter flight, no possibility at all of transferring to a scheduled flight, so sorry. Miss Maurice? Well, she'd check in a moment, when she had dealt with this other matter –

And at last she did, grudgingly, running her blood-red finger nail slowly down the lists, sighing heavily to show how put upon she was.

'Miss Maurice, you say? Yes, here we are. A double booking, Miss Maurice, Miss Olaf. Yes, they both caught the flight. Message? No, absolutely no messages. Now, if you'll excuse me please. I do have other things to deal with – *good* afternoon!'

She stood there in the middle of the concourse trying to sort it all out. Birgitta Olaf gone to Florence? How could that be? Hilda had said nothing about Birgitta going. And why hadn't she left a message for her, been anxious? And what would she do without the money?

It wasn't until she got home to Hackney that she remembered that her suitcase was on the plane. Then she cried.

14

Mr Wooderson sat down, baffled, and Hester leaned back and hissed, 'I did warn you. I told you there was probably more to it than I knew. I did warn you.' For the first time there was an edge of annoyance in her whispered voice, and Wooderson didn't look at her but ruffled his papers and then turned and spoke in a sharp undertone to his junior.

Hildegarde on the other side of the court allowed herself to look across at Hester. That had been a *mauvais quart d'heure*, she thought and was irritated at herself. That was just the sort of fancy phrase Hester used to come up with, meant to make you feel stupid. It had been a bad moment. Say it how it was.

She looked at Sylvia, now making her way from the witness box to the rear of the court, wanting to smile encouragingly at her and show her gratitude. He'd done his best, that pompous sod behind Hester, to get the story out of her, but she'd stood there and stonewalled him a treat. She deserved a thank you. But Sylvia went past her and didn't look at her, and Hildegarde let her eyes slide across her to Mel, sitting glumly waiting for – what? Poor Mel, she thought. For the first time, he's a bit out of his depth. Stupid bastard. Good old Sylvia.

Sylvia. She turned her head, wanting to catch her eye, to get across to her how much she really appreciated what she hadn't said, but she was sitting stolidly beside Auntie Fido who was saying something softly and neither of them would look at her. Stupid, stupid, *stupid*, she thought savagely, and looked over her shoulder at Jordan-Andrews. 'Well, now what?' she whispered. 'What happens now?'

Jordan-Andrews shook his head repressively and Hildegarde grinned mockingly at him, and sank back into her own thoughts. It was amazing there'd been no trouble with Sylvia, really. But she'd gambled on that. She'd told Jordan-Andrews she could be trusted not to throw any shit in the fan – and she grinned yet again as she remembered how his lip had lifted at the expression – and she'd been right. 'Sylvia, let *me* down?' she'd said. 'Never. No way. She couldn't.'

But once, it had been a near thing.

'Do not forsake me oh my darling . . .
Wait – wait alone.
I do not know what fate awaits me,
I'll lie a coward in my grave . . .'

She did all she could to make it right for her. They'd spent the whole morning in the galleries, starting at the Uffizi and ending at the Pitti Palace, and she'd stood and let her rabbit on about the Botticellis, even managing to bite her tongue when she said something sentimental about how like the Primavera she looked. Not easy.

They'd walked in the cool bustle of the straw market, leaving the din and the flies and the stink of drains out in the hot sun of the narrow streets and, still feeling full of bonhomie, Hildegarde had bought her a box made of Florentine red leather studded with flat headed brass nails, and Sylvia had stood in the dim light and clutched it to her narrow chest and said over and over again, 'Oh, thank you Hilda – Hildegarde, thank you. It's lovely. *Thank* you –'

And then back to the Boboli Gardens and dinner in the Piazza della Signoria and giggles over *spaghetti carbonari*, trying to loop the slippery strands over their forks and in an odd way Hildegarde had quite enjoyed it. Sylvia was maddening in her adoration but at the same time it was pleasant to make someone happy. And making Sylvia happy was very easy.

But the sightseeing and the giggling had to stop eventually. They went back to the hotel and Hildegarde said easily, 'Well? *Gelati* on the terrace or *spremuta di limone* in the lounge?'

Sylvia shook her head, almost apologetically. 'I'd as soon have a cup of tea in my room, to tell you the truth,' she said. 'I'm a bit tired.'

'It's been a long day,' Hildegarde said heartily.

'Yes. And all so sudden, too.' Sylvia looked at her doggishly, and the familiar prick of irritation made Hildegarde's lips tighten. 'I still don't understand. And though it's been lovely and everything, I still feel awful. I mean, it was dreadful last

140

week, dreadful. I can't tell you how awful it was, and not know-ing what had happened and the money and my luggage and all.'

'We'll get your tea,' Hildegarde said. 'I'll explain then. You'll understand, once you've had your tea. We'll sit on the terrace, shall we? Under the vine –'

They brought them tea in heavy white china cups, lukewarm and with the tabs of the tea bags hanging over the edges, and Sylvia fussed over them a bit, very English, and Hildegarde sat and smoked a cigarette and watched her in the dappled light filtering through the leaves and wondered how a woman who had started out so well could have become like this. She'd been really interesting once, she thought. Talked about art and pic-tures and made me interested. What happened to her?

'Well?' Sylvia said after a while, sipping the tea and staring at her over the edge of the cup. 'You said you'd explain.'

Hildegarde put her own cup down and sighed. 'Okay, explain, explain. Look, I needed to come out here to buy some designs and some stuff as well. They've some good fabrics and shoes and knitwear. But here, my duck, there're no short cuts. Italian designers are as sharp as bloody needles and if I want the stuff I've got to pay for it. One hell of a lot. So, I deal with a few of them coming to London, but what I need obviously is to come here, see what's happening, get the feel, right? And then I've got to buy. Raising the money to buy isn't that difficult – but getting it out is something else. So I worked it out – if I can go through passport and currency control after someone else has been pinched I've got a good chance of being ignored. So –'

'So you arranged for me to be the one who was pinched? Oh, Hilda, really! What a rotten thing to do –'

'Rotten to do, or rotten to do to you?' Hildegarde said and laughed.

There was a little pause and then Sylvia said, 'Well, to me, I suppose. I'd like to feel you knew it was wrong anyway to do such a thing, breaking the law – but to do it to *me* – I thought I was your friend.'

'Let's not get sloppy, for Christ's sake, Sylvia,' Hildegarde's voice hardened, took on its cutting edge. 'It's enough, isn't it? I've made it all right? Sent you another ticket, got you here? And you've had a good day today, haven't you?'

Sylvia looked at her for a long moment and said helplessly,

'You think that made up for it? After all that happened last week?'

'Well, hasn't it? You're here, aren't you? I promised you a holiday in Florence. Well, all right, this is Florence, *Firenze*, in sunny Eetaly! What more d'you want?'

Sylvia shook her head, her mouth drooping with self-pity, and Hildegarde felt her own jaw tighten again. 'There's more to it than that. You make it sound like just paying off a debt of money.'

'Oh, don't worry about *that*! You'll get your money back! I'm not interested in robbing you, you know. I get my kicks a different way. Pinching tuppence ha'penny from you won't get me far –'

'It's a bit more than tuppence ha'penny to me. And anyway, that wasn't what I meant.'

'Listen, Sylvia, at under five hundred quid it was cheap, you hear me? I got three thousand out here, three *thousand*. That's what you call an investment. I'll get it back nine times over and more. Just like you'll get your bloody three hundred back.'

'That isn't what I meant,' Sylvia's voice was the same but there was a whining quality about her that was making Hilda more and more irritable. 'I mean, what about a person's *feelings*, what about someone who loves you and wants to look after you and always has, and who suffers dreadfully if –'

'Oh, Jesus H. Christ! I've had enough! I told you. I used you to help me sort out a problem. Terrible thing, so I didn't tell you every detail in advance! If I had, you stupid cow, you'd have ruined it, don't you know that? You're so bloody transparent, you'd have ruined the whole thing. So – I didn't tell you, and because I didn't tell you, it worked out right. You'll get your money back, you're here, so stop belly-aching –'

Sylvia was crying helplessly, sitting holding her cup between both hands and letting the tears run down her cheeks unchecked and with her nose running too, and Hildegarde couldn't look at her. It always happened like this, however good her intentions when she started out. She tried to be good to her, tried to be kind, and what did she get but this sickening devotion and grizzling and helplessness?

'Listen, Sylvia.' She leaned forwards in her chair, staring at her very directly. 'If you don't stop this you can go and get

142

stuffed, you hear me? I can't stand this sort of yuk – either shut up or get the fucking hell out of my sight –'

'You wouldn't say that to that Birgitta,' Sylvia said, her voice thick with misery. She sniffed and swallowed and now Hildegarde got to her feet, taut with rage.

'You stupid, jealous *bitch*,' she said and her voice was very low and so full of threat that Sylvia actually shrank back. 'You jealous dyke, you! So Birgitta came here with me! So bloody what? What's it got to do with you? Eh? What skin is it off your nose? Did I ever make you any promises, did I ever try to pretend anything? You know I didn't. Don't you dare to throw Birgitta in my face, do you hear me? Don't you *dare* –'

Later that night, after she'd calmed down and when Birgitta was asleep in the twin bed beside her, she lay and stared at the ceiling and thought for a long time and then sighed sharply, and got up and pushed her feet into her mules, tangling her toes in the feathers and swearing under her breath. It would be boring and there'd be recriminations and apologies and tears and comfortings but she'd have to do it. Sylvia was much too involved with everything, the business as well as this damned trip, to be allowed to go on crying into her solitary pillow too long. She'd have to put it right.

So she went padding away down the dimly-lit corridor with its smell of old marble and sour Italian cigarettes to Sylvia's room, leaving Birgitta snoring softly in the twin bed, her yellow hair tangled over her face. At least Birgitta didn't get jealous, she thought, suddenly tired, as she gently pushed Sylvia's door open and stood there in the darkness listening to her soft sobbing. If I had to keep soothing her as well, Jesus H. Christ, I'd never get any work done.

'Sylvia?' she whispered. 'Stop crying, you silly fool. I'm here. Stop crying and move over.'

Sammy, beside Bonnie, with Stanley sitting heavily on her other side, shifted in his seat. His buttocks were numb, and his feet were cold, and he'd forgotten to pee at lunch-time, what with looking after Bonnie and trying to control his anger with Stanley. He stared down the court and estimated the effect his departure would have. Would the judge get testy and demand

143

all the on-lookers be thrown out? He cast his mind over the little he knew about judges and the law and imagined a roar of, 'Clear the Court; clear the Court!' and grimaced. It wasn't like that. Only one day he'd been here, and even he could see it wasn't like that.

He got up and said softly to Bonnie, 'I'll see you later. I need to get a breather,' and she looked up at him, startled, and he smiled as reassuringly as he could. She's not really well, his physician's voice said inside his head. I'd like to get a blood picture. Bit anaemic, maybe. More likely to be depressed.

Outside in the corridor there was bustle and busyness and he stood for a while, glad to be on his feet, and stared vacantly down the long hallway. Now what? Should he go home, forget the whole damned business? He hadn't really thought about it in any detail, had assumed the whole thing would be over today but obviously it would not. The case could go on for days, a whole week maybe. He hadn't that sort of time to waste. He couldn't possibly sit through all of it. Go away home now, maybe, come back the day after tomorrow? But suppose it all ended tomorrow? He imagined Bonnie, suddenly, standing in the witness box white-faced and with the skin under her eyes creasing as she concentrated, trying to find the honest answer that would hurt no one, and he knew he couldn't do that. He'd have to be here all the time. He'd call the hospital, tell Agnahotri he'd have to manage, he was needed for a – what? – for a family crisis. That's what he'd tell them. A family crisis. Anyway, they were as much of a family as he had. It had been years now since there'd been anyone else.

The court door whispered open again behind him and he looked round and it was Auntie Fido, leaning heavily on her stick, with Sylvia solicitously holding her arm.

'Sammy,' she said after a moment as she looked up and saw him looking at her. 'Sammy. It *is* you, isn't it? I haven't got my glasses on.'

'Yes,' he said. 'How are you, Miss Morris?'

'Terrible.' Her voice took on a dying cadence. 'Terrible.' She brightened then. 'It's me arthur-itis you know. Terrible pain, terrible. Are you a specialist now, Sammy?'

'Not in arthritis,' he said quickly and then, a little ashamed, 'I can arrange for you to see someone who is.'

'That would be nice,' she said, almost eagerly, and then sighed and began to move again, awkwardly, and Sylvia held on to her arm, hindering her more than helping, but meaning well. 'I haven't seen you in a long time, Sammy.'

'It's been difficult. You know how things get sometimes – busy.'

'I know, I know. You all grow up, have your own lives to lead. Leave us old ones behind, eh, Sylvia? Thank God we still have each other to hold on to, Sammy, me and Sylvia. God alone knows the trouble we'd be in without each other, eh Sylvia? Oh, I tell you Sammy, 'f I'd 'a known how it'd all turn out, how they'd be, what'd happen, I'd 'a given up years ago. Years ago, I'd 'a given up –'

'We'd better hurry,' Sylvia said and smiled apologetically at Sammy. 'They might want you to give evidence soon.'

'Yes,' Auntie Fido said and smiled, suddenly coquettish. 'Must find the little girls' room quickly. Some things no one can do for you, eh Sammy?' and she went hobbling stiffly along the corridor and he watched her and felt the tightness in his throat again.

OCTOBER 1952

'I'll be loving you, eternally,
With a love that's true, eternally . . . .'

It was cold, and he stood with his hands folded in front of him, trying to put the right expression on his face. He wasn't sure quite what sort of expression should be there really; he'd never been to a funeral before, after all. How could he know?

Again he became aware of the cold and he moved his feet awkwardly on the gravel, and Hilda turned and looked at him, and sketched a wink and he was outraged. She meant well, he was sure, but winking at him, at his father's funeral?

One thing about it all, it was suitable weather. The sky was a heavy icy grey, and the wind was so sharp that his eyes had been watering ever since he'd got out of the car. People had looked at him with respect and sympathy on their faces as he'd wiped them with a large handkerchief and he was embarrassed, wanted to tell them all it was the cold and not to do with his father at all.

145

But he couldn't do that. It would embarrass them too much. So he mopped his eyes and tried to look suitably wooden, and his feet ached with the cold.

They walked back from the graveside faster than they had paced the gravel paths there, first himself with the rabbi in the black cassock beside him and then Auntie Fido and the three girls and then a sprinkle of total strangers. He'd seen them in the little bare building where the service had been held and used the time while the rabbi muttered and intoned to look at them, trying to work out who they were. None of them looked familiar. They weren't any of the Sunday afternoon tea-drinkers of years ago, nor did they look like busy Party men. Just rather dull little people, men and women in dull clothes with dull faces.

He stopped thinking about them now as the little party came back to the bleak building where the service had been held, and the strangers melted away into the grey afternoon as dully and as silently as they had come. The rabbi murmured something and he misunderstood at first, and then, scarlet with embarrassment, put his hand in his pocket and settled up. It was extraordinary how many people had had to be paid. His father would have been furious about that.

'What now, Sammy, dear? What will you do now?' Auntie Fido was standing beside him and peering up at him with her face full of sympathy. She looked absurd, he thought, for the cold had made her skin slightly blue, and the network of red veins on her cheeks and on her nose shone through the beige make-up, which had streaked on them and made them look more noticeable than ever. Her mascara had smudged too, whether because she had wept with the cold, or because she had wept for his father he didn't know. But he found her tears touching and smiled at her.

Hester was standing beside her, and now she said tartly, 'What d'you mean, what'll he do now? What he's done for years! Live in his own flat! What else should he do?'

'Well, I don't know,' Fido said, and her voice trailed away apologetically. 'I thought, his mother maybe –'

'Don't be stupid,' Hester said. 'Sammy, are you going to drive straight back to Town? I've got an audition this afternoon. At Lime Grove –' Her chin lifted with excitement as she said it.

He looked at her and his teeth grated against each other. This was one hell of a time to parade herself.

'No,' he said. 'I'm going to drive your aunt back to Hackney. And anyone else who wants to go.'

Hester looked at him and he stared back, his eyebrows a little raised. She was the only one who looked good in this weather. She had on a long coat, with a high shawl collar that framed her face, and a soft floppy hat that looked like a shower cap into which she'd tucked most of her hair. Her angular face peeped out between the cradle of cloth, white and cold, but not made ugly by it, as was Fido's and his own. For a moment he hated her for her poise, her total lack of self-consciousness.

'As you like,' she said. 'I can take the underground. Give me a lift to the station.'

'Me too,' said Hilda. She was rosy and sparkling in spite of the apparent effort she had made to look suitable for a funeral. People turned and looked at her as they reached the car park, at the long black coat with the huge silver buttons and the round black cap with the even bigger silver button on its crown, under which her hair had been brushed out like a halo. 'I've got to get back to Chelsea.'

'It was good of you to come,' Sammy said. He didn't mean it to sound bitter but it did, and he was ashamed of himself. 'Really,' he said and smiled and nodded. 'I appreciated it.'

After the girls had scrambled out of the car and disappeared into the tube station at Stanmore, they drove in silence for a while and then Auntie Fido said timidly, 'The rabbi was good, Sammy. He said very nice things about your father.'

Sammy laughed. 'The old man'd be furious if he knew. He hated religion. Swore it was everything that was evil. He never cared about what happened after death – said when you died that was it, and to hell with what happened. But all the same, he'd have been furious to know I'd buried him with all the trappings like that. A rabbi. Oh, he'd have been furious!'

'Oh.' Auntie Fido considered that for a while and he drove on, through Edgware, pushing his way through the heavy afternoon traffic. 'Why did you, then?'

'I don't know. Insurance, I suppose. He said there was nothing afterwards. I don't think there's anything afterwards. But still – insurance.'

'You never know, do you, Sammy? You never know how life

will turn out,' Auntie Fido said sententiously and sighed deeply. He said nothing and she sighed again. 'Do you, Sammy?'

'No,' he said unwillingly. Oh, do me a favour, no armchair philosophy. I'm not in the mood. Do me a favour.

'I tell you, Sammy, 'f I'd 'a known, all those years ago, how my life would work out, I'd never have let it happen. I'd 'a done something about it. But we never know.'

'No,' he said as repressively as he could. 'Are you warm enough? I could put the heater on higher.' They'd reached the Edgware Road, and the traffic clotted and slowed up, and he began to work his jaw muscles the way he always did when he was in a hurry and couldn't get going, and then made a conscious effort to relax. He'd finish up with masseter muscles like an American gum-chewer if he wasn't careful.

'I was such a girl of course,' Auntie Fido was saying, staring mournfully out of the car window, her hands clasped on her lap in front of her as primly as though she were being interviewed. 'But there they were, three little mites, orphaned and with only me to care for them. What else could I do?'

She looked up at him then so intently that he had to turn his head to look back at her. They were held at the traffic lights at Colindale behind a huge lorry turning right. Bloody hell, they'd be here all day at this rate. God knows when we'll get to Hackney.

'I was really very pretty then, though you might not think it now,' she said and looked at him almost pleadingly, begging him to contradict her. Irritated and tired as he was, he could not let her down.

'Of course you were,' he said heartily, too heartily. 'You still are.'

'Silly boy,' she murmured, well pleased. 'But sweet really.' There was a silence again for a while and then she said a little timidly, 'Er – what about your mother, Sammy?'

'What about her?'

'Is she – did she – was she very – oh dear.'

'She doesn't know he's dead, if that's what you mean,' Sammy said, trying to keep his voice neutral. Everyone knew now about her, ever since the day she'd suddenly gone completely out of control, had chased his father with a hammer and the police had been called. The whole damned neighbourhood

148

knew. Anyway, why should he care? He was qualified, doing well, and as an educated man knew better than to be ashamed of the fact that his mother was mentally ill. Stark staring bloody bonkers, where's the stigma in that? 'I explained of course, but she's very – she's too ill to understand.'

'I dare say Bonnie'll go on visiting her, all the same,' Auntie Fido said after a moment. 'She's a dear good girl, is Bonnie.'

'Yes.' The traffic was moving better now. Over the North Circular. Here comes Finchley.

'They're all good girls. Clever as well. Hester's very clever.'

'Yes.'

'Oh, 'f only their poor dear mother and father had lived to see them grown up! Hilda so pretty and so talented, and Hester doing so well –'

'Yes.' He said it deliberately this time. If only he had a car radio! That might shut her up. 'f only!

'I've done my best for them. Gave up my life, really,' the monotone went on. 'Mind you, it hasn't been easy. It hasn't been easy at all. I missed out on a lot. I mean, I could have done a lot of things, 'f I'd 'a had my chances. Well – it doesn't do to sound boastful, but I had my offers, you know. I had my offers!' And she peered up at him roguishly over her smudged mascara.

'I'm sure,' he said savagely. 'Now, I'll have to concentrate on the road here. The traffic really is shocking –'

But she went relentlessly on and on. ' 'f I'd 'a put myself first, why, I'd 'a gone out to America just after the war. I had an offer you know, a very good one!' She sighed. 'But there, I had the girls and someone had to look after them, and I couldn't expect someone else to take them on just for the love of *my* blue eyes!' Again the giggle and the sideways glance. 'So, I did what I could, made a nice home for them. I do like things nice, and with three girls it's important to make sure things are nice, isn't it? It's too easy to be sloppy and let things go. A little refinement stretches even the thinnest of purses, so I always told them. And ours was quite thin. Though there was the insurance, of course –'

For the first time she was silent for a while, a brooding silence, and he was grateful for it. But as the car reached Marble Arch she said abruptly, 'Hester – has she ever said anything to you about that?'

149

'About what?'

'Insurance. Money and so on.'

'No.' He was genuinely surprised. 'Why on earth should she?'

'I don't know. I just wondered. Mind you, 'f I'd 'a thought that –'

'Miss Morris,' he said suddenly, and it was as though it was someone else who said it, not him, as though it was another harsher man whose voice came hard and cold into the stuffiness of the car. 'Do you know why the girls call you Auntie Fido?'

She giggled. 'Isn't it sweet and silly? I just laughed and laughed the first time I heard it – it was Hester, I think, bless her. Yes I think it was – my name's Freda, of course, but I dare say they thought this was easier to say, or more – you know. Nicer.'

'Really?' he said, and still his voice was harsh and cold and somewhere deep inside him was a smaller worried Sammy trying to shut him up, telling him not to be such a bastard just because he was cold and tired and trying to push his way through heavy traffic on a bitter December afternoon while his father lay newly buried in ice-cold earth at Bushey. 'Is that what you really think?'

She looked up at him. 'Why? What do you mean?'

'They call you Fido,' he said deliberately, wrenching the wheel round at last to push the car into Park Lane, 'because of your maddening trick of always saying " 'f I'd 'a known this, 'f I'd 'a done that, 'f I'd 'a thought of the other." It drove them mad.'

'Oh,' she said. And not another word, all the way back to Hackney.

15

'All right, then,' Wooderson said. 'We'll go through it all as fast as we can. We want simply to establish that you are a well-respected journalist, that you don't have to scrabble in the gutter to get a story –'

'It's where the best stories come from,' she said, and laughed.

'Hester, for heaven's sake!' Willy Rundle's jowls quivered with impatience. 'You're being much too flippant about all this. You have to realize she can take you to the cleaners if they find for her! Do stop and *think*.'

Hester looked at him coolly and then shook her head. 'You stop and think, Willy. I'm not bothered *that* much about her damned charge –' and she flicked her thumb and finger scornfully,' – because we've got dynamite in our locker. Right, Mr Wooderson?'

'The financial aspect? Well, yes, it could be quite startling. But you must understand, Miss Morrissey, that that line of evidence may be disallowed. If you wish to make a claim of your own, a different case, a different court, well enough. But it is this case and this court with which we now concern ourselves. And Mr Rundle is right. You are indeed on very thin ice. Exceptionally thin.'

JJ made an odd sound, half cough, half laugh. 'She's been prancing around on the thinnest ice you'll ever see all her working life, Wooderson,' he said. 'And dragging a few of us with her. I wouldn't fret any about that.'

Wooderson looked at him with studied dislike. 'Mr Gerrard, do let me remind you that in some ways you are at greater risk than Miss Morrissey. The plaintiff has a grievance against both of you, even though you are not named in this case and although it is Miss Morrissey who carries the burden, you are there in the background you know, you are very much there.'

'Christ, do I know!' JJ said savagely. 'She's had me by the short and curlies for more years than I care to remember. And still has.'

'I love you too, dear,' Hester said sweetly. 'May we now get

151

back to the matter in hand? *Me*, baby? Thanks a lot. Now, Mr Wooderson, what is it you want? All I need is a straight briefing.'

'Before I tell you the ground I would like to cover, do let me remind you, Miss Morrissey, that Jordan-Andrews will be cross-examining. He may touch on areas that –'

'Jordan-Andrews?' she said and laughed again. 'Oh, I'm very scared of *him*! I've eaten his sort before now, on toast without any butter. Don't you worry about his cross-examination. I'm not. Any more than Sylvia Justin seemed worried about yours.'

Wooderson's face mottled an ugly red and JJ grinned at Hester. 'Hester Morrissey, you're a Grade-A bitch.'

'Mmm. Aren't I the lucky one? All right, Mr Wooderson, let's have a run through, shall we? Time's getting short.'

'We'll start at the beginning. How you first became involved in the – ah – media –'

'Christ! Right at the beginning? Amateur theatricals and all that?'

'Amateur theatricals and all that, indeed, if that was where it began.'

OCTOBER 1946

'Everything will come right, if you'll only believe the Gipsy
She can look in the future and drive away all your fears . . .'

The tram bucketed and creaked through the fog, and she sat on the top deck, swaying with it and looking at her reflection in the opaque window. Her mouth was lovely, she decided, heart-breakingly lovely. The curve of her cheek – no, wrong word, the sculptured line of her cheek – below the chiselled bones that framed her eyes, held mystery. Her hair – she turned her chin a little more and looked at the reflection of her hair and after a moment looked at her mouth again. Hair, after all, was not the be-all and end-all. Lovely mouths, on the other hand, especially heart-breakingly lovely mouths, really had an effect on people.

A man in a yellow oilskin raincoat came lurching along the tram, coughing and spluttering with the exertion of climbing the stairs and looked at her and then pushed himself into the seat next to her. She made a little *moue* of distaste and moved closer

152

to the window, and the man coughed again and reached in his pocket and pulled out a crumpled packet of cigarettes.

' 'ave one?' he said after a moment, and she looked down at the packet and then with an ostentatious turn of her head out of the window. Player's Weights. No class, some people.

He shrugged at her silence and lit one for himself and as the smell of the tobacco drifted across she opened her bag with an elegant turn of her wrist and took out her own cigarettes, a neat pack of Craven A. The man watched her as she took one out and put it between her heart-breakingly lovely lips and then struck a match for her. But she ignored it, carefully taking her own matches from her bag and striking one with a little flourish.

He got up then and moved down the tram and she sat and smoked happily, blowing the grey vapour out through her nose with some skill, and feeling good. That had put him where he belonged. No class, some people.

At the Settlement hall there was only one light burning in the lobby and she went straight into the ladies' and took off her coat, combed her hair, doing the best with it she could. Here, in the fly-blown mirror, she didn't look as good as she had in the tram window and she stared at her face dispiritedly for a moment. Heart-breakingly lovely like hell. I look like – well, I don't look like people ought to look when they're sixteen. Bony face, thin mouth – she pouted a little and then gave up. That made her look worse.

But she had style. That was worth much more. Style. She looked down at her dress and untied the wide sash belt. Auntie Fido had made it and pronounced it sweetly pretty and on some people it would be, all full-skirted green flounces. On Hester it looked awful.

She twisted the sash round her head twice and tied it at the back, tucking in all her hair and looked again, and slowly her mouth curved and looked lovely again. With her hair out of the way her face was all bones, like Greta Garbo, and full of excitement and the dress hanging straight down made her look fragile and boyish rather than lumpy. Style, she told herself and went into the big hall.

He was just putting on a record, and the music started, da-da-*da* da-da-da-da-da-da-da-*da* and she pirouetted and then marched across the dusty floor towards him.

153

'In the mood!' she called. 'That's what I am – in the mood!' and he responded at once, came towards her with a matching pirouette, and they danced, stamping and twisting and performing mightily for each other.

Glen Miller ground to a pulsing hiss and he went to wind up again and turn the record over but before he could set the needle in the groove she called out dramatically, '*Qui va la?*'

' "A friend!" ' he shouted back, striking a pose.

' "Discuss unto me – art thou officer, or art thou base, common and popular?" '

' "I am a gentlemen of a company –" '

They went right through the scene, taking a couple of steps towards each other with each line, until by the time he reached, 'It sorts well with your fierceness!' they were standing very close together.

She stood there in the echoing silence of the dusty hall staring at him. He had a nice face, she thought. A nice soft sort of face that looked as though it would be pleasant to touch, and she put out her hand and set one finger on his cheek and his eyes widened a little, but he stood still. She could see a minute reflection of herself in his eyes with the green sash tied round her head making a sharp dot of colour and she looked good, tiny and interesting and good, and she let her hand fall on his shoulder. Still he stood there staring at her and very deliberately she put her other hand on his shoulder and moved closer.

'Young lady, if I didn't know better I'd say you were trying to make a pass at me,' he said after a moment and she giggled.

'How could you ever get such an idea in your head?'

'I'm not sure. There are signs perhaps? Straws in the winds, scents in the breeze, rustles in the undergrowth, ripples in the reeds –'

'People who talk can't kiss,' she whispered in her best Lauren Bacall voice; she was getting good at the husky bit, tightening her throat quite easily.

'And why would a little girl like you want to kiss a middle-aged man like me?' He was still standing easily but somehow there was a rigidity about him, as though he were holding her at arms' length and her confidence began to waver. It had seemed too easy to work on him. She'd realized when she first joined the Settlement Players last spring that he was better class than

154

the rest of them, as well as being the most important, and built on that, quoting Shakespeare at him, making drawling Noël Coward jokes and complex, in-turned epigrams. He'd responded beautifully and they had worked up a nice little situation, playing together with great glee. The 'clever pair' they were, the 'only ones who understood' the 'gold amid the dross', and the jealousy of some of the other people in the company had shown her very clearly what a success the whole thing had been.

And yet now, for the first time, he wasn't playing the game properly, and she looked at the little reflection of herself in his eyes and said uncertainly, 'Little? Middle aged? Such words! I'm Eliza Dolittle, you're Professor Higgins –'

He laughed then. 'Me, make *you* over? That'll be the day! Me and whose army?'

That was better. 'It needs no army.' Again the Bacall voice and a gentle sway nearer. 'Just you.'

'Now, look, ducky, you're a nice little girl, but don't start games you can't finish.'

He pushed her away, not too gently, and she stood there feeling her face red with shame, and as soon as she knew it was shame, it turned to anger. No one did that to Hester Morrissey, she told herself, saying the words fast inside her head. No one did that to Hester Morrissey.

'What's the matter?' she said, a hard thin voice now, nothing Lauren Bacall about it. And then, remembering a jeer she'd heard someone throw at a man outside a pub, a jeer that had led to a noisy fight which had made Auntie Fido hurry the three of them away, tutting and exclaiming, she said, 'What's the matter, love? Got the wrong bits and pieces for you, have I?'

Until that moment she had genuinely not known what the taunt meant, but she could still see the terror and rage that had filled the face of the man it had been hurled at, and now she saw the same expression on Harold Myton's face. He had started back towards the gramophone but now he turned and came back across the room to stand in front of her with his face twisted and grey with fury and said in a very flat voice, 'You – don't ever say a thing like that again, you hear me? Don't you ever. Not to me, not to anyone else. Because if you do, I'll get you put away. I'll tell your family and everyone else that you're a tart, that you're not safe where men are, you hear me?'

She stood and looked at him for a long moment and then her mouth curved very slowly.

'So that's the way of it, then! You the sort that'd rather be a scoutmaster! What are you doing hanging around a lot like us then? More girls than fellers here!'

His hand came round before she had closed her mouth, and her head snapped back as his hand made contact with her cheek, and then behind them they heard the door to the lobby bang open, and the voices of three of the girls who always arrived together.

And immediately, as though they'd rehearsed it, they were in action. He put his arms round her, held her close, and bent her back as though he were about to embrace her with great passion, and pushed his head down against hers. But it was an actor's kiss. Their lips were nowhere near each other, but she knew it looked good from the door. And it hid her face.

She heard the giggles, jumped back from his grasp with every sign of dismay and threw her hands up to her face, covering both cheeks as well as the marks his fingers had made and stared at the newcomers, who were standing goggling at them.

'Oh, no!' she cried, her voice high and shrill. 'Oh, how *awful* –' and turned and fled, running down the hall to the stage and to the dressing room beyond with every semblance of girlish confusion.

By the time the marks of his fingers on her cheeks had faded and she came back he was handing out the acting editions; they were planning their new spring production tonight, were all set for casting, and there was a lot to do.

She walked through the giggling staring girls as insouciantly as she could, and went and stood beside him, and they were both very aware of eyes on their backs.

'I was thinking,' she said quietly. 'I mean, what you said about me being only a little girl. I am, aren't I? Sixteen. And you're nearly forty.'

'Thirty-three,' he said. 'Look, I'm sorry. You got me at a bad moment. Didn't mean to lose my rag.'

'Doesn't matter,' she said sweetly. 'Funny, isn't it? Either way you're in dead stooch, aren't you? I mean, if I say you did something to me you shouldn't, and me sixteen, there'll be no end of trouble, won't there? And if you tell 'em you didn't, then I'll have to tell 'em the reason you didn't was because I was a girl, won't I? I mean, either way. Either way. And those others saw us. Didn't they?'

Considering the people she was up against were all more experienced than she was it was a big part she got once he started casting. But as she said to him, you might as well begin the way you meant to go on.

'So, you felt an interest in a dramatic career very young,' Wooderson said smoothly and she nodded, sweeping her lashes demurely on to her cheeks. 'Now let us move on. Your first professional engagement, Miss Morrissey. That was in the theatre, was it? Or as a journalist?'

'Neither, actually.' She smiled up at the judge, who stared stonily back. 'Television. It wasn't what I wanted precisely but this isn't an easy industry so like most people I accepted what work I could get, and kept my eyes open for something more suitable –'

OCTOBER 1953

'We're perfect young ladies, preparing to take
Our places among the noblesse,
Perfect young ladies preparing to make
The most of the charms we possess . . . .'

'Bloody hell!' the girl with the red hair said. 'Powder-puff dolls!'

'That's about the size of it,' Hester said, and leaned forwards and peered into the mirror.

'Honestly, how could they?' the red-headed girl said and looked sideways at the silent one, a blonde with fluffy curls and a short upper lip.

'How could they what?' Hester was still staring at her face. Perhaps if she used more colour in the base that would fill her out a bit? It would have to be clever, to get past the make-up girls who always had such cock-eyed ideas of their own.

'See you as a powder-puff doll, sweetie,' the red-headed girl said and laughed. 'I mean, you're more the intellectual type, aren't you?'

157

Hester looked at her through the mirror, consideringly. She'd known there'd be problems over this. It had taken every atom of personality and push she had to get herself cast at all, and she'd had to work ludicrously hard to get herself noticed in the middle of all those dancers. The audition had been littered with them. Girls who'd been going to dancing schools – one, two, three, hop, *that's* it, dear – since they were three years old, girls whose one ambition in life was to make the turntable on *Sunday Night at the London Palladium*, girls who spent a fortune getting their teeth capped for perfect smiles. She'd been desperate for the job; for seven years she'd been trying to get something, anything, and this was the first real sniff she'd had. And she'd got it. One of the three girls in the Doll's House Theatre, BBC *Children's Hour*, six weeks and the option of another seven if the viewers liked it. The viewers – moronic five-year-olds; Christ, to have to work and want and push so hard to get a job like that.

But now she'd got it somehow, and she still wasn't there, still wasn't safe. The other two were looking at her with those pretty blank faces and shiny long-lashed blank eyes, and hating her because she was different. Different meant frightening. And she was frightened enough herself already; she was no dancer, she'd never had the one, two, three, hop, *that's* it, dear, training they'd had. She was going to have to busk it somehow, my God, was she going to have to busk it. She needed their support, all she could get –

Still looking at the red-headed girl through the mirror she let her lips droop. 'Nor can I, to tell you the truth. I'm amazed the nice girl you were talking to – the one with the lovely figure – didn't get it. I mean, why me? She was lovely.'

'Best friend,' said the red-haired girl, a little mollified. 'Marvellous, she is. Could do the splits when she was four.'

'I'm sure she could,' Hester said fervently. 'Honestly – unless they wanted me as contrast. You know, the funny-looking one to make the best of the two pretty ones? Could that be it?'

She smiled at them tremulously, looking from one to the other.

There was a pause and the red-headed girl said, 'My name's Glenda. This is Dorrie. You ought to try some green base, you know, on your nose. It'll take some of that redness out.'

'Oh *thanks*,' Hester said fervently. 'Thanks ever so. Will you show me how?'

Still she wasn't exactly home and dry. They were mollified but it would take very little to start up the animosity again, and she didn't fancy that. Animosity was boring, made it hard to get people to dance to your piping. The ideal answer, she thought, as they went through their moves at the second rehearsal, would be to get these two pushed and two new ones in. Then, as oldest resident she'd be in charge. Much neater.

Thank God for moronic five-year-old viewers, she thought, as she sat in the canteen over soggy sausages and chips and listened humbly and with every sign of total absorption to Glenda's chatter about her hectic private life and her Boy Friend What I Flat-Share With, and her sniggers and giggles, as well as Dorrie's lugubrious accounts of her problems. BBC producers worry about moronic five-year-olds and even more about their mothers. So when she'd got enough facts clear, like the Boy Friend What I Flat-Share With's name and where Dorrie's illegitimate two-year-old lived with his grandma, she phoned the Diary people at the *Evening Standard*, and the features people at the *News of the World*, who were very interested to hear about the private lives of two of the BBC's Doll's House Theatre Powder-Puff Dolls. It made a nice story for a dull edition, for both of them, with the *News of the World* splashing it quite big on page five, with pictures that Glenda and Dorrie had been delighted to let them have, seeing they hadn't been told what the piece was all about.

It was much easier once Carole and Cheryl took over.

16

'How do you think she's coming across?' Bonnie said, lingering in the doorway.

The court had adjourned early, half way through Hester's evidence, and they were free to go, all of them, but she had made them linger. The thought of the evening ahead had come into her mind, of Warren and Daniel nagging and the girls too, and Stanley sulking; she had closed her thoughts away, but she had lingered all the same, first telling Stanley she had to go to the loo, then remembering her gloves left behind in court, now standing here on the steps assaulted by the noise of the Strand with Sammy on one side and Stanley, impatient and scowling, on the other.

She looked from one to the other with a slightly desperate brightness, wanting to talk. 'I mean,' she went on, 'I just couldn't recognize any of it. I can't pretend I knew everything that happened – I was busy with my own life, after all. But I knew some of it. She talked a bit – but today, it wasn't at all like that, like the way it used to be.'

'You don't expect her to tell the truth, do you?' Stanley said. 'Look, Bonnie, do me a favour. Let's go home and talk there! I've got a lot to sort out for tomorrow, John's coming round to collect the papers he'll need to carry on for me. Bad enough I've got to waste all day tomorrow here, do we have to hang around now?'

'No – of course not,' she said, and moved forwards, but not quickly, looking at Sammy, still standing there with his coat over his arm. 'I just thought – and I haven't seen Sammy for such ages – Sammy!' She said it suddenly, not looking at Stanley. 'Come home with us. Have dinner, yes? Then we can talk, and Stanley can do his work –'

'Bonnie, for Christ's sake!' Stanley said loudly and then shoved his hands into his overcoat pockets. 'Can we go home already?'

'That's kind of you, Bonnie. I wouldn't want to put you to any trouble,' Sammy said. 'I'll drop in later, maybe. Have a cup of coffee –'

'No, come now. I'll drive you. I'm parked at Brewer Street.'

'I'm parked down at Shoe Lane.'

'Oh. All right then – you can make your own way, can you? You've got the address? Just off Hale Lane, the Mill Hill end –'

'I know. Well – all right. Thanks. I'd like that. I'll be there a little after you, then?'

'As soon as you like,' Stanley said savagely, and waved his arm furiously as a taxi came trundling up from Fleet Street, its light on. 'Come *on*, Bonnie. And I'll drive. I want to get home tonight, not tomorrow morning.'

Going home wasn't nearly so bad now she knew Sammy was coming. If she cut the steaks carefully, and please God that stupid au pair had got everything else right, and opened a couple of tins of that special consommé and put some sherry in it, that would stretch it nicely. And with a bit of luck the children wouldn't hang around and she could talk to Sammy. About Hester, and the way she'd been in court, not like Hester at all. Quiet and reasonable, but altogether –

She shivered suddenly, sitting there beside Stanley as he pushed the car urgently up the Edgware Road. Suppose she won? How would Stanley be then? And suppose she lost? How would any of them be then?

She made herself relax, breathing deeply. She'd missed her meditation this afternoon, and she felt the lack of it. But after dinner, Sammy would be there, and he'd help her understand. He'd tell her why it was all happening. Why Hester had seemed so odd this afternoon. Well, not odd precisely, but not the Hester Bonnie thought she knew. But Sammy, who had known them all so well, who had been one of them really, he would be able to explain. Wouldn't he?

FEBRUARY 1943

'I'll be with you in apple blossom time.
I'll be with you to change your name to mine.
Church bells will chime, you will be mine,
In apple blossom time . . . .'

161

They had had a lovely afternoon, though it hadn't started out well at all, Bertha thought.

She'd hung around the school gates after they came out at dinner-time, because they were still only going in the mornings, even though the raids hadn't been so bad lately, and some of the evacuated children were drifting back to London, and filling up the classes again. She'd been annoyed about that, when they first started to come, annoyed that they used the things and the rooms and the playgrounds that the regulars used. They'd been away all safe in the country, staying in bed all night, and now it wasn't so bad they were coming back and spoiling it all for the rest of them.

Then she hadn't been annoyed, but quite proud because there were so many things the evacuated lot didn't know, and she could tell them about. It made up for a lot, that did. But not for the way they weren't allowed to use the same playground as the boys any more. Now they were all girls together in the old infants' ground, and the boys used the other side. That was miserable, because it meant she couldn't accidentally see Sammy at playtime every day. She had to hang around the gates pretending to be doing something else, hoping he'd come out and see her, and talk to her.

Today he had and for a little while it had been lovely, standing there and talking about nothing much, really. But only for a little while. Hetty had come and walked right in among the boys, as calm and easy as you please, calling his name, taking no notice of the jeers and giggles the other boys threw at her.

'What are you doing here?' she said when she saw them, stopping in front of them and standing with her hands in her pockets and her legs apart, staring at Bertha from under her straight dark brows. 'Eh? What are *you* doing here?'

'I'm talking to her,' Sammy said flatly. 'What d'you want me for?'

Hetty stood and glowered for a moment, looking from one to the other, and Bertha stared back at her, her eyes wide and limpid.

She'd never asked Sammy to keep quiet about their meetings in the park, and the times they went to the pictures and, giggling, slid in through the exit doors when other people came out, and the times they walked around the streets, just talking.

She never told him that Hetty could be very nasty if she thought other people were trying to take things away from her, and certainly never told him that as far as Hetty was concerned he was one of her things. But he seemed to know anyway, and didn't tell her. Bertha knew he still took her out sometimes, to the pictures, to the park, but she never thought about it. It was one of those things that happened, and thinking about them didn't help.

'I want to go down Ridley Road market,' Hetty said after a moment. 'Miss Cooper was telling Mrs Caister they've got some apples. You got any money?'

'Ninepence,' Sammy said after a moment. 'But I need it.'

'Well, I've got one and a penny,' Hetty said, surprisingly, Bertha thought. She didn't usually let people off that easily. 'Come on.'

She turned and slid her hand into Sammy's elbow, proprietorially. 'Go on home, Bonnie,' she said. 'I'll see you when I see you.'

'You come too,' Sammy said, and made an elbow and after a moment, Bertha put her hand there and Sammy began to walk, leaving the other boys and their jeers behind. Bertha was red; she was the only one who seemed to care, or even to have noticed.

'What d'you want *her* to come for?' Hetty said after a moment, and Sammy tightened his arm against his side and her hand in a friendly way, to reassure Bertha, and she wanted to giggle. 'Why shouldn't she?' he said. 'She likes apples, too, don't you, Bertha?'

'Bonnie,' Hetty said almost absently, and they walked on in silence for a while, past the shops with their glass windows criss-crossed with sticky brown tape and the piles of sandbags and the hurrying people.

Bertha stared up at the sky, milky blue and cloudless, blinking in the thin February sunshine and staring at the big fat barrage balloons, bobbing lazily at the ends of their cables. Like great silver fish, she thought. Fat, friendly, silver fish. They made her feel safe and comfortable, even though she knew the planes had still come and dropped bombs right through the middle of them. They just looked so nice.

By the time they got to Ridley Road it was all settled. Hetty had decided to be the Big Sister giving an outing to her little sister, and Bertha played along contentedly enough. It was worth it to be with Sammy.

So they walked in among the stalls, and she smelled the rich, earthy smell of potatoes and the tighter, harsher reek of onions and enjoyed the rumbling in her belly. Being hungry was an interesting feeling and she didn't mind it as much as she used to. And as she always seemed to be hungry these days, it was just as well.

They couldn't get any apples. There was a long queue for them and Hetty made Sammy and Bertha stand in it and went to the front to look at the stall, and assesss their chances of getting any. She came back, and turned down her mouth and shook her head.

'There's only about ten pounds there, honestly,' she said loudly. 'Most of the people here won't get served – they'll all be gone.'

But no one budged, the old women standing stolidly with their plaited straw bags in their hands staring ahead and shuffling slowly forward.

Hetty said quietly, 'We might as well go, really. They've got some, but it won't go far. I'd as soon have some carrots anyway.'

So they bought carrots, big fat ones, and Sammy used his pen-knife to scrape off the worst of the dried mud, and they chewed them and Bertha felt better as the rumblings in her belly stopped.

They wandered past the rubbish stalls and the old clothes women, laughing at the customers and pretending to pinch things, and once Hetty actually did, an old hat with a ratty-looking red feather in its greasy band. Sammy tried to make her take it back, but she laughed at him, dancing along backwards in front of him, holding it high in the air, daring him to snatch it from her. But he knew better than to play that game, and just paced along, dignified and silent, with Bertha hanging on to his arm equally silently.

'I'm going to give it to Auntie Fido,' Hetty said, and bundled it up and shoved it into the belt of her dress. 'Tell her I thought she'd like it and that was why we came down here. She'll like that, silly cow!'

164

After a while they were tired of the market and went back towards the school, cutting across the bombed-out site where Sophie Simmons's shop had used to be. It was getting on for four o'clock now, and already the light was thinning out, threatening the long night ahead.

It was Sammy who stopped, sat down on a pile of bricks, first heaping them up into the semblance of an armchair, and Bertha immediately copied him, making herself another chair, so that she could sit facing him.

Hetty stood and jeered for a while as they worked, pretending to throw stones at them, but always missing, and then, when they sat down, shrugged her shoulders and made a chair of her own. But being Hetty, she did it the fast and easy way, pulling a piece of plank from a heap of rubble and balancing it over some piles of shattered mortar.

Sammy laughed at her and she laughed back and for a moment they were locked together, the two of them, and Bertha in her neat brick armchair looked at them and felt bleak and alone, shut outside all by herself.

But it was only for a moment, because Sammy turned then and looked at her, and smiled and she felt better.

They played 'I Spy' and then 'Film Stars' giving each other initials and saying 'warm!' and 'cold!' as they tried to guess who it was.

'GG.'

'Man or woman?'

'Woman.'

'Does she look like me?' This from Hetty.

'Cold, cold, cold!'

'Greer Garson.'

'Cold, cold, cold!'

'Greta Garbo –'

'Now it's your turn.'

'DD.'

'Donald Duck!'

'Oh, you're mean! It's not fair! You should have asked some questions first!'

And then they sat in silence and ate another carrot each, and Bertha leaned back carefully against her bricks and pretended she and Sammy were married and Hetty was their little girl and

165

the war was over and they lived in a nice house like the big ones by Victoria Park.

'Let's play "Tomorrow",' Hetty said suddenly.

'I don't know it,' Sammy said. 'Do you, Bertha?'

'She's just made it up, I expect,' Bertha said. 'Haven't you, Hetty? She's always doing that.'

'Hester,' Hetty said, but not nastily. 'Yes, I just made it up. It's a good game. You have to say what will happen to a person tomorrow. And the person who it is has to say true or false, and false wins and changes places. I'll start. Sammy, tomorrow, you will be –' She looked at him sideways and grinned. 'Tall!'

He looked at her scornfully. 'True. Anyone can see that. So what's so clever about that?'

'Bonnie, tomorrow you will be – um – still saying, "I'm sorry," all the time.'

'Soppy,' Bertha said. 'False.'

'No, it's not,' Sammy said. 'I bet you will, Bonnie. You're always saying it, even when it's not your fault.'

'Well, I'm only trying to be polite!' Bonnie said hotly and looked at him appealingly. Stay in the middle, Sammy. Don't take her side.

'What's polite about saying sorry when you don't have to?' Sammy demanded. 'That's just silly.'

She felt her face redden and it came out before she could stop it. 'I'm sorry, Sammy –'

Hetty crowed. 'See? So it's still my turn. Sammy, tomorrow, you will be – you will be – let me see now, tomorrow you will be – clever! You'll be a doctor. Or very rich. Or famous.'

'Or all of them,' Sammy said, and he was quite serious. 'True.'

'Still my turn. Tomorrow, Sammy, you will be –' Hetty stopped and grinned and leaned forwards and whispered in his ear, and Sammy went very red, and pulled away from her.

'False!' he said loudly. 'I've told you, don't talk that way. It's –'

'You'll still be saying common the day *after* tomorrow, you will!' Hetty said and she bit into her carrot again, her teeth big and gleaming in the dull afternoon.

There was a little silence and then Sammy said suddenly. 'D'you know what you'll be tomorrow, Hester?'

She sat there, attentive and waiting, her jaws moving rhythmically and noisily over her carrot, staring at him and he shook his head, almost impatiently.

'I'm not playing now. I'm asking you. Do you know? Really know?'

She chewed thoughtfully and swallowed, still staring at him, and then nodded her head. 'Yes, I know. I know what I want, and if you want a thing a lot you can get it.'

'Just by wanting?' Bertha said.

'Yes.' Hetty didn't look at her. She was still staring at Sammy. 'Just by wanting.'

'What do you want, then? To be rich? Famous? To be a doctor like me?'

She shook her head. 'You won't ever be rich or famous, Sammy. Not being a doctor. You're the sort that wants to be a doctor round here.'

She waved a comprehensive hand, and they all looked up and stared round at the rows of narrow terraced houses and heaps of broken masonry and the people moving through the grey streets, themselves almost as grey as the pavements.

'It's only in stories that people get anything out of being that sort of doctor,' she said. 'The sort of stories they keep trying to make you take out of the library. To be a rich and famous doctor you have to go to Harley Street and look after rich and famous people.'

'How do you know?' Sammy said and she laughed.

'I read the *other* books. I know. So I'm not going to be like you.'

'Well, then, what are you going to be like?' Bertha said and Hetty turned and stared at her.

'Not like you,' she said with sudden rage in her voice. 'Not like you, dreaming and being frightened and waking up screaming.'

Bertha drooped her head, and looked at her shoes, side by side in the dust, and at the mottled pattern on her legs and thought, please don't tell him, please, don't tell him.

Last night had been dreadful. She'd dreamed it again, and it had gone on and on, and she hadn't been able to wake up at all, not until the water had risen almost to her nose, and then when she did she had found out she'd wet the bed and the others had shouted at her, and Auntie Fido had come in and there'd been all that fuss about changing the sheets. Awful that was. Wetting the bed when you were eleven, going on twelve. Please don't tell him.

'Well, she can't help it if she gets upset!' Sammy said, and he put out one foot and kicked Bertha encouragingly and she looked up at him and grinned. 'It was a terrible thing to have happen to your Mum and Dad and I'm not surprised she has nightmares. I would too, if it was me.'

'She told you she has them? My, you're lucky! She's always kept it a big secret before!' Hetty said jeeringly and stared at Bertha with her eyes narrow and slitty, the way Bertha most hated. But then she looked at Sammy again and her face smoothed out.

'You want to know all about what I'm going to do tomorrow?' she said, and now her voice took on a dreamy note. 'I'm going to be famous. Really *famous*. They'll turn round in the streets and they'll look and they'll say, "There goes Hester Morris," that's what they'll say. "There goes Hester Morris." Anywhere in the world I go, any country anywhere, America and Australia, it'll be the same. "There goes Hester Morris." I'll show them.'

'Show who?' Sammy said and he sounded a little breathless, as though he were there with her and all the people in the streets turning round and pointing her out to each other. 'Who will you show?'

Hetty blinked and looked at him almost blankly and then shook her head. 'Everyone,' she said vaguely, 'Just everyone.'

But Bertha knew. She knew who Hetty wanted to show. The ones who whispered behind their hands about the poor Morris girls, poor little things, both parents killed, you know. Auntie Fido's friends who sighed and twittered over Poor Auntie Fido, her life ruined by her duty to the three orphans. Everyone whoever felt sorry for them. Everyone they ever met. Bertha knew.

And suddenly she wished she was in bed, that it was night time and she could turn over and put her arm round the sleeping Hetty, and feel her skin warm and close. There were times when Hetty turned over too and cuddled close, seemed to want to feel the warmth they could grow between them, seemed to want to feel the joined-up-ness that Bertha felt sometimes.

'How will you be famous?' Sammy said, matter of factly.

'On the films!' Hetty sounded grand, now, and her voice seemed to change, to become deeper and thicker, and more la-di-da. 'That's how.'

'Rich as well, then,' Sammy said. And laughed. 'You're really daft, Hester, honestly you are. What makes you think anyone'll ever let *you* be on the films? You've got to be –'

He stopped, and the unspoken words hung between them in the darkening afternoon. 'You've got to be taught how to act,' he went on lamely. 'And where can you learn that, round here? With a war on?'

'What you mean is you've got to be pretty,' Hetty said and didn't seem a bit put out. 'Well, I'll tell you something, Sammy Sternberg. You can be anything you want to be. And when I'm ready, if I want to be pretty, I will be. Just like that.'

'Hilda says she's going to be rich,' Bertha said suddenly. 'Will she be rich, Hetty – Hester?'

There was a silence for a moment and then Hetty said, 'Yes, she will. That's what she wants more than anything. So she will.'

'What do you want more than anything, Bonnie?' Sammy said and she felt her face go red.

To be the girl he loved better than anyone, that was what she wanted. To be the girl loved best by lots of people, but most of all by Sammy. She shook her head and then shrugged. 'Don't know.'

'Then you won't be anything at all.' Hetty said witheringly. 'Nothing at all. Not till you want. Go home, Bonnie. Auntie Fido'll be moaning and you'd better go home and tell her we're coming. Go on.'

'Why should I?' Bertha said, knowing she'd do it eventually, but playing for time as Sammy got up and began to dust down his trousers which had mortar dust on them. '*You* go.'

'Do as you're told,' Hetty said sharply. 'Or you'll know the worst of it. Go on now. I'll be there soon. I want to talk to Sammy. It's private.'

She went, dragging her shoes through the dust even though Auntie Fido would moan about that when she saw them, leaving them standing there on the bomb site, staring after her. It had been a nice afternoon till then.

They never played 'Tomorrow' again, though. At least, not with her.

17

The crowds were satisfyingly thick as they left the Law Courts, and they only had to stand poised on the top step for a few moments to be sure everyone had seen them before they ran, heads down, for the kerb and the car.

They both signed autographs, which helped. JJ had had a bad day, one way and another, and if they'd made a beeline for Hester and paid too little attention to him he'd have lost his cool, he knew that. But he leaned back in the car now and looked at her as the driver pulled the wheel round and took them out into the clotted traffic going down Fleet Street, and grinned easily.

'So? Enjoyed yourself today, have you?'

She shrugged. 'I didn't look for pleasure.'

'That solicitor of yours – what's his name – Rundle. He's a Grade-A shit, isn't he? Hanging on to your ear all day.'

'Grade-A shit he may be, but he knows his stuff.' She was staring out of the window, abstracted, and he began to feel irritable again.

'I hope I'm not boring you,' he said loudly and she turned her head and stared at him.

'Boring me? Not particularly. Why?'

'You're not exactly with me, are you? It's like talking to the back end of a bus.'

'I'm sorry,' she said and he was mollified by her uncharacteristic softness. 'I'm a bit – I don't know. It's been a funny day. That court was full of people I used to know so well and hardly ever see any more. Odd.'

'How d'you mean, odd?'

'How long since you saw your mother?'

'My *mother*? Christ, I don't know! Yonks ago. What's that got to do with anything? She's sitting there in her bloody Welsh valley happy enough, I dare say. Costs me enough, that's for sure. What's she got to do with –'

'Imagine if she'd been in court today. Imagine if you'd looked round and seen her staring at you.'

He laughed at that. 'Impossible.'

'Maybe. But impossible things happen. I looked round and there was Auntie Fido. Christ, JJ, I haven't seen that old bitch in years – years and years and *years*. And there she was as large as life and twice as ugly and d'you know something? It was just like it was last time. I looked at her, and I was so angry I could have – oh, it was odd. Very odd.' And she turned her head and stared out of the window again.

There was a silence for a while as the car wheeled left past St Paul's and then he said abruptly. 'What are you doing this evening?'

'I don't know. Hadn't thought about it. Could work, I suppose.' She seemed to be lightened by that thought. 'Yes, I could work –'

'What at? We're off the air this week, thank God, and the terrorist story is as far on as we can get it – we've got to wait to see what Bloch digs up in Frankfurt, and there's no point in going any further on the Hampden hospital business until Peter has –'

She shook her head, amused. 'You are funny! There's more to life and work than *Spectrum* you know! I've got more irons in my fire than are dreamed of in *your* philosophy.'

Now he was really angry. 'Oh, I see! Working on the Great British Novel again? How many does this make? GBN mark seventeen or eighteen?'

She was still amused. 'So the last effort didn't work as well as it might. But this one will. I'll be leaving *Spectrum* next year.'

'Just like that?'

'Just like that,' she said coolly.

'I wouldn't throw such valuable dirty water away until I was absolutely sure my bucket full of clean would wash me so well,' he said savagely, anxiety pulling at his belly. 'You've got yourself a nice soft option where you are, and don't you forget it.'

'You're the one who needs to remember it,' she said, and looked at him sideways, her eyes glinting a little in the dimness of the car. 'Because without me, you'd have one hell of a problem keeping up your ratings, and well you know it.'

'Like hell I do. I was doing that programme before you turned up and don't you forget it.'

She laughed aloud then. 'How could I? I dragged it screaming into the top ten, remember? In fact, top five, as I recall. *And* it wasn't all that difficult.'

DECEMBER 1956

'... *you think there's nothing wrong, you string along, boy,*
Then zap! You're cooked, you're hooked,
You're caught in the tender trap ....'

The Christmas issue of *Pendulum* hit the bookstalls the first week in December, and right from the start it was a winner. The mix was superb. A crisp analysis of the Suez crisis jostled with an interview with the new, raw young playwright, Osborne, who was packing them in at the Royal Court; a heart-rending account of the sufferings of a couple of refugees from Hungary, who got out just after the Soviet tanks got in, elbowed a profile of Peter Twiss, Test Pilot Extraordinary; a detailed description of the way the Calder Hall nuclear power station was going to revolutionize the lives of Mr and Mrs Joe Bloggs ran alongside a light-hearted piece about what Christmas greetings celebrities were going to offer their American friends over the new transatlantic phone service. There was a full page review of Colin Wilson, as well as half a column about his book *The Outsider* and a wickedly funny short story by Angus Wilson. The artwork was brash and full of excitement, the advertising lavish and altogether, JJ thought, sitting in the City TV Club over a large gin and tonic, a nice production. I think I'll get the editor in, do a probe into Magazines Today, Are They At The Crossroads?

And then he turned the page and saw it: 'The Show Band Popsie. A Look Behind the Cameras at City's Blockbuster'.

He began to read with a wry smile on his face. Just like Hester, he thought, to get herself in the first issue of what was going to be a big 'un and keep quiet about it till it came out. With a bit of luck, she's mentioned me, he thought. With a bit of luck.

She had, and as he read he felt his face tighten, felt the muscles under his skin crawl against the bones, pulling his lips down into a tight grimace, and narrowing his eyes. He knew there were people watching him, people who had already read the damned thing and who would want to gloat, and he couldn't

173

do a thing about it, flicking his eyes over the page with such speed he almost felt sick.

' . . . she has the authentic appeal for 1957,' he read, 'with her lavish but young clothes, her *soignée* look, above all her refreshing honesty. She talks of her friends, her private life, her vision of the future with the same disarming candour she uses when she talks about her taste in literature and the arts. I spoke to her of her friendship with the TV pundit, J. J. Gerrard, who is another of City's stars, albeit occupying a lesser place in their firmament . . . .'

JJ clamped his jaws hard and tried to loosen his shoulders, but he couldn't. He was as taut as the mainspring in an alarm clock and could almost hear himself twanging.

' . . . with some trepidation. After all, there has been some ill-natured gossip. I need not have feared. She gave me one of those brilliant smiles of hers and said simply, "We have a working relationship – and it works on *every* level. I never believe people who tell you they have platonic relationships, do you? We don't, JJ and I. And it's great." "No rivalry?" I ventured. No tension between them about their different ratings? After all, not many men like to have the woman in their lives shine more brightly than they do. J. J. Gerrard, whose programme *Spectrum* is required viewing for any journalist and which I for one never miss, strikes me as a strong man, one not given to being in anyone's shadow . . . .'

He relaxed a little. Whatever bitch Hester had said, at least this journalist whoever he – she? – was had the wit to recognize truth and value when it was shoved in front of him.

' . . . and she shook her head, giving me a sturdy denial. "JJ hasn't a jealous bone in his body," she averred. "He does his job, I do mine, and we both know that that's the way we like it." '

Better and better, JJ thought and began to smile again. For a while.

' "Mind you, I'm not sure that in some ways he doesn't share the opinion of some pseudo-intellectual types, and think being the Show Band Popsie is easy. I know it isn't. Quite apart from the need to have a positively encyclopedic knowledge of the whole popular music world – its lesser lights as well as its stars – I have to project personality and involvement to a very mixed audience in a way that is acceptable to all of them. It can be tough, really tough. I'm quite sure that it's easier to present a story about the latest developments during, let's say, the current International Geophysical Year, than to put over an hour of mixed rock and roll, jazz, ballads – the audience for the Geophysical Year programme don't need any help, you see. They can understand just like that. But to involve – deeply involve – an audience that runs from the top of the land – I'm told they watch regularly at the Palace – down to kids in the lowest stream of a secondary modern school in a slum, that takes a different sort of effort. Much greater, frankly." '

I don't believe it, he thought, and the muscles in his belly tightened now. She can't have said all this. But if she didn't, where did this stinking journalist get the idea from? She can't be trying to push herself in on *Spectrum*, she *can't*.

But she was.

' . . . I liked the idea, and said so. It seemed to me a most intriguing thought, I said to her as she poured me another cup of tea . . .'

I'll bet, JJ told himself furiously. I'll bloody bet –

' . . . to imagine City setting up a swop. You on *Spectrum* one week, J. J. Gerrard on the Show Band show the next. That would be compulsive viewing.' She just laughed, leaning back easily in her elegant chair. "I don't know," she said modestly. "That's up to City, of course. I don't run the programmes – I just present them." But she looked wistful, I thought, as her eyes strayed to the window of her chic Chelsea flat, and stared out at the snow-filled skies above . . . .'

'Well, JJ? What d'you think of the idea?'

He looked up, blinking, and saw Coleman Lewis, and at once his face smoothed out. The man was going to need some careful handling. Oh, Christ, Hester, you bitch, why did you have to do it? Couldn't you at least have talked to me, warned me? To drop me in the shit like this. Christ, what did I do to deserve it?

'What idea, Cole? Have a drink? Yours is Bacardi and coke, as I remember – Sam, Bacardi and coke for Mr Lewis, and fast about it –'

'You've read it of course – yes, I can see you have. And I must say it's a great promotion notion!' Lewis lowered his bulk into the chrome and leather chair, which creaked a little in protest. 'Worked up properly, we could double the ratings for both shows in two successive weeks. I like it, I really like it.'

'Like what, Cole?' JJ said with studied nonchalance, and looked down at the magazine on his lap as Lewis pointed at it. 'Oh! You mean this chatter of Hester's about coming over to *Spectrum* one week?' He laughed indulgently and made a face, indicating dubiety, a willingness to try anything new, amusement at the pretensions of a silly little pop music madam, all at once. 'I could bring her over to take part in a discussion on – what could we call it? – ah, The Pop Culture – get in a couple of new-wave sociologists, a musicologist, perhaps, from one of the newer red-bricks – could be quite interesting –'

Lewis shook his head, and drank half his Bacardi and coke in one swallow. 'You didn't read it right, JJ,' he said. 'She's come up with a fantabulous idea – a straight swop between you. I really like it. Thought I'd take it upstairs, run it up the flagpole, see who salutes, you know? She's timed it like a pro, she really has. A pro PRO.' He laughed fatly, and finished his drink. 'Here we are about to push the spring schedules, looking for ideas, and she comes up with a humdinger of a gimmick. I think they'll like it upstairs, I really do. Don't you?'

'Frankly no,' JJ said savagely. 'From where I'm sitting it looks vulgar, cheap and a certain candidate for failure. You're more likely to kill both shows than lift the ratings of either of 'em if you do any such dam' fool thing.'

Lewis raised his eyebrows and stood up, puffing a little with the effort. 'Like that, is it?' Well, JJ, I've always been straight, as well you know. And I tell you straight now that if that's your reaction, I know we're on to a winner. They'll love it upstairs, just love it. So think about it a bit more, will you? Handle it right, and it'll do you no harm. But I wouldn't be too opposed, not in front of the front office, anyway.' Again that fatuous laugh, and JJ held his jaw firm and stared at him in silence. 'Because I reckon it's going to do us very well indeed.'

And he went lumbering away, nodding and becking at the people he passed, leaving JJ sitting with his gin and tonic in his hand and so filled with rage and plain cold fear that he couldn't trust himself to raise his glass to his lips, in case his hand would shake with it all. The bitch, bitch, bitch. He knew what was going to happen now, and there wasn't a thing he could do about it. Except join in, and play it her way.

They sat in silence for the rest of the journey, each staring out of their windows at the traffic and the hoardings and thinking their own thoughts. It wasn't until they reached her flat in Limehouse and the car had stopped and the driver sat waiting to see where he was to go from there that she seemed to be aware of anything outside herself.

She yawned suddenly. 'Coming in?' she said after a moment, and he looked at her and at the back of the driver's head and lifted his eyebrows, and she shook her head almost imperceptibly. 'Drink, maybe. That's all,' she said. 'Give you a chance to unwind. Dave'll wait, won't you, Dave?'

'Yes, Miss Morrissey,' the driver said stolidly, and turned off his engine. 'I'm on the middle turn tonight. Goin' off duty at 'arf past nine, so it's up to you. Mr Lewis said as I was to keep the car for both of you as long as you wanted it.'

'You'll get away on time,' she said crisply and opened the door and swung her legs out to the pavement. 'Right, JJ? Come on then. Get yourself a beer, Dave. There's a pub over there, got real ale, your actual CAMRA stuff.'

He stood in her big living room staring out over the river. The window filled the whole of the end wall, and the first time he'd gone there he'd felt drawn to it, felt he could topple off the edge through the glass and down into the water below without so much as a whisper. It had almost frightened him, so powerful was the pull. Now he was used to it, and could sit anywhere in the room and just watch the wrinkled elephant-skin surface of the river and the silly fussy boats, and relax.

She brought him his gin and tonic and then kicked off her shoes and stretched out on the heap of crimson and blue cushions that filled one corner of the room. There was a gas fire burning in the grate, with real red and yellow flames licking false logs and he stared at it and thought suddenly, She's like that. She burns and flickers and lights everything round her, warms it sometimes too, just a bit, but none of herself is ever consumed.

He turned his head and looked at her and he felt it again, the lift of excitement that she could always create in him and with it came anger and self-pity and he said harshly and with conscious

177

self-dramatization, 'I wish I'd never met you, Hester Morrissey.'

She smiled at him, lazily, like a cat. 'Most people feel the same way.'

'Why?'

'Why do most people wish they'd never met me, or why do I have that effect on them?'

'It's the same thing.'

'If you think that then you don't think enough. No, you fool. The people who wish they'd never met me are the soft ones, the give-at-the-knees ones. I'm tough and pushy and greedy and I've got a lot of living to do. The people who don't wish they'd never met me, the ones I prefer, they recognize that. And they don't hate me for it. You wish-I'd-never-met-you types, you're soft and –'

'Christ, but you're a ball crusher!' he said, stung, and again she smiled that triangular cat-like smile.

'I was about to say, soft and human and compassionate and lovable. Much better people than I am, or the people I like are. We're the baddies, sweetheart. You're the goodies.'

'Me, a goodie? I should live so long!'

'But you are, you know. Oh, I know, you're as devious as every other bastard in this bastard business. You'd screw your own grandmother on air, as long as you got a nation-wide hook-up for it. You'd probably do it for a regional programme, come to that. As long as there was an audience you'd be in there screwing. But you didn't start out that way.'

He got up and went and refilled his glass, and came back to his sofa, bringing the bottle with him. She shook her head when he lifted it at her invitingly.

'No, I didn't, did I?' It was almost as though he couldn't remember. But he could, of course. He'd been red hot with it. Rage and compassion. The Poor, the Hungry, the Downtrodden, they were all his, every one of them, and he'd come down from university, sparkling with his new degree, draped about with the polish of Oxbridge education, and gone head first into the BBC and splattered his compassion about all over the further education department. But no one had been out there listening so he'd moved on, and City had given him his first success with *Probe* and he'd had a marvellous time.

178

Far, far away, down the long corridors of the past he watched himself, young and earnest, perspiring a little, thinner and more wiry, and oh, so *sure*, lambasting all of them. Politicians and con-men and insurance salesmen and front organizations for pressure groups from the Right, the Left, the Moderate Centre, he'd slaughtered them all for their venial ways, their mixed-up motives, their taste for money and display and their muddled thinking.

She watched him as he sat and stared into his glass, and said with real gentleness, 'I'm right, aren't I? You cared once, didn't you? You were going to change the world. You're still like that, somewhere underneath all that has happened to you since. You've been ruined, of course, by all of it. Cameras and make-up and being recognized by strangers. It's made you like the rest of them. But underneath, you're still the caring sort, you poor bastard. Me, I'm not. I was what I am when I started in this business. I'm one of the people who make television the cesspit it is. I'm about as deep as a cathode-ray tube, about as soft and about as human. But I'm just as clever as the bloody tube, just as cunningly put together –' She stretched and laughed again, lightly, her voice sounding mocking. 'Jesus, how I do run on! One day's exposure to the Might of British Law and I wax right philosophical!'

But he was interested now, and looked at her and said, 'Why? I think you really are as tough as you come on. But for Christ's sake, why?'

'Put it down to painful childhood experience,' she said lightly. 'Are you nearly finished with that gin? Because Dave'll be sitting down there chuntering and –'

'You don't give a shit for a bloody car driver, lady,' JJ was getting pugnacious. Gin often had that effect on him. 'What childhood experience?'

'Sometime when you've a year or two to spare, I'll tell you all about it,' she said and got up. 'Good night, sweetheart. I'm going right now to take a shower. I am then going to make myself a nourishing egg flip, and write a chapter of next year's runaway best seller. You do what you like, but keep out of my way. And don't think you'll get laid if you hang around, on account of I'm not interested.'

'You always do this,' he complained loudly, feeling aggrieved tears rising in his throat. 'As soon as we start being real people, start talkin' about ourselves, you go an' sheer off, and won't talk. S'not fair. It's not right to treat a man like that. I want to know about you, everythin' about you. An' every time we get anywhere near each other, you go and –'

'Get Dave to stop and buy you a hamburger on the way home. You're half pissed already and you'll need something to sop it up. Go on, buster, get going.' And she disappeared through the bead curtain that led to her bedroom and bathroom.

'Hester!' he shouted after her, almost despairingly, and she called back, 'See you in court!' And he heard the water start to run and swore and went out, slamming the door behind him. Bitch Hester. If only he could love her as little as he liked her.

18

Sylvia always put Radio Three on as soon as she came into the kitchen in the mornings, because they played such lovely easy music, Tchaikovsky and Brahms and even Strauss sometimes, and Fido, when she came creaking in ten minutes later, always changed it to Radio One with its thumping, whining pop. Then Sylvia would change the station again, apparently casually, as she went from the kettle to the electric toaster, and, equally casually, Fido would turn it off altogether. It was a ritual they went through every morning, and like so many other aspects of the life they shared, they never talked about it.

Today they sat and ate their wholemeal toast and bran flakes – so vital for good health to take care of the bowels – and drank their decaffienated coffee in an even greater silence than usual, both sunk in their own thoughts. And then Sylvia looked at the clock, the one shaped like a frying-pan with flowers painted where the numbers ought to be, and stood up and began to clear the dishes.

'We'd better put a move on, dear,' she said, clattering the plates into the bowl in the sink. 'It was quite crowded yesterday and it wouldn't do not to be able to get a seat. Would it?'

'I don't think I can go this morning,' Fido said in her special I'm-so-weak voice and leaned back in her chair, putting one hand on her chest and staring at Sylvia. 'I'm not well, I've got such a heaviness in my chest, and I had palpitations again last night. I didn't call you because I didn't want to disturb you, but I felt dreadful, absolutely dreadful, and I thought my time had come, I really did. I don't think I ought to go this morning.'

Sylvia managed not to show her irritation. 'Look, dear, we've been through all this. You'll have to. They said they might want to call you as a witness and if they do, you've got to be there. You can't just say, "No thanks, I don't feel like it," can you? I know it isn't easy, seeing Hester again after all this time, but I had to do it, didn't I, even though Hildegarde was there –'

'It's got nothing to do with Hester!' Fido said shrilly, and began to knead her chest with one gnarled fist. 'I told you, I feel

181

ill. 'f I'd 'a called you in the night the way I wanted to, you'd 'a seen for yourself and you wouldn't ha' let me get up this morning, let alone being so cruel as to make me go. It'll be the death of me, that's what it'll be, the death of me –'

'There's nothing to be afraid of!' Sylvia said, and dried the last cup and went to hang it on the Easiwerk. 'I've told you, whatever she says, she can't do anything to you. It was all a long time ago, and anyway it's got nothing to do with this case.'

'It has,' Fido said, and began to weep, the big oily tears sliding down her face unchecked. 'It's about money, isn't it? Hester gets all upset over money, she always did, and she hasn't changed. I tell you, she'll start all sorts of things up again and have me put away, and I'll die, I really will die, honestly I will. Sylvia, please don't make me go, please don't.'

'I'm not making you do anything, dear,' Sylvia said, in the special voice – all sweet reason and common sense – that she had learned to use years ago as a teacher, and now often found herself using for Fido. 'I'm just trying to explain to you that this is a situation you can't escape from. That the law of the land can't be gainsaid. If they want you to be there as a witness, then there you must be. Or go to jail for contempt of court. Then you really would be in trouble.'

Fido got to her feet, stiff and awkward, reaching for her stick and sniffing dolorously. 'If I have a heart attack and die right there in front of them, it'll be on their heads, that's what it'll be, on their heads. I didn't ask for them to bother me, did I? I don't ever ask anyone to bother me. I didn't ask them to kill my brother and leave me with three orphans to bring up. It wasn't my fault – and how was I supposed to do it without any money, anyway? It's not my fault –'

JULY 1964

'It's been a hard day's night,
I've been working like a dog.
It's been a hard day's night,
I should be sleeping like a log . . . .'

'I didn't ask them to leave me with you three to bring up, did I? But someone had to look after you, and how was I supposed to

182

do it without any money, anyway?' Fido said piteously and turned her head to look at Bonnie. But Bonnie shook her own head and said nothing, looking at Hester.

'Jesus God, woman, will you listen? I'm not saying you shouldn't have used the money to look after us. It's the fact that you *didn't* that makes me puke, the fact that you –'

'Hester, that's enough,' Bonnie said firmly, and looked at Sharon and Daniel sitting on the floor and ostensibly playing with their bricks, but staring wide-eyed and interested at their aunt. 'If you can't keep this discussion on an adult basis, then I'm afraid you'll have to go – I won't have the children upset by –'

'Oh – Bonnie, for God's sake, stop being so *wet!*' Hester said but she dropped her voice. 'Can't you see what all this means? We were – all those years, when we were kids, all the years when I was going around with my arse hanging out, and she was sitting on bloody thousands of our money – *our* money –'

'I don't see how you can say it was only our money, Hester,' Bonnie said, trying to be reasonable. She was watching Sharon and Daniel, wondering whether it wouldn't be better to call the au pair and have her take them out for a walk, but there'd be a fuss, with the children whining and the au pair sulking because she was supposed to study in the afternoons, and then Hester would probably lose her temper even more and the children would finish up more upset than ever. And then Warren would be coming in from school and demanding all sorts of attention – oh, damn it, why had she asked Auntie Fido over this afternoon in the first place? And why did Hester have to pick today of all days to find out all about this ancient history?

'Look, Hester,' she said now, trying to be very calm without sounding as though she were wheedling. 'It's all so long ago now anyway. What does it matter, after all? We're doing all right – more than all right, Stanley's got more than enough for us, and you and Hilda couldn't be doing better, could you? So –'

'That's not the point,' Hester said, and threw herself into the big armchair by the fire. 'If someone's robbed you, they've robbed you. It doesn't matter when they did it, or what your situation is, robbery is robbery –'

'It wasn't robbery.' Auntie Fido began to cry, wiping her eyes on the back of her hand and snorting a little. 'It wasn't. I was

183

just a girl on her own, just a girl –'

'Some bloody girl,' Hester said. 'Thirty-five-year-old spinster, dried-up old virgin, the best thing that ever happened to you was us –'

'That does it,' Bonnie thought, and got to her feet.

'Sharon, Daniel,' she said brightly. 'Come along and I'll ask Inge-Lis to take you down to the ice-cream shop for a walk. You can meet Warren coming out of school first, though, and all get ice cream together –' She couldn't disapprove more of bribery like this, tutted as much as anyone when she saw other less careful mothers stuffing their children's mouths with tooth-rotting sweets and ices, but there were times when it couldn't be helped.

By the time she got back to the lounge, having compounded her bribery by giving Inge-Lis an extra evening off – and Stanley would have something sharp to say about that, but what could she do? – Hester was marching up and down with her hands shoved deep into her jacket pockets. She was wearing one of the new short-skirted suits, its skimpy hem half way up her thighs, over white net tights and white boots. The suit was white too, and her face above it was ravaged and tight. Altogether she looked like an elderly child, Bonnie thought, and felt better about her own sensible tweed pinafore skirt and woolly jumper. Anyway, when you've got three children and you're pregnant again you can't go around looking like a fashion plate. At least Hilda wasn't here to make her feel even more dowdy; that was one comfort.

'Thank God you've got rid of them,' Hester said when she came in. 'Now we can talk like people. Listen. Bonnie. Let me tell you what –'

'I don't want to know,' Bonnie said, almost surprised to hear the determination in her own voice. 'Honestly, I don't want to know. I mean, what on earth possessed you to go digging around in the first place? It's the maddest thing I ever heard after all these years –'

'It's a story I'm doing for *Spectrum*,' Hester said impatiently. 'About post-war credits and war-time compensations – I thought, where better to start an investigation than into the affairs of my own parents? Maybe they had credits lying around waiting to be picked up – oh, boy, did they ever! Not that this

184

bitch here would leave anything lying around for long. You're a
bloody scavenger, you know that? The sort of animal that goes
creeping around corpses to see what it can pick up for itself –'

'Oh, stop it, Hester, for pity's sake,' Bonnie said wearily as
Fido began to wail again. She was beginning to feel sick again.
This was turning out to be a rough pregnancy. 'What's the use,
anyway? It's not as though you can get it back now. Nothing can
make up for what's past –'

'You're damned right it can't!' Hester said. 'My God. When I
remember –'

Looking at her, at her tight hard face and the blaze in her
boot-button eyes Bonnie could suddenly feel it. It was as though
she could, for the first time, get inside her sister's skin. All the
years when she had been trying so hard to make it, to be an
actress.

She remembered the way she would work all day and half the
night at dreary, dirty jobs, washing up in grubby tea shops, or as
a casual chambermaid in one-night-stand hotels near Victoria.
She remembered the way she would go out on mornings when
she had an audition organized, her head poised on her neck with
such springiness it looked as though it would leap off and
bounce ahead of her like a rubber ball, and how she would come
creeping back to the Hackney house with her face grey with
fatigue and misery because she hadn't got the job.

She remembered how she was when she did have some sort of
part, in tatty little films and cheap fit-up productions touring
schools where the audiences couldn't have cared less about
what they were watching; how she would go on working in those
horrible cafés and cheap hotels in all her free time, to get some
extra money, because none of the jobs paid enough to keep her.

And how Auntie Fido would moan. All the time, moaning.

'Why can't you get a nice job, Hester, like the others? You
used to have a lovely job in that nice clean office with the record
company, and gave me a bit more money to keep you with. But
you gave that up to go and be in some silly play that didn't last a
month – why don't you go back to them and tell them you're
sorry? Tell them you won't do it again? You can go on with
those nice Settlement Players, get it out of your system that way
– how would it have been 'f I'd 'a done what you're doing, done
what I liked instead of worrying about looking after all of you?

Eh? How would it have been? I can't feed you on air, you know, money doesn't grow on trees –'

And Bonnie herself, filled with compunction about poor Auntie Fido trying to make the money stretch to feed them all and always failing, would give her more, leaving herself so short that sometimes she had hardly any underwear and what she had was so shabby and patched it hardly held itself together. She'd given money to Hester too, saving it by walking to work instead of getting the bus, telling her casually that she'd had a bonus from the shop this week, or had made some commission, and Hester would take it and mutter ungraciously, but it made Bonnie feel better about the whole problem.

Only Hilda had gone sailing serenely through it all, impervious to both Fido's moaning and Hester's grim misery. She always had clothes to wear, and seemed to eat better than any of them. But then she, of course, had Sylvia to worry over her. Lucky Hilda. Not so lucky Hester and Bonnie.

Bonnie looked now at Fido sitting by her marble fireplace, on one of her expensive armchairs, her feet on her top-quality Wilton carpet, and felt a sudden lift of anger. Had she done what Hester said she had done? Had she really kept them half starved and skimped on everything, in spite of having plenty of money to take care of them? And Heaven help her, was she still doing it? Oh, God, what will Stanley say?

'How much did you say it was, Hester?' she said suddenly now, and Hester looked up, aware of the change in her tone, and said in a flat voice, 'Five thousand pounds.'

'Five thousand. – five thousand. If you'd only spent five pounds a week out of it, Auntie Fido, we could have lived decently.' Bonnie said. 'You always said you only had what the Board of Guardians allowed you, and the money from the Orphan's Aid Fund – until you started to get National Assistance and went on and on about that –'

All those shameful years when social workers would come and look at the Hackney house and assess whether they had a right to more. The way they would look at the plastic flowers in the white and red kitchen and the little plaster ornaments of kittens sitting winsomely in shoes, and Fido would say pathetically, 'I try so hard to keep it nice for them, poor little orphaned girls –' and how the social workers would smile and write their reports and she'd get a little more. All the time, wheedling and lying and trying to get just a little bit more. 'And why not,' Auntie Fido would say. 'It's supposed to be a welfare state, isn't it?' And would buy more silly plastic flowers and plaster ornaments from the market stalls. But no more food, no clothes.

'Five thousand,' Bonnie said again, and shook her head and sat down heavily in the other armchair.

Now Auntie Fido began to cry in earnest, seeming more alarmed by Bonnie's reaction than Hester's enraged attack, and the two sisters sat there while she cried, her face twisting into a smeared, red-nosed map of ugliness.

She looked up at last, wiping her pouchy eyes and sniffing unappetizingly, and looked at Hester who stared back at her with such an expression of cold dislike on her face that she flicked her gaze away, and looked at Bonnie instead. 'Try to understand, Bonnie,' she said piteously. 'You're the only one who ever cared – try to see it, please try. 'f it'd been you, what would you have done?'

And now it was Fido's skin Bonnie slid into, Fido's misery she felt, Fido's fears that filled her. Thirty-five, desperately trying to be bright and young and live with the knowledge that no man had ever wanted her and no man ever would. No future and no past either upon which to draw. Only a cold empty plain stretching bleakly ahead. A plain with nothing on it at all. No comfort, no peace, no love, nothing.

And then her only brother is killed and leaves behind him three small girls and five thousand pounds in insurance money. Five thousand pounds –

'It must have made a big difference to you,' she said now, staring at the twisted old face in front of her. 'Five thousand pounds.'

'It was all there was for me, Bonnie. All there was. I was on my own, wasn't I? I knew what happened when children grew up. They just went off and left you. My brother did it to my mother, and then she died – what was there for me if I didn't have that? I knew you'd all grow up to hate me, children always do, and all there was was that bit of money. There wasn't anything else for me, nothing at all. I knew they wouldn't let you three go without, the Board of Guardians, the Funds and all – so

I thought, there wasn't no will, just the insurance money and the man said to me, use it for the children, to look after them and to look after yourself of course and I thought, if I can get money for them from somewhere else the insurance money'll be mine. It was mine, mine by right – I gave up my life for all of you, I did. Gave up my life –'

The tears started again, thick and noisy, and Hester got to her feet and started to march up and down again, energy streaming out of her painfully, making Bonnie tired just to look at her.

'You see, Bonnie? She admits it! The bitch stole our money from us. Five thousand. It could have – Christ, when I think the difference that'd have made ten years ago, when I was trailing round those bloody agents' offices, wearing rags that bitch there cobbled up out of curtain remnants from the stalls in Ridley Road – when I think –'

'I know,' Bonnie said, trying to feel for Hester again, but with Fido's misery still lingering in her mind. 'I know, Hester. But she did try, I suppose. I mean, we had somewhere to live, we didn't die of hunger, did we? And she did her best – she did make things for us, didn't she? Dresses and that –'

'Because it was the cheapest way to do it, that's why! Because even *she* wouldn't have the brass gall to send us out in rags – and once we started earning, Jesus Christ, but didn't she skin us! Jesus Christ, but didn't she get her whack! All those years, never a penny to call our own, when I remember it – hunger and guilt and rage and wanting – oh, I'll never forgive you, you hear me? If you die tomorrow it won't be too soon for me. For the rest of your stinking lousy life, I hope you rot. I hope every bone in your body aches, that every day should be riddled with pain and disease – I hate your guts, I always have and I always will, and I'll never forgive you, never –'

It was like a tidal wave, as though all the years of resentment had at last broken their banks and come pouring out and Bonnie stared at Hester, at her twisted face and her open mouth and thought, 'She'll kill her, she'll kill her –' and she stood up and went towards Hester, her hands held out, and then stopped because suddenly Hester was crying with great tearing sobs and holding her hands in front of her face.

Bonnie stopped, amazed. Hester, crying? Hester had never cried. In all the years she had never seen Hester weep, and she felt enormous embarrassment, as though she'd suddenly taken off all her clothes and squatted on the carpet to empty her bowels. It was disgusting, it was obscene, she couldn't look. And suddenly her own eyes were filled with tears and she put her arms round her sister and tried to hold on to her.

But Hester recovered, almost as suddenly as she had lost control, and she raised her chin and said loudly. 'Listen, bitch – listen. You give me that money, you hear me? All of it. Every penny. Or I'll hound you through every court there is –'

'You can't.' Fido was sitting very straight, staring at her, and looking back over her shoulder Bonnie thought – she's all right. She's not upset at all. She's all right.

And it seemed as though she really was, for her blotched colour was fading and even her tear-draggled eyes looked almost normal. She was staring at Hester with a kind of triumphant gleam in her eye and her mouth was curved downwards but it looked like a smile.

Hester cried, Bonnie thought, and let her go. Hester cried, and now Fido's all right. Because Hester cried.

'You can't,' Fido said again. 'The insurance man said, all those years ago – there wasn't no will, neither of them left no will. Just each other to benefit, and they both died, so no one was named. He said I was to sign for it, since I was his sister, and anyway I was looking after the children. I asked him most particularly. It was legal. *I* signed. And it's all put away safe, you couldn't get it no matter what. It's all put away safe for when I'm old and on my own. None of you would care when I was old, I knew that. I'd got to take care for when I was old, didn't I? So I did. None of you would care –'

'Stanley's been giving you money every week since we got married.' Bonnie said loudly. 'Every week.'

'I knew it wouldn't last. Not till I was old,' Fido said, the whine coming back into her voice. 'Don't you turn on me, Bonnie. Please don't you turn on me.'

'She'll never speak to you again as long as she lives,' Hester said. 'Any more than I will. Right, Bonnie?'

'Oh, Hester, for God's sake.' Bonnie was tired now, all the way through to her middle, tired and bored and sick. 'It's over. Auntie Fido, put your coat on. I'll take you to the station –'

'I'm telling you Bonnie, you'll never see me again if you see her.' Hester's voice was loud and harsh. 'You choose. Me or her.'

'To tell you the truth, Hester, I don't care if I never see or hear from either of you again. I've had enough of the pair of you. Go home, will you? I'm not feeling very well.'

19

Breakfast again, thought Bonnie, staring out of the window at the garden. The days turn round faster and faster, and suddenly it's breakfast-time again, and it's like it's only a couple of hours since I last watched Stanley shoving muesli into his mouth as though he hadn't eaten for a week. At least the kids aren't squabbling this morning. That's something to be grateful for.

It's a lousy life. The words seemed to come into her head the way a stranger suddenly walks into a room and makes everyone there look up and stare. It's a lousy life.

She went on staring out at the garden, where the rain poured down relentlessly on the carefully-trimmed azalea bushes and the lilacs, and sent rivulets of grey water trickling across the patio. How can you say that? a little voice somewhere deep in her mind said. How can it be a lousy life when you've got so much? This house and all that's in it, your clothes, your au pair, the children, the car –

You see? The strange voice started again. You see what I mean? Of course it's a lousy life when the only way you can justify it is by making an inventory of your possessions. And think about that inventory, ducky, just think. The children come one hell of a long way down the list, and your husband – ha! Your husband is nowhere.

'No!'

Warren looked up. 'What's 'at?'

She looked at him blankly and shook her head, embarrassed. 'I'm sorry. I was thinking – I didn't mean –'

'Listen, Bonnie –' Stanley finished his muesli and reached for the toast and marmalade. 'I don't want you to go to court today. Yesterday was bad enough. I'll be there from the start so there's no need for you to go. Stay home.'

'No,' she said. And listened to the little voice in her head again. The children come one hell of a long way down the list, and your husband – ha! Your husband is nowhere.

'What d'you mean, no? I've told you, there's no need for you to go.'

'Need has nothing to do with it. I want to go.'

'Oh, do me a favour, Bonnie. Be your age! I've told you –'

She looked at him, at his mouth full of toast and his champing jaws and shook her head, cool and relaxed. It was as though she were someone quite different. A lovely feeling.

'I heard you – and I'm telling you, I'm going. It's as much my affair as yours – more, in fact. They're my sisters. So I'm going.'

Sharon had put down her paper and was looking at her, her head on one side and her eyes a little narrowed.

'How can it be more your affair than mine? Whose money was it, for Christ's sake? Eh? Answer me that? Whose money was it?

She leaned back in her chair and thought of last night, of Sammy sitting there talking to her for hours after Stanley had gone off to deal with business again, sitting there in the kitchen with his elbows on the table and talking to her about his work, about his plans for the future, about her psychology course and her meditation, about plays and books and himself again, and felt his strength filling her. And she smiled, a wide serene smile.

'Mine. Mine and yours. It's law, now, you know. I own half of everything. Half the house, half the money. So you can say the money Hilda had came out of my share, if you like. If it'll make you feel better.'

Stanley stared at her, his jaws still rhythmically chewing and then he swallowed and shook his head.

'I've got no time to waste on such rubbish. I've told you. I don't want you to go. It's a waste of time, bad enough I have to be there.'

'Actually, you don't have to be there,' she said, remembering Sammy again, building her own strength by thinking of his face. 'I told you, in law the money is half mine anyway. So, you go to the factory, instead of wasting your time at court, and I'll be there. If they want a witness, I'll be there. They haven't actually said they want either of us, of course. But if they do –'

'You're mad,' he said flatly and stood up. 'I've better things to do than stand here and argue with a mad woman. You want to go to court? So go already. Go and watch your precious sisters make bloody exhibitions of themselves, much I care. I try to protect you, you don't want it, so much I care – are you coming, Sharon?'

Sharon shook her head, still staring at her mother. 'No, I think I'll go my own way. Like Mum,' and she giggled suddenly and Bonnie looked at her and Sharon grinned. 'Attamum!'

Warren looked up from the *Daily Mirror*. 'So what's going on here? Women's Lib, all of a sudden?'

'All of a sudden,' Bonnie said, and stood up. 'I'm going to get myself ready for court. If anyone wants a lift into town, I'll be leaving in about half an hour. Oh – and I might not be back for dinner. I might go out.'

'Hey, hey, what's all this?' Sharon was still staring at her mother. 'I mean, stand up for yourself by all means, but suddenly you've got dinner dates? What is all this?'

'It's that bloody Stermont,' Stanley said. 'That bloody know-all Doctor Stermont, goes on television, talks a lot of socialist rubbish about private patients. Never could stand the man – right from the time I first knew him, he was trouble. Take no notice, Sharon. Your mother wants to make a fool of herself with such a one, she's welcome. For my part, I'm going to the factory. And I don't know whether I'll be in this evening either. See how you lot like that!' And he went, slamming the kitchen door viciously behind him.

There was a little silence and then Warren said abruptly, 'Is that true?'

'Is what true?' Bonnie was standing by the kitchen door, waiting to hear the front door slam behind him too so that she could go comfortably upstairs to change, not have to see him on the way.

'About that fella that was here last night. Is he – I mean, are you –'

He looked at her with his face a little crumpled, the way it used to look when he was five years old, and she wanted to put her arms round him and cuddle him better. 'No, of course not, silly boy. He's an old friend, that's all. An old friend.'

'Still and all; you're not being like you usually are this morning, are you?' Sharon said, and she stood up as the muffled slam of the front door came pushing into the room. 'And he *was* here last night. I liked him. How come I haven't met him before, if he's such an old friend?'

'We lost touch,' Bonnie said after a moment, and went out leaving them staring after her. 'Don't worry about tonight. I suppose I'll be here at dinner-time. I always am, after all.'

JUNE 1956

'Love and marriage, love and marriage,
Go together like a horse and carriage,
This I tell you, brother,
You can't have one without the other . . . .'

'I feel such a *fool*,' Bonnie whispered. 'And I've got all sorts of spots on my face and I know I look awful.'

'You look as awful as every bride. Which isn't awful at all, and well you know it,' Sammy said, and reached forwards and tweaked her veil. 'Though how you can tart yourself up in all this pagan stuff is beyond me.'

'Well, Stanley, and his family –' Bonnie said and went to the door and peered out through the little crack. 'Oh, ye gods, look at them all! Hundreds of them. I don't think I can stand it, marching up the aisle in between all of them. *Hundreds* of them –' And she pulled her dress down at the hips, trying to feel comfortable. All that vilene and lace and satin – it felt ridiculous.

'Where's Auntie Fido?' Sammy said. 'Isn't she supposed to be here by now?'

'I don't think so. She's got to be up there on the thing with the rabbi and Stanley's people and all that – oh, Sammy, I do feel awful.'

'Why? You wanted to get married, didn't you?'

'Yes – no – I don't know – I sound as silly as I look.'

'Well, there's no point in nattering on about it now, is there? Here you are, and here I am and how I ever got conned into taking part I'll never know –'

'I had to have someone to give me away.'

'It's a horrible idea,' he said almost violently, and went to look through the crack in the door.

'Oh, please, don't start all that again. I know how you feel about weddings and all. Leave it at that.'

She looked down at her dress, trying to see herself inside it,

194

and she couldn't. Under all that lace and satin there couldn't be a real live human skin. It had to be celluloid and smooth all over, like a kewpie doll. I'm a shocking-pink kewpie doll, she thought and wanted to giggle and looked brightly at Sammy instead. 'What you would have done if you'd married Hester after all, I can't imagine –'

He stood very still at the door, with his back to her.

'Married Hester? Who said anything about marrying Hester?'

'You did,' she said. 'You asked her. I heard you.'

He turned then and looked at her and she felt her face go crimson. 'The blushing bride, is it?' he said, his tone light. 'But you're not blushing for the usual reasons, so maybe it doesn't count. What did you hear? When?'

She began to twiddle with her bouquet. 'Will it be much longer? Won't they come and call us soon?'

'When they're ready. What did you hear?'

She was silent for a moment and then shrugged. It was her wedding day today. What the hell, it couldn't make any difference.

'I was in the kitchen. You two were in the hall. You asked her to marry you. Ages ago.'

She lifted her chin and looked at him and his face seemed remote and shimmery and she thought, the veil's supposed to make me look younger and softer, not him. 'I cried and cried.'

'Did you? No more than I did. Why did you cry?'

She made a little face. 'I had an awful crush on you.'

'Crushes do make you cry. I had one on Hester.'

They were silent for a while, listening to the crunch of footsteps outside the little room as guests marched into the synagogue, hearing the crows of greeting, the shrill cries of children being shushed by their mothers. It was stuffy in the little room and smelled of old prayer books and wet shoes and rust.

'Are you over it?' she said suddenly, watching his face. She felt safe behind her veil, unobserved and secret. 'Your crush?'

'Of course.'

'Why "of course"?'

'Aren't you over yours?'

'I wouldn't be here if I weren't,' she said after a moment.

'Then the same applies to me. She'll be here today with that Gerrard, won't she? If it mattered, I wouldn't be here. Anyway it's all an aberration.'

'What is?'

'Romantic love.' He went again to peer out of the crack in the door.

'Of course it isn't. It's the only thing that makes it possible, love and –'

'Makes what possible? Sex? Take it from me, Bonnie, you can have smashing sex without love. Better sometimes.'

Now she reddened the way brides were supposed to, and bent her head and he laughed then, a sharp jeering little note that was very unlike him. 'Shouldn't I have said that? Do you mean to tell me that you're shy about talking about it? Hasn't the splendid Stanley initiated you yet into –'

'No!' she said fiercely. 'D'you think I could stand here dressed up like this if – if I hadn't the right to?'

He stared at her, and shook his head slowly. 'Honestly, Bonnie, you slay me. You're like something out of – I mean, how can someone like you be so damned conventional?'

'What do you mean, conventional? What about you? Who asked a girl to marry him instead of going on so hole in the corner, being so grubby, so messy? Who wanted to hold his head up with his wife beside him? Conventional!'

'You *did* listen, didn't you? he said after a moment, almost lightly. 'Didn't miss a word. Did you peep as well?'

'Don't be disgusting!'

'What's disgusting about it? It's only sex. Stupid sex. Almost as stupid as romantic love.'

'You're just being hateful!' She turned her head, looking for a mirror. 'My veil's slipping.'

'If I was a symbolist, I'd read a lot into that,' he said. 'Listen, I'm sorry, Bonnie. Put it down to emotion, will you? I've know you three as long as I can remember. You're all part of my life, and it's funny to be standing here pretending to be a father to you, waiting to prance down an aisle in a religious building I despise and hand you over to some bloke I don't like much and who doesn't like me. No, don't look like that. There's no reason why we should like each other. We're chalk and cheese. All I mean is – I really care a lot for you, funny old Bertha. Honestly,

196

I do. And seeing you all dolled up in that ridiculous gear –
really, it's so *silly*.'

'Stanley's mother bought it for me,' she said, looking down at
the stiff folds of lace-covered satin and the tulle trimming at the
hem. 'So I shouldn't disgrace them. It's no disgrace to be poor,
they all say, but they do all they can to hide it.' She smiled up at
him, a little lopsidedly. 'I do feel so odd. So silly. You're right.
It's all silly. Sammy, let's go away. Let's walk out of here and go
away and do –'

The door opened and a man in a dirty black cassock fussed in,
and at once it was all flurry and excitement and it was all happening. The months of planning, of sitting listening to Stanley's
mother and aunts talking about invitations and seating plans
and presents and clothes, the weeks of Stanley's complaints
about the workmen at the house and the price of carpets and
built-in furniture, the long afternoons spent trailing around curtain departments and china departments and dining-room-suite
departments, all of it culminated in a rush and bustle to push her
out of the little room and into the rain-streaked lobby outside,
on into the synagogue reeking of wilting gardenias and lilies of
the valley and furs out of mothballs and human sweat.

This isn't me, she thought, clinging to Sammy's arm. This isn't
me, as the rabbi muttered incomprehensible words at her. This
isn't me, as there was a tinkle of breaking glass and people
shouting, 'Mazeltov.' Oh God, who is this stupid person standing here with sweat running down between her breasts, under
tight lace-covered satin and a veil? Who the hell *is* it?

Her head was aching long before the reception was half over.
She concentrated on it, willing it to go away, and people jostled
her and shook her hand and told her she looked lovely, a real
vision of a bride, may all her years with the lovely Stanley be
happy ones, and she nodded back at them, willing her headache
to go away.

At last it went away and she began to liven up, feel better. It
was really rather marvellous to have all these people around
her, wishing her well. Marvellous to look as she did, for now
when she caught a glimpse of herself in the peach mirrors which
lined the ballroom she looked slim and yet curvy, really quite
pretty.

She looked round then for people she wanted to see, but

Hilda was dancing with all sorts of different people, looking incredible in crimson, with her hair a vivid blonde halo round her face, and Hester – Hester, Stanley said, had had to go early.

'She said she's got a programme to do,' he said, his lip curling a little. 'You were over the other side, talking to my father, and she said not to disturb you, she'd be in touch when we got back from Majorca. Frankly, I'd have thought for her own sister's wedding she could have made an effort, asked for the time off. Working, she said! On a Sunday afternoon?'

'They do, often,' she said, and looked round the crowded room again. People were dancing, talking, eating – the eating seemed never to stop – and she wondered where Sammy was in all that.

'The man she was with. Are they engaged?'

'Oh, Stanley, love, I don't know. Those television people – they're funny. They don't go in for engagements all that much.'

Stanley made a little face. 'Television people they may be, but she's your sister. How come a decent girl joins in on such behaviour?'

'I didn't say she did,' Bonnie said patiently. He was working up to one of his niggles about her family, and she really didn't want to have to deal with that. Not on her wedding day. 'I just said, they don't go in for engagements. And it takes two, doesn't it? Like it takes two to make a wedding.'

He smiled then, relaxing. 'Yes,' he said and slid his arm round her waist. 'It takes two.' His voice deepened, took on that vibrant note. 'When tonight comes, Bonnie – tonight – can you wait?'

She just smiled, and turned her head as an elderly man came up to claim with noisy jocularity his right to dance with the bride, and tried to ignore the sinking feeling Stanley's words had created in her. It was Sammy's fault, she thought angrily, as she smiled at the old man steering her around the dance floor with exaggerated Charleston-style steps which she almost had to skip to avoid. Talking like that about sex, he'd made it all seem grubby and horrible. It's his fault. I must find him and tell him I hate him.

But she couldn't find him, and when the last guests were leaving, and she was standing drooping a little with tiredness, shaking hands with them all, she asked Hilda, almost the last to go, where he was.

Hilda grinned and said airily, 'Oh, he left ages ago. Told me to say goodbye and that. He's going to the States, he said, next month. Did he tell you? Got some sort of grant to do a special course in Baltimore. Lucky bastard.'

She kissed her cheek, briefly, and looked up at Stanley, who was looking down at the deep plunging neckline of her dress with an expression that seemed compounded of equal parts of disapproval and lasciviousness. 'Take care of her, now, Stanley, me old friend, you hear me? Us sisters, we stick together, and if you treat her wrong, I'll be after you with a whip.'

'Promises, promises!' Stanley said, giving in to the lasciviousness and grinned, and Hilda reached up and kissed his cheek noisily.

'I'll see you when you get back, Stanley. Might be able to put another little bit of business your way, you never know! 'Bye Bonnie. See you –'

It's funny, Bonnie thought, parking the car at Brewer Street again. Twenty-two years. The last time I saw him was at my wedding, and now here he is turning up again in time for the divorce.

And she couldn't imagine where the idea had come from, because whoever had said anything about divorce? It was unthinkable. Yet she'd thought it.

20

It's getting sharper, Bonnie thought. They've been messing about till now, just like kids paddling at the edge of the beach, but now they're right out there, in the deep water. Mixed metaphors, she told herself then, and almost smiled. She was feeling different too; stronger, more aware of herself, better able to cope.

Cope with what? she thought as Jordan-Andrews got into his stride, opened out his questions to Hildegarde. With all the answers. The answers to the questions why. Mr Hermann was right. If you keep on asking why, eventually you get the true answers, and then you can handle yourself better.

All right then. Why do you feel so good this morning? That's easy. Because Sammy said he'd be here again. Because I haven't seen him for years and years, and now I'm seeing him again and I like it.

Why did you think about divorce this morning? You've never thought about it before. Haven't I? Maybe I have but didn't listen to myself thinking. She wanted to smile again, but shook her head a little, trying to clear it. The air was thick and muggy already and she ought to concentrate on what was going on.

'– at what point, Miss Maurice,' Jordan-Andrews was saying, 'did you realize that the programme you were watching had anything to do with you?'

'Not for quite a while. I was intrigued, of course, when they said they were doing an item on an international dress designer, and using actors – I mean, this was usually a documentary programme, not a drama one. Everyone knows that. So after it was announced, I watched.'

'Did you watch it alone?'

'No. My associate, Melvin Bremner, was dining with me. We watched it together.'

'Your associate?' Jordan-Andrews said smoothly, and Hildegarde swept her lashes down and then smiled at him, wide-eyed and ingenuous.

'Yes. We work together. But we've been friends too, for many years.'

There was a little snigger of laughter from the back of the court and the judge looked up, frowning. He looked soggy and tired, his eyes peering balefully from between pouches of pallid skin. The snigger whispered away to silence.

'So. You were dining together, a peaceful Sunday evening, watching television, no thought of – ah – trouble, not expecting any unpleasant experiences.'

'Not at all. I was expecting to see an interesting programme. And of course to see my sister. I am a great admirer of her work.'

'And then what happened?'

'Well, the programme began, and it was all so *odd*. Instead of the usual studio with big armchairs and the name of the programme up behind them – you know how it always looked – there was what was supposed to be a work room in a couturier's. All rather absurd, really. And then Hester – my sister – appeared and started this "Once Upon A Time" thing.'

'There was no attempt to convince viewers that what they were watching was a true account? They told it like a story? A children's story?'

'Yes. The names they used were story-like too. They called the couturier "Queen Stitch" and the designer "Little Slavegirl" and stupid things like that.'

'But you were in no doubt at any time that the characters as portrayed on the screen were supposed to be yourself and others with whom you were involved, and the events described were a thinly-veiled account of some actual happenings – as well as some that never occurred?'

'M'lord,' Mr Wooderson was on his feet, looking bored. 'My learned friend is leading the witness disgracefully –'

'We need no overblown adverbs, Mr Wooderson,' the judge said. 'The court is well able to observe what Mr Jordan-Andrews is doing. What do you say, Mr Jordan-Andrews? Surely Mr Wooderson is right?'

'M'lord. Perhaps I could deal with it this way then. Miss Maurice, will you please tell the court in your own words what you saw as the programme progressed?'

'I saw characters portrayed on the screen who seemed to be

supposed to be me and the people with whom I was involved,' Hildegarde said promptly. 'And the events described were a thinly-veiled account of some actual happenings as well as some that never happened.'

Again the whisper of laughter, and this time the judge said nothing but looked sharply at Hildegarde, and Bonnie thought, 'Silly, silly! That was clever, but silly. The jury didn't like it –'

It was extraordinary. This ought to matter to her, dreadfully. She ought to be cut to ribbons by it all, for wasn't it her sisters who were at loggerheads, wasn't her own husband involved in the whole sordid business? Wasn't it likely to lead to such an explosion that none of them would ever be able to talk to the others again? It all ought to matter, yet here she was, coolly assessing points as though it was a tennis match at Wimbledon. Oh, well played, sir. Oh, dear, bad shot, bad shot.

There was a movement along the bench on which she was sitting, and she looked up and there was Sammy, smiling a little lopsidedly at her and sliding along to sit next to her. The court was less crowded this morning. Maybe the rain had kept the gawpers away, and she was glad of it. She put out one hand, touched his sleeve, happy to feel the wetness against her fingers and bubbling inside with the sheer pleasure of seeing him. Mad, really, after all these years.

'We will go through in detail, Miss Maurice, the ah – the happenings that did *not* occur in reality. The matter complained of, in fact. But let us now establish one important fact. At what point did you think that you were being defamed – that you personally were being held up to opprobrium and disgust in this programme?'

'I must object.'

'I am with you, Mr Wooderson. Mr Jordan-Andrews, I feel you should be rather more careful.'

'M'lord. Miss Maurice, at what point did you realize that you were not – ah – watching only a child's story?'

'When I recognized the clothes.' Hildegarde's voice hardened and some of her insouciance fell away. She was beginning to be angry again, and it showed in the lift of her shoulders and the tilt of her head. '*My* clothes, on that programme. And supposed to have been designed by a character called Little Slavegirl and

202

stolen by Queen Stitch. That was when I knew what was going on.'

'Definitely your clothes?'

'I never forget what my own designs look like. It doesn't matter how old they are, they're mine, and I recognize them.' She gave a hard little laugh, and then said, 'I'd be more likely to forget the face of an old boy friend than to forget what my designs looked like.'

Silly, silly! Bonnie, watching the jury, wanted to shout it at her. That was very silly. Hildegarde seemed to realize it and recovered. 'I mean no disrespect to old friends when I say that. It's just that the things one has created, sweated over – they're part of you. Like your children. Unforgettable.'

'And there on the screen you saw your own designs?'

'I did. They had what was supposed to be a show – models parading. Very badly done it was. And every one of them wearing a Hildegarde suit, or a Hildegarde dress, and with Hildegarde accessories. If a TV set could transmit smells, then they'd probably have been wearing Hildegarde perfume as well –'

'Let us confine ourselves, Miss Maurice, to what you observed and what actually occurred, not to hypotheses. All the clothes were your designs?'

'Every one of them. And then I got confirmation.'

'Confirmation?'

'I have a friend – someone I've known for years. Works in the wardrobe department at City Television. He told me. Every one of the clothes used for the programme was a Hildegarde model. He'd had special instructions –'

'Please, Miss Maurice, you must stop,' Jordan-Andrews said hastily. 'There are rules about hearsay evidence which must be observed. We have already heard from other witnesses about this matter. There is no need for you to add to it. I wish you now simply to tell the court what you did then –'

NOVEMBER 1972

'Once I was climbing the garden wall
Slipped and had a terrible fall,
I fell so hard I heard bells ring,
But I kept a-hold of my ding-a-ling-a-ling ....'

'I don't *believe* it.' Mel said and sat there as she switched off the set and stood beside it staring down at the blank screen. 'I just don't bloody believe it!'

'Shut up,' Hildegarde said. 'I'm thinking.'

He sat and watched her standing there against the television set and staring down at it, and felt a sudden lift. To see Hildegarde set back on her heels – now, that wasn't something that happened often. To see her actually having to stand and think, and not come up with the fast answer, the immediate response, the quick way to make a profit out of every situation; boy, that really was something.

He leaned back on the sofa, luxuriously stretching out his bare legs under his kaftan. It might be one kind of pleasure to see Hildegarde in a dilemma, but it meant the loss of another kind. He'd not be getting anywhere with her tonight. A pity, because it had started out hopefully, finding her already wearing that wraparound thing that made her so available, the one Birgitta had made all those years ago, and pleased with the Greek food he'd brought. He'd changed his own clothes and then they'd sat in her huge living room in each corner of the big tweed-covered sofa, eating pitta and doner kebabs with their fingers and drinking her favourite bubbly, and she'd giggled and let him paddle around a bit under the wraparound for a while. It had looked hopeful and he felt good and randy. No risk that he'd have any trouble tonight. That episode was good and over. Wasn't it?

But then she'd insisted on watching the programme first and they'd both sat and laughed to start with. And then had become silent. The actress they had to play the Little Slavegirl – she'd been the first shock. Moon-faced and with a wig – it had to be a wig, because no one could look that much like Birgitta – the long yellow hair – and that awful Scandinavian accent. And then the one playing Queen Stitch, in incredible, outrageous clothes, an absurd collection, one on top of the other, waistcoats and skirts and shirts all higgledy-piggledy, but every one of them a Hildegarde.

And then Hester. Sitting there dressed up like a waitress in a *bierkeller*, all criss-cross tied black waistcoat over frilled white blouse and dirndl skirt, sitting there reading from a vast tome labelled *Stories of the Wicked World*, wide-eyed and innocent, reading out the story of Queen Stitch and the Little Slavegirl.

'– and because this is a story of the big wicked world, my little dears,' she'd said, closing the book and staring into camera with a lugubrious expression. 'Because it is really a true story and not a let's pretend, there isn't a happy ending. The poor Little Slavegirl didn't win happiness and wealth and the hand of the Handsome Prince while nasty Queen Stitch was felled, snicker snack. No, my dear little listeners, it was not so. For it was the Little Slavegirl who sank without trace, while Queen Stitch flourished and went on from strength to strength. So are the ways of the wicked, wicked world –'

Hildegarde moved now, came back to the sofa and sat down, still staring blankly at the television set and then she shook her head sharply and said loudly, 'Phone her, Mel. Phone her at the studio. Tell her you're on your own, that you've just seen the programme and that you know that when I find out about it, there's going to be one hell of an explosion. Got that? Then tell her –' she leaned forwards. 'Tell her like this –'

'You bastard,' Hester said, and her voice was very controlled. 'You lousy, stinking, hateful –'

'I've heard it all before,' JJ said, in high good humour. 'Forget it, there's a love.'

'Why didn't you tell me? To set me up like that – Christ, what did I do to deserve that sort of –'

'Oh, come off it! What did *you* do? When I think of some of the strokes you've pulled in your time, when I think of the way you've –'

'All right.' She was very tired now, could feel the ache creeping up her bones. 'All right. We'll forget the ancient history. Just tell me why you did it.'

'Okay. I'll tell you. I get this incredible story, right? I am told – and never mind how or who, because that's classified information – that Hildegarde Maurice who is making money and spending it like there's no tomorrow, is no designer. That every garment she brings out has been designed by other people who get bugger-all for their efforts. And that at the beginning the stuff that really got her noticed was designed by a girl called Birgitta Olaf. Are you with me?'

205

'I'm with you. But you're talking out of the back of your neck. She's always been terrific, Hilda has. When she was a kid she had an eye for colour and –'

'Spare me the touching reminiscences, already. Just listen. No, wait – tell me this first. Do you remember this Birgitta Olaf?'

'Of course I do! A great gloomp of a girl, used to moon around after Hilda – she'd have driven me clean out of my attic, but Hilda was good to her, gave her work. But her design? Not as long as she had an arse to sit on! She made an occasional dress for Hilda, but as a person she was too dull to breathe –'

'Not so dull, believe me. As I got the story. She was very very clever. Odd, but clever. Some of her ideas were way ahead of themselves. So way ahead no one'd look at 'em. Except Hildegarde Maurice, of course. Your little sister. Who took 'em, hung on to 'em and years later used 'em. Anyway that's the story as I got it, and I was interested. But I've got a problem, haven't I? There's you.'

'Oh yes – you've got yourself a problem, I promise you. You've got yourself one hell of a problem, because don't think I'm going to let you get away with what you've done here tonight –'

She stood up, and whirled about the office, her face white with fury. 'Christ, dressing me up like this, like some bloody refugee from *Children's Hour* –'

'Which you are, powder-puff doll!'

'– and then shoving me in front of a camera with that stinking script in my hand – who wrote it? It had to be you! Half literate, about as clever as a worm in a bag, great stuff, that'll get you an OBE, that will!'

He was still full of good humour, sleek and happy. He hadn't enjoyed a programme so much for years.

'Insults will get you just where they always have, my darling. Now you need 'em and they still aren't working! Poor little dear. Hurt your feelings, have I?'

'I'll tell you this much. You've done more than hurt Hilda's feelings. If she's seen this – well, even if she hasn't, someone else will have done, and they'll fill her in. And then God help you. I may be tough, JJ, but that one – she's going to eat you alive, you know that? She is going to mash you so small you won't know what hit you –'

'I'm shaking in my shoes! Anyway, sweetheart, even if she does – I'll have you by my side, won't you? In case you've forgotten, *you* were presenter on this one, not me. You were the one who sat there and told it like it was! Me, I was standing by, ready to take over with my item about the dockers and the strike, remember? You were in the hot seat –'

She was still now, standing there in her absurd costume and staring at him. 'I should have seen it,' she said at last. 'Never once, never ever, have I gone on without a rehearsal. Never. And I come back from that lousy no-good story about the National Theatre, and – how did you persuade Juniper to do it? He's not had an original thought for years, so you were the one who put it to him. So how did you persuade him?'

'Juniper does as he's told. He always has, he always will,' JJ said happily. 'I told him, it's your sort of story, and when he chuntered on about rehearsal I told him you'd be livid if you ever heard that he'd said you couldn't do a straight scripted item to camera without a rehearsal, you with all your experience! So –' He shrugged. 'That's how it happened.'

She could say no more. She just stood and stared at him again, but soundlessly this time. He'd set her up. He'd pushed a story through under her nose, without her knowing anything about it, arranged to have her sent out on another item, just so that when she came back this one could be shoved into her hands, and she would go on camera and not have a clue what was happening.

Oh, Christ, she thought. Did Hilda see it? Is there any chance she didn't? That none of them did, that she'll not know? Tonight's TV's as dead as mutton by Tuesday, maybe she won't know, maybe –

'No need to look so sour, ducks!' JJ got up, picked up his clipboard and stood smiling benignly down at her. 'So you've been clobbered, the way you've clobbered other people before now. You've been set up the way you set me up. This'll make up for the way you got yourself on to this programme in the first place. You're in the hard news medium now, little girl. No Powder-Puff Doll and Show Band Popsie rubbish here. It won't wash. Here, you've got to remember, if you can't stand the heat, stay out of the kitchen.'

'Can't you find any older clichés than that? Like the buck stops here? Or –'

'Oh, you can sneer, sweetheart! So, maybe I'm not the genius you are! Maybe I can't twist words and play games with meanings the way you do! I'm just a poor bloody journalist doing the best job he can – and when I uncovered that story about your sister, I knew what'd happen if I tried to run it with your knowledge. You'd have found some stinking dirty trick to get the story killed. Wouldn't you? Of course you would. So, me, I settle down to finding a nice dirty trick of my own and wait for the right time to use it. I waited a long time but it was worth it. And the longer I waited, the more I fancied getting you in the line of fire when the shit hit the fan. And you've got to admit, sweetheart, did I ever do it. Did I ever!'

'You're a fool,' she said curtly. 'You've taken on someone you don't know the first thing about. She'll have the balls off you.'

'No dear. *You*. You're the one who presented the item, remember?'

'Yes, and you, you poor half wit, *wrote* it. Remember that! And when her legal types come sniffing round – which they will, JJ which they will! – they'll find out. I may be in the line of fire, but you're right there beside me, buddies to the end.'

'Oh, come off it.' He was at the door now. 'There's no way she's going to get legal with you. Her own sister? How can she? Admit it. I've got my story out, and you're the one who helped. This is the first time you've been dropped in it – and it was high time. Now go home, get your rage off your chest, and next week we'll start again, with a better relationship, I trust, dear one. A better working relationship which is one compounded of respect between equals, rather than petticoat dominance by a queen bitch! Take your punishment like a man, little one. You're always saying you work and think like one. Now behave like one. Be a gent!'

And he went, slamming the door behind him.

21

'We will now go through, Miss Maurice, some of the episodes depicted on this programme, which bore no relationship at all to truth, especially those involving Miss Birgitta Olaf –'

'My Lord, I must object yet again.' Mr Wooderson sounded theatrically weary now, and Jordan-Andrews shot him an acid glance and then looked appealingly at the judge.

'M'lord! I really must ask to be allowed to present my client's case! These constant interruptions on the most minor points –'

'Not minor, as I'm sure your lordship will agree,' Wooderson said, making great play with his gown as he rose. '*Far* from minor when such leading questions are constantly being put to witnesses –'

Sammy stirred uneasily beside Bonnie and she looked at him enquiringly. He made a little face.

'Are you all right?' she whispered.

'A bit low on air, I think. Feeling a bit off. I'll be back.'

He slid along the seat and went out of court and she watched him go, her forehead creased, as Wooderson's and Jordan-Andrews's voices rolled heavily over her. She turned her head again to look down the court, trying to concentrate; they'd reached an important part of the trial, a desperately important part and she ought to be alert. She'd felt herself stiffen as soon as Birgitta's name had been mentioned, but now her anxiety had shifted, was focussing on Sammy somewhere outside.

Hildegarde was standing there in the witness box, looking rather amused as she stared down on the two counsel still arguing tediously over an abstruse point of law, and for a moment Bonnie felt her own gorge rise. How dare she look amused? Angry, yes, worried, yes, but amused? Don't look like that, she wanted to shout at her. This isn't bloody funny! It's dreadful, absolutely dreadful, and they're going to dig over that poor creature's past and yours and it's nothing to laugh at. And Sammy's feeling it too. That's why he couldn't stay here and watch you.

How she knew that she did not know, but the knowledge was there. It wasn't lack of air that had sent Sammy out to the echoing terrazzo halls outside. It was the weight of memory.

She gathered all her energy into her legs, and stood up, smiling apologetically at the people she passed, and slipped out. The corridor outside was dim and for a moment she had to peer to see anything, and then she saw him, sitting on one of the stone benches, leaning back with his head against the wall and his eyes closed, and she went over to him and sat down quietly and put her hand over his.

He opened his eyes and looked at her and smiled. 'Hello.'

'Hello.'

'You feeling queasy too? Did you have breakfast?'

'Yes. Did you?'

'No.'

'We'll go and have some coffee now then.'

'You'll miss what's going on.'

'To hell with what's going on,' she said sharply and had to consciously control her voice to keep it from shaking. 'All this bloody stuff – I'm sick of it.'

'That sounds very positive. For you.'

She looked at him and frowned a little. 'How do you mean?'

'As I remember you, you were always the quiet one. The peace-keeper. Always had a placatory note in your voice. Whenever you said anything you had your mental hands folded supplicatingly. Prayerful Bonnie. And yesterday –'

'Yesterday?' she said after a moment. 'What about yesterday?'

'I was going to say you sounded the same. And you did all day. And when Stanley came. But last night you didn't. More like just now. Positive.'

'I'm learning,' she said and let go of his hand, suddenly awkward. 'It takes time to get the learning done, though.'

'Yes.'

He closed his eyes again and then after a moment took a deep breath. 'Come on. We'll go back. I'm all right. It was rather self-indulgent of me to come out at all. It wasn't anything physical, you know.'

'I know.'

'How can you? You weren't there, were you? In Paris? Of

course you weren't. There was only me. Apart from them, of course. So how can you know? Hildegarde isn't exactly the sort of girl to let down her back hair and have a heart to heart with her nice big sister, is she?'

'No,' Bonnie said. 'But I knew. Not all of it, of course. But I knew.'

'Did you know I was there?'

'No, I didn't know that. But that it was all – awful. That I know. Even peace-keepers have eyes and ears. And they think sometimes, too,' she finished with a little flash of malice and he smiled at her and took her hand and tucked it into the crook of his elbow.

'Well, whatever you knew, or thought you knew, come back into court. It won't be very agreeable, but hearing it'll be better than sitting out here imagining it.'

Hildegarde was talking when they went back in. She was standing with her hands resting lightly on the edge of the wit- ness box and talking easily and calmly about what had hap- pened that October, seven and a half years ago.

OCTOBER 1970

'What do you get when you fall in love
You only get lies and pain and sorrow . . . .'

'But why should they come?' Mel said again, and looked gloom- ily at the make-shift rails stretching round the room, at the heaps of clothes still piled on the bed, at the dressing table and its piles of order forms.

'Listen, have I been wrong yet?'

'Not that you've ever told me.'

'Very clever. You know bloody well what I mean. Whether I've told you what I'm doing or not, have the books ever shown that I've been wrong?'

'There's always a first time. And this is going to be it. Why couldn't you have done it properly? There's our own show rooms, our own –'

'Whose show rooms?' Hildegarde said, and there was a dangerous note in her voice.

'All right – *your* own show rooms, *your* own models. You could do it properly. Make a good job of it. Though why you

211

want to get involved in *prêt-à-porter* is beyond me. You're making a marvellous living as you are, marvellous! You're on top of the couture tree in London, you've got a list of clients everyone envies you and –'

She stopped hanging clothes and turned and looked at him, her hands clasped in front of her. She was feeling good; it showed in the way her eyes glittered, the bounce of her hair, the way her skirts curled around her as she moved and he looked back at her and said it before stopping to think.

'Honestly, Hil, can't you stop, just for a minute and see sense? What've you got to go on flogging yourself stupid for? What more do you want that you haven't got? That fantastic flat, the cars, the clothes, you've got some marvellous gear, marvellous, what *more* do you want out of it that you haven't got? Let it go already – let it run itself, marry me, we'll settle down, we can run the place with our eyes shut, go on as comfortable as you like –'

She stood and stared at him and he stared back, beginning to feel better. He hadn't meant to say it; he never did, but every so often it came out of him like an explosion, his need for her, to have her marked as his, all his. Sometimes she laughed at him, sometimes she swore at him and told him to shut up, but this time she was just staring at him. He stared hopefully back.

'You know, Mel, you're a real disappointment to me,' she said at last. 'I thought you were a man going places, you know that? When I first met you, I thought, here's a guy who knows where it's at. Here's someone who's as hungry as I am. And look what you've turned out to be! As easy to satisfy as a cat with a bowl of milk, you are. You've got about as much spark in you as Bonnie has! All you can think of when it gets hot, when it gets interesting, is some lousy little suburban house full of shrieking kids and the stink of cooking. Christ, but you're a disappointment to me!'

'So what do you think you are to me, for God's sake? I think I've got someone who's a woman and she turns out to be some sort of she-wolf. Kids and you? Any child you had you'd eat alive. You look like a woman, but Christ, you're –'

'Go on, ducks, insult me!' She turned back to the rails again, began hanging the clothes with meticulous care. 'Say I'm like a man – go on, insult me!'

212

'There're men who'd be ashamed to be as hard as you are.' Now he sounded merely petulant and she laughed, still working with the clothes, tweaking, arranging, selecting colours with her eyes a little narrowed.

'No they wouldn't. There's not a man anywhere who wouldn't admire the sort of man I am, wouldn't want to be like me. I know what I want, I go out and get it and when I've got it, I enjoy it. Until I don't want it any more and then I get rid of it and start again. That's what every last one of you would like to be, and you know it, poor damp little Mel! And shall I tell you something else? The reason you're still hanging round me, the reason you're here right now is because I'm the sort of man you'll never be! And sexy with it. Poor little Mel!'

He sat in sulky silence for a while. They'd been through it so often, her jeers, his anger; there was no sense in taking it any further. Because she was right; he was fascinated by her, by the drive in her, the push she had.

He'd had it once, been eaten with it, but he'd lost it with her. There were times when it sparked again, flared red in his sky, even made good things happen – he thought of the time, all those years ago when he'd raised their first big finance, and grinned inside his head – but they were getting fewer and fewer.

'That'll do it,' she said at length. 'That'll get 'em!' She stood back and looked round the room, and then went over to the window sill and picked up the vase of roses he'd brought her. 'Get rid of these, will you?'

He stared. 'Get rid of them? Why?'

'Because they look too fancy, that's why,' she said impatiently. 'Oh, Christ, have I got to spell it out? Listen –'

She stood there with the vase in her hand, the red delicacy of the hot-house roses looking incongruous against the harsh black she was wearing.

'Listen, and get it right, because I shan't tell you again. I want to open out from the bespoke to the ready-to-wear – but *big*. I'm sick of making individual garments for stupid women with more money than sense, ugly women who can't wear clothes however fabulous they are. I'm going *big* – and that means ready-to-wear. But I'm going to do very expensive ready-to-wear. The very top of the trade. No rubbish, none anywhere. One of my dresses'll retail at hundreds of pounds off the peg. In the States, they'll cost more dollars than most men like you earn in a week. Top stuff. And the people who want that sort of stuff are here in Paris, right now, looking at St Laurent and Courreges and Balmain and the rest of them. They're here as much to rip them off as anything else – they'll get cheap copies made of the stuff they see, and flog it hard. So I'm going to give them something better to rip off. They've been asked here, special appointments, and they'll come –'

'Who? The press? The manufacturers, the –'

'No, you fool, the *buyers*. The big ones. Neimann Marcus, Saks, Harrods – the big ones. I found out who was here, where they are, and they've all had a quiet tip-off that there's some great stuff lying around in a tatty tourist hotel – not Georges Cinq, but a dismal two-star nothing place off the Place Clichy – and they'll come. They've had the big boys up to *here* – the salons, the fancy-schmancy music, the razzledazzle. They'll come here, you'll see, and they'll find me, simple little expensive me, in a crowded hotel room, with rails of fantastic, incredible, fabulous stuff. And they'll buy. I'll tell them the prices and they won't turn a hair – they'll be queueing to buy. Just you watch me. Just you *watch* me.'

Her head was up and her eyes glittered so ridiculously that he wanted to laugh. She looked like a child waiting for Christmas, desperate with anticipation and absurdly touching, and he felt the bewilderment spin in his head and tried to hold on to practicalities.

'And who's making this stuff you're selling? Neimann Marcus you say? Can you meet the sort of orders they can place when they get going? Harrods you can supply, I suppose – one store, it's not so difficult. But if you're after the big American fish, you've got a lot of grafting to do.'

'It's done,' she said contemptuously. 'When did I ever do anything that wasn't properly planned? I've got 'em set up everywhere. There's three out-workers in Ireland, all set. Working already on some stuff. The stuff I know they'll buy. I've got a place going down in Camberwell, that Greek, you remember her? Stella Arionopolis – she wanted money to start her own place? Well, she's working for me now. Oh, believe me, it's all going. I'm ready to hit 'em so hard they won't even feel it and they'll love me for it –'

He shook his head. 'How? In Christ's name, how did you get all this set up without me knowing? I do the books, I handle the tax, the money –'

'You?' She looked at him and grinned, and then carried the roses to the bathroom, and put them on the floor in the corner. 'Listen,' she said over her shoulder, 'You're so easy to hide things from it's boring. I set up the money for this myself. It's all *mine*. Every bit of it. No rake off for you or anyone. Not even the taxman.'

She came back into the room laughing, bright eyed again. 'I've got the tax side so organized they won't get so much as tuppence ha'penny out of this little lot. It's all mine –'

He shook his head, still staring at her. 'And what'll you do with it? You're loaded already. Remember me? I do the books – I know what you've got already. Why more?'

She grinned again. 'Poor little Mel!' she said. 'You really are poor little Mel, aren't you? If I have to tell you why, ducks, you couldn't even begin to understand. Now get going, will you? This lot I handle on my own.'

She was right, of course. As she said herself, she always was. He met her that evening in the bar of the hotel where they were sleeping – much less tatty than the one she'd chosen for her sale room – waiting for half an hour after the time she'd said she'd be there. And then she arrived looking as sleek and self-satisfied as he'd ever seen her, and as she moved through the foyer towards him he felt it again, that twist of need for her. But there was no way he was going to let her know of it. Not him. Not this time, anyway.

'Oh, Mel,' she breathed, looking up at him with her eyes wide, and across the foyer a middle-aged woman looked at them benevolently and he wanted to shout at her, This is money, lady! It's only ever money that makes her look like this. Never men, never me – 'Mel, you never saw anything like it! I had 'em fighting, I swear it! Look –'

She pulled a small writing-pad from her bag and thrust it into his hands, and he looked at her and then at the pad, and opened it. Page after page of figures, model numbers, sizes, colourways, prices – the totals were incredible. He'd never seen an order book like it.

'They're all sure?' he said after a moment, awestruck. 'No welchers?'

'This lot?' she crowed. 'Welchers? Look!' and she dived into her bag again and this time it was a billfold she showed him, and he riffled through the cheques in it, his face rigid as he tried to count up the amounts in his head.

'I told 'em. No deposits, no orders.'

'And they – but they couldn't have – I mean, God, in *this* business? Deposits? You must be mad to even think they'd ever –'

He looked down at the billfold again, stupefied, and she laughed, a long ripple of laughter that made the middle-aged woman look up again, and then she leaned over and kissed him, throwing her arms round his neck with the abandonment of a schoolgirl.

'But they did, didn't they? There's money there, Mel, my darling, real hard money, and it's all mine. Every bloody penny of it. Every last bloody penny – come on! We're going out, we're celebrating, we're living tonight! And tomorrow, I'm starting again! There's more where this came from. They're clamouring for my stuff, you know that? They're going mad for it –'

That night they made love, one of the rare times when she actually seemed to enjoy it, rolling around on the bed and dragging him breathlessly with her until his head spun and he was so exhausted he didn't know how he kept his eyes open; for she seemed insatiable. It was as though all the hunger that filled her, the need in her that he was always aware of in their business dealings had converted itself to a physical lust, and concentrated itself deep inside her body. She almost ate him alive, and it frightened him and invigorated him and sickened him and then exalted him until they both fell asleep in a welter of blankets, tangled together like kittens in a basket.

When he woke she was gone, and he extricated himself from the mess of the bed and went blearily to the bathroom.

She'd left a note for him.

'Don't come near me all day,' it said curtly. 'I've got money to make, and I'll do it better alone. See you here tonight.'

The day seemed to stretch ahead interminably. He showered and shaved, ate breakfast and wandered off on a desultory

216

round of the tourist spots, feeling thick and depressed. It was as though he were her dog, a puppy dog she alternately petted and ignored, and when he was being ignored he fretted, was lonely, even pined. A hateful feeling. The Tour d'Eiffel and the Arc de Triomphe stared bleakly back at him, shrouded in his own misery.

So hateful that when he saw her walking composedly along the Faubourg St Honoré he shouted and waved, as pleased to see her as if she'd been his oldest and most beloved friend.

'Birgitta!' he bawled. 'Birgitta!'

People turned and looked at him as he waved and shouted again, but she seemed not to hear him and he dodged out into the traffic to a cacophony of horns and screams from the cab drivers to the other side of the road and seized her elbow, breathless and beaming.

'Birgitta! What in hell are you doing here? Hildegarde didn't say you were coming! I thought you were staying in Oslo for good. What are you doing here in Paris of all places?'

She looked at him owlishly, apparently unsurprised to see him. Time hadn't changed her much. She was still dumpy, moon-faced, hiding her inexpressive eyes behind the sheets of sleek yellow hair.

'I am here to see Hilda,' she said, and looked round to his other side. 'She is here with you, yes?'

'Yes – I mean no. I mean, we're here together for the shows but today she's – she's busy. It's good to see you! Have you had lunch? Come on, I'll take you to the Crillon, we'll live a little.'

'Thank you. No. I wish to see Hildegarde,' she said, and her sing-song accent began to grate on him as it always did. 'Where is she, please?'

'I told you – busy today. You'll have to wait. Like the rest of us.'

'I have come from Oslo especially.'

'I know, Birgitta. Christ, I heard you! But she's *busy*, and you ought to know better than any of us that you see our Hildegarde when she's good and ready and no other time. So come and eat lunch and tell me what's so urgent!'

Unwillingly, she came, and he took a perverse pleasure in choosing the most expensive place he could, the most expensive food. But she sat and looked dully at the *escargots* the waiter put in front of her, and shook her head when he tried to urge her to eat them, showing her how to hold the snail shells. He was pressing, but she just shook her head dumbly.

He let her be and ate greedily himself, mopping up the garlicky butter with his bread, chewing noisily, and she sat and watched him and seemed not to hear his talk about the crowds in Paris for the big shows, the way they'd had trouble getting on a flight, the extra payola he'd had to find to get them into a hotel, let alone the extra room she'd wanted for business –'

She seemed to wake up then. 'An extra room? For business? Why is this?'

He shrugged, circumspect suddenly, looking at her over his napkin as he wiped his mouth. 'Hildegarde business,' he said lightly. 'You know what she is. Does it her way, tells afterwards.'

'I have been in Oslo alone for over a year now,' she said suddenly. 'I am making the knitwear, buying it, shipping it over to her. Over a year.'

'I know,' he said and leaned over and patted her shoulder. 'You've been doing marvellously too – marvellously. Your figures go up every month. Great work.'

'I am tired of being alone in Oslo. I wish to see my Hildegarde.'

It was as though she were not aware of him. She stared at him, her round blue eyes opaque and only just visible behind that ubiquitous hair, and her face remained clear of any expression.

'I need to see my Hildegarde and I telephone and they say she cannot speak, she will call back. She never calls back. For three months she never calls back. I am anxious. So I go to London and they say she is here.'

He looked at her, frowning. 'D'you mean you just took off and went to London? And then came here? Just like that? She'll go mad –'

'I am mad. I am very mad,' she said dully, and there was no humour in the contrast between her voice and the words, but there was a very real menace and he looked at her, his gaze tight and watchful.

'Mad at Hildegarde?' he said, after a moment.

'Yes. She says to me when she sends me to Oslo, every month she will come to me or I to her. I am to stay in Oslo for the

218

business but every month we meet. And it is over a year. I wait no more. I am mad. I must see my Hildegarde. You will tell me where she is.'

'Where were you going when I saw you?' he said after a moment. 'You can't tell me they told you in London where she was. They couldn't have. They don't know.'

'No, they did not tell me.' She looked down at her plate where the waiter had set an omelette and she suddenly began to eat it, with great gulping bites, seeming not to taste it. 'I am going to the big houses – Courrèges, St Laurent. They will know if she has appointments there. They will tell me.'

He shook his head, half in exasperation, half in amusement. 'You're a goer, I'll give you that.'

'A goer?' Her mouth was full, and he looked away. She had never had any of the social graces.

'You know what you want and go for it. Like Hildegarde.'

She shook her head. 'No, I am not like Hildegarde. But she is mine and I want her and I am mad. A year is too much. Too much. Where is she?'

He looked at her and slowly his lips curled. Hildegarde with her jeers and her notes in bathrooms. Hildegarde in her tatty hotel room selling God knows what to the big buyers, getting them to put their money where their mouths were. Hildegarde looking over her shoulder, seeing the door open, seeing Birgitta there. A delicious thought.

'I'll take you,' he said loudly. 'I'll take you to her. Have some pudding first. You'll enjoy it. A *crème caramel*?'

22

The court room smelled disagreeably of wet cloth and hot radiators, and Mel shifted awkwardly in his seat. His behind was numb, almost as numb as his feelings. He cared more about such physical sensations than about anything else that was going on, even though he knew in a cool academic way that there could be trouble for him in what might come out. He was almost ashamed of caring so little, but there it was; his numb behind mattered most of all right now.

Until he turned his head and saw him. There had been a little flurry at the door and at once he'd turned to look, to give himself something to do, and there he was, that bloody doctor looking much the same as he had the night he'd arrived in that sleazy hotel room. Rumpled and sardonic, he'd stood there and stared round and just said, 'Well? I'm here.'

OCTOBER 1970

'I'm on your side . . .
When time goes by
And friends just can't be found . . .
Like a bridge over troubled water,
I will lay me down . . . .'

He'd been buoyed up with his own devilment all the way from the Crillon to the hotel – and they'd walked all the way through the pushing crowds and over the traffic-shrieking roads – until he reached the door and then, as he pushed against the stained glass to let Birgitta walk stolidly in ahead of him, his mood had plunged. It was as though the wine and the food that had bubbled him along so joyously had evaporated, gone twisting away like a wreath of grey smoke, and he felt sick and empty.

'No – Birgitta,' he said urgently. 'I must be mad. You know what'll happen – I must have been mad to even think of it –'

But she just looked at him round the edge of her hair and went up to the desk and the fat man behind it.

220

'*Mademoiselle Maurice, s'il vous plaît,*' she said and Mel wanted to laugh at the thick accent and careful enunciation, but the fat man just grunted, '*Vingt deux,*' and jerked his head towards the staircase, and she turned and went across the little foyer, her heels clacking against the cracked tiles of the floor.

He went after her, and as they reached the first turn of the stairs, took hold of the iron balustrade in front of her, trying to stop her going any further.

Someone was coming down and they both looked up as a man in tight pale-blue trousers and a white cashmere sweater, bedecked with silver chains, went by on a wave of Canoe after-shave, and Birgitta frowned and pushed Mel's hand away with a sharp twist of her wrist that made him yelp. The man in the blue trousers looked back over his shoulder at them and made a face expressive of disdain, and Mel felt his own face harden with embarrassment.

She went on, climbing lumpishly and as expressionless as ever and he went after her. Maybe he could still stop her? 'Birgitta,' he said again, but she ignored him.

The door to room twenty-two was half open, and he could see Hildegarde standing by one of the dress rails, her head down over a writing-pad she was holding in her hand, and once more his belly contracted with sickness. This time it stayed that way. He felt dreadful.

Birgitta stood in the doorway and stared at Hildegarde, and he looked at her too over Birgitta's shoulder and she looked up, her face smooth. There was not a flicker of emotion as she saw them.

'Well, well. Birgitta,' she said after a moment and bent her head again to her writing pad. 'Imagine seeing you here. Mel, I told you, I'll see you tonight. Get the hell out.'

'She insisted,' he said, and pushed Birgitta ahead of him into the room, closing the door behind him. That glance of disdain the man in the cashmere sweater had thrown at him still hung in the air, and he felt a deep need to shut all three of them away from staring eyes. 'I bumped into her, maddest thing ever, there she was, Faubourg St Honoré, large as life, twice as natural. Looking for you. All the way from Oslo –'

'Be quiet, will you?' Hildegarde said, and her voice was bored. 'You're rabbitting on like some half-witted old woman.'

'Yes,' Birgitta said unexpectedly. 'Be quiet. Go away. We do not need you.'

'Bugger that for a lark!' he said and at last a new feeling began to fill him, making him feel better. Anger, and masculinity. He lifted his chin, tugged his tie for a moment. 'Jesus, who the hell do you two think you are? Do this, do that – I'm not your bloody lapdog, either of you, so if you don't like my company you can fuck off some place else. I'm staying here.' He thumped down on to the bed and glared at them but they ignored him. Birgitta was staring at Hildegarde.

'You said every month, in Oslo, or in London,' she said. 'Every month. It is one year and never once. I am mad. I am very mad.'

'You're mad to come here, that's for certain,' Hildegarde said coolly. 'This is business, work, money. Not the place for one of your over-heated scenes. Do me a favour, Birgitta. Go home, go to London if you like and wait there. I'll be back by Friday, Saturday maybe. Then you can make scenes as much as you like. I'll explain it all, make it better. There's reasons.' She smiled suddenly, a bewitching little girl smile, her head on one side. 'I always do, don't I? Make it better?'

'I am very angry,' Birgitta said woodenly and Mel looked at her, seeking for evidence of her rage, but she stood there with her bag held neatly in both hands, her feet rather too far apart and her hair hanging dully on each side of her face. Angry? Would she know what it felt like?

Hildegarde shrugged and turned away, beginning to riffle along the lines of garments on the rail behind her. 'So you're angry. Hard luck. Me, I'm busy. That's my problem. Do me a favour and go away. Go where the hell you like – it's no skin off my nose. You want to make a scene? Okay, I'll play your scene game, but when I'm ready. In London, on Friday or Saturday. But not now. I've got work to do. A lot of work.'

Birgitta said nothing. She was standing even more still, if that were possible, and Mel looked at her and felt a little ripple of fear. Her face was still blank but now her whole body seemed filled with menace.

Hildegarde seemed to feel it too because she looked back over her shoulder at Birgitta and then, following the line of her stare, at the clothes on the rail in front of her.

As though it had been shouted aloud, Mel knew she'd made an error, as big an error as she'd ever made. And she was aware of it, too.

She turned then, moving forwards towards Birgitta, her hands held out, but Birgitta ignored the gesture, pushing past her to the rail, dropping her bag on the floor and taking off one of the hangers.

She stood there and stared down at it, and so did Mel and Hildegarde, all three of them silent, listening to the sound of traffic from the street two floors below and an incomprehensible shouting of voices coming from somewhere along the corridor outside.

They all stared at the clothes on the hanger. A pair of widely-cut culottes in thick white suede. A waistcoat in the same white, but with a crimson leather flash across one breast. A crimson leather jacket with huge sleeves lined in the white suede. And dangling from the hook by their laces, crimson boots with deep-cut white suede cuffs.

'I make this design in 1961,' Birgitta said, and her voice sounded almost conversational. 'I remember. It is the year we have a holiday in Rapallo.'

'Not at all,' Hildegarde said lightly. 'In sixty-one? Darling, you must be mad! Nine years ago? Who'd have thought of such a thing then?'

'I did,' said Birgitta and dropped the hanger, letting it go as casually as though it were a piece of dirt and she reached for another. A dress in chiffon, creamy white, its hem dropping at different levels, sleeves a cascade of frills. '1956,' she said, 'when I make your sister's wedding dress,' and dropped that too.

There was a short silence, and then Hildegarde laughed and went over to the bed where Mel was still sitting and with a jerk of her head made him move over.

She sat down, leaned back on her elbows and stared up at Birgitta, smiling.

'So. You've seen a couple of things that are a bit similar to ideas you had umpteen years ago. So what? There's no patent in ideas. None at all.'

'There are others here,' Birgitta was flicking hangers along the rails, and they clicked the way her heels had done on the

223

tiled floor of the foyer, and Mel watched her, his hands lying relaxed on his lap.

'You're getting positively paranoid,' Hildegarde said lightly, 'and boring. I've told you – go away.'

Hildegarde turned and looked at her, and blinked rapidly a few times, as though she were trying to rid her eyes of flecks of dust.

'Is this why you do not come to Oslo, do not let me come to London?'

'Oh, stop going on so, Gitta! It's bloody boring, I told you – *boring*. Who needs it?'

'You are taking from me the designs I make all those years ago. All these, the best of these, they are mine. You told me when I did them I am mad, that they are ugly clothes, that no one will ever wear. You tell me they are rubbish, and I say I throw them away and you say you keep them for sentiment.' She laughed then, and Mel thought, I've never heard her laugh before. 'For sentiment, you said.'

'Oh, shut up, Gitta! I told you –'

'I tell you something, Hildegarde. I tell you now. If you had said to me, ever, I love you, Gitta, I love you very much, give me the designs, I give them to you. You know that?'

Hildegarde said nothing, her eyes holding their gaze on Birgitta's face.

'If you say to me now, Gitta, I love you, I want these designs should be mine, you can have them.'

Mel looked at Hildegarde sitting there so still beside him, leaning back on her elbows, and she turned her head and looked at him, her eyebrows a little raised.

'Aren't you getting hot under the collar yet? Or are you going to stay and watch the whole thing? Getting a kick out of it, are you?'

He shook his head and looked again at Birgitta, who was now standing beside the little dressing-table, staring down at the clutter of make-up and needles and thread and scissors and scarves and oddments of jewellery.

'If you say to me now, Hildegarde, I love you, then they are yours.' She did not look up.

'So, I love you, I love you, I love you! Big deal! What good is that to you? D'you believe me? Anyone who ever believes me

224

when they're talking about love has got to be out of their tiny minds. Love! It's a load of shit. You hear me? A load of very old shit.'

She got up and went over to the rails and bent to pick up the clothes and Birgitta said loudly, 'Leave them there!'

Hildegarde looked up at her, and then shrugged and crouched and began to put the chiffon dress back on its hanger.

'If you do not leave them there, I kill myself. Right now. Right here,' Birgitta said and Mel, his eyes on Hildegarde, grinned. It was so funny, straight out of one of those awful foreign films at the Cameo Poly they used to go to with Hester sometimes. He tried to catch Hildegarde's eye, to share the joke with her, but she was still fiddling with the clothes.

'You hear me?' Birgitta said.

'I heard you.'

'You do not care?'

Hildegarde looked up then, still crouching beside her clothes, and Birgitta, her hands held tightly across her chest, blinked again.

'You're a fool, Birgitta. You eat yourself up with loving and caring and all the rest of it, go through Christ knows what hell and then get even more miserable because I don't do the same. And you're supposed to love me! You're supposed to want only the best for me, to see me happy! That's what love's supposed to be for. You said that often enough! And now, because I don't get screwed up the way you do, you're more miserable than ever. Honestly, you're like a cheap film.'

She did see the joke, Mel thought. She did see it.

'You do not love me,' and now Birgitta's voice was flat and dull again.

'I don't love anyone. I don't believe in it. It's against my religion,' Hildegarde said, and though her tone was flippant there was a contempt deep in her voice that made Mel feel cold again.

'You do not love me,' Birgitta said, and she moved slightly so that Mel turned his head to look at her. She was standing with a pair of big scissors held in her hands, looking down on them, and Mel thought, stupid, such a stupid bad film.

'Don't be daft,' Hildegarde said sharply and without looking at her Mel knew that she was watching Birgitta too.

225

Birgitta moved slowly, almost casually, lifting the scissors with both hands, holding the points over her belly, just where her white blouse met her dull grey skirt and then as easily and as offhandedly as though she were slicing a loaf of bread she brought them down, and the points slid forwards and inwards and he stared, puzzled and interested, until he saw the blood come moving up along the shaft of the blades, outwards, spreading slowly across the white blouse.

He looked at her face then, and her eyes were wide and for the first time in all the years he had known her there was an expression there, a recognizable change on the flat features. She looked surprised and irritable, as though someone had interrupted her when she was busy and she opened her mouth as though to speak. But she didn't speak; she seemed only to hiccup a few times, and then she opened her mouth wider and it was full of blood, and then Mel was sick, horribly sick, sitting there on the bed with his hands on his knees and staring at Birgitta leaning against the dressing-table with her mouth full of blood.

It was Hildegarde's fury that brought him back. She hit him, her hand stinging his wet face to awareness, and he got to his feet, clumsily trying to clean himself with the counterpane, pulling it from the bed awkwardly, and she pushed him aside and went to Birgitta and took her by the shoulders and propelled her towards the bed, making her walk. And Birgitta walked, her eyes wide and very blue in her pallid face, and blood trickling down her chin.

He was shaking now, feeling cold and empty and horribly tired, wanting desperately to lie down somewhere and go to sleep. But she wouldn't let him. She grunted words at him, pushed him, kicked him once, and he did as she told him, dazed and silent.

And then at last Birgitta was in the bed, and her clothes were off, and he couldn't remember who had done that for her, and he was in the bathroom washing himself, scrubbing his bare chest furiously to get rid of the reek and the mess.

'What shall we do? What shall we do? What shall we do?' The sound of his own voice surprised him, and he looked at Hildegarde who was standing beside the bed looking down at Birgitta. 'Hildie – Hil, what are we going to do?'

'Shut up. I'm thinking,' she said, not turning her head.

'We'd better get a doctor. Get the police, get someone –' he was babbling, and he was suddenly ashamed and turned back to the basin in the bathroom and began to wash his shirt, rinsing it carefully under the running water.

'Not the police,' she said, and came into the bathroom. 'She's alive. Not the police. And God help you if you say a word to anyone, you hear me? I'll kill you myself, and I'll make a bloody sight better job of it than she did –' She looked back over her shoulder at the figure on the bed, surrounded by rails of dresses and coats and trousers, their colours filling the room with a soft radiance. 'Though at least she waited till the last appointment had gone. That's something – put your shirt on.'

'It's wet.'

'So, it's wet. You won't die or melt though you're soft enough – put it on.'

He did, shivering again as the cold wet poplin crawled against his skin.

'A doctor,' he said then, buttoning the shirt with shaking fingers. 'I'll call the concierge and ask for a doctor.'

'You'll do no such thing. I told you, keep quiet about this. We've got to keep it quiet.'

His teeth were chattering now. 'K-k-keep it quiet? How the hell do we do that – that? She's got to have a doctor, right away, she probably needs an operation. What do you mean, keep it quiet? I'm ringing right now, the concierge, right now –'

'No!'

He stood still, looking at her. 'Then what do we do?' He knew he sounded stupid and helpless and didn't care. 'She's got to have a doctor.'

'She'll have one,' she said, and went back to the bed and leaned over Birgitta and looked closely at her face. She was lying with her eyes half open, and as Hildegarde leaned over her the lids lifted and she looked up and grimaced and said something in a hoarse voice.

'What was that?'

'I don't know. Since when did I speak Norwegian? Anyway, she's alive – the stupid –' and then she reached forwards and took her by the shoulders and lifted her and shook her, so that the yellow hair swung backwards and forwards.

227

'You stupid, stupid cow – what did you have to do that for? Did I ever do anything to make you do that to me? You bitch, you stinking –'

Mel could do nothing. He stood and watched, feeling his shirt wet on his chest, and Hildegarde shouted and shook the lax shoulders and shouted again, a stream of abuse coming out of her mouth, so thick and choked with fury that the words were undistinguishable, and somewhere along the corridor outside someone shouted back, and other voices were raised, expostulating, enraged.

She stopped at last and stood there, her back bent and her hands still on Birgitta's shoulders and then Birgitta smiled, the pale white lips lifting and she put up both hands and tried to put them over Hildegarde's.

'I love you,' she said after a moment, and closed her eyes, and Hildegarde made a thick sound in her throat, and wrenched her hands away.

'Silly bitch,' she said again, but this time it was cool, unemotional, and she picked up the phone from the rickety table beside the bed and jiggled the rest.

'*Allo – allo – ah, enfin – écoutez! Il faut que je parle avec Londres, tout de suite. Vous pouvez me – avec Doctor Stermont – oui, Doctor Stermont lui-même à sept neuf zero deux huit deux huit – oui – Londres, Angleterre – immédiatement –*'

It took them half an hour to get the call through. And it took Sammy twelve hours to get to them.

Mel had been dozing in a chair beside the bed and he woke suddenly, aware of his stiff aching back and blinked at the door, and there he was, rumpled and sardonic, his coat over his arm. He stood there and stared round and said abruptly, 'Well? I'm here.'

23

The court was very still now. The little movements that rippled through the full benches, the whispered colloquies, the self-important bustling of the ushers, all had ceased. The whole court seemed focussed on Hildegarde in the witness box and on the wigged and gowned figure beneath her, questioning, probing, digging for elucidation, over and over again.

'You must explain this very clearly, Miss Maurice, in the light of the evidence we've already heard. You say Miss Olaf attempted suicide, there in your hotel room in Paris?'

'Yes.'

'Why? Did she give you any inkling of her mood, her emotional state?'

'She was upset,' Hildegarde said and hesitated, and only her eyes moved as her gaze swept along the double line of jurors, assessing them. 'She was very Scandinavian.'

'And what does that mean, Miss Maurice?'

Hildegarde sighed sharply, a little intake of breath that could be heard all through the court. The daylight was beginning to dwindle now, and someone switched on the overhead lights and suddenly the windows seemed to darken as the rain thickened against them. But the air inside was still stuffy, still smelled of wet fabric drying in the heavy atmosphere.

'You must remember that when we first met we were little more than children. Seventeen – eighteen. An awkward age. She had no friends in London. I helped her. She was grateful. She got – she developed a *schwärmerei*.'

The bewigged head turned, and Jordan-Andrews said smoothly, 'I think, for the benefit of the jury, we should clarify that, Miss Maurice.'

'She got a crush on me,' Hildegarde said loudly.

The jury moved, rustling on its benches, and the judge turned his head and looked at them, frowning.

'She fell in love with you?' Jordan-Andrews said.

'Foolishly, yes.'

'Was her affection returned?'

'Only as friendship.'

'You mean that this was not a sexual relationship?'

'Is that relevant?'

'You are answering the questions of your own counsel, Miss Maurice,' the judge said, 'I think you should remember that.'

'Oh, well, all I can say is, not on my side.'

'You felt no – ah – physical attraction to her?'

'None at all. I was sorry for her.' Cool contempt filled her voice again, and the jury looked away from her and Bonnie thought again, stupid. Don't be stupid.

'Why? What occasioned your pity?'

'She had aspirations to be a designer, but she wasn't very good. She had a few ideas, but she couldn't carry them through. Couldn't make them work. I encouraged her all I could, gave her a job when I started my own business, but it was obvious to me she'd never be a success as a designer in her own right.'

'She never designed anything you would wear yourself?'

'Oh, she did sometimes. But between her design and the garment I wore there were changes. *My* changes. Lots of my special touches. The touches that make a Hildegarde design what it is –'

'So you never stole any designs from her? As was implied in the TV programme which is the subject of this – ah – action?'

'Never!' Now I know what ringing tones mean, Bonnie thought. She said that in ringing tones. Beside her Sammy put his hand out and set it over hers.

'You are on oath, Miss Maurice, and you maintain you stole *no* designs from her?'

'I did not. Ideas come to people – it happens to all of us – we get the same ideas at the same times. But it's what we do with them, how we use them, how we see the original inspiration through from drawing-board to clothes on a woman's back – that's what makes a design. And I never stole such a design from Birgitta Olaf.'

'Yet she attempted suicide in Paris that autumn. Why was that?'

'I told you – she had a crush on me.'

'But why should that make her desire to take her life? You say yourself she had developed this – ah, this feeling for you in

230

her late teens. At the time of which we are speaking, she was a woman of almost forty. No longer a teenager. She had had this crush for half her lifetime. Why should she choose this moment to destroy herself?'

There was a little silence and then Hildegarde lifted her hands in a little gesture of puzzlement. 'I just don't know. I've asked myself over and over, but I just don't know. I thought all was well. She was my Norwegian agent, sending me new fabrics and knitwear ideas as they appeared there, she had a nice flat in Oslo, a good salary. I thought all was well. And suddenly she turns up in Paris, in a state, in the middle of vital business dealings, and does this terrible – this thing. I never understood it. I still don't. But I'm sure of this –' she leaned forwards, looking down at Jordan-Andrews very seriously – 'it was nothing to do with me. Nothing at all.'

Jordan-Andrews looked at the jury and then bent his head to his papers, shuffling them a little, giving the twelve of them time to absorb her words, and she stood up straight again, and looked at them. They did not look at her.

'Now then, Miss Maurice, I think we must go over the happenings of those painful few days. Miss Olaf stabbed herself with the scissors, and was clearly very ill as a result. What did you do?'

'I got her to bed, and made her as comfortable as I could. Then I sent for medical help.'

'Ah, yes. You sent for medical help. A French doctor, I presume?'

'Oh, no!' She sounded quite shocked. 'I was much too concerned about her – I couldn't have let her be seen by a foreigner! No, I sent at once for an English doctor, someone I could really trust.'

'All the way from London?'

'Yes.'

'That was very – how shall I put it – that sounds a very expensive thing to have done.'

'Birgitta was my friend,' Hildegarde said with conscious dignity. 'She also worked for me. I could do no less.'

'I see. How long did it take him to arrive?'

'He got to the hotel the next day, very early. And it was worth waiting for him, because he really was the best there was – an old friend, Professor Stermont, you know. Professor Sampson Stermont.'

'I'm leaving on a jet plane,
Don't know when I'll be back again.
I'm leaving on a jet plane . . . .'

He stood at the door and looked at them sitting there in a pool of light thrown from the bedside lamp, and felt the hope recede like a tide that left him beached and helpless. It had been absurd, the whole thing. There he'd been, sitting in his cluttered little office at the hospital, battling with a paper he was working on for the *Lancet* on the role of enzymes in the lysis of thrombi after myocardial infarction, and she'd phoned. It had been as ridiculous as something out of a cheap romance and he'd risen to it like a fish to a fly. 'I need you. Please come.' That was all she'd said, and it had been enough.

And now there she was, fast asleep in an armchair with that damned lawyer sitting beside her, staring at him stupidly, looking rumpled and dirty in a cluttered room that smelled of sweat and vomit and perfume. It was disgusting and he felt his gorge rise, and turned back to the door. Whatever it was she'd wanted, to hell with her. To come this far for such a reason had been mad; to go home to work again would be the only sanity.

But she woke and saw him and at once was on her feet, coming round the edge of the bed with her hands outstretched.

'Sammy, oh Christ, Sammy, am I glad to see you – quick, come and look at her –'

He turned back and blinked at her and then looked at the bed and for the first time realized someone was in it.

'What is it?' he said stupidly, and shook his head to clear it. He was tired; he'd sat at Heathrow for two hours stand-by waiting to get on to a flight, and then it had been delayed by a lightning strike of the maintenance engineers, and he'd slept only fitfully in the narrow hard-backed seat. Everything seemed very effortful now, far away and effortful. 'What is it?' he said again.

'Birgitta. Come and look at her, for God's sake.'

232

He went to the bedside and sat down on it and looked at the face on the pillow. She was pale, and her eyes were half open, a narrow rim of white showing beneath the lids. She was breathing unevenly, deep sighing breaths alternating with periods of rapid shallower breathing.

'She's anaemic,' he said automatically, and reached for her pulse. Thready, rapid, missing occasionally. 'Very anaemic.'

'She's bled a lot,' Hildegarde said impatiently, and pulled the sheet downwards and he saw the wound under her ribs, rough and jagged. The pallid flesh swelled up on each side of the rawness, puffy and blood-stained.

'Dear God, what happened?' The fatigue was gone suddenly. His concentration was all in his fingertips and his eyes as he delicately touched the skin round the wound and then moved his hands over the belly beneath it. 'She's bled into the peritoneum – what in God's name did it?'

'Scissors. She –' Hildegarde stopped and he looked up at her but her face was in the shadows.

'She what?' He could hear his own voice, incisive and medical and was almost amused. All the time since she'd called him he'd been obsessed with thoughts of her; even while he'd tried to sleep on that damned plane he'd dreamed of her, dreamed he was touching her, holding her, making love with her at last, and now here he was talking to her like a doctor.

'Stabbed herself,' Mel said, and his voice pulled Sammy back sharply and he turned and looked at him and Mel said quickly, 'She did it herself. We weren't anywhere near her. She just took hold of the bloody scissors and shoved them in herself – it was – Christ, it was awful!'

'How long ago?' Sammy looked at the wound again, at the crusting of blood on the edges and touched it gingerly, very aware of his unwashed hands.

'About – oh, around half past four yesterday afternoon.'

'Half past – but it's almost six in the morning now! Why isn't she in hospital? Who's seen her? Treated her?'

'We sent for you,' Hildegarde said.

'You sent for me? You mean no one's seen her? She's been like this all this time and you didn't get a doctor to her? Are you mad?'

'No, I'm not mad!' she said in a harsh undertone. 'And for

Christ's sake keep quiet. This isn't the sort of hotel where they pay much attention to you, but if you wake too many of them at this hour of the morning there'll be all hell let loose, and then we'll really be in trouble. For God's sake, Sammy, have some sense! The silly bitch stabs herself with my scissors, in my hotel room – am I likely to start a great hoo-ha over it? We've got to get her to London fast, sort her out, get the whole thing dealt with quietly –'

'So that's why you sent for me?'

'Of course. Who else, for God's sake? You're the only doctor I know well enough to come so far, and who'd keep quiet about it –'

He stared up at her with his face as expressionless as he could make it. She's done it again, he was thinking. She's done it again.

'I've got nothing with me,' he said after a moment. 'You – Bremner – go to a pharmacy, get me some things. I'll do what I can –'

He took his note-book from his pocket and began to make a list of what he needed, struggling a little to remember the French for cotton wool and gauze and dextrose, and Mel took it and went, and they sat and listened to his footsteps receding along the corridor outside.

'Has she talked at all?' he said after a moment, and she shook her head, and went round to the other side of the bed and sat down in the armchair, and leaned forwards to look down at the pale face on the pillow. He looked too, and then back at Hildegarde. She seemed as fresh and comfortable as though she were newly slept and bathed. Her streaked fair hair leaped round her head in its usual halo, her skin was smooth and matt, her eyes clear and bright.

She felt his gaze and looked at him and smiled, her teeth glinting a little in the lamplight. She looked like a twelve-year-old again.

'I am glad you came.'

'To get you out of trouble?'

'Of course. But to see you as well. You're always such a comfort.'

'Like a hot-water bottle.'

She sighed then, and stopped looking like a twelve-year-old.

234

'Oh, ye Gods, Sammy, not now, do me a favour! You always get so bloody personal –'

'I would have thought myself entitled, this time.' His voice was carefully controlled. 'You phone me. You tell me in that special voice you put on that you need me, that I've got to come, please don't make you wait, come now. You *need* me. I would have thought after that I was entitled to take a personal interest.'

She giggled. 'Oh, love, I'm sorry, but I had to get you here, didn't I? And I couldn't risk that bloody concierge listening and hearing it all if I'd told what I really needed you for. I know they're thick, but they're sharp enough when it comes to something that could be of advantage to them – and a story like this, Christ, can't you imagine what a dog's breakfast the papers'd make of it! I had to get you here –'

'So you used my favourite bait.'

She leaned back in her chair so that her face disappeared into the shadows again. 'I don't understand you, I really don't. As long as I can remember, you've leched for me. When I was a kid you used to watch me. You were always watching me. I used to watch you doing it. And when I got older – you made such heavy weather over it all! Hester, you said, and then worrying about me being a virgin – oh, you were ridiculous! You could have had me any time at all those first few years, you know that? But no, you wouldn't – and even now – for years it's been the same. You want me, you can have me as far as I'm concerned but when it comes to it, there're always reasons. You're like a woman when it's sex, aren't you? Always screwed up about love and other people and right and wrong – a bit more screwing and a bit less screwing up'd do you a power of good – mind you –' she laughed then, softly, '– if you weren't like that, I wouldn't have such effective bait, would I? It's funny really. You make me throw out lures, just so that you can agonize over them and not follow up. You're a funny sort of wanker, Sammy, you know that? You tease yourself – real kinky –'

He couldn't look at her, because he knew she was right. She knew him better than he did himself, knew what made his whole body concentrate itself into an ache of need for her, knew how to cloud his thinking and bewilder him more than anyone else. Hester had been his first woman, and he'd learned about his

235

body from her, found out just what he was capable of from what he could do to hers. And Bonnie – she had always warmed him, made him feel comfortable and relaxed and important. A splendid feeling, always. Bonnie had wanted him as he wanted Hildegarde. He knew that. He'd known it before she had, poor child.

He sat and looked down at Birgitta's pale sweating face and thought of Bonnie, comfortable Bonnie with her apologetic eyes and hopeful smile. Bonnie who was the only one of the three who really gave him the one thing he craved more than anything else. Being loved. He must have been mad to let her go, mad to have even looked twice at her sisters, because hadn't Hester laughed at him and left him behind and didn't Hildegarde play with him like a cat with a spider?

He yawned suddenly, cracking his jaw, and she laughed.

'So much for medical drama!' she said. 'I'd imagined you'd come bursting in here waving instruments and have her sewn up and bandaged and all the rest of it in no time. And here you sit, yawning like a baby –'

'There's damn all I can do,' he said harshly, hearing his own voice crackle against his ears. 'She's too ill for any miracles to be done here and now. I'll give her some parenteral fluid, if your friend manages to get hold of the stuff on my list, put on a dressing, keep her alive. It's the best I can do. Then it's got to be a hospital and surgery. She'll be bloody lucky if she survives.'

'There's no way she goes into hospital here,' Hildegarde said loudly. 'She goes home, and we get her into hospital there. No silly questions asked, understand me?'

'You're a fool,' he said flatly. 'It can't be done.'

'It can. It almost is. I made arrangements yesterday afternoon, waiting for you. Called the airline, told 'em I've got a sick woman who'll be travelling with her own doctor. There's a certificate you'll have to sign accepting responsibility – I've got it here. Then they'll take her. This afternoon.'

'I'll do nothing of the sort. Do you think I'll take on the responsibility of shifting someone as ill as she is, when there's perfectly adequate surgical help available here? You're right out of your mind.'

'You're blustering,' she said coolly. 'You know damned well what'll happen if we go to a French hospital. Questions and

236

investigations, Christ knows what. D'you want to see me in front of one of their bloody magistrates? In one of their prisons?'

'Stop dramatizing. It won't be anything of the sort –'

'But it could be,' she said softly. 'You couldn't take the risk for me, could you?'

He knew he was defeated long before Mel came back with his parcel from the all-night pharmacy in Place Clichy. He always was when it was Hildegarde.

The journey back to London was nightmarish for him, but not for her. She was cool, more worried about her cases full of clothes and getting them back through customs than about Birgitta on her stretcher with the intravenous dextrose and chloride solution that Sammy had managed to rig up somehow. He sat and worried, sick at himself for the way he'd let her manipulate him again, sick with rage because she so patently didn't care, sick with anxiety about the sort of reception he'd get at his own hospital when he arrived with so odd a patient.

But as ever, she had been right. The casualty people didn't turn a hair when he told them his friend's colleague had been injured in Paris, and they hadn't wanted to risk seeking French medical help for her. As far as they were concerned, his friend had been totally right to be so mistrustful, for who in the world could possibly be better than an English surgeon?

They stood there in casualty, he swaying with fatigue, watching Birgitta at last being wheeled away to a surgical bed and she laughed, very softly.

'You see, Sammy? It's worked out fine, hasn't it? She's here, and there's been no fuss and –'

'And if she dies? If she dies because she'd been bleeding too long and because she didn't get the treatment she needed in time, what then? Will you still say it's turned out all right?'

'Probably,' she said. 'If she dies, it'll be meant, won't it? Things work out the way they have to. They always do.'

'Don't you care about anything, about anybody?' He said it suddenly, letting his anger pour out of him. 'Birgitta loves you – I've known that for ever, and so have you. The poor stupid creature thinks the sun rises and sets in you. I can remember, when you were kids – years ago –'

237

'Yes, we all knew about poor old Birgitta.' She turned and began to walk away and he followed her out into the leaf blowing road where the red buses ground their way with English stolidity past the lorries and cars and he thought, this morning in Paris. Now here. It's a mad world!

'But it wasn't my fault, was it? And anyway she got something out of it in her own way. I mean, if getting hung up on me gave her something to be interested in, it can't be all bad.'

He stopped then, standing in the middle of the pavement and put his hand on her arm, making her turn round to look at him, and she stood there very straight in the grey afternoon looking exotic and frightening and yet achingly familiar.

'Hildegarde – Hilda – how can you be as you are? When people love you and show it, how can you be as you are? Birgitta, that Bremner, even me – Fido and Sylvia – people who love you. Lots of them. How can you be as you are to them?'

She looked at him, smiling a little, her head to one side as though she were really thinking seriously about what he had asked her, but he didn't really believe she was. Until she stopped smiling and pushed her hands into her pockets, automatically taking on the sort of pose the model girls used when they showed her designs.

'How can I be as I am?' she said. 'It's the only way to be. It's the only way that makes sense. You lot, all going on about love and needing and caring – it's so stupid. Where does it get you? Where did it get Birgitta? People say they love you, but they never do. They love themselves, seeing themselves in your eyes. That's what they love – themselves seen in your eyes, their own bodies felt in yours. Who needs it? I don't. I've got more sense. I learned a long time ago it isn't safe to love people. They leave you. They drop you right in the shit if you love them. I stopped loving people after my mother and father dropped me in the shit, getting themselves killed. It just isn't safe.'

'Getting themselves killed?' he said, almost wonderingly. 'Getting themselves killed?'

'They shouldn't have,' she said loudly, 'but they did, and that's the end of it. Thanks for your help, Sammy. I'll be seeing you.' And she went, walking easily along the wide traffic-heavy road with her leather bag swinging over her shoulder, and her yellow head bobbing vividly against the monochrome of the buildings.

You won't, he thought. I won't ever again come when you call. I'll never want you again, I swear I won't. That's it. I've finished. I'll never see you again.

He didn't see her again, not even when Birgitta died. Not until the case came to court.

But he never stopped wanting her.

24

The luncheon adjournment left them all edgy, from the ushers to the judge himself. It showed in sharp movements and slightly raised voices and a certain amount of irritable pushing as people shuffled out of court.

Bonnie and Sammy went in search of lunch together as a matter of course, neither finding it necessary to discuss the matter, although Sammy asked briefly whether Stanley would be coming to court today and she answered even more briefly that she did not know.

It was too wet to consider the Temple Gardens. They stood poised on the steps looking out at the hurrying umbrellas and the swish of windscreen wipers and Sammy said, 'We could try a pub.'

'Lovely,' she said very aware of being a little daring. Respectable women married to respectable men like Stanley didn't go to pubs. 'I'd really enjoy that.'

The pub, battered and old, and down an alley in Covent Garden, was noisy with journalists roaring at each other and damp with men in dripping raincoats talking earnestly with their heads close together, and he settled her at a small table and went off in search of shepherd's pie and lager, leaving her to patch her make-up and to try not to think about what was going on.

But it was impossible not to. She looked at her face in the mirror of her compact, and tried to see it objectively. Not too lined, considering her age. Quite good really. Smooth, just a little crêpiness of the eyelids and the corners of her mouth. Her hair was good – well it should be, the amount her hair-dresser took from her each week – and though she was plump she was firm. She didn't have that melted-wax-doll look so many women in their forties had. Her face wasn't falling off its bones.

What does it matter what you look like? You're a married woman, a mother of a splendid family, what does it matter?

It matters because of Sammy. Because I want him to think I look good.

Good?

Interesting. Attractive –

Attractive? Now, there's an odd thought for a respectable married woman. Especially one who thought this morning about divorce.

Shut up. Shut *up*. I'm not interested in the answers to why any more. I'm not interested.

'Mustard? This looks as though it could do with something to improve it – probably got a lot of soya in it.' Sammy put her plate in front of her and she looked at it and then smiled up at him.

'It smells great. Don't bother with mustard. Not worth the effort –'

They ate in silence and, though the pie was rather nasty, she was too hungry to care and gobbled it quickly.

'Junk food,' Sammy said gloomily. 'This damned case – I've eaten nothing but rubbish since it started.'

'It's only the second day.'

'Is it? It seems like an eternity.'

'Sammy –'

'Well? Spit it out.'

'Oh, it doesn't matter. None of my business, really.'

'All right, it isn't. Still, ask it.'

'Why did you come? I mean, you weren't – what's the word – subpoenaed. Were you? Why did you come? You must have known it'd well – upset you.'

'The solicitors asked me if I'd be willing to give evidence. I said I'd rather not, and in the end they said it would be all right but it would be handy if I kept myself available. Anyway, I was interested.'

'That's understandable, I suppose. But – risky?'

'Risky?'

'You've never exactly had much pleasure from us all, have you, Sammy? Looking back. There's so much I didn't understand that I do now.'

'Do you? Really? I don't think anyone can know what it was like for me then. What you were like.' He leaned back against the grimy wall behind him so that his head was incongruously framed by the pictures of boxers that hung there and stared at her over his lager glass. 'I was bedazzled by you all, I think. Quite bedazzled.'

241

'Why? There was nothing very special about us. Just three kids living with an aunt –'

'There was more to it than that. Ye gods, but there was more to it! Fido herself – that extraordinary mixture of meanness and keeping up appearances – it fascinated me because my mother – well, never mind her. Not now. And then you three –'

'I loved you very much, Sammy,' she said suddenly. 'Did you know that?' And then as he looked at her she shook her head and put her hand to her mouth. 'Oh, my God, what have I said?'

He smiled at her, that sideways closed-lipped smile she was beginning to recognize as very much a part of the new Sammy. 'Nothing you shouldn't. Yes, I knew. And I think I –'

'Don't say you felt the same about me because you didn't.' She said it almost violently, although her voice was low. 'Because you didn't. It was Hester and Hildegarde you cared about. You were mad about them, one at a time and both together.'

'Yes, I was. One at a time and both together – and it was hell.' He leaned forwards, and made her look at him. 'You know that? It was total misery.'

'Then why did you put up with it? Why didn't you just go away and stop coming round? You never seemed to be anywhere else but at our house.'

'I couldn't. I was – I told you. Bedazzled. But you mattered too. I remember so many good things about you, Bonnie.'

'I know.' She stood up and smoothed her skirt, not looking at him. 'Nice, comfortable, easy things. Not being bedazzled, though.' She looked up then and made a little face, half smile, half apologetic grimace. 'I've never been bedazzled. It must be interesting.'

'Not when the dazzle goes out. Then it leaves a – hell, I'm getting maudlin. Let's stop this, shall we? To hell with yesterday. It's now, isn't it? Now that's important?'

'It will be when this damned case is over. If it ever is. It seems to be going on and on – and it's all about yesterday. Things that happened and should have been forgotten.'

'Birgitta – she should have been forgotten,' he said after a moment.

'Yes. That was – did it all make sense to you, what she said in court, Sammy? About it being Birgitta's own fault?' It was important to her that she should know his opinion, and she looked at him very earnestly.

'Nothing is ever Hildegarde's fault, is it?' He stood up and collected his still-dripping umbrella from behind their table, helping her into her wet coat. 'Things just happen around her.'

'They always have. I – we don't see much of each other, you know. Not these days.'

'I know.'

She looked up at him, frowning. 'How do you know?'

'I see Hester from time to time. She tells me.'

'Oh.' She shivered suddenly in her wet coat. 'It's getting late, isn't it? I think we'd better be going back.'

'Yes, I suppose so. Here, you take my umbrella. I can manage –'

It wasn't until they were back in court again and the counsel were moving into their places that the chill between them went. Sammy said something about J. J. Gerrard; Bonnie, polite but a little remote, still trying to cope with the wave of feeling his casual mention of Hester had aroused in her, said, 'Oh, have you met him?'

'Of course.' He looked at her and then smiled. 'Or don't you watch the programme regularly? I'm on quite often. Medical spokesman and all that.'

She half-turned in her seat so that she could look at him foursquare. 'You're on *Spectrum*? I didn't – we don't see it often. Stanley thinks it's boring – I didn't know. Is that where you see Hester?'

'Where else?'

'Of course. Where else?' And she settled herself in her seat again, feeling better. Even when Hildegarde, who was still giving evidence, started to answer Wooderson's questions the glow of comfort stayed with her. For a while, anyway.

DECEMBER 1955

'You load sixteen tons, and what'ya get,
Another day older and deeper in debt.
Don't call for me brother 'cos I can't go,
I owe my soul to the company store . . . .'

The party had been going on for a couple of hours when Stanley and Bonnie arrived. They'd had to go first to his father's cousins in the Bishop's Avenue, in Hampstead.

'They're important people to us, Bonnie,' Stanley had said. 'And even for your sister and her party, I don't offend them. Besides, it's all right – we can Go On.'

He'd said it in capitals; taking a pride in being so in demand that they went to two parties on the same evening, finding it smart to arrive so late that everyone knew they'd already had a wearying round of socializing. Bonnie smiled indulgently when he said such things. It was so very Stanley and she found it rather endearing.

Hester's party had been announced as an UnChristmas Party, and was being held in a coffee bar in Shepherd's Bush. It took them some time to find it, and when they did and pushed their way through the heavily-curtained door that led into the noisy, smoky room full of people it took them a few moments to see what was going on. And then Bonnie saw the cut-outs on the walls of Easter bunnies and daffodils, and pulled on Stanley's arm.

'Look, Stanley – d'you see what they've done?'

He peered through the smoke, a little irritably. 'What? Daffodils? Why daffodils?'

'It's an unChristmas party!'

'What's daffodils got to do with Christmas, for God's sake? Oh, hello, Hildegarde. Didn't know you'd be here – who are all these people?'

'Hello, gorgeous! What kept you so long? These people? Oh, they're special – television and all that. *Very* special! None of your old rubbish cluttering up Hester's party – except us, of course –'

She linked her arm into his and pulled him forwards. 'Come and get a drink. She's got some Midsummer Punch – Gawd knows what Midsummer Punch is but she's devised it. I reckon the joke's getting a bit thin on the ground, myself, but when Hester gets a notion into her head there ain't no holding her. Come on, Bonnie – Mel's here somewhere –'

Bonnie followed them, grateful for the wake they left behind as they pushed through the tight-packed people, trying to see Hester. She wanted to talk to Sammy about her wedding, about giving her away, and the sooner she did it the better. And where Hester was, Sammy was sure to be.

When they reached the corner to which Hildegarde was making her way, however, there was only Melvin Bremner looking sulky and Birgitta sitting as silent as she always did, and Bonnie smiled at her uneasily; she was always such an uncomfortable girl to be with. Birgitta nodded back and said nothing, and Bonnie sat down and left it to Stanley and Hildegarde to do the talking.

They did, with Hildegarde pouring glasses of a pink, vaguely fruit-flavoured concoction from the jug on their table and shouting above the roar of the skiffle group in a far corner, playing *Rock Island Line* with a particularly heavy thumping on its washboards. Bonnie gave up trying to listen after a while and watched the people around her.

An odd lot, she thought, with their exaggerated versions of the current look; a girl in a wide skirt with what looked like a dozen rows of frilled petticoats beneath went whirling by, dancing with a man in trousers so exaggeratedly cut that they looked like a caricature of every menswear shop window in London. Silly, really, she thought. Why try to look so different to everyone else? Why do people have to show off so much?

Hildegarde was still talking to Stanley, her head very close to his. Mel on her other side was looking sulky and Bonnie began to feel uneasy. They shouldn't have come on here, really. It would have been better to stay in The Bishop's Avenue with the relations, who were dull but weren't threatening in the way this place and its people were. There she'd felt safe, cared for, at home even though it was a ridiculously rich house and the people were even more ridiculously rich. At least they didn't deafen you with their noise, and didn't come between a couple who'd arrived together.

Stanley leaned forwards over the table and tapped her on the arm. 'Listen, Bonnie, Hil says there's another room upstairs, quieter, and she and Mel want to talk to me about business. I'm going up – you don't have to if you don't want to –'

'I'll come,' she shouted back firmly, and stood up, while Hildegarde, leaning across behind Stanley's back, said something to Mel. He looked alert and interested for the first time and stood up too, and after a moment so did Birgitta. But Hildegarde said something to her and she stood there for a second, quite still, and then sat down again. And the four of them again pushed their way through the crowded room, this time with Mel holding Bonnie's arm.

Upstairs the sound of the insistent thumping of the music could still be heard but it wasn't as deafening, and they found a corner where there was room for all four of them. On each side Bonnie could see couples locked together, some leaning against the walls, others curled up on the floor, and she didn't want to look. When Stanley wanted to neck at parties like this, she hated it; it wasn't that it embarrassed her, she'd tell him earnestly. It was just that it was too personal, too important to share with a crowd like this. But here, she had to admit it. She was embarrassed.

So when they started talking, Hildegarde and Mel, she listened, not because she was interested, but because it was better than being aware of the couples.

'Look, like I told you, Stanley, I could do very well, very well indeed – but not as I am now,' Hildegarde was saying with great seriousness, leaning forward with one hand on Stanley's arm, and looking up eagerly into his eyes. He watched her, a half smile on his face, enjoying her importunity. 'I'm as far as I can go the way things are – I raise a bit more finance every time, but it's peanuts, it's never more than peanuts –'

'If we could capitalize properly, Maddern, we could start something really lucrative,' Mel said, his voice smooth and professional. 'I've done what I can, but the facts are that real capital isn't easy to come by – not on a long-term basis. What we need is some money we can rely on for a long time. An open-ended term.'

'I've managed to build a base capital of my own of a thousand,' Hildegarde said, and Stanley's eyes narrowed suddenly. Bonnie turned her head and looked at her sister. Hildegarde with a thousand pounds? Where did she get a thousand pounds from? Her chest lurched with fear suddenly; had she been doing things she shouldn't? People at the shop talked about the sort of slippery customers they knew who raised money the wrong way. Hildegarde?

'Incredible, Maddern, incredible business head on this girl,' Mel said. 'I tell you, she's parlayed thirty quid into a thousand in just a couple of years – some business woman –'

'If I can do that with thirty in a couple of years – well, less, really – imagine what I could do with another couple of thousand for a long term,' Hildegarde said, and her voice was low and coaxing. 'Imagine, Stanley! And you'll be in on it.'

'What are the terms?' Stanley said. 'How much, what return, what period of loan?' His voice had a crackle and liveliness in it that Bonnie had never heard before, and she looked at him and felt a sudden lift of pride and pleasure in being his girl. He looked even more handsome than he usually did, with his jaw-line crisp and hard, and he caught her eye and gave her the ghost of a wink. He was obviously enjoying himself hugely and she was happy for him.

She looked at the others then, at Hildegarde's glitter, for she seemed to be as vivid and as light-reflecting as a piece of tinsel, and then at Mel, his head up and his eyes alert over the Black Russian cigarette he was smoking. They were all enjoying themselves hugely, and she felt forlorn for a moment, outside and unwanted. They were playing a game of their own which absorbed them and she wasn't; she was the outsider, alone and lonely.

'A thousand,' Hildegarde was saying. 'Not an enormous sum, is it? Not for someone in your size of business.'

Stanley shook his head in mock despair. 'A grand? Darling, even for a sister-in-law that's asking too much. In fact, it's downright chutzpah! You expect me to match your own stake? Come on, doll! Let's talk reasonable!'

'Five hundred,' Mel cut in smoothly and shot Hildegarde a warning glance. 'Of course we don't expect to have our own equity totally matched by any one investor. Bad business, that – Hildegarde should know better. I tell you, Maddern, as a money woman, she's a brilliant dress-maker –'

'And who parlayed thirty into a thousand in two years? Who made the whole thing possible at all?' Hildegarde flashed and he held up one hand soothingly.

'No need to get into a flap, darlin', none at all! Maddern and I – we speak the same language. Listen, Maddern, we want five hundred, unlimited term, only to be repaid when the business is clearly in a position to make such repayment without detriment to its further progress, at a rate of interest' – he paused for dramatic effect, and then said portentously, '– at a rate of interest – compound of course – rising throughout until it reaches the level in force at the time of repayment.'

There was a short silence, and Bonnie could hear whispers and giggles from the couple nearest to her, and reddened. If only the music downstairs would start again.

'Let's get this clear,' Stanley said slowly. 'You want five hundred, to be repaid only when *you* say you're in a position to repay it, never mind whether I need it or not, and with no immediate return during the years of the loan – however long they may be?'

'Yes, I know. It sounds crazy – until you think it through. Listen, Maddern, what's five hundred to you right now? Peanuts. With a business like yours it's got to be peanuts. You won't even notice it.'

Stanley lifted his shoulders and lit another cigar, his eyes bright above the flickering match.

'So you feel nothing now – but in time to come when your little sister-in-law here has turned it in to big money, and you get it back – then you get compound interest at a rate then in force. Not the three per cent that's bank rate now but at whatever it is then. It's rising steadily, Maddern. By the sixties, the seventies, who knows – five or six per cent. Maybe even more! Work it out – how can you lose? It's like an insurance policy with every bonus there is! It's the best deal you can get with your money. Believe me, the time will come when you'll wish you'd put in the thousand. But you're right, of course. We've got to spread the equity –'

I wish I understood it all, Bonnie thought. Equity, bonuses, interest. I'm stupid, I don't understand money.

But Stanley did, and he was sitting there with his cigar in his mouth looking at Mel and with his eyes bright and sharp, and after a while he nodded.

'Okay, Hildegarde, okay. You've got yourself a deal. January first, that's when. We'll date it January first next year, keep it tidy, and draw up a document –'

'Mel can do that,' Hildegarde said, leaning back, relaxed, her sparkle somehow dimmed. 'He's a lawyer.' She looked round the room, peering at the couples, trying to see who was there and Bonnie thought, she's bored now. The game's finished –

248

Mel and Stanley were still playing, though, and went on for a long time, as Mel scribbled on a sheet of paper he'd taken from his pocket and Stanley leaned over it, jabbing with his finger, changing words, altering phrases, until at last they were both satisfied. Stanley looked at Bonnie and winked again.

'Listen, this is shocking, eh doll? I take my fiancée to a party and end up talking business! No way to treat a lovely girl! Come on, sweetheart, we'll go downstairs and dance, eh? Or –' he peered round, 'Stay up here maybe! Here looks a good place to stay –'

'We'll dance,' Bonnie said firmly and stood up. 'Are you coming down, Hildegarde?'

'In a minute. I want to talk to Hester –' She looked up at Stanley. 'Glad you opted in, gorgeous. You'll be glad of it, one of these days!'

'I'd better be!' Stanley said and winked at her, and then laughed. 'Or maybe I'll be coming round to get my debt paid off in kind, eh?'

'With a sister-in-law?' Mel said and grinned. 'There's a name for that Maddern!' and Bonnie reddened. They were only joking, she knew that, but she didn't like it. It was supposed to be clever, that sort of joking, but she hated it, always had.

'I think Hester must be downstairs,' she said. 'Haven't seen her since we got here – we really ought to say hello, Stanley. I mean, it's her party –'

'Coming, doll. Got to shake hands with a friend first. Where's the bog, Bremner?'

Mel jerked his head, and Stanley went, edging his way past the interlocked couples with loud and flowery apologies. Mel stood up, smiling down at Hildegarde.

'I'll see you later,' he said. 'I've got people to see – things to do.'

'Keep in touch,' Hildegarde said briefly and he grinned at her, and went, slapping Bonnie casually on her shoulder as he went by.

Hildegarde yawned, and stretched and then stood up too. 'Tell Stanley I'll see you both later,' she said. 'I've got to go down – have a good Christmas,' and then she too was gone, leaving Bonnie standing there waiting for Stanley and feeling more lonely and apart than ever. A silly way to feel, really, at her own sister's party, she told herself. Ridiculous. I must find Hester and talk to her. And Sammy –'

But by the time Stanley came back and they were able to get downstairs, Hester and Mel were sitting in a corner with their heads together talking. Hildegarde had disappeared and there was no sign of Sammy anywhere. Somehow there seemed no point in staying there any longer.

25

'We come now to matters involving the financing of your business which is highly pertinent, Miss Maurice, to the case in hand. I want you to tell the court –'

'Yes,' Hildegarde said loudly and looked at the jury, turning her head well round so that they could see she was looking at them. 'I think it's very important. I think I was defamed as part of an attempt to make me give them money they aren't entitled to and –'

'Miss Maurice, you really must wait for my questions,' Jordan-Andrews said, mildly reproving. Wooderson looked half asleep, but his glance was sharp with amusement as he looked at his opponent. Such a client to have! his expression said. Such a client!

'I'm sorry – it's just that I feel very strongly –'

'Yes, I am sure you do. We will explain to the jury how strongly you feel, and why, but in the proper manner. Now, Miss Maurice, you have told us how your business found some of its early capital from Mr Stanley Maddern, and your sister Mrs Bonnie Maddern.'

'She wasn't Bonnie Maddern at the time,' Hildegarde said quickly. 'They were engaged, that was all. It was all his doing, the loan.'

'You think that is an important point to make?'

'Of course I do! To listen to some people, you'd think I was trying to rip off my own family. And I never did. I truly never did. I just gave them an opportunity. An opportunity to profit from my hard work.'

'I see. You borrowed money, then, from Mr Stanley Maddern, who later married your sister, and from Miss Hester Morrissey, your sister?'

'Yes. They were both given the same opportunity –'

'You arranged both loans yourself?'

'Not exactly. I was there when the loan with Stanley Maddern was arranged, but Mel – Mr Bremner dealt with Hester by himself.'

'Melvin Bremner –'

'My financial adviser,' Hildegarde said smoothly. 'A lawyer, you know, and very knowledgeable about money. Much better than me. My job really was to do the creative work. He was always responsible for the money side.' She looked down at the body of the court, and Bonnie followed the line of her gaze and looked at Mel, sitting there with his arms folded and his head poking forwards. Even from the back she could see the tension in him. His shoulders were tight and his head seemed to tremble faintly as though she were looking at him through a heat haze. Here she goes, she thought. Here she goes, doing a Hildegarde, dropping him right in it.

'I see. So, you had nothing to do with the discussions about the loan obtained from Miss Hester Morrissey?'

'Nothing at all,' Hildegarde said loudly and with great satisfaction. 'Nothing at all.'

JANUARY 1956

'I know a dark, secluded place,
A place where no one knows your face . . . .'

'I don't care how you do it,' she said impatiently. 'I've got enough to worry about right now. There's that fabric to get in from Ireland, and that bitch in Islington is trying to carve me up over cabbage. Cabbage! I told her when I took her on that every inch of the stuff was spoken for, and if she didn't get the right number of garments out I'd sue her, and she's still trying it on –'

'What d'you mean, cabbage?' Mel said, diverted.

'Oh, the CMT people think it's their perks –'

'You'll have to explain more if you want to make sense to me. I'm a lawyer, remember? Not a bloody tailor.'

'Jesus, what does it matter, anyway? I'm trying to tell you, I've got enough to deal with myself without having to beat my head over Hester. Leave me alone, already.'

'I have to know. I have to know everything about this business if I'm to be any use to it at all. I keep telling you that. It's no use trying to keep me in a box, Hilda, and the sooner you learn that the better. You can run Birgitta the thick like a puppy on a string, but I'm an equal partner. I have to know *everything*.'

252

She looked up at him then from the drawing of a coat she'd been working on and grinned. 'Oh, but you're jealous, aren't you? Go on, admit it. Confession's good for the soul! You're as jealous as hell.'

'Of Birgitta?' he said putting on a cool, mocking voice. 'Jealous of that one? Do me a favour! I was bored out of my mind with her before I even met you, ducky. Bored out of my *mind*. If she wants to play kisses and cuddles with you that's your affair. I'm not interested, believe me I'm not.'

She leaned back, twirling her pen in her fingers, and looking up at him from beneath half-lowered lids in a way he always found uncomfortable.

'Don't look at me like that! I'm telling you, I couldn't care less.'

'Not even about me?' she said softly. 'I believe you when you say you don't care about Birgitta – I mean, who could? I can't imagine how you ever did –'

'She was an easy lay,' he said loudly.

'Okay, I'll grant you, an easy lay. But be honest, Mel. You do care about how I feel about Birgitta, don't you?'

He shook his head impatiently. 'You know bloody well I do! D'you have to make a complete monkey out of me? I told you – you know what I told you.'

'You tried to get me to go to bed with you,' she said. 'That's telling?'

'That's telling,' he said. 'Actions speak louder than words.'

'Oh, there's a lovely original thought! Actions speak louder than words! Who'd ever have thought of putting it so elegantly? Oh, Mel, you are remarkable, you know.'

'Eh?' He stared at her and shook his head, again feeling the muzziness in it, and she laughed.

'You want to know about cabbage? I'll tell you. When I hire a CMT firm – cut, make and trim – I take 'em sufficient yardage for say, twenty completed garments. Okay? If they can get out twenty-one then the extra one is regarded as their perks. That's short for perquisites. P-E-R-Q-U-I-S-I-T-E-S. Me, I don't approve of perks. They're robbery. I pay for my cloth and I intend to get every last inch out of it. So, when that back-street madam tries to tell me she can't get out fifty garments when I know it can be done, that tells me she's trying to cook up some cabbage for

herself. Okay? D'you quite understand now? I hope so –
because I've got work to do, and I'd like you to go and do yours.
Which is to talk to Hester about a loan.'

'You're a bitch, you know that?' he said and could feel his
voice trembling in his throat. 'A Grade-A, first-water, double-
dyed –'

'Yes, dear. As you say, dear. Three bags full, dear. Now will
you go and see Hester? And if you do well, why, maybe I could
get away for the week-end after all.'

He stared at her, almost helpless with his anger, but at the
same time his senses let him down, for the mere thought of
going down to the coast with her for a couple of days was
enough to make him feel randy. And she knew it.

'I might not be available,' he said savagely, and took his hat
and went, knowing she was sitting there and laughing at him.

He took her out to eat, choosing an Italian restaurant in Soho.
He thought she'd like that, and it would be a chance for him to
display his own sophistication. She was, after all, an actress and
had appeared on television at least six times. She was worth
making an effort for.

He picked her up at the house in Hackney, very aware of
being watched from behind the net-curtained front-bedroom
window. She came swinging out of the door, very nonchalant,
and he registered her grosgrain silk duster coat and the long
umbrella in its striped cover with the matching cravat tied
oh-so-casually round her neck, and felt good. She'd gone to a
lot of trouble to look nice for him and that pleased him. He
looked at her covertly as he drove up to town, and she sat very
relaxed and at home staring out a little scornfully at the pedes-
trians, and decided that she didn't look all that bad after all.

The first time he'd met her he'd thought her really plain and
even wondered whether she could be Hilda's real sister at all.
Hilda with her big blue eyes and her fair hair and her luscious
shape couldn't have come from the same source as the bony,
gawky sharp-featured Hester. Even Bonnie, the dull one, was
more interesting. She had a great shape on her, big bust and
nice tight behind, even though she was so dim and got embarrassed so easily. But this one he'd thought an acid drop as soon
as he'd met her, a real acid drop.

254

Until now. Now she looked exciting and a little mysterious and he began to relax. He'd been dreading tonight, dreading having to persuade this odd girl to lend them money, had been sure she'd react as he had to Hilda's refusal to join in the negotiations, with suspicion. And the thought of spending hours in the company of someone so unsexy had filled him with gloom. But now, he let his movements become a little more florid as he changed gear, so that his hand apparently inadvertently touched her thigh. She was wearing a tight blue dress under the duster coat, and it was slit to show a lot of beige stocking, and he liked that. He liked it even more when, far from changing her position to shrink away from his hand, she seemed to relax in such a way that her thigh came closer, was easier to reach.

The restaurant he'd chosen was just right, he decided as they gave up their coats to the waiter. Small tables with candles stuck in Chianti bottles heavily encrusted with the sculpture of wax drippings, the smell of rough red wine and garlic and Continental cigarettes, all very intimate.

He ordered for them both, loudly, choosing *stracciatella*, *scallopini* with *tagliatelle*, *salata verdi*, *zabaglione*, and a bottle of Lacrima Christi, allowing the Italian phrases to loop themselves lusciously round his mouth, and then caught her eye and wondered for one uneasy moment whether she was laughing at him. But she smiled and the doubt passed, and they sat and drank martinis while they waited for the food, and talked.

He didn't bring up the subject of money for some time. They talked first of her career. She'd had three TV jobs, one after the other, over Christmas, two of them for children's TV admittedly, but not bad, and there was an audition coming up soon which sounded hopeful.

'Is it always like this?' he asked, genuinely curious, and filled her glass.

'Always like what?'

'You know – out of work a lot. Hand to mouth.'

'Of course it is! I do better than most – there are people I know who've been signing on at the Club for months on end. I do at least get the jobs sometimes –'

'The Club?'

She laughed, a hard dry laugh. 'Labour Exchange. Didn't you

255

know that? It's the likes of you, working hard, paying your taxes dutifully, who keeps the likes of me in dole money. Doesn't it make you sick?'

'No. Should it?'

'You'd be surprised how many people it does, *and* who don't mind telling you so! I've been told we're parasites, that actors should be exempt from the dole, left to starve if they won't work at other jobs like being a dustman or a char, oh, some lovely things! Tax-payers, you see. They reckon they've got a right to say what the hell they like. If you don't, believe me, you're unusual.'

'I'm a very unusual tax-payer. I don't believe in paying any. So I don't.'

She looked up at that, staring at him over the lifting candle-light. 'You don't?'

He grinned. 'I most definitely don't. That's a mug's game.'

'How do you do it?'

'That'd be telling,' he said lightly. 'More salad?' He pushed his bowl towards her, and she took it, finishing it with despatch.

'There are ways, you know, to make money do all sorts of things.' Once again he poured wine into her glass and then after a moment's hesitation waved to the waiter and ordered another half bottle. 'It's not something that just lies there, as far as I'm concerned. It has to work for its living.'

She laughed. 'And there's me thinking all these years that working for your living was what got you the money. And now you're telling me it's the other way about?'

'It certainly is.' He leaned his elbows on the table and propped his chin on his fists. 'As I see it, any mug can work. Any idiot can go and wear out his body – and it's the only one he's got, remember – with the sort of manual labour the majority go in for. So, I get hold of the money and then let the money do the work.'

'Just like that?'

'Just like that.'

'Tell me how.'

It couldn't be better, he thought jubilantly. Short of putting the words into his mouth she couldn't have made it easier for him. 'Investment,' he said aloud, and shut his mouth like a trap, putting on his can-I-trust-you face.

'Stocks and shares,' she said after a moment, and began to eat the rich sticky *zabaglione* the waiter put in front of her. 'Wall Street crashes, bulls and bears. Not my sort of thing at all.'

He laughed at that, indulgently, as one would laugh at a pert child's mispronunciation of a long word. 'Bless you, no! There's more to investment than stocks and shares and that sort of thing! That takes specialist knowledge and a hell of a lot of capital to get anywhere. It'll be a while before I'm ready for that. No, I was meaning private investment. Spotting a bit of talent, putting it to work for you and your money.'

'Like an angel?' She sounded very cool, very relaxed, and he began to feel at a disadvantage and his mouth tightened a little. She seemed to be aware of his discomfort and smiled at him. Her skin seemed translucent in the candlelight and her eyes much bigger and darker.

'That's a bit of theatre slang,' she said. 'Angels are the people who put money into shows, back them, you know? Then they get out a share of the profits to match the proportion of the money they put up. I'm only just finding out how it works myself. Anyway, it's private investment.'

'Private gambling, my dear,' he said, and leaned back expansively and waved at the waiter for cigars. 'I wouldn't put my money in shows, not ever. That way lies nothing but big losses. Only the insiders make any real money that way – and in that field I'm no insider. In others, however –' He selected a cigar, and went through the agreeable fuss of piercing it, lighting it, rolling it between his lips luxuriously. 'In others I know my stuff.'

He looked at her then and the smoke from his cigar, fragrant and blueish grey, wreathed over the candle and made her look softer and more desirable than ever. He began to concentrate. Hilda and money, that was the object of this exercise.

'What sort of others?' she said softly, and began to play with the wax on the Chianti bottle, making molten little rivulets slither down the gullies and ravines that had folded themselves round the base. 'Do tell me. You never know. I may be rich one day, want to make some of my money earn its living.'

He leaned forwards, confidential and friendly, his eyes wide with candour, his mouth set in a frank honest smile, his jaw line crisp with determination and reliability. It was a look he'd been cultivating for years. 'Well, your little sister, for a start.'

There was a short silence and then she said softly, 'Hildegarde? Your girl friend?'

He was sidetracked at once. 'Did she say she was my girl friend?'

'Oh, we don't discuss you, my dear Mel! I wouldn't do that! But you and she – you are, aren't you? A pair?'

He made a little face. 'Sometimes.'

'Oh, naughty Hildegarde! She really is very naughty –'

'How do you mean?'

'A tease, I'm afraid.' She shook her head a little mournfully and looked up at him, her eyes as wide and honest as his own. 'So much charm, you see, such lovely looks. She is rather beautiful, isn't she? Quite heart-breakingly lovely. But it's spoiled her. Lots of attention does spoil a girl, I think. Don't you?'

He was nonplussed, staring at her while she still played with her candle wax. The rivulets were thickening, building up into a peak as the wax hardened. It was beginning to look quite vulgar. He looked away from the wax, up into her eyes.

'She's quite a worry to me, you know. I mean, as her older sister – and no parents – it's a responsibility.' She still sounded mournful.

'It must be.' His voice was a little hard now. This conversation was going all wrong. He didn't like it. And again, as though she were thinking his thoughts for him, she spoke the words he needed.

'But we really mustn't talk personalities, must we? You were saying about Hilda and my money earning its own living? When I have some, of course.'

'Yes –' He gathered the shreds of his concentration again, and leaned forwards. 'Yes, Hilda. She's very clever, you know. Got a marvellous business head on her. She's running a nice little business already – well, of course, you know that, don't you?'

'I don't know a lot.' She was watchful now, her eyes fixed on his. 'Tell me.'

He told her, and she sat and listened to his account of fashion shows and new designs, out-workers and CMTs, profit margins and cabbage. He sounded very knowledgeable and she sat silent, her face absorbed.

258

'Well, well,' she said softly at last. 'Imagine little Hilda having all that. It's really amazing. And the rest of us absolutely broke to the wide. Not tuppence to bless ourselves with.'

He leaned back, well pleased with himself. He was in control again now. 'Oh, come on, Hester – let's not kid each other. You're doing all right! You may be out of theatre work a lot, but you do other jobs, don't you? Hilda said. And to look at you – your clothes, your style – you can't cry poverty to me.'

'Can't I?' She sounded quite differently, suddenly. 'Can't I just! Shall I tell you something? This – all of it, dress, coat, bloody umbrella – borrowed. The lot. One of the girls at the office. I –' She smiled as suddenly as she'd shown her flash of anger. 'I wanted to impress you.'

'You have,' he said after a moment, and stared at her, and then felt her knee against his, its pressure unmistakable, and knew his face suffused a dull red.

'I'm glad. I like you,' she said simply and returned her attention to the candle wax. But her knee still pressed against his.

There was a silence as he sat and thought, trying to catch hold of the words that were pushing their hectic way through his mind. One minute she was all sophistication and worldly wisdom, the next the little waif, wanting to be taught, displaying her poverty with total ingenuousness. And then she was the siren sending out strong messages of allure. He blinked and moved his knee experimentally, allowing them to fall apart more widely and at once her leg moved forwards and to his amazement he felt her stockinged foot pushing against his crotch as she leaned back and smiled at him, languorous and very relaxed.

'Why did you ask me out tonight, Mel?' she said softly, and he too leaned back, allowing his body to move forwards a little, increasing the contact between himself and her foot.

'Because I like the look of you –' he said, and she laughed, low in her throat, a thick soft sound that he found very exciting. He'd eaten well, but not too much and the wine was moving agreeably in him. He felt more comfortable than he had for a long time.

'Liar,' she said softly. 'You wanted to borrow money. Hilda told you I was working, that Christmas job I'd had had paid well, and that maybe you could borrow as much from me as you did from Stanley.'

He didn't move, but his concentration shifted from his crotch to her words. 'How do you know about Stanley?'

She laughed again, that same soft thick sound. 'Bonnie, dear boy! You must never underestimate little Bonnie! She may be the quiet one, the ordinary one, but I tell you, one of these days she'll set us all on our ears. Bonnie told me. I knew as soon as you called me why you wanted to take me out tonight. It wasn't for the sake of my beautiful blue eyes, was it? The ones I haven't got?'

'Why did you come then?'

'Maybe because I like the look of you?'

There was a little silence and then he laughed, making his own voice as soft and throaty as he could. 'This is funny, you know that?'

'Funny? How?'

'Hilda. She thinks –' He shrugged. 'Let's just say it's funny.'

'I'm falling about. Mel –'

'Yes?'

'Let's talk more about this business of loans, shall we? I may be broke, but I have my sources. I might be able to get my hands on a bob or two. Or even three. Let's talk about it, shall we? Because if Stanley Maddern is in Hilda's business, I reckon I ought to be in too. Because although Stanley isn't exactly my idea of the ideal man – good in the body maybe but thick in the head – one thing he does have is a well-developed sense of cash. So I don't intend to be left out. Let's talk about it.'

'With pleasure,' he said, and leaned back even further, allowing his legs to stretch out, and his behind to slide forward on his seat.

'That's what I meant,' she said softly. 'With pleasure. I can't say my place or yours, because mine – too many people about. Sisters, you know? So it'll have to be yours. Pay up Mel, and let's go. Shall we?'

26

'It's like I've done this every evening for – oh, almost for ever,' Bonnie said, standing on the steps of the Law Courts and looking out into the Strand. 'You know – like those films we used to go to when we were children. They'd show you a tree with its leaves growing and then the blossom and then the leaves falling off to show time going on – I'm talking nonsense, aren't I?'

'Yes,' Sammy said. 'But I know what you mean. These couple of days – they've stretched, gone a peculiar shape. More like a hall of mirrors than a tree.'

'Now who's talking nonsense? A hall of mirrors?'

'Distortions. I keep seeing things, things I remember, all twisted and odd.' He sounded very flat, standing there and staring into the rain-washed street, his coat bundled untidily over his arm. 'We were kids, and I knew you all, and we spent a lot of time together, and – all this talk in court makes me remember. I keep remembering whole scenes. I seem to watch us all doing things, being children, and every one of them is peculiar – every one of them threatens me with what was to come –'

He stopped and she said nothing, standing there beside him and looking up at him, willing him to go on unprompted. He felt it and looked down at her and smiled. 'It's as though I can remember fears and feelings I didn't have at the time. Today gets all mixed up with yesterday. Distorted.'

'Me too,' she said and took her hand from his arm, pushing her fists down into her coat pockets. 'I keep seeing me and Stanley – the children, too, and Hester and Hildegarde – I keep seeing us dancing and marching round each other in patterns. Like the ones we used to do with those stupid playground games. Nothing looks the same any more. Not me, not Stanley.' Her voice dwindled away, and after a moment he put his hand on her elbow.

'Come on. We ate rubbish at lunch-time, so I'm going to get you a decent meal now.'

'Sammy, I can't. I must get home – the children –'

261

'Children? How old's your youngest, again?'

'Thirteen.'

'At that age most of the people we were at school with had started jobs.'

'Not really,' she said mildly. 'We left school at fourteen, unless we were brilliant like you, and got scholarships. Or clever like Hilda and got teachers to look after us and send us to college.'

'Don't split hairs. The point is, she's not a baby, is she? And the older ones'll be there. And Stanley. And that au pair. You're not precisely abandoning them all to starvation and misery if you come out to dinner with me, are you?'

They were down the steps now, on the pavement, and he was holding her quite close, his hand firm against her arm, and she put up her umbrella so that they could both huddle under it. People pushed past them, and they stood there feeling the rain on the back of their necks and looking at each other.

'It's – I want to,' she said. 'I want to a lot. I'd rather spend the evening with you than do anything else. That's why I don't think I should.'

'Why not?'

'You know bloody well!' she said, and there was a note of hysteria in her voice and he held on to her arm even more tightly. 'I'm frightened, Sammy.'

'Why?' he said again and she put up one hand and pushed the wet hair off his forehead.

'You're as bad as Mr Hermann. My analyst. All these whys.' Her voice was unsteady.

'You'll have to answer sooner or later, won't you?'

'Must it be now?'

'I think so. I think it might be easier. In the long run.'

She closed her eyes, smelling the traffic grinding heavily along the road beside her, hearing the roar of voices and engines, the noise of London lapping her round. 'Because these two days have reminded me. Because these two days have made me see things about being married to Stanley that I've known all along and didn't want to think about. Because I had a hell of a crush on you, a long time ago and never really got rid of it. What more do you want? Shall I get down on my knees on these wet paving stones and plead to be allowed to go on living my life the way it was? I was managing fine, I was really managing very well indeed –'

'Were you? I'm delighted to hear it. Will you be able to go on managing so well, even if you don't come to dinner with me?'

She shook her head. 'I don't know. How can I possibly? But I ought to try.'

'Why?'

'Oh, ye Gods, Sammy, get off my back, will you? I told you –'

He began to walk, turning west, curving round into the Aldwych. 'We'll have a drink at least. You can't go now, not till we've talked a bit. I – damn it all, I didn't mean this to happen, you know that? I've been sitting there beside you for two days, watching them both, remembering how they both tied me in knots, and how you didn't and feeling them let go and you holding on and knowing what a bloody mess I'd be making if I went on – a mess for you, I mean, and I swore to myself I wouldn't, I swore to myself I'd see you politely to your car and then go back to the hospital and not come to court tomorrow and never say a word. I really meant that, you know? Damn you, Bonnie. You've changed. You're a different person and still the same one. It's a very difficult mixture.'

'I'm not sure I know exactly what you're talking about,' she said carefully, trying not to stop him, glad to be going to have a drink with him. A drink could do no harm. None at all. And she'd told them she might stay out tonight anyway, hadn't she, all those years ago this morning?

'I'm just talking,' he said. 'I'm just talking. Come on. We can get something here –'

As they disappeared into the big swinging doors of the Waldorf Astoria, Mel leaned forwards in his seat and peered out of the taxi window, wiping his hand over the glass to clear the mist.

'There's your sister,' he said. 'Bonnie. She looks good, doesn't she? I saw her in court. I wouldn't have known her.'

The taxi curved left, moved into the traffic making for Waterloo Bridge and the church in the middle of the road obscured his view, and he leaned back again.

'Bonnie? She never looks any different,' Hildegarde said absently and didn't turn her head. 'She's like God Almighty, the

263

same yesterday, today and for ever. And about as comfortable to be with.'

'That sounds very bitchy. What has Bonnie done to you, for God's sake? She's not involved in this business, after all. It's Hester, not Bonnie. Remember?'

'And Stanley,' Hildegarde said, and her voice was tight with control. 'Bonnie's husband, *remember*? He's as much involved in this bloody rip-off as anyone —'

'What do you mean, rip-off? Come on, Hildegarde, calm down! I told you — I got the money tied up so tightly no one can ever get a fraction of it. There's no way anyone but me could ever work out what the business is worth. I've spread it everywhere, as thin as you like. It's not as though Maddern and Hester have a leg to stand on, even! You're suing them, remember. Well, Hester anyway. She's the one who's involved in this defamation business. Her and Gerrard. She's the defendant, not you. The worst that can happen is that you lose, and have to pay costs. Not cheap, I grant you, but nothing like as big as the cut they were after originally. And after all this is over, they'll think twice before they attempt to use the courts to get any money out of us. I've told you, I've worked out what they're entitled to, and that's all they'll get — it's around three and a half thousand each, which is enough, I know. But it's not what they're asking for, and it's all they're going to get. So calm down, will you?'

'Calm down?' The taxi swerved out of the heavy traffic turning on to the bridge and she was thrown against him, and he held on for a moment, revelling in the smell of her, until she pulled herself back, furiously. 'Calm down? When that bitch is trying to rob me? She always did. If it was mine, she had to have it, no matter what. Ever since I can remember. Even that poor old cow Sylvia, you know that? She set her up with Auntie Fido, would you believe it, with Auntie Fido! She hates Fido almost as much as she hates me, and that's saying something — but she finagles and twists Sylvia round her finger until the daft creature doesn't know whether she's on her head or her heels, and finishes up living in that muck heap in Hackney. All to do me in the eye, you know that? All to make problems for me —'

He sat and looked at her, and after a moment shook his head. 'I'm glad I never had brothers or sisters. When I was a kid, I felt deprived, I really did. But looking at you – Christ, I'm well out of it –'

She was silent, staring broodingly out of the taxi window as they pushed their way past Charing Cross. It was as though he hadn't spoken.

'No matter what it was,' she said suddenly. 'She was jealous. She was always jealous. She's still jealous.'

'Oh, I don't know,' he said, still watching her. 'She's doing all right for herself, after all.'

It was odd to see her like this, ruffled, angry. She who had always been so offhand and casual about everything, who even when they were making love could suddenly talk about business, remind him to chase up money, organize a tax meeting – to see her like this was almost alarming in its strangeness. Something particular had got under her skin, something about today's evidence, and he tried to think back, work out what it was. It had been a tough day, a hard day, and tomorrow could be worse, but all through so far she'd been flippant about it all, told him it was good publicity, that in the long run it would improve the business. But now, suddenly, she was different. Uptight and – he shook his head, puzzled, and stared at her.

She turned her head then and looked back at him, her blue eyes seeming as hard and opaque as pebbles. 'Mel!' she said, and her voice was equally hard. 'I want to know. What did happen? When she loaned you the money?'

He blinked. 'Nothing happened. She loaned the money. That's all. I brought it back to you, didn't I? You got it – what are you talking about now? Jesus, Hildegarde, it was over twenty years ago! What are you talking about, what happened?'

'With you and her? I never gave a damn before, but now – I want to know. What happened?'

'I told you. Nothing happened. She just –' His voice dwindled away. 'She just loaned me the money.'

JANUARY 1956

'Let me go, let me go, let me go, lover,
Let me be, set me free from your spell . . . .'

He couldn't quite believe it. He'd thought himself an experienced man, someone who had forgotten more about sex than

265

most people would ever know, but within ten minutes of letting them both into his flat, he was nonplussed. She came on so fast; made for the bed room unerringly, was out of her clothes and tugging at his before he'd had time to catch his breath properly. And then, when they were on the bed, she did things, gave him sensations, that he'd never shared with anyone but himself. He'd been a bit ashamed of some of the fantasies he'd had about sex, to tell the truth, over the years, yet here she was, calm as you like, making them into reality.

After a while they lay smoking and he was blissfully sleepy, wanting only to lie there with his limbs warm and relaxed, his muscles quiescent. But she was as whipcord taut as ever, and lay on her side, her head propped up on one fist, her elbow making a deep dent in the bed and he looked at her and thought – she's got funny breasts; huge nipples, not much else, nothing to put your head against and nestle. Sometimes Hildegarde would let him put his face between hers, breathe the warmth of her, make himself feel at peace that way, and he loved it. She wouldn't play the Momma for long, admittedly, but when she was in the mood at least she had the equipment for it.

Comfortable though he was he couldn't resist the little wave of malice that rose in him and he said lazily, 'You and your sister – you're quite different, aren't you?'

'How?' She seemed relaxed and unthreatened.

'Oh, shape, for a start.' He smiled and put his hand out and with one forefinger touched a nipple. 'Now, you, you've got big teats, but not much to hang 'em on.'

'True enough – Hilda always was one of your pneumatic ladies.' She sounded judicious, very objective, and he was a little surprised. Most women resented being compared with other women. 'Mind you,' she went on, 'you should see Bonnie. She really is one of your earth-mother types. Billowy, that's Bonnie.'

He squinted up at her, the smoke from his cigarette wreathing round his eyes. 'Don't you mind?'

'What, not having huge knockers? That'd be daft. I never waste time mourning over what I can't have. If it's available I go and get it, and if it's not –' she shrugged and rolled over until she was lying on her front, her head turned so that her face was very close to his. He could smell her breath, faintly garlicky, but not

266

disagreeably so. She put out one hand and rubbed his belly and then cupped it over his crotch.

'That's friendly,' he said.

'I'm very friendly. What else is different about me?'

'So you do care?'

'How d'you mean?'

'I thought you were a bit too good to be true – letting me compare you with your sister, not minding. I'd have thought most girls would do their nuts.'

'I'm not most girls. Would Hildegarde do her nut?'

'I don't know. We've never discussed you. I mean, there's never been any need, has there? As far as she's concerned, she's the only lady named Morris I've ever played naughty games with.'

'Is that how you see it? Naughty games? I don't.'

'Well, how else can I? I'm not married. So it's not kosher, so it's naughty games.'

'Balls to that! Married, not married, what's that got to do with anything? Sex is like eating. You've got to do it to keep alive. Sometimes you just stoke yourself with any old thing, sometimes you choose someone special to share a meal with, and then it's a super meal, with all sorts of fancy touches – like this –'

He put his cigarette out just in time, because again she was all over him, as eager and as busy as she'd been when they'd started, and just as clever, because to his own amazement she brought him to her own pitch of readiness very fast, lifted him to an almost painful climax and then left him breathless and stranded, still lying on his back – he'd stayed so throughout – with his arms flung wide.

'Boy,' he said after a while. 'Some dinner! Do you usually eat as well as you screw?'

'If I can get it,' she said coolly. 'Me, I like the best of everything, but like I said, what I can't have I don't cry for. Where's the bathroom?'

She came back wearing his dressing gown and sat on the bed beside him, and he woke from his doze and stared up at her, bewildered. 'Hildy?'

'Go on – she never lets you call her Hildy, does she?'

He blinked and sat up, yawning. 'I'm sorry. I forgot where I was for a moment. I'm sorry.'

'Sorry I'm here? Sorry we did it? Sorry I wasn't Hilda? Sorry we've stopped? Take your pick.'

'Sorry we've stopped – but I couldn't start again.' He held his hands in mock surrender. 'I have to tell you, ducky, that you've won this round. I thought I could go it, but you – boy, you're something very special –'

'As special as Hildy?'

'I'm getting really confused, you know that?' He went to wash too, talking to her over his shoulder as he splashed himself with cold water, threw talcum powder around, climbed into his best black pyjamas.

'If you mean you can't work out whether I'm jealous of my sister or not, then you needn't bother. Jealous I'm not. Competitive I most certainly am.'

'What's the difference?'

'Jealousy means eating your heart out for what you can't have. Competitiveness is my way – taking it if you can get it, abandoning it if you can't in favour of something better, and more available.'

'Did you want me? I mean, let's not beat about the bush. I've been seduced.' He came in from the bathroom and struck a pose, one knee bent, one wrist elegantly drooping. 'Honestly Orficer, it wasn't my fault, I mean, Orficer, truly, truly, the lady just – oh dreary me, the lady just *took* me, you know, Orficer?'

She laughed. 'And you just a lawyer! Should have been an actor, like me. You'd knock 'em in the aisles down at the Old Vic.'

'And sign on at the Club every week? No thanks, sweetheart. Not for little Melvin Bremner. I like my cash coming regular and rich. Like my women.' Again he smirked at her.

'Will you tell Hildegarde about this?' She was lying on his bed, her hands behind her head and the dressing gown spread negligently about her.

'Well, now, I hadn't given the matter much thought. Do you want me to? Is that what all this was about? Yah, yah, yah, I got your dolly, I got your dolly?'

'You can be really perceptive sometimes, Mel. For a lawyer.' She got up and went over to pick up her clothes from the floor

268

where she'd dropped them, and began to dress. 'Would you believe I don't care one way or the other? For me the pleasure of winning a competition is that I know I've won it. I don't need a lot of other people clapping or booing to prove it. Hildegarde might mind, of course. She can be a right grabber, can my little sister.'

'Grabber?'

'What's everyone else's is hers, what's hers is her own. She mightn't give a tuppenny damn about you, but she'd be livid if she thought anyone else was getting any joy out of you, specially me. She resents me, you know? I've got as much drive and push as she has and –'

'Who said she doesn't give a tuppenny damn about me?' He was sitting on his bed, staring at her with a sulky look on his face, and she laughed as she caught sight of his expression.

'God, I don't know! Maybe she adores you! I'm just explaining how she is. Not making any value judgements about the quality of your personal relationships. There, doesn't that sound good? Real strong language that. Value judgements –'

He stared at her, still nonplussed. She seemed to slide from mood to mood without being aware she had done so. She threw words around like confetti, but when they hit you, they stung.

'Hadn't we better talk money?' She was dressed now, and although he was decently covered he felt very much at a disadvantage. Her clothes looked sleek and good on her, and his black pyjamas which he'd thought so very elegant seemed sleazy, shouting that they were made of cheap rayon and not expensive silk.

'What?'

'Money, dear. That loan. What's in it for me?'

He shook his head, pushing his own mood back into a business one.

'In the long term, a lot,' he said, and smoothed his hand over his head. 'Er – five hundred pounds is what Stanley's put in. Are you interested in matching that?'

'Might be. What will it be used for?'

'We reckon the time's ripe for getting out of the mass market, and into the better end. There're premises in Buckingham Palace Gate I can get reasonably, and use as a show room and workshops. We'll build our own clientele –'

'Do you say *we* when Hildegarde's around?' She laughed at the look on his face. 'No, I rather thought not. Anyway, bash on regardless. She's going to go in for the haute couture, is that it? Fat women from Edgware who spend a lot in cash and so-called society types whose cheques bounce but give the place a bit of class?'

'Something like that,' he said sulkily. She could be as sharp-tongued as Hildegarde when she tried.

'Right. What are you offering, then? What's the return?'

He explained, carefully, repeating word for word what he'd told Stanley at her party in Shepherd's Bush and she listened, not appearing to concentrate particularly but not missing a word. And when he'd finished she nodded.

'I'll come in. But I want the thing worded differently. I want the same sort of deal that angels get on a show. D'you understand?'

He was suddenly feeling very tired. It had been a long day, and for all his air of knowingness and worldly experience she had put him through sexual athletics that had drained him, and he yawned hugely. 'I'll bring the document to Hackney – tomorrow night – we can sort it out then –'

'No. I'll come here. Around eleven – then you can spend the evening with Hildegarde as usual, can't you? I'll bring the money, you bring me some sort of document. But remember – I want an angel deal. Not the sort that Stanley's got.'

'Tomorrow,' he said, wanting to get her out as soon as possible, aching for bed. 'Tomorrow. We'll sort it all out then.'

27

No one could doubt his unease. He stood there fiddling first with his wrist watch, then putting both hands on the edge of the witness box, then tweaking at his jacket. His forehead shone a little greasily, and his upper lip was beaded with sweat.

Wooderson looked up at him and sighed and then bent his head to his papers once more. The overhead fluorescent lights were already on and the rain was beating as relentlessly as ever against the windows. It had been misery driving in this morning with the traffic nose to tail everywhere, and even more misery trying to park. There was hardly anyone in court who wasn't edgy and sour, and the judge looked more irritable than any of them. All they needed was a tense witness who wouldn't answer properly, who'd get questions tangled and fall over his tongue.

'Mr Bremner,' he began ponderously. 'I want you to tell us about the finances of the business Miss Hildegarde Maurice runs. You are in charge of all financial operations, I understand?'

'Er – yes –' Mel's voice was thin and almost inaudible and he tried it again and it came out sounding rough and harsh, and strangely that seemed to comfort him. He gained confidence.

'Yes. Right from the beginning. I've been her financial adviser, dealt with the accountants, the contracts, the books –'

'I see. You have special training for such work?'

'Special training?'

'Your professional qualifications, Mr Bremner. Can you elucidate?'

Mel's forehead smoothed at once. 'Oh! Oh, yes. I'm a Bachelor of Laws. London University. Graduated 1952 –'

'But never practised?'

'Not in an *ordinary* practice. No. Certainly not.' The fat man beside Hester looked up at him and his expression was flat and cold and Sammy nudged Bonnie, amused. 'That'll endear him to this little lot,' he whispered.

'Hush,' Bonnie said, and squeezed his hand. From the

moment they'd met at the entrance to the courts they'd been light-hearted, standing there dripping and laughing at each other's wetness, giggling at others in the same state. They hadn't talked at all about last night and what Stanley had said when she got in at midnight. Sammy hadn't asked, and she hadn't volunteered. There was no point in it.

'You joined Miss Maurice's firm immediately upon qualifying then?'

'No way! She hadn't got a firm then! No, I went to the contracts department of a bank – just for a year or two. For experience, you know. But I advised and guided her from the very start, as soon as she started running a business at all. I was always very involved – even before I joined her full time, always the one who knew about the money and the contracts and so on –' He seemed suddenly to recover himself, to realize where his boasting was leading him. 'Not that I was in sole command, of course. Miss Maurice – she was the final arbiter, she was the one who decided everything, who insisted on being responsible for everything. I just guided and advised.'

'You just guided and advised. I see.' Wooderson said heavily, and rustled the papers in his hand.

'What's all this about, Bonnie?' Sammy whispered. 'They seem to be making a lot of fuss about money – what was it all about? Do you know?'

She turned her head and looked at him, and wanted to touch him, wanted to stroke the untidy hair away from his forehead and had to hold on tightly to her control of herself to prevent it. It was mad, quite absurd, to feel like this. At her time of life, and a meditator and going to an analyst and all. To feel like this was irrational and dangerous and absolutely marvellous.

'Some of it,' she whispered back. 'Not all, but some. They tried to get it back, you see, only they wanted it on a percentage basis. Not just as a loan – there was a hell of a row about it –'

DECEMBER 1970

'Like a circle in a spiral, like a wheel within a wheel,
Never ending or beginning on an ever-spinning reel,
Like the circles that you find, in the windmills of your mind . . . .'

272

'Will you look at this, Bonnie? Just look – go on, read it –'

She pushed her sun-glasses more firmly on to her nose, and took the newspaper from him and obediently began to read the article he was thrusting his index finger at, squinting a little as the shadows from the tree under which she was sitting made patterns which danced on the print.

It was hard to read; the financial pages which were all Stanley ever read of the Sunday papers had always bored her, and this piece seemed to be as dull as any of them. Hardly worth the expense of buying a copy flown in from London. For the pesetas he'd spent on this, she could have got another one of those little Spanish dolls for Tracy. Oh dear, Tracy, she thought. Are they all right? I should have told Stanley I couldn't go, should have stayed at home with them. It's not fair going away without them this time of the year –

'Well? What d'you say *now*? You and your wait and see, leave it alone –'

Guiltily she concentrated, and read the article again, properly this time instead of just letting the words slide across her eyes.

Fashion was Big News, it said. British fashion was going to conquer world markets yet again in the near future. Three top firms had gone into Europe in a big way, were chalking up incredible sales. Hildegarde Maurice –

She didn't have to struggle to concentrate now, and read the article to the end, carefully, and then folded the paper and gave it back to Stanley.

'So, now what do you say? Did you see what it said? Annual turnover of three-quarters of a million – did you see that? Seven hundred and fifty thousand pounds – and that's what they admit to! Your sister's a bloody sight too fly to let all her profits appear on the books. There's more behind than there is in front, I'll bet you. Or damn near – so now what do you say?'

'Stanley, what are you going on about? Your own business is doing very well, we don't go short of anything, the children, thank heaven, have all they need – why do you have to be so – so – oh, I just don't understand it.'

'Talk to you, talk to a fool,' Stanley grunted and sat there in the deck chair, his legs stuck out aggressively on the footrest, the sun umbrella throwing a green light on to his face.

He looked good; his weight had gone up some, admittedly,

but he was still handsome, with his dark crisp hair and heavy face, and his body was in good shape. He could still make her feel good too; she looked at him there and remembered last night and having sex with the light on, and how nice it had been. It was always nice on holiday; that was one of the reasons they always tried to get their winter break, to enjoy themselves a bit. So Stanley always said, winking at their friends when they told them they were off again, buying himself new shirts with matching shorts in outrageous prints he'd never wear at home in Edgware, not even beside the swimming pool they'd put in last year. And now he'd gone and ruined it all, insisting on buying that wretched paper, insisting on reading the financial pages.

'Oh, I'm sorry, Stan, honestly I am, but I just can't get worked up about it all. If you want the five hundred back, then take it back! You don't need it, but take it back! She's been doing well for years now, and I'm glad for her, I really am, and I thought you were too. Why do we always have to have this – this moan every time there's any mention of Hildegarde's business? Is there something wrong with our own business that it gets under your skin that way? All I ask is to be helped to understand.'

He looked at her and then, as though making up his mind, nodded, and put his feet firmly on the terrace and leaned forwards. The green glow of the umbrella shifted from his face, bathed his shoulders, and he squinted at her in the sunshine.

'Okay – okay, I'll tell you. And hear me out, and don't tell me I'm some sort of pig, some villain because of what I say. Because I can tell you, your sister agrees with me – Hester agrees with me.'

'Agrees about what?'

'About the way this loan – the loans we both made – ought to place us. Now, listen carefully. I know you're not interested in business and I've never talked to you about it much, because you've got your own business to keep you busy, me, the kids, the house – but this you've got to understand. When I lent your sister that five hundred pounds fourteen, fifteen years ago it wasn't so easy to put my hands on such money as it is now. It was real money then – today, five hundred – it's not so much. But then, it was more. It was more to me, and it was one hell of a lot more to her. Right, I lend her this money, your sister

Hester lends her the same, and it's one lousy deal we get. One lousy deal. That Mel Bremner – well, I should have seen through him. But then, I was younger, more trusting, and she was your sister, for God's sake, and this was your sister's boy friend –'

'I had nothing to do with it all,' Bonnie said mildly. 'I remember – it was between you and Hildegarde. She went straight to you, never even told me she was after a loan, I mean, I didn't ask you to help her –'

'I didn't say you did. Just that when I lent it, I had all this in my mind. So we agree, Hester and me, we agree to this really bad deal. They can have the money as long as they need it, we can't call on it until such time as they reckon the business can stand it and all that time we get nothing.'

'Not nothing, Stanley. The interest – I remember about the interest.'

'Oh, sure. It sounds good, eh? Compound interest at two-and-a-half per cent over bank rate, adjusted as the rate goes up or down. Sure. You know what that adds up to now? Peanuts! I tell you, they've had our money all these years and we get peanuts back – when we get it back.'

'You can have it whenever you want it, I should think.' She picked up the paper again. 'I mean if this paper's got it right, what's five hundred to each of you to Hildegarde now?'

'That's my point, that's exactly my point! She could have paid us back any time this last ten years – and you know something? I'd have taken it, taken my interest, and wished her well. Never given it another thought. But no, as long as we didn't ask, we didn't get. And when I said to you – how often I said to you! – we should get our money back you'd say, "Let it go, wait a bit, who needs it?" – Didn't you? You can't deny it.'

'I'm not denying it, I just never thought it mattered that much. I never thought it was worth making an unpleasantness over. After that business with Auntie Fido – oh, it was all such a mess! And I thought, forget it, maybe you'd forget it, because you said yourself, what's five hundred pounds to you, now? There's Hildegarde, not married, only herself to depend on, and I thought –'

He leaned back at that and laughed aloud, his face creasing into white lines through his tan. 'Hildegarde, a poor little spinster? Listen, Bonnie, if you can believe that, you can believe anything.'

She made a face. 'Well, I know. It's a bit daft – but I just didn't want a fuss. I can't bear fusses –'

'Well, there'll be more now, I'm telling you.' He sounded grim. 'Because I've had it right up to here. I've had enough of your poor little spinster sister Hildegarde, who's about as helpless as a tarantula. And with Hester's help, we're going to sort it out. We're going to sort it out good.'

'How?' She was uneasy and he shook his head.

'That's my affair.'

'No it isn't. You said you were going to explain. So tell me.'

He was on his feet now, picking up his glasses, pushing his feet into his sandals.

'You'll make a fuss telling me not to make a fuss. You're better off out of it, after all.'

She got up too, and together they began to walk back to the hotel. 'Look, Stanley, you started all this – started telling me what you were going to do. You can't just go all mysterious on me now. Not here – not while we're on holiday.'

She was holding on to his arm, looking up into his face, deliberately wheedling. She didn't know why it mattered to find out what he was going to do, but matter it did, and she pulled on his arm again.

'All right. All right, I'll tell you. I'm going to phone Hester in London. I'm going to tell her about this report if she hasn't already seen it. And I'm going to suggest that we make a claim on our loans.'

'What sort of claim?'

'Not now, I won't tell you now. Tonight, after I've talked to her, found out a couple of things from my office, checked with the accountant, tonight, I'll tell you. Listen, you go shopping now, all right? You said you wanted to go shopping for the kids. So go. Here's money – that be enough? Okay, take another thousand – this money, it's like shopping with old bus tickets – I'll see you here afterwards. In the bar, before dinner, okay? Don't talk to any strange Spaniards –' And he was gone, in high good humour, making his way to the telephone kiosk on the far side of the great marble-floored foyer.

She dressed, and went shopping. There was nothing else to

do, after all. But all the time as she walked through the little streets that hung on the hillside beneath the cathedral in Palma, she was abstracted, finding little pleasure in buying dolls for Tracy and clothes for Sharon and bits and pieces for the boys. Suddenly Stanley was being threatening, and it wasn't a posture of his that she found familiar. Overbearing, thoughtless, about as sensitive as a tortoise – these things she had discovered about him a long time ago. But he'd never posed any sort of threat, never made her feel at all alarmed. Until now. His blustering, his occasional roars of temper at the boys, all these had been easy to tolerate, for the children showed the same sort of behaviour and she'd learned over the years how to soothe them. She soothed him the same way.

But now she felt tense and worried and teased away at her mind, trying to work out why. But she couldn't; all she knew was that tangling with Hildegarde had always caused trouble when she was a child, when they had all lived in that house in Hackney, and she felt deep inside that she was as dangerous to peace of mind now as she had been then.

For years Stanley had muttered about that stupid loan, had moaned about being used, about being treated like a door-mat, about people who didn't pay back their debts just because they thought being family made them exempt, and she'd been able to deflect him. But this time she knew it wasn't going to work. He'd had too much time, sitting here in a Majorcan hotel, to think about it, too much time to spend making calls to London, showing off his busy importance to the hotel clerks. This time he was going to do it.

And he did. He was in a towering mood when they met in the bar, full of *bonhomie*, laughing and talking to the other guests, being Stanley the Happy, Stanley the Big Businessman, Stanley with the Lovely Wife. He greeted her solicitously, fussing over a chair for her, taking her parcels and imperiously calling a page boy to take them to their room, ordering her drink with a great deal of fussing with the barman about how much orange to put in the gin, how it had to be freshly squeezed. Oh God, she thought. What has he done, what's happening?

It wasn't until they went into dinner though, that they could talk, because there were so many fellow guests about all wanting to join them, to bask in his jollity; and then she had to go

277

and dress. But at last, over the consommé, they were out of others' earshot.

'Well?'

'Well what?'

'You know perfectly well what I mean! What did Hester say? What did the accountant say?'

He put down his spoon, beaming at her. 'A lot. A hell of a lot, and I'm here to tell you that Bremner is going to have his tail so roasted he won't know what hit him. He's going to squirm – and Hildegarde won't be that happy either, and you might as well know it now as later.'

'What are you going to do?'

'We're claiming that as we both put up twenty-five per cent of the original capital – Hildegarde had just a thousand, remember? – we're entitled to twenty-five per cent now.'

'In interest? Oh, come on, Stanley, that's –'

'Not interest. The firm. We want a quarter each of the firm. It's ours. We own it.'

'You're mad,' she said incredulously. 'You've got to be stark staring mad! How can you expect Hildegarde to give you that sort of – Hester said the same? You're mad!'

'No one's asking her to give it. It's not a gift. It's what we're entitled to, and we're going to claim it. Go to court if we have to. No, don't look like that. Go to court, I said and I mean it. Hester's the same. She's as sick as I am. All these years and we carried the burden, and what return did we get? Well, we're going to get it now. Once we get back to London, I'm going to see Bremner and give him the chance to settle out of court. But I'll warn him – and I'm warning you – that we're not bluffing. Hester had seen the paper too, and she was as angry as I am. Now, we're together on this, there won't be any stopping us. Will you have some of the salad with your veal? No? Then I will. Waiter!'

28

Tension was definitely rising now, and Bonnie let go of Sammy's hand. It seemed all wrong, somehow, with Mel up there talking about Stanley, and Stanley not here to know about it, to defend himself. Defend himself? Silly thought. He had nothing to be ashamed of, nothing to defend, not in a legal sense, of course. Did he?

It was ridiculous how pat it happened; there she had been thinking about him, and there he was, coming through the door of the court. There was room for him; the weather seemed to have helped keep the gawpers away, and there was none of the undignified fussing there had been on the first day. He just walked in and sat down at the end of the row she and Sammy were in, crossing his knees a little awkwardly in the confined space, staring stonily at the court in front of him.

She leaned forwards, and hissed, 'Stan!' and he heard her at once. She could tell that by the way his ears seemed to lift against his skull, and she almost wanted to giggle. Being able to waggle his ears had been one of his party tricks, long ago. But it wasn't funny now, because after a long moment he just turned his head and looked at her coldly and then looked back at the court again. He was still angry about last night, she thought. Oh God!

Sammy beside her sat very still, and she could feel the tightness in him, and for one brief second she wanted to move away from him, wanted to go and sit beside Stanley and make him feel better. He was her husband, he was entitled to her support, whatever happened he was entitled to that, or what was marriage about, after all? But then she looked at Sammy's profile, and thought absurdly – but I've known Sammy longer. As though that had anything to do with it.

She didn't move. She just sat there beside Sammy, feeling the tension in him, and feeling the waves of cold Stanley was throwing out. It was all very uncomfortable and she thought suddenly, I wish I was Hildegarde. I wish I was like her and didn't care, and never felt anything for people. It must be marvellous to be like Hildegarde.

'Mr Bremner.' Counsel was probing now, peering at the man in the witness box as though he were a rather unpleasant specimen under a microscope. 'The matter of these loans – as I understand it you made a different arrangement with each of these creditors without telling them so, and yet allowing them to believe they had the same – ah – deal. Is that so?'

Mel was sweating again. 'I don't know what you mean,' he said, and his voice had a sulky not in it. 'I was asked by Hildegarde – by Miss Maurice – to arrange two loans, both for the same amount. I did. Five hundred pounds each, it was.'

'Yes, Mr Bremner. That is not in dispute. What *is* in dispute is the fact that with one of these loans – that with Mr – ah – Stanley Maddern, Miss Maurice's brother-in-law –'

'Not at that time,' Mel said swiftly. 'He wasn't her brother-in-law then.'

The silken arm waved that away. 'The loan from Mr Maddern was taken on the understanding that the capital sum would be repaid at some unspecified later date and that compound interest at a varying rate, depending on bank rate, would accrue. But the loan from Miss Morrissey now, that was different, was it not? You entered into quite another arrangement with her.'

'I can't remember,' Mel said loudly and Wooderson peered up at him and shook his head sadly.

'Now, come, Mr Bremner. Are you asking the court to believe that matters of such great importance could possibly slip your memory? When in addition the question of the loans and the agreements made about them was brought to your notice in quite recent times? Around the time of this television programme the content of which we are here in this court to consider?'

'My memory's all confused,' Mel said, and looked down at his hands on the rim of the box. 'It was all such ages ago –'

'And yet you are the firm's financial adviser and guide! Come, Mr Bremner, I invite you to cudgel your memory, to bring back into recollection these important facts. For if you do not, the jury, I am sure, will draw their own conclusions. Now, let me help you. In the very early part of 1971, you were called upon by Mr Stanley Maddern and Miss Hester Morrissey, were you not? In your offices in Lower Regent Street – I am sure you recall that afternoon –'

JANUARY 1971

'All day long I'd happy, happy be,
If I was a wealthy man . . . .'

It had been a cold morning, and he'd told the girl to bring an extra fire into his office from the big show room, and now he'd got a really comfortable fug built up, and was sitting happily in his shirt sleeves, his feet up on his desk and dictating long memos into his brand-new German dictating machine.

It wasn't an easy one to use, and the secretaries always got the tapes snarled or accidentally wiped them because they couldn't follow the instructions, but he'd refused flatly to buy any other kind. This one looked what it was – expensive, the right equipment for a really successful yet still up-and-coming young executive to have in his office. It went with the furniture, the heavy black leather and the Danish teak and the big modern paintings on the wall.

Privately he thought the paintings a load of nonsense with their swathes of colour and peculiar shapes and nothing you could call recognizable in them, but that didn't matter. The man in the gallery at Beak Street had told him they were the very latest of their kind – and at those prices they ought to be – and they certainly impressed any visitors that came in. What with them and the three phones in different colours he was happy. Sure, some people sneered at such offices; he wasn't stupid, he knew there were some who just laughed but the people he cared about, the people who mattered to him, they were impressed. And that was what it was all about.

The intercom buzzed and he swore and flipped the switch. 'I told you not to interrupt me!' he bawled. 'What the hell do you –'

'There's two people here who said you'd see 'em and that you'd be as mad as hell if I didn't say they was here. So what am I supposed to do? Send 'em away and have you start shouting about that? For two pins I'd –'

'Oh, all right, stop moaning!' This girl was getting too

281

damned big for her boots. A couple of lunches, the odd dinner and she thought she was a partner. 'Who is it?'

'Maddern and Morrissey. Man and woman,' the intercom snapped.

'Maddern and – oh!' He sat and thought for a moment. 'Yes, all right. Sorry I shouted. Tell 'em I'm a bit tied up at the moment, send 'em in in a minute or two, when I buzz –'

He arranged his desk, spreading the papers as far as they would go over the wide teak expanse, and then ran his hands over his hair, ruffling it to a really hectic rather than merely busy look. After a moment's thought, he pulled his tie loose, too; shirt sleeves alone wouldn't make entirely the right impression.

He buzzed and they came in, Hester first, looking extraordinary in a plaid suit with the trousers ending three inches above her ankles, to show thick white socks and high heeled wedge shoes. He grinned; she'd got that straight out of *Vogue* and it really wasn't for her at all. Not at her age. She had to be forty, if not more. After all, Hildegarde was thirty-eight, though she'd kill him if he told people that.

'Hey, this is a great treat!' He stood up, deliberately pushing his papers aside with a for-you-even-desperately-vital-matters-can-wait gesture. 'Just passing, or what?'

'Or what,' Hester said, and sat down, stretching out on the big black settee.

'Thought we'd just come, rather than make an appointment, Bremner.' Stanley said, and sat down too, stretching his arms across the back of the settee and Mel looked at them both uncertainly for a moment. They looked cat-like, satisfied, and yet alert. He smelled tension.

'Well, whatever it is, it's great to see you!' he said heartily. 'Sherry? Whisky? Name your poison.' He went over to the big cabinet and casually pushed up the front to show the vast mirror-lined interior with its tightly-packed array of bottles.

'Sugar-free tonic,' Hester said. 'Same for Stanley. He's beginning to bulge a bit.'

He fussed with glasses and ice and lemons, chattering busily about the last time he'd seen them both, which was at Warren's barmitzvah.

'A lovely party, beautiful, really classy, people are still talking

282

about it.' But they made no response, just sat and listened and watched him, and took their drinks from him.

He sat down again behind his desk, leaning back expansively. 'So? To what do I owe the honour? Business of some sort? Must be – or you wouldn't be here, I suppose. I mean,. for the purely social – by the way, you know Hildegarde's away? In the States. One of those fantastic selling trips of hers. If she doesn't come back with enough work to keep all the factories going full blast for the next year, quite apart from the heavy home and European demand, then I'm the Chancellor of the Exchequer. And you can't get anyone dafter than that!' He laughed loudly and drank some of his whisky.

'Maybe it's just as well she's away,' Stanley said. 'You might find it simpler to cope with this matter on your own –'

'Stanley, let's not be devious,' Hester said, her eyes on Mel. 'We came now because we knew Hildegarde was away. It suits us better to deal with Mel. And it'll probably suit Mel better too.'

'You'd better put me out of the misery of my ignorance,' Mel said lightly, very aware of her fixed stare. 'So what is all this? Going to put the bite on me for some charity affair? Believe me, I'd be glad to –'

'Charity? Don't believe in it. It's against my religion,' Hester said. 'No ducks. This is strictly personal. It's about the money we loaned you a while back. I'm sure you remember it.'

He felt his face go red, and was furious with himself. But it was unavoidable; as soon as she'd said it, he'd remembered. There had been only those two episodes, those two evenings in his flat all that time ago and never again had he got her into bed with him – not that he'd tried, what with Hildegarde to think about and all – but he'd never forgotten it. And now he remembered it so vividly that he felt a physical response, and he jumped up and went over to the drinks again, needing to be busy.

'Freshen your glasses? Not that it's easy to freshen tonic water,' he said over his shoulder and refilled his own glass a little recklessly.

'I see you do remember,' Stanley said, and laughed suddenly. 'Did you ever forget it? I mean, how come you never offered to pay it back? You'd made it, you and Hildegarde, very quickly.

You were daft, really weren't you? Sitting there with a couple of liabilities like that hanging round your neck, when you could have been shot of the pair of us years ago –'

'Stanley, shut up a minute, will you? Let me do some talking – I'm also a person,' Hester said, and she grinned at Mel. 'Aren't I, Mel?'

'Whoever could doubt it?' he mumbled, drinking again, as much to hide his face as because he wanted the drink. This was stupid; what with the heat of the room and the unusual alcohol he was beginning to feel a bit odd, sparkling round the edges, hot and sticky.

'The thing is, Mel dear, we've been thinking. We've been thinking that you owe us quite a bit. When you borrowed that money, and we were both so young and poor – weren't we, Stanley?'

'Oh, very young and poor.'

'– finding that money for you wasn't easy. It was very hard, in fact. Do you know I had to borrow it for you? No, don't look like that – I did. Paid it back long since, of course, but there it was – I borrowed it. And it wasn't easy. And then I left it to you to pay me back at the time that was right for the company. That was the deal, wasn't it? You'd pay us back when doing so wouldn't harm the company –'

'Which was any time this past ten years or more,' Stanley said, his voice smooth but pugnacious for all that. 'Right, Bremner?'

'Well, yes, I suppose so. But there –' He smiled uneasily. 'To tell you the truth, both of you, we never gave it a thought! I mean, there you both are, riding high, doing marvellously well, making a fortune, your furniture advertised all over the shop, Stan, Hester on TV so often you can't go to the lavatory without being nagged for your autograph – what do you want with a few hundred quid? So I suppose we forgot it. But look, now you've mentioned it, of course – naturally. I'll have our people dig out the agreements, work out the interest – cheques by the end of the week, no later – my word as a businessman –'

'No thank you, Mel,' Hester said sweetly. 'No cheques.'

He was really puzzled now, and again hid his face in his glass, took a long drink.

'So what do you want? You're going round in circles, Hester, to tell you the truth, and with so much to do –' He waved his hand expressively over his desk.

'No circles. Straight to the point,' Stanley said crisply. 'Let's not be devious, right, Hester? Okay, Bremner. When you borrowed from us, what we gave you represented a quarter of your total capital. That's what we want now. A quarter.'

'A quarter of what?' He stared at them. 'I don't know what you're talking about.'

'A quarter of the company shares, dear boy.' Hester said. 'I know you're a private company, so there'll be no hassles over shareholders – just provide us with what we're entitled to, which is a quarter of the profits – net, of course, not gross. We don't want to be greedy! – and we'll leave our capital in. But if you'd rather, why, then just put your people on to assessing the capital worth of the firm, and we'll put *our* people on to scrutinizing as well, and we'll take the cash, and let the future go.'

There was a little silence and then she added with an air of fine, judicial calm. 'Not that I don't think we'd be mad to take our capital out. I mean, as you said yourself, the business is booming. If we stay in, just taking our share of the income, we'll be better off in the long run. But there, we're not difficult to deal with, are we, Stanley? We'll settle for whichever it is you want to give us.'

From that point on, Mel felt he'd lost control; if he'd ever had it. At first he blustered, then he laughed, then he blustered again, but they just sat and looked at him and let him talk on, sipping their drinks quietly, making no attempt to interrupt him.

He spluttered into silence at last, and drank the rest of his glassful, and shook his head, trying to clear it. Goddamn it, he must have been mad to drink whisky at this time of the day, mad to have even agreed to see them. They'd have to go. Right now, they'd have to go.

'I can't talk any more about this now,' he said, trying to sound belligerent, but even in his own ears seeming to bleat. 'I've got work to do, people to see – you'll really have to excuse me –'

'Right now, we will,' Hester said calmly and stood up, and now it was Stanley's turn to bluster.

'What d'you mean, we will? I've given up God knows how many important appointments to fit this in this afternoon. D'you think I'm going to just –'

285

'Stanley, dear, don't let us be silly,' she said and her eyes were very bright, Mel thought, sparkling in her bony face with a glitter that was full of threat. I don't feel well, he thought. I really don't feel well.

'What do you mean, silly? If you think that I –'

'Silly because he can't do anything right now, can he? But he knows what we want. Don't you, Mel? And he knows what will happen if we don't get it –'

'What do you mean, what will happen?' Mel was almost surprised to hear his own voice.

'Why, dear, we'll have to make our claim official, won't we? In court and so on. It'd be a great shame – tragic, really, quite apart from the embarrassment of it. All our *private* business trotted out in a court of law – you'd hate that, Mel, wouldn't you? Especially as I should imagine you've done some very clever things with the firm's money as far as taxes and so on are concerned. I can't believe that the profits we read about are the whole of the story. I mean, knowing how clever you are. It's my guess there's all sorts of things that you'd rather have kept quiet – business as well as personal.'

She was looking at him now with those sparkling eyes wide and bright, and for a moment he could see Hildegarde's face there, and again felt a wave of nausea.

'So you see, Stanley?' she went on. 'No point in staying here and ruining poor old Mel's afternoon. After all, he's got business to do for us as well as himself, hasn't he? The more he works, the better reward we get for our investment. So we'll go away. But we'll be back in a few days to see what arrangements you've decided to make. Mel. Dare say you'll want to fill Hildegarde in on it all, won't you? Well –'

She grinned a wide happy grin that made her face as engaging as a child's.

'Well, on most of it! So long, Mel. See you in a week, or thereabouts – come on, Stanley. I'm ready for some tea. Take me to that place in Bond Street – I'm feeling greedy for cream cakes.'

He sat for a long time after they'd gone, staring out of the window, trying to relax and let the whisky die down in him. But after a while he went to his private filing cabinet in the corner and fished a key from his ring and unlocked it. And found the copies of the documents he'd signed with them both, all those years ago.

They were as bad as he remembered them. My God, he must have been mad, stark staring mad to have agreed to them, but he had, so what was the use of worrying about it now? Anyway, that was the way Hildegarde had wanted it.

'Get me some money I don't have to worry about,' she'd said. 'I can't be doing with quarterly interest bills, or people breathing down my neck. Offer 'em what they want in interest, anything they want. I'll be able to sort them out in a few years, anyway –' So he'd done just that.

'Oh, Christ!' he said aloud, and went over to the window and struggled to open it. He needed air, and he needed it badly. The window opened at last and he leaned out, swallowing the cold diesel fumes in great gulps. He remembered now the few times when he'd reminded her, told her to pay them back, but she'd laughed at him.

'What's the hurry?' she'd said. 'Why should I give anybody what they're not asking for? Listen, when they want it they'll come for it. Till then, mind your own affairs. My sisters are happy enough to mind theirs –'

Silly bitch, he thought savagely, silly bitch. Now look what she's done. She should have realized that bastard Maddern would try something like this sooner or later. Not that his deal really stood up to his claim when you thought about it. Hester and her claim he would not, could not, think about.

Below him the buses ground heavily on and taxis and vans grumbled at cars and motor bikes, and he stared down, half dreamily. People used to jump out of windows like this when they had business worries, he thought, and then shook his head again. Stupid!

He lifted his eyes and across the road he could just see the clock on the second floor of the huge carpet show rooms there and he blinked at it. Half past two. That means half past eight this morning in New York.

He began to feel better at once. Hildegarde. She'd have to know anyway, and the sooner the better. If anyone could sort this out, she could. He'd ring her, right now, in New York. They were her bloody relations, let her sort them out.

He enjoyed the little flap of making the call, finding out the

287

number of her hotel, getting on to the operator, and then hearing the exotic accent so clear, so near. 'Plaza Hotel,' it bleated. 'Good morning. Can I help you –'

And then he heard the distant ringing as they called her room and imagined her, in her shower probably at this time, walking out, dripping and naked, and he liked imagining that, standing there in London on a cold afternoon and seeing her in her dripping skin in New York.

There was a rattle and then he heard her. 'What is it?' She sounded cold and remote and he wanted to reassure her, make her feel good.

'Hildegarde!' he cried. 'Hello, darling. It's me. Mel. It's great to hear your voice –'

'Who? Mel? Are you mad, phoning at this hour? It's half past eight, for Christ's sake.'

'You usually get up early, though, don't you, on working trips?' He wanted to conciliate her so much, wanted her to sound happy to talk to him.

'Well, what is it?' Her voice was as cold as ever, and the little bubble of pleasure that had been in him collapsed, leaving only the sour smell of whisky and the feeling of nausea again. He was tired, very very tired, too tired even to try.

'I've just seen Maddern and Hester,' he said baldly. 'They want a quarter each of the company for that loan they made at the start. They say they're entitled. It was a half of your capital.'

'They said *what*?' At last the cold had gone from her voice and he found a certain satisfaction in the edge of anger he could hear now.

'You heard me.'

'Oh, my God, did you ever hear anything so bloody stupid in all your –'

There was a rattle again, as though she'd dropped the phone and he said urgently, 'Hildegarde? Are you there? Hilde –'

'Oh, Jesus, this is one hell of a time to go talking,' he could hear the deep masculine tones as clearly as though they were in the next room. 'Come back to bed, baby. I got better things to do than talk –'

He stood there holding the phone in his hand and staring out of the window at Lower Regent Street, and the sick feeling thickened, became more urgent, and he hung up the phone and

288

turned and almost ran to the cupboard in the corner that hid the washbasin and stood there for a long time, his head bent and his face wet with the sweat of it all.

He came back to his desk shakily, and sat down, and let his thoughts twist in his mind, running about after each other, half-formed words tumbling over themselves. She had some other man in that hotel room with her. After all these years when she knew how much he needed her, how hard he worked for her, she'd taken another man into her room with her.

He let the hate rise in him, lifting over his belly into his chest, just as his nausea had, and then, as it broke in his mind, he knew suddenly just what to do.

If she could do things behind his back, things like that, there were things he could do, too. There were things she wanted to hide from him? Great. Let her try. There were things he'd helped her to hide for years, from all sorts of people, but not any more. Now he'd tell the world, tell it how it was, that's what he'd do. He'd tell them all, everything, about the way this bloody business built itself. About Birgitta, all of it. He'd show her, her and her men in her hotel rooms –

He reached for the intercom, and pressed the buzzer.

'Here, bring me the phone book, will you? No, I'll look it up for myself. What? Oh, A to D. Right away.'

He found the number, and dialled it on the green phone, the only one that didn't link with the switchboard, the only one he could make private calls on. And by the time the girl at the other end answered, 'City Television. Good afternoon,' he knew exactly what he was going to do.

29

'I'm not sure I can work out what's going on,'
Sammy said. 'So, I'm damned if I can see how the jury can.
They sit there looking blank, just staring, and I think, what the
hell can be going on in their heads? Can they really work out all
this stuff about loans and who said what to who, and what it's got
to do with the case anyway? It's not as though money was even
mentioned in the defamation writ. Or have I forgotten? It's all
so woolly –'

They'd chosen to have a better lunch today. He'd booked a
table at Rules, and now they were sitting in the corner looking
at the actresses performing for each other and the journalists
making the most of their expense accounts and pretended to eat
jugged hare.

'It's all part of the parcel,' Bonnie said, almost dreamily. It
really doesn't matter. All I can think of is that I'm sitting here
with Sammy and feeling just the way I used to feel all that time
ago. Nothing else really matters. Not even what Stanley said.

'Bonnie?' he said a little more loudly. 'Did you hear me?'

'Not really.' She looked up at him, anxious suddenly, and put
down her fork. 'Sammy, what are we going to do?'

'I don't know.' He too stopped eating.

'I'm not imagining it, am I?'

'No.'

'Sometimes I wish I were. I lay awake last night and I
thought, you're just imagining it. It's just a silly fantasy, a
middle-aged mummish fantasy, all because you've met an old
friend and you want to be seventeen again. That's all it is, I
thought. I wanted it to be just that, I really did. Last night. I'd
be safer –'

'If it's a fantasy, I'm in it with you.' He leaned across and
picked up her fork and put it into her hand. 'Do me a favour –
eat your lunch. I don't want to sound like Stanley, but at the
rates they charge here I'm going to be aggrieved if you haven't
even eaten anything.'

'You too, then.'

'Me too.' He began to eat, and she did as well, surprised to find herself enjoying the sensation of the food in her mouth.

'Come to my place for dinner tonight,' he said suddenly and then laughed. 'That makes me sound obsessed with food, doesn't it? I'll try again. Come to my place tonight. Don't go home. Come to me.'

She sat very still, staring at her plate. And then tried to shake her head, tried to say, 'No. I can't. Stanley, the children.' But the words wouldn't come out right.

'Tracy's staying with her friend tonight. They're going on a school trip tomorrow.'

The words sounded silly, and she tried again. 'The others – I don't know what they're doing.'

'You could try starting to live your life without immediate reference to other people, Bonnie,' he said a little sharply. 'The sky won't fall in if you do. You don't always have to worry about the children and Stanley.'

'Of course I do!' She was angry then. 'Christ, if you can't understand that, then you can't understand anything. And I thought you did. That's one of the things that have been feeling so good these past days. Thinking you understood –'

'Oh, of course I do! I'm just trying to tell you that you don't have to feel so guilty after all! That you're talking about a bunch of grown-up people – well, all but one of them – who live *their* lives their way without reference to you. I'm trying to tell you that you can do the same.'

'How do you know they make no reference to me?' She was defensive now, clutching at the crumbling edifice of twenty-two years spent worrying about other people. 'Of course they care about me. Why do you try to take that away from me?'

'I'm not trying to take caring away. Just guilt. If they care for you, as *you*, and not just as someone who does physical things for them with food and clothes and – if they care for you, no one can take that away. They always will. They may get angry and they may be hurt, but if they care properly – if they love you they will. That doesn't change. But if it's only guilt in you that holds them then you don't need it. Or them. Come to me tonight. Come home.'

'Home,' she said and sat still, thinking of her living room with its smoked-glass tables and tiffany lamps. 'Your place, home?'

'It is, actually.' He leaned back in his chair. 'It really is. I may be a man alone, but I'm not entirely helpless. It's comfortable. Not as elegant as your house, I grant you, but comfortable in my sort of fashion.'

'I'm sure it is.' She was abstracted again, trying to hold on to the pattern of her life. Middle-aged women didn't just casually go home with men they weren't married to and stop worrying about feeding their family the way they had for years and years. Middle-aged married women didn't suddenly do things like going to bed with other men, even if they had known them for years and years. Anyway, she'd be shy. Christ, but she'd be shy. She was older now, with stretch marks and rather sagging breasts. How could she let him know what had happened to her body this last twenty-two years? Especially as he hadn't known it before. Oh, Sammy, why didn't you ever know it before?

And who said anything about going to bed, anyway? He just said to come home with him. He came home to us the first day, so today I'm going to return the compliment – oh, God, I'm going round in circles –

'You'll come, then.' Sammy said, a statement, not a question.

'I'll phone them. I'll have to phone them.'

'Of course. No one would expect you to do otherwise. What will happen this afternoon, do you suppose? Will Mel Bremner still be giving evidence?'

'I think so. They didn't say he'd finished, did they? I – I listened but I didn't hear properly. I really tried, but it didn't go in properly. But I think it's still Mel. I remember now. No – they were talking about the time when Hester went to see him, after she and Stanley went to see him the first time. Wasn't that it? Have I remembered right?'

I'm gabbling, she thought, just gabbling. I'm embarrassed. It's the silliest thing that could happen. I'm embarrassed by Sammy. It's mad and I'm mad, and I wish I knew what was going to happen.

'That was what it was, when they adjourned, wasn't it? Hester going to see him on her own. That's what Wooderson said, anyway –'

'The minute you walked through the door,
I could see you were a man of distinction,
A real big spender . . . .'

'Don't look so suspicious, Mel!' she said and pinched his arm so that he winced; not that anyone would be likely to notice in the hubbub around them. The foyer was full, and he tried to tighten his muscles to make himself smaller in order to keep away from the pressure of bodies and voices. Because they weren't his sort of bodies or voices; most definitely not. These people were so bearded, so scrappily dressed, so shrill, that he felt uneasy and he twitched at his tie and pulled his jacket into place. Beside their blue jeans and filthy cardigans he looked peculiar and that was infuriating, because he was the normal one; they were the oddballs.

'I was just thinking how nice it was of you to ask me,' he said, trying to be smooth. 'I certainly wasn't looking suspicious – just appreciative!'

'Been here before?' They were pushing their way through the crowd towards the door, and he looked around at the raw brick walls and the slightly self-conscious squalor of the posters and shook his head.

'No. Always meant to, of course – but you know how it is –'

'Go on with you! You know bloody well that Shaftesbury Avenue's the be-all and end-all of the theatre for you. Maybe Drury Lane, for a big one – you wouldn't be caught dead in a dump like this usually.'

'Well, it's not exactly convenient, is it? I mean, Camden Town –' They were in through the doors now, and the boy in tattered jeans who took their tickets leered at her. 'Evening, Hester! Coming where the real art is, then? Take care – you might catch something!' and she smiled back, bright and professional.

'Little shit,' she muttered, as they made their way through the rows of seats. 'So bloody clever –'

He was glad of her discomfiture; it made him feel more on an equal footing. Ever since she had phoned him and told him imperiously that she had tickets for the Roundhouse and she'd pick him up at the office he'd been tense. Did she know already what he'd done?

Now that he'd had time to cool down he'd realized he could have started something much more upsetting than he'd meant to. Gerrard, once Mel had managed to get through to him had listened, and made non-committal noises, asked for a few names and dates and phone numbers and then said crisply he'd 'look into it'.

Since then Mel had heard nothing. Not a single word. And neither had he heard anything from Stanley and Hester. Weeks had gone by, and he'd been confused and anxious and yet soothed by the passage of time.

Hildegarde had come back from her trip, in a state of huge delight at the sales she'd made – it had been one of her most successful trips ever – and somehow they'd never talked about the man in her New York hotel, never said anything at all about his call to her. They'd just picked up as usual, and that had been that. Except for the lingering memory of that damned half-drunken phone call. And as time had gone on that too had begun to fade.

And then Hester had phoned him, and he could still feel a little of the chill the sound of her voice had created in him. What the hell was she up to? Theatres? They'd never been out to theatres, or anywhere else, come to that, and here she was, buying theatre tickets for him.

They settled themselves in the third row, and he wriggled uncomfortably on the canvas and metal seat. 'Why do these arty places always have to be so bloody uncomfortable?'

She was reading the programme and didn't look up. 'Arty, the Roundhouse? Hardly! It tries to be, I grant you, but it doesn't often manage it. As for uncomfortable – I've known worse. You ought to try the Edinburgh Festival Fringe sometime.'

'I'm not likely to, am I? I'm just a hard-nosed businessman, remember?' He was nettled, feeling cool amusement in her. 'Just a Shaftesbury Avenue type.'

She looked up then. 'Got under your skin, did I? Well, maybe I meant to. That stupid kid got under mine, so I passed it on. Silly, really.'

He was mollified at once. She seemed to be putting herself

294

out to please him now, the way a woman ought to with any man, and he patted her hand. 'Apology accepted. So tell me about this show. What is it?'

She looked down at the programme again. 'Musical comedy about premature ejaculation.'

He stared at her and then shook his head. 'I don't believe you.'

'It is, though. I told the author – I can see there's comedy in the situation, but to music? And J. J. Gerrard – you know JJ? He said he could understand doing it to music but what's so bloody funny?'

'J. J. Gerrard. Why should I know him?' He was acutely uncomfortable.

'Oh, I don't know – lots of people do. He's one of those people who get around. I just thought you might have met him.'

He looked at her sideways, and then relaxed. He found her confusing, threatening, and bewildering, but this time she was not trying anything on. Her comment about JJ really had been mere idle chatter. Whatever tonight's meeting was about, it wasn't to do with his call to City Television; and he began to feel better. She'd tell him soon enough what it was all about, no doubt. Meanwhile, he'd sit back and watch the show and stop worrying. Why should he worry, after all? No one could do anything to upset his apple cart. It was much too firmly set on the road to success. And enjoying the thought of his own cleverness, he sat back and watched the show.

He enjoyed it a great deal. It wasn't at all arty, but very much his sort of show, clear story line, lots of jokes, easy music and sexy with it, and he laughed a lot, very loudly. At the interval they drank gins in the untidy, noisy bar and shouted banalities at each other and then went back and he laughed a lot more. By the time the show was over he felt relaxed, comfortable and had almost forgotten his earlier uneasiness. Until they were having dinner.

She hadn't asked where they were going, hadn't even left it to him to suggest going on to a meal at all. She'd just led the way across the road to a Greek restaurant where the *bazoukis* were noisy and the smell of charcoal-roasted lamb and oregano almost overwhelming, and he was a little irritated at that. He'd gladly have taken her somewhere good, like the Caprice or the

295

Trat. She didn't have to treat him like a cheapskate, using such a place as this.

But the food was good and he softened as he ate fried squid and *taramasalata* and drank cheap white wine. Not elegant, like the Caprice, maybe, but it had a raffish charm of its own. He murmured the words under his breath; raffish charm.

'Heard any more from Stanley?' she said suddenly and at once the pleasure was gone. He was again alarmed and watchful.

'Stanley?' he said easily, and ate some more *pitta*, chewing the thick putty-like stuff with concentration. 'No, why should I?'

'Oh, come on, Mel! Why should you? Don't you remember why we came to see you that afternoon last month?'

'Last month? Oh, that!' He swallowed the bread, feeling it stick a little in his throat. 'Was I supposed to take that seriously? I never gave it another thought – just one of those silly things people say, I thought –'

'If you'd thought that, then you'd be a fool. And since I know you're not, then I know you didn't think that. We meant every word. Every bloody word. Certainly Stanley did.'

He looked at her over the rim of his wine glass. She was leaning back against the red-flock wallpaper staring at him, her eyebrows slightly cocked and he took a deep breath.

'So? What am I supposed to do now? Burst into tears? You know and I know that it's all a lot of crap – absolute crap. There's no chance of you getting any such cut and well you know it. We'll pay back your loan. In fact, if you like, we'll pay it back at double. Can't say fairer than that. You helped us find capital when we needed it and no one can say Mel Bremner is mean. I know what's due to genuine help. I appreciate it. Your sister – she's different. I'll have to work on her, and that's the truth of it. I don't have to tell you about Hildegarde, though, do I? Tight as a duck's arse, and that's watertight –'

He was talking too much and he knew it, but he couldn't stop himself. If she'd started talking this way as soon as they'd met it would have been different; he was keyed up and ready for it then. But now, what with a large whisky before he left the office, and two gins in the interval and now this wine, he was feeling less in control than he should be. He ought to see his doctor. He hardly drank at all, hardly anything, but just one drink and he felt queasy. It wasn't easy to do himself justice feeling as he did.

He filled his glass again and then grinned at her, trying to look easy and comfortable. 'But I'll deal with Hildegarde, as I said. And I'll send both of you cheques. I worked out what was due to you, and what with the fluctuations in bank rate and all – well, call it three and a half thousand, and that's erring on the generous side. So, I'll send you cheques for seven thousand apiece. Not bad for an initial outlay of five hundred, eh? You can't complain – you really can't complain –'

'I never complain. I get what I can, and ignore the rest,' she said and then smiled. 'Stanley, however, is different. It's taken every bit of skill I've had to hold him off your back this past month, you know that? He was all for putting his lawyers on to it right away.'

He stared at her, his mouth a little open. 'Why?'

'Why have I had to work so hard at it? Because he is one very angry man, that's why. Because –'

He shook his head. 'Why have you been trying to stop him? I mean, I thought you two were in this together, against me? And Hildegarde, of course.'

She laughed softly. 'Now, whatever gave you that idea? Silly Mel! Do I look like the sort of woman to go in for that sort of alliance? With *Stanley*? Do me a favour!'

He shook his head, bewildered. 'You came to see me together. You did say then – what the hell did you say? You've got me in a flat spin, you know that?'

'It suited me to come with him, that's why. But I'm not in cahoots with him and never you think it. You've got two distinct problems, my little Mel, with us. His problem, and my problem. And they're different because our deals were different. Remember?'

There was a little silence and then he nodded heavily. 'I see. You're going to press your claim, is that it? You're going for the quarter share?'

'I've got the right to, haven't I?'

'Right? I wouldn't call it that –'

'Oh, don't filibuster, Mel, please! You signed a deal with me. I've got my copy here –' she tapped her jacket, '– and I know you've got yours tucked away somewhere. If I want to press for

297

it, I've got a quarter of the business. And you know it.'

There was a short pause and then he said heavily, 'Are you going to?'

'That all depends.'

'On what?'

'On how co-operative you are.' She leaned forwards. 'Look, Mel, I'll tell you the scene as it appears to me, okay? I'm not exactly short of cash at the moment. I'm doing reasonably well – but this is a funny business I'm in, and high as I may ride now, this time next week I could be flat on my fanny, and no one'd remember I'd ever been on my feet. I have to think of the future. I'm on my own, no one to lean on, no one to rely on but myself. Bonnie's got her Stanley, Hildegarde's got you – and her business. Me – I'm just me. If I don't work, I don't eat. And I've got to make sure all my exits are covered, to coin a cliché. Okay. Now, I've got a highly dubious document that you signed at a time when we were – shall we say, going through a period of close friendship. If I choose to stand on my rights, take that document to court, I could maybe make it stick. Chances are I couldn't – possibly, they'd throw it out as undue influence or some such. The thing is, however, what it would do to *you* if I went to court? If Stanley went to court? I know Stanley would lose, of course. He hasn't got a toe to stand on, let alone a leg. But he can be manipulated, can Stanley. He'll do as he's told. And I'll see to it that he does –'

He shook his head again. 'I thought I was as twisted as a corkscrew, but you – you've got me beat ten times over.'

'Compliments will get you nowhere. Just listen, will you? I'm saying that I'll keep Stanley off your back in exchange for a certain amount of future security. I'm not asking for a quarter of the business. Jesus, what would I want with that? I'd have to be out of my mind. Tax troubles, the lot. No, lover. All I want is a living wage. My sort of living wage. You put me on the payroll – and keep Hildegarde out of it, because that one'd grudge me the price of a coffin – put me in as a couple of secretaries and a driver or something – and pay me a regular five thousand a year. Tax paid. I want no problems, just a regular comfortable sum I can rely on.'

'Five – are you mad? She'd never fail to miss a sum like that on the payroll!'

'You weren't listening. Put me in as three or four other people, I said. You can do it – pay tax for them, deduct stamps for them – it can't be that difficult. Then she won't notice it. And with a payroll like yours – how many people do you employ?'

'I don't know,' he said, trying to sort out his thoughts, stalling for time. 'I'm not sure –'

'Oh, come off it! Unless you want to make me really angry! I'm telling you. I can make big problems for you, Mel. Or keep them away from you. It's in my hands to make or break you, and I'm offering you a respectable way out. Now think about it! How many people are there on your work force?'

'About five or six hundred, in the UK. More than that in Ireland,' he said sulkily.

'And you couldn't absorb four false employees? Pull the other one! It'll play you a symphony.'

'Why should I? What's in it for me?'

'I won't sue for the quarter of the company. I'll get Stanley off your back. Hildegarde'll never know how it was you came to sign that deal in the first place,' she said promptly, and then laughed aloud, a sound of such sheer enjoyment that the men playing the *bazoukis* looked across at her and nodded and grinned cheerfully and played even more loudly.

He sat quietly, staring down at the table, thinking. Hildegarde, hearing about all that time ago, Hildegarde throwing him out, and then what? Because she would and he was still no more than an employee. No partnership agreement ever. She'd always shrugged it away, like the family's loans. If she found out and chucked him, then what? Quite apart from the way he needed her, felt about her, wanted her. This bitch Hester, this bitch, she had him curled up on toast and she was enjoying it. Bitch.

'How can you keep Stanley off my back?' he said suddenly. 'If I do agree?'

She laughed again. 'I have my methods, Dr Watson! I have my methods! I can handle him yesterday, today and tomorrow, amen. If I make a promise it's kept. And right now I promise you that either you do it my way, or you're in it up to your neck. It's up to you.'

'I do it your way.'

'Five thousand a year.'

'Tax paid?'

'Tax paid. Straight into my account.' She reached into her bag and took out a piece of paper, pushed it over to him. 'You'll find all the information you need there. Right. That's settled then. It's a weight off my mind.'

She stood up and waved at the waiter who ran to fetch her coat, and Mel stared up at her, bewildered again. 'Where are you going?' She looked down at him, shrugging on her heavy coat. It was a thick fur-lined Burberry.

'To take a weight of Stanley's mind,' she said. 'And yours at the same time. See you around, Mel. Glad you liked *Maybe That's Your Problem.*'

'What?'

'The show,' she said. 'That was its title. *Maybe That's Your Problem.* Well, we've solved a couple of ours tonight, haven't we? Very apt. Pay the man, will you, darling? I have things to do. Goodnight.'

And she was gone, leaving him staring at three men playing *bazoukis*.

30

When Bonnie and Sammy got back to the Law Courts they were breathless, for the time had gone so quickly and the restaurant had been so full it had been impossible not to be late, and they went through the long echoing terrazzo halls at a lope, he holding her elbow in a firm grip that impeded rather than helped her; but she would not have had him let go for the world.

They stood outside the court for a while, gasping a little because he held her back, and she nodded. It wouldn't do to go bursting in panting like a pair of greyhounds.

Someone came bustling out, papers in his hand, and the door swung and for a brief second she saw inside and then felt a sharp lurch of surprise. Was that Stanley walking down from the benches at the back, towards the witness box? The door swung closed and she looked over her shoulder at Sammy.

'Did you –'

'Yes,' he said. 'We'd better go in.'

They went in, bobbing their heads awkwardly at the judge and sliding into their seats, and as they settled themselves she looked down the court and there he was; she hadn't imagined it. Stanley was in the witness box, taking the oath.

'I thought he'd gone,' she whispered idiotically to Sammy who just shook his head repressively, and she subsided, trying to organize her confusion.

Stanley had got up to leave the court half an hour before the luncheon adjournment, and she had leaned forwards and whispered quickly, 'Stanley?' and he'd jerked his head at her, and obediently she had got up and followed him out.

Standing out there in the dimness of the corridor, with incurious people hurrying past them she had looked at him and felt a pang of remorse. He had looked tired, his face hard and with the lines seeming deeper than they usually did. But that was because of his anger with her, not because of any real distress. She'd told herself that firmly and looked up at him and said, 'Are you going?'

'I have things to do at the office,' he'd said harshly. 'Listen. I don't know what's got into you since this case started. I don't know what that Stermont is up to, and I don't care. I just want you to know that I'm not in the mood for any more of your nonsense, you understand me? I don't expect to be treated like a stranger by my own wife. I'll see you at home, at the usual time, and I expect to see a decent meal on the table and the children waiting for me. Understand?'

'The children?' she'd said. 'I can't promise anything for the children. Not even Tracy. She's going to the Lyndsay child's tonight. As for the other three, they're young adults now, Stan. If they're in they're in, if they're not, then they're not –'

'I'm not paying for a hotel there, not for them and not for you. Be there, *all* of you, or there'll be trouble. I've had enough.' And he'd gone, leaving her standing and staring after him and feeling curiously detached. Poor old Stanley, she'd thought as she'd gone back into court, and slipped back into her place next to Sammy. Poor old Stanley.

And she had forgotten his anger, and her remorse, forgotten his commands, forgotten all about all of it in the comfort of sitting with Sammy at Rules and pretending to eat jugged hare. Until now.

Looking down the court at him there in the witness box, the Bible in his hand, repeating words after the man standing gabbling in front of him, he looked tired and vulnerable and once again that stab of remorse came, and she looked sideways at Sammy, almost resentfully. Why had Sammy had to come to court at all? If he'd stayed away, the whole thing would have been so much easier. It would have happened, and there would have been bad feelings and tension, of course there would, but she would have known where she was. Would have still been herself.

Still have been alone and shut in, she thought, as Sammy turned his head in response to her glance and smiled fleetingly. Still would not have known how much living with Stanley is all wrong for me.

Counsel was on his feet, staring sternly at Stanley, and for a brief moment it was as though she were inside his skin, standing up there and feeling everyone's eyes pressing heavily on him and she shivered, and Sammy put his hand over hers comfort-

302

ingly. He knows, she thought. He knows. That's one of the best things about him. He always knows.

'Mr Maddern, in the matter of this loan –'

The questions came crisp and fast, with Stanley answering in monosyllables at first but gaining confidence as they went on, and he became expansive, adding extra information, much more than he was asked for, and Bonnie felt anxiety thickening in her chest again. Watch it, Stanley, watch it. You're going to fall into some sort of trap, I know you are. I don't know why you're up there, but there's trouble in this for you. Please be careful.

MARCH 1971

'You don't have to say you love me, just be close at hand,
You don't have to stay for ever, I will understand . . . .'

'What did you tell Bonnie?'

'Bonnie? What should I tell her?' He seemed genuinely surprised at the question.

Hester smiled. 'Well, I'm not married, so maybe I wouldn't know. But I'd have thought that any wife would want to know where her husband was going at eight o'clock on a Saturday evening.'

'I told her it was business. She knows about business – I see people at all sorts of times, all sorts of places. She knows.'

'Does she know I'm the business? Does she know we're meeting here?'

He looked sulky for a moment. 'No.'

'Why not?'

'Listen, Hester, why the cross-examination, for God's sake? What does it matter? I'm here, we're going to talk business, so what's it got to do with Bonnie? She's taken the kids to the theatre, as a matter of fact. She likes doing that. She's a very good mother –'

'I'm sure she is.'

'– so, like I said, why the nagging?'

'Because I need to know where I am,' she said and smiled easily. 'And if you haven't told Bonnie you're here then I know exactly where I am.'

She got up and went into the kitchen and he sat and looked round at her living room. A funny-looking place for someone

303

with the sort of money she must be making. No style at all, just cushions all over the floor – couldn't she afford decent furniture? – and curtains that looked as though they were made out of mattress ticking. They covered one whole wall, and the stripes seemed to dance in his eyes as he looked at them; very nasty.

He turned awkwardly on the big sofa she had put him on to. It was the only piece of real furniture in the room, big and soft, and he didn't feel as comfortable as he did on his own tightly-upholstered furniture at home. At home you knew you were sitting on something, because a Maddern chair was a *chair*; here it was like sinking into a bag of feathers.

She came back with a tray in her hands and he looked surprised.

'Supper,' she said briefly, and put it down on the floor at his feet. A bottle, its trickling surface announcing how chilled it was, a plate piled with rolls of smoked salmon, thin bread and butter.

'There'll be some roast duck after this,' she said, and expertly eased the cork from the bottle, catching the shower of sparkling wine without wasting a drop. 'You'll like it.'

'I thought you said out to dinner?' he said uncertainly, staring at the food. It looked good, but there was something threatening about the tray. It had little legs that folded away, like the tray they had for their bedroom, he and Bonnie, when they wanted a cup of tea and biscuits last thing. What with the softness of the sofa, and the intimacy of the tray, he was embarrassed.

'I thought it'd be easier to talk sensibly here than in a crowded restaurant where there are too many people interested in other people's business,' she said easily, and gave him the glass. 'I didn't think you'd fancy that any more than I would. Anyway, you get better value for your money when you eat at home. Lemon with your salmon?'

They ate, and he began to relax. What was there to be embarrassed about, for God's sake? If a man couldn't have a simple meal with his sister-in-law as part of a matter of business it would be a poor show. A poor show, he repeated deep inside his head, and drank the wine thirstily. It tasted good, sweetish and fruity, and he liked it.

304

'Asti Spumante,' she said watching him. 'I had a feeling it was your sort of thing. Was I right?'

'Dead right,' he said. 'Dead right. I like something I can taste.'

He looked at her over the edge of his glass as she put more salmon on his plate. She looked nice, not as angular and funny as she usually did. She was wearing an odd garment, not exactly a day dress, not exactly an evening one. Soft and shimmery, it fell in thick green folds from her shoulders to half way down her calves, making her look approachable and feminine. Not at all as she usually was. Usually she looked sharp and horribly aware, but tonight she was different.

'You phoned very late last night,' he said suddenly. 'I mean, I've been trying to get hold of you for over a week, and then you ring at gone eleven. Lucky I wasn't in bed.' He sounded faintly reproving.

'I hadn't realized how late it was,' she said, and smiled up at him over her shoulder. She was filling his glass again. 'In my job, Stanley, time is peculiar. I work when everyone else is relaxing, sleep when everyone else is rubbing noses on grindstones. I don't always remember what it's like for people in other – ah – fields of endeavour. Forgive me?'

'Of course,' he said, a little grandly. 'Of course. I wasn't in bed, after all. I was working. In my study. Very much a field of endeavour.'

'So late? I'm not the only one who has to put in a lot of time –'

'You're not kidding! Listen, let me just tell you –'

He launched into an account of the week he'd just had at the factory, of the urgent trip he had to make to Tilbury because of a crazy mix-up over a consignment of timber from Denmark, about the argument he'd had with the purchase tax people, about the way he'd had to deal with some of the men at the factory who'd started some rubbish about wanting to get a union branch going, and how he'd had to sack three good cabinet-makers as a result.

'Believe me,' he said earnestly. 'Believe me, it's no picnic running a business like mine. They're all out to screw you, every damned one of them, and you have to be on the *qui vive* the whole time. Always on the *qui vive*.'

She listened, eating, quietly nodding, not interrupting, and he

305

felt more relaxed still. In all the years he'd been married to
Bonnie, he'd found this sister of hers hard to get on with; one
minute laughing, seeming normal and friendly, and the next
coming out with some sharp remark that made his face redden
with anger and discomfort. She had a nasty line in jeers, had
Hester, and hadn't been afraid to display it. But she seemed
now to have eased up, to have softened, become more like a
woman, what he would call a woman, and he smiled as she came
back from the kitchen with two plates with neatly-carved duck
piled on them and chipped potatoes.

'Finger foods!' she announced gaily. 'Who needs to fiddle
with forks? We'll take it easy. Have a napkin,' and she put the
plates on the tray and then leaned over and tucked a napkin into
the collar of his shirt, and spread another on his lap. She smelled
good, soft and flowery, a scent he liked.

She took the tray away when they'd finished, clearing up with
despatch and he liked that too. No messiness about her; he
couldn't abide messiness. He'd had to work hard teaching Bonnie how to be organized the way he liked when they first married. Hester seemed to know without being shown.

She came back from the kitchen with a couple of towels in her
hands and sat beside him on the sofa.

'Give me your hands,' she commanded and without stopping
to think he held them out, and she took them and used one of
the towels, damp and warm and faintly scented, to wipe away
the remains of the duck and potatoes.

He sat and let her turn his hands from side to side, enjoying
the sensation of being looked after, feeling comfortably drowsy
from the food and drink, but not too drowsy. It was a feeling of
physical comfort, a moment of simple pleasure that was all too
rare. Why didn't Bonnie do caring things like wiping his hands
for him?

She dried them equally carefully and that was agreeable too,
feeling the soft warmth between his fingers, and then she turned
and leaned over and used the damp towel on his chin and round
his mouth, and dried him. He just lay back on the sofa and let
her, looking up at her face so close to his. A nice face, really.
He'd never really looked at it, but it was a nice face. The nose
was neat and well chiselled. He liked the thought. A well-
chiselled nose; Bonnie's was a bit on the thick side. Her eyes,

306

too, looked nice, long and slitty and shining moistly. Her mouth was slightly curved, the lips a little apart and her tongue caught between her teeth as she concentrated on drying him.

It seemed the most natural thing in the world to put one hand behind her head and pull her closer and kiss her.

There was a startled response from her when she seemed to tense against him and then, almost as though it were against her will she softened, became yielding, and he kissed her with increasing urgency.

When he let her go he smiled, a lazy smile of the sort that befitted a man who could so quickly overcome a woman's natural scruples about being kissed by her sister's husband.

'A little family salutation,' he said with his voice pitched deliberately low. 'A little thank you to a delightful sister-in-law for a delightful supper.'

'I'm glad you liked it,' she murmured. 'I tried to think of what you'd like.'

He hadn't really noticed her stretching out on the sofa beside him. The thing was so huge and so soft that half an army could have climbed on it and he'd not have noticed. So he told himself as he felt her close to him, smelled the thick flowery scent of her, and felt her breath warm on his cheek. But there she was, familiar and yet a stranger, comforting and yet exciting, a combination of feminine attributes that as far as he was concerned were irresistible.

Even if there'd been any need to resist them, which there wasn't. She seemed happy to co-operate, not exactly pushing him away, but not being too eager. He couldn't have borne that; a woman who made the running in sex always struck him as perverse. There had been times in the early years when he'd had to rebuke Bonnie for being too willing, too much in advance of him. A man needs to lead the way, he had told her, a man has to be in charge, it's part of his nature.

He didn't have to tell Hester that. She seemed to know, being delightfully uncertain as his hands moved across her body, and yet yielding to the effect of his caresses with gratifying speed. A splendid woman, he told himself, marvellous, super, everything a woman ought to be. Even if she was his sister-in-law.

It seemed to be the most reasonable thing in the world. Why

shouldn't they see more of each other? They weren't doing any harm; she seemed to need him, and it gave him pleasure to pleasure her, for he knew he did. She was always the same soft, doubtful but persuadable creature she'd been on that first occasion, but she showed her gratitude for the joy he gave her in a way that made him feel good. She would whimper a little, clinging to his arms with her soft grip as, with her head thrown back, the look of ectasy appeared on her face. And then she would subside, all soft and crumpled, and he would finish, feeling masterful and good. Not at all like Bonnie who when she climaxed would arch her back and grimace so that her face looked quite ugly. She'd sweat, too, and sometimes red blotches would appear on her skin and he'd never really found that attractive. Women shouldn't be so obvious; Hester was never obvious, never sweated, never grimaced or yelped. Just those soft whimpers and gentle yet firm fingertips on his biceps.

And Bonnie never seemed to notice anything, never seemed surprised when he said he was going out, even when he decided a week-end would be fun. She'd accepted the need for him to go to Denmark to see about raw materials without a question. Business was business after all.

He'd been more than a little put out when at the last minute Hester had had to let him down. There he'd been in the most expensive room in the most expensive hotel in Jersey – there was no risk of anyone he knew ever seeing them there; who among his set went to such places, for God's sake? Paris, now that would have been a risk – and she'd phoned. Work, she'd said. A special programme, what could she do?

That had been bad, that week-end. He'd sat there on the beach or on the hotel terrace, wanting to go home, wanting Bonnie, wanting the children. He must have been mad to let this whole situation develop anyway. Business was one thing, but one way and another the business bit had lapsed. He'd tried to talk about their plans regarding Hildegarde, had tried to pin her down about what she wanted to do, but somehow it always slipped away in kisses and softness, and it didn't seem to matter.

But this week-end it mattered, and he sat in the sunshine of Jersey and glowered at the holiday-makers and thought about Bonnie and Hildegarde and Hester, and was far from happy.

But then it had been all right after all, for she had arrived suddenly on the Sunday morning after he'd already spent two days on his own, and was sitting in his room thinking of how to fill the hours until his flight left. And she had arrived and they had spent the entire day in bed.

He'd initiated her, that day. Taught her things she didn't know, and she'd been shy and had even wept a little at one point, but he hadn't hurt her, not really. And at the end of the day, as they sat side by side in the taxi going to the airport she had clung to him, and told him she would never forget it. Not ever.

And that had been a marvellous thought, that he had been able to make this sophisticated woman, this creation of television who knew all sorts of men, who obviously was worldly wise, sit up and take notice. That had been a marvellous thought, and it had pushed the simmering anger about Hildegarde and her damned business deep down into his mind for a long time. Somehow, in that magical summer of 1971 pleasure had seemed to be more important than business.

The pleasure had even lingered on through the rest of the year, and into the following spring. And then the programme happened. Then he sat beside Bonnie watching TV, as bored as he always was at home these days and watched her talking about Hildegarde. After that, business was as important again as it had always been.

31

She was shaking, all the way through to the middle of her body. She could feel the trembling in her belly and put her hand over it, trying to control it. The worst part of it was she didn't know what the trembling came from. Fear? Anger? Relief? Because after all that, how could he stop her, how could he dare to stop her? He'd stood in the witness box and talked so much that the whole picture had shivered into place. The pieces of her private jigsaw puzzle had slithered about and slotted into a total vision of the life she had led with him, and it was hideous.

'Not a pretty sight,' she said idiotically to Sammy. 'Not a pretty sight.'

They had come out of court and were sitting on one of the stone benches outside. He had taken her out as soon as Stanley had said it, as soon as they had both realized what his evidence meant.

'Do you want to leave now? We could be away before he comes out.'

She shook her head, just sitting there with her hand over her belly.

'I wouldn't talk to him here, Bonnie. This wouldn't be the place.'

She shook her head again.

'Does he matter so much? Is that why you're so upset?'

She found her voice at last. 'Matter? I don't know what it means any more, I – he's been my husband for over twenty years. What was I supposed to do? Not care that he – that my sister – that – of course it matters!'

'I'm using words badly.' He sounded pedantic, as though he were lecturing a room full of bright but under-informed young-sters. 'I'm sorry. What I meant was, are you upset because you love him? Do you feel deprived by his behaviour?'

'Deprived?' She frowned and clasped her hands on her lap. Thinking about it, talking about it, eased the shaky feeling inside. 'I can't remember – it was 1971, he said, didn't he? I remember that summer. The children – they had a lot of illness

310

that year. Picked up a virus from somewhere and one after the other, they were ill. I was up most nights for weeks and weeks, and – I worried about him, you know that? I worried about him because he was randy, he's always been randy and there was no way I could – I wasn't the accommodating type, never was. I had to join in, had to be as hungry as he was, had to be a part of it. I couldn't just oblige him – and that summer, I was so tired I just went right off it. And I worried about him. And all the time he and Hester –'

She turned her head to look at him, and when she saw the expression on his face she stopped sharply. He looked pinched and white and the word slid into her mind. Stricken. He looks stricken.

'It matters to you,' she said, and felt the sick trembling start again. But now she knew the cause. It was fear. Fear of losing Sammy, when she'd only just found him again. Fear of losing the future that had filled her fantasies for the past two days, fantasies which had come to be more important than any reality ever was. He looked stricken, and she felt sick.

'Hester,' she said. 'Hester. You're upset because it was Hester.'

He still just sat and looked at her, saying nothing, and she wanted to hit him. She, who was never aggressive, who always controlled her anger, wanted to hit him, and she felt her hand go up as though she were about to, but it degenerated into a silly half wave, and she said again, 'Hester. You still want Hester.'

He shook his head then, and opened his mouth and closed it again, and her anger gave way to a tired pity, and she sighed deeply, a shaky breath, for the trembling was still there. But it made her feel better.

'Poor Sammy. Still leching after Hester, after all these years. And me, still mooning after you. It'd be funny if it wasn't so silly.'

'It's not Hester. It really isn't Hester,' he said. 'D'you think I don't know about Hester? D'you think she wasn't screwing around all those years ago? Of course she was – people don't change, you know. Not really. She was a whore when we were kids, she always has been and I imagine she still is.'

She wanted to giggle at the word. It sounded so prissy.

'But you still want her, for all that.'

311

'I don't think so. I really don't think so.' He was looking better now. 'I've been worrying about that. Thinking about you and the way it's been here and how you've been, and I've been worrying about me and both of them.'

He stopped and looked down at his hands on his lap, lying loose and ungainly on his thighs. 'It wasn't just Hester, you know, when we were kids. It was both of them. Hildegarde as well.'

He looked up at her then and tried to smile. 'I admired you, and I felt good with you, and comfortable with you. But it was Hester who made me feel so hopeless – so desperate. It was exciting, feeling like that. Lurching from day to day not knowing where I was with her. It was living, you know? And Hildegarde – she made me exhilarated. Nothing complicated about her. She just went after me as though I were raw meat and she was starving. I had to hold her back, protect her from herself. That made me feel – oh, great. Very adult. Until later, when I just couldn't. There was something about her that – well, never mind now. But the exhilaration was always there with her. You see? Both of them were much more – oh, it's impossible to explain it. I felt it all the time then and I've been feeling the left-overs ever since. It seemed to me that there wasn't a hope in hell of me ever being like other people and having a wife and children – because I was stuck with three separate people. What I wanted was something impossible. Something that was all three of you in one – until just then.'

'Until when? In court? Until Stanley said he'd been –'

He shook his head. 'No. Until you started talking about sex with him. I don't know quite what I'd imagined your life had been. I didn't think about it – but I suppose I'd seen you as one of those women who lie back and think of England. You know? I see them in my clinics all the time. Back-aches and belly-aches and blood pressure and faces as flat and empty as their hopes are. No joy in their own bodies at all. And I suppose I thought it'd been like that for you, and I wanted to make it better for you. Christ, talk about arrogant! I was going to rescue you, out of the pity of my heart. I was going to sweep you into bed and give you the joy of having sex with the person you'd always wanted. Galahad and King Cophetua in one splendid parcel. Charming, isn't it? And then you said you liked sex with him.

312

You did say that, didn't you? You said you liked sex with him, and it all went haywire –'

She put out her hand and then took it back, not touching him. 'Jealous? Were you jealous?'

There was a silence as people went past, oblivious in their busy-ness, and they watched them go, leaning back against the stone wall. After a while he said. 'Yes, I think I am. I think I'm jealous.'

She had no time to think about that, to savour its meaning, for behind them the door swung and there was a bustle as people began to come out.

'They've adjourned,' he said and stood up, tugging at her arm. 'Come on. I don't think I could stand it, a confrontation here. I really couldn't stand it –'

She smiled at him, feeling a great wave of warmth for him. 'I'll cope,' she said. 'Don't worry – I'll cope –'

They were coming out in a little rush now, people pushing past them hurriedly, and she was about to turn and follow them, taking Sammy with her, when at the tail of one little group Hester appeared.

She stood and looked at Bonnie, her head tilted to one side and Bonnie stared back, trying to assess her. She's my sister, she thought. You can't get much closer a relationship than that. My sister, and she's looking at me as though I were a stranger and that's as it should be, really, because she's a stranger to me. There's so much I don't know, don't understand.

'Well, Bonnie?' Hester smiled and moved forwards easily, and behind her her counsel came through the door, with the fat solicitor beside them.

'Have you met my team, Bonnie? No? You really must. This is Mr Wilmshurst, the junior counsel acting for me in this epic affair. His leader is Wooderson – he's a notable silk, they tell me. He's still in court nattering to someone. Altogether they're the best that money can buy –'

She grinned sardonically at Wilmshurst who looked stony and nodded briefly before hurrying off, his pupil beside him. Rundle the solicitor showed signs of lingering and Hester said sharply, 'I'll see you in the morning, Willy. Family business to discuss. Goodnight.'

'Not a good idea to discuss a case like this at this stage –' he mumbled and she shook her head irritably.

'Oh, Willy, go away! You're a bore – go and phone JJ. He needs encouraging to come tomorrow. He's as much a part of this business as I am, and I want him here. Go and tell him.'

Rundle went, going back into the court, trying to look both dignified and affronted and for a moment Bonnie wanted to turn and follow him. She looked at Sammy, but he was fully in command of himself now, standing there with his hands clasped loosely in front of him and his raincoat bundled untidily over them. He was staring at Hester, but his expression showed no tension at all. He appeared slightly bored, polite, relaxed.

And then the door swung again and Hildegarde came out, her chin up and a half smile on her face. Mel was behind her, and he seemed uneasy as he caught sight of Hester and said awkwardly in a voice that was too loud for comfort. 'I've got to make those calls – really very important – see you downstairs –' and he went scuttling off, walking fast and swinging his arms in a travesty of relaxed movement. He looked as stiff as a toy soldier and Bonnie wanted to giggle again.

' "When shall we three meet again, in thunder, lightning and in rain –" ' Hildegarde said, striking a pose, and looking at Hester. 'Did I get it right, dear? You should know –'

' "When the hurly burly's done, when the battle's lost and won –" ' Sammy said and all three of them turned and looked at him, startled. He looked back at them and made a little face, half smile, half grimace.

'It's really odd, looking at you three. So different, yet so obviously sisters,' he said in a conversational tone.

'It wouldn't be a bad thing for you to go, either,' Hester said. 'Go on, Sammy. There're things we've got to talk about.'

'There's nothing you have to say that can't be said in front of Sammy,' Bonnie said, hoping she sounded cool, but knowing her voice was tremulous.

'No? Have you two made it, then? Got him into bed at last, have you?' Hildegarde said, and Bonnie tightened her mouth.

'Dear Hildegarde,' Sammy said. 'You don't change, do you? Still the same sweet thing you always were.'

'And what about you?' She sounded equally sweet. 'Still the disappointed virgin?'

314

His face mottled and Hester said, 'Not as I remember him, my duck,' and laughed.

'Look, if this is what this is going to turn into, I'm going right now.' Bonnie said loudly. 'It's been a long time since I got any sort of pleasure out of this sort of discussion, if I ever did, and I'm damned if I'm going to put up with it now. If you've something worthwhile to say, either of you, then get on with it. But neither Sammy nor I have time to waste on this sort of juvenile niggling. Right, Sammy?'

'Right,' he said, and she moved closer to him.

The other two stood and looked at them and she felt good, really good. And with the feeling of pleasure came pity.

'Look, I'm sorry, honestly I am, that this whole mess has blown up,' she said impulsively. 'I wish you could have settled it some other way. I'm sorry for the part Stanley played in it and –'

She had genuinely forgotten, just for a moment, about Stanley and Hester and now as she remembered she stopped speaking.

There was a little silence and then Hester said, 'Look, Bonnie, I want you to know – there was nothing personal in it. I wasn't trying to break you up or anything. I don't want him – I'm fine as I am. It's just that it was expedient. At the time it was the only way I could – arrange things. Try to see that. It wasn't personal.'

'Not personal?' Bonnie looked at her and tried to see her as she had been when they were children; the big one, the one who made things happen, the one who looked after the three of them. And she had, in her own peculiar fierce way. 'I suppose not. But it's extraordinary how you've always got yourself involved in the men in my life, haven't you? You got rid of David Spero and –'

'He was no use to you. I knew. It would have been a disaster for you. That was why,' Hester said swiftly.

'Would it? The same sort of disaster it's been anyway?'

'Really?' Hildegarde said curiously. 'Was it? I thought you were happy. I thought you had all you wanted. Rich husband, the children, the fancy house, the whole boring bit. Wasn't that what you wanted?'

'I never knew what I wanted,' Bonnie said. 'I never did. I'm beginning to, though, I think. Just beginning to –' and she slid her hand into Sammy's elbow.

Hildegarde looked at him and again produced that sharp little smile.

'Christ, you're just as wet as you ever were,' she said disgustedly. 'If the best you can want is *Sammy*.'

'Don't you –' Bonnie began and Sammy interrupted her smoothly.

'Tell me something, Hildegarde. I've always wanted to know – why are you always such a bitch? Do you get pleasure from being hateful? From saying the cruellest things you can find to say? What does it do for you?'

She seemed to consider the question seriously. She was leaning against the wall now, the fluffy halo of her hair glowing against the grey of the stone. She looked much younger than her forty-three years, with her smooth round face and her taut body.

'I've never had to be anything else,' she said after a while. 'I suppose most people have to flatten the things they really think and not say them, because of being afraid of upsetting people. They have to be kind and friendly and nice and all those tedious things just to get on. Me, I've never had to.'

She tipped her head sideways, and laughed, looking at Sammy. 'It's true, isn't it? No matter what I said, or what I did, you always came back for more, didn't you? Everyone always does. They always have.'

It's true, Bonnie thought, looking at her. It's really true. All her life people have cared about her and been fascinated by her and done what she wanted just because it was what Hildegarde wanted. She never had to ingratiate herself with anyone. Never had to try. She had always been completely free, free of any fear of loss, free of any longings. Always she had what she wanted when she wanted it.

'Lucky Hildegarde,' she said, and Hildegarde's eyes flickered towards her and then away.

'Yes,' she said lightly. 'I am, aren't I?'

'If that were true you wouldn't be here in court,' Sammy said flatly. 'You're sueing Gerrard and Hester for defamation of character, so you value your good name, or you wouldn't be here. So, if you value that, it means you care about others'

316

opinions of you – which again means you would put yourself out to get good opinions, if they didn't come as easily as they always had.'

'That may sound beautifully logical, Sammy, dear, but it isn't. You've missed something out. Money. Money – now, that I *do* care about. Money's real, you see. So anything that affects money I get interested in. That's why I'm sueing Hester, and she knows it, even if you don't. That't right, isn't it, Hester? It's money that's at the root of this business. She was bleeding me, bleeding my business. I found out, and I didn't like it. So I decided to put a stop to it. That's all. There's no malice in it, is there, Hester?'

Hester was standing with her hands thrust deep in her jacket pockets, smiling a little and she turned her head and looked at Hildegarde and laughed softly. 'Oh, I wouldn't be so sure, ducks, I really wouldn't be so sure. I think it's very personal, you know that? I think it's the same as it was when we were children. You discovered I had something that you thought belonged to you. And you wanted your own back. In every sense of the word.'

'Something that belonged to me? You mean Mel?' Hildegarde shrugged. 'He couldn't matter less. He never could. No one ever does – I told you. I don't believe in wasting energy about people. They let you down if you do. They all care for me, and that's good enough. I don't want any more than that.'

'Really?' Hester said softly. 'Really? I find it hard to believe –'

'You're a fool, Hester,' Hildegarde said lightly. 'You really are. You're doing a turn-about. You're the one who's eaten with jealousy of me, of Bonnie too. You always have been. If we had anything, the silliest toy, whatever it was, you had to have it too. If you couldn't get it, then you'd break it. I remember. I remember very well. That's why you went after Mel and why you went after Sylvia. And Stanley. They belonged to us, to me and Bonnie, and that wouldn't do for you. *You're* the eldest. *You're* the one in charge. You had to have it all. You've been wearing blinkers all your life, you know that?'

I don't believe it, Bonnie thought, standing there and watching them. I don't believe it. They're grown women and they sound like children, squabbling over conkers like shrill schoolgirls in a playground. It's mine! It's not! It is! It isn't! I don't believe it.

'Even Birgitta,' Hildegarde was saying. 'Even her, you tried to get away from me, didn't you? You tried very hard to get her away from me –'

'Birgitta?' Hester sounded genuinely puzzled. 'I never had anything to do with her. I don't know what you're talking about –'

'Oh, yes you do. You know. They told me at the hospital, after she died. She was there for three weeks and you visited her, tried to get round her. Did you think I wouldn't find out? Of course I did. They told me at the hospital. After she died they told me my sister used to visit her.'

'That wasn't Hester,' Bonnie said wearily. 'It was me. She sent me a message.'

She felt them all looking at her then, Sammy too, and she blinked and looked round at him. 'Why look at me like that? Was it so odd? She was ill, she was alone in London, she was unhappy. She got them to call me. So I visited her.'

She saw from out of the corner of her eye the court door open again but she didn't look to see who was coming out. There was an odd tension there between them all, and she couldn't recognize it. It was different from the way they had been before; sharper, and she wanted to understand it, but she couldn't. She was very tired, suddenly. Very tired.

'I visited her,' she said again, a little more loudly. 'I couldn't do otherwise, could I? Poor creature, she was so unhappy –'

'You didn't tell me,' Sammy said.

'Why should I? Since this case has started there's been so much to talk about. Too much. This – I never saw any reason to tell you. But now you know, what difference does it make? I visited her, she talked to me. That's all.'

'It makes a lot of difference,' someone said behind her and she turned and looked up at Wooderson with the fat solicitor just behind him. Wooderson was a tall man, and in his wig and gown seemed taller still, and she felt herself quail a little and stepped back, almost defensively. Stanley was standing behind Rundle, but she hardly noticed him.

'I beg your pardon?'

'It makes a lot of difference,' Wooderson said again. 'You

318

could tell me the state of Miss Olaf's mind at the time of her death? You could tell the court of what she said?'

'The court?' Bonnie said, and felt cold. 'I have nothing to tell the court.'

'Oh, I think you have, you know. I think you really must, in fact. Don't you agree, Rundle?' Rundle nodded, his jowls swinging a little, and Bonnie wanted to laugh for a moment. 'It is, of course, up to Mr Rundle to arrange this, but it does seem to me to be a matter of some importance. After all your sister is accused of defaming Miss Maurice's character by dealing publicly with matters that pertain to Miss Olaf's death. So I really think Mr Rundle and I must ask you to come into court as a defence witness tomorrow. Justification, you see. Would you not agree, Miss Morrissey? I am sure you will, in fact –'

32

In the end she spent the night with Auntie Fido and Sylvia at the Hackney house.

Sammy had tried to persuade her to come home with him at first. 'I've got a spare room, you know,' he'd said with some acerbity when she'd responded with a swift refusal almost before he'd got the words out of his mouth. 'I'm as aware of the situation as you are, my dear, and I'm not about to use this as an excuse to go in for the big seduction scene – I've got some discrimination, for Christ's sake.'

'I know,' she'd said wearily. 'It's nothing to do with that. It's Stanley. How could I go home with you, after today?'

'And how can you go home with him?' he'd said.

And of course, he had been right. The thought of being obediently there, with the decent meal on the table, even if the children weren't there too, was unfaceable. So she phoned home and told the au pair what to cook, and left a message for Sharon and Warren, and phoned Daniel's school. And then instead of phoning a hotel to book a room, which she'd planned to do, she suddenly found herself dialling Auntie Fido's number, heard her own voice saying she wanted to come over, would it be all right?

It was all as though it were someone else doing it, not her, as though she were a little grinning observer sitting high in the corner of the phone box looking down at the tidy Bonnie standing there, dialling, pushing coins into the slot, talking, talking, talking.

When she came out of the phone box and stood in the street outside, pulling on her gloves, he reappeared. She hadn't really thought about him, hadn't really thought about anything. She was going to have to be a witness in court tomorrow, her own home was a place she felt she couldn't go to, how could she think about him?

But he was there, and she was quite glad to see him. 'I thought you'd gone home,' she said and pulled on her gloves, stretching the leather meticulously over her fingers as though their smoothness were the most important thing in the world.

'I will, when I know you're all right.'

'I'm not helpless,' she said, almost sharply, and he smiled at her in the yellow sodium light of the street lamp and shook his head.

'I didn't suggest you were. I was just indulging myself. I told you this afternoon – I'm jealous.'

'What?' She was puzzled, digging back into her memory. 'This afternoon?'

'Stanley and sex. Me. Jealous,' he said and she giggled.

'You sound like Tarzan.'

'Yes, I know.' He put out one hand as though to take her arm, but she pulled back. 'I suppose I'm being stupid but I'm as confused as you are.' He dropped his hand and they both pretended the moment of denial hadn't happened. 'Will you be all right?'

'I don't know. I just don't know. I never really thought they'd ask me to give evidence. Can I refuse, Sammy? Could I, do you think?'

'Would there by any point?'

The spark of hope that had flared in her spluttered and died. 'I suppose not.'

'What will you do, then?'

'I'm going to Auntie Fido,' she said. 'I'll pick up the car and go over to Hackney.'

He smiled again at that. 'Back to the womb?'

'Fido? Hardly. She's about as comforting as –'

She stopped and then shook her head. 'That's what all this is about, Sammy, isn't it? This whole bloody case, the whole lousy business.'

'How do you mean?'

'It's about not having a womb to go back to. About being orphans. It sounds so silly and mawkish, and when Mr Hermann used to ask about it, I'd get so angry with him –'

'You've lost me.'

'My analyst – the man I've been doing this psychology course with. He said he thought a lot of my – confusions – are to do with having my parents killed the way they were. I told him it was silly, because it was all so long ago, all forgotten for all three of us. But it isn't forgotten, is it?'

He was silent for a moment and then he said, 'No, I don't think it is. You don't ever forget some things,' and he turned his head and looked down Fleet Street, bright and noisy with evening traffic, towards the huge black building where his father had talked to him about yellow journalism, all those years ago, and thought about his mother sitting and muttering in her scruffy kitchen and Bonnie looking after her, and shook his head again. 'You don't ever forget. Come on, I'll see you to your car.'

Sitting in court next morning with her eyes sandy with tiredness, for she'd slept badly in the cold little room with its hardly-ever-used lumpy single bed, she refused to think of the evening before. Of the way Fido's whining had grated on her ears, the way Sylvia's too-bright kindness had made her throat constrict with irritation.

She'd phoned home in the morning at what had seemed the safest time, while Stanley would still be in the bathroom, all ready to apologize to the children, even to try to explain a little, but they hadn't even noticed she hadn't been home. Daniel had gone to a club evening with some friends straight from school, and was surprised when he found out where she was, and Sharon hadn't given her absence another thought, she told her cheerfully, because she'd had a date last night anyway. Only Warren seemed to have been aware and that was because he'd wanted to borrow some money. But he'd got it from the au pair, so that was all right, he told her, and she hung up feeling curiously disconsolate. It wasn't that she wanted them to be miserable without her, of course she didn't. But it would have been something if just one of them had missed her. Maybe Stanley had? But that was a thought not to be entertained.

When the time came for her to go into the box, it wasn't nearly as bad as she'd thought it would be. It was like waiting to go into hospital to have a baby, thinking what it would be like to have an injection for the pain, to feel the needle sliding into your arm, but when it came to it, you hardly felt a thing. And she walked through the court and up the steps of the witness box with quite a steady gait, pleased with herself for being so calm.

But then they gave her a card to hold and read and the book to hold and she discovered how much her hands were shaking.

She had to rest her wrists on the edge in front and make a real effort to get the words to come out of her mouth. 'I swear by almighty God –'

Almighty who? she thought as she picked her way laboriously through the oath. What do I know about almighty God, and what does almighty God know about all this nonsense? As if he hadn't better things to do. It's all so silly, so puerile. And a word she'd once heard an American friend use came into her mind. Cockamamie. A lot of cockamamie nonsense. She wasn't sure what it meant, but it sounded right.

Wooderson was quite conversational, asking her all sorts of questions she hardly understood, and sometimes she said, 'Yes,' and sometimes, 'No,' letting the responses come on their own, and he seemed happy enough, nodding his head so that the silly tails at the back of his wig bobbed and then looking down at his papers and questioning again.

But then he started to talk about Birgitta, and then it became clear in her mind. Then she remembered, and it was just a matter of helping all of them to remember too.

NOVEMBER 1970

'And any time you feel the pain, Hey Jude, refrain
Don't carry the world upon your shoulders,
For now you know it's a fool who plays it cool
By making his world a little colder . . . .'

She felt a little guilty because she quite liked the smell of the place. Most of her friends, the mothers she met at the school gates and the coffee mornings, the charity organizers hated hospitals and said so, loudly. They were so very dramatic about how much they'd gone through when they'd had their tonsils and appendixes done, how dreadfully their aunts and mothers had suffered when they'd had their hysterectomies, that she felt there was something shameful about enjoying the clean, crisp smell of disinfectant and floor polish and the bright, bustling cheerfulness of it all. Hospitals were such young places, full of bright-faced girls in fancy uniforms and bouncing young men in swinging white coats and it was they, as far as Bonnie was concerned, who set the pace, and made a hospital an interesting place to be. She never really thought about the patients, and

323

even if she had, she would have visualized them as smooth-browed pleased-with-themselves new mothers, for all her own experience had been as such a patient herself, or a visitor to one.

But this time was different. This time she sat in the stiff waiting room with its uncomfortable straight-backed armchairs in green uncut moquette and old copies of *Punch* and *Country Life* on the table and enjoyed the smell, but not the feeling of apprehension that was in her. Why on earth should Birgitta have sent for her? She'd known her for years, of course, but only in the most semi-detached sort of fashion. As far as Bonnie was concerned, Birgitta had just been a part of Hildegarde, a silent if bulky shadow who was sometimes there and sometimes wasn't, and made no impact either way.

A nurse appeared at the door, smiling and apparently friendly, but invincible behind her starched apron. She would give so much and no more; friendly surface sympathy, but no soft places anywhere to weep on.

'Mrs – ah – Maddern, is it? Miss Olaf's visitor?'

'Yes.' Bonnie stood up at once, obsequious and anxious, and was irritated by her own reaction. This girl wasn't much more than nineteen; why should a married woman and mother of four feel so inferior in her presence? The nurse took it for granted, however, and with another of her bright smiles led the way along the corridor to the ward, her rubber heels creaking against the wooden floor and her bottom waggling provocatively under her apron. Does she know she looks like that from behind? Bonnie wondered, and if she does, why waste it on me? Practice, probably –

Walking past the other patients was awful. They lay there, some asleep, some staring at her, some looking right through her, and she felt big and lumpy and felt her cheeks redden. She was grateful to reach Birgitta's bed, and sat down on the slippery wooden stool the nurse had pulled out from beneath it, fussing a little with her gloves and bag.

The nurse went away and left them there, cocooned behind a screen. A yellow screen with folds of fabric pulled tightly between the struts and she thought absurdly of the old films on late-night television. They used to show the credits over fabric folds like that, sometimes.

She had to look at Birgitta then. She couldn't stare at the screen all the time. So she turned her head.

Birgitta was lying tidily with her head in the exact centre of the pillow. Her hair had been tied with little pieces of white bandage into bunches on each side of her face, and that should have made her look younger, but it didn't. She looked old and heavy, the skin of her cheeks seeming to have been thrown up into ridges with sharply-shadowed valleys running alongside them.

Bonnie stared at her and tried to see the blank-faced girl she had known, the one with the down-turned sulky mouth and the blue eyes hiding behind swinging curtains of yellow hair, and couldn't. This was a woman, a tired old woman with narrow lips and dried out skin. But she couldn't be that old – thirty-five? Thirty-six? She was Hildegarde's friend, after all.

Birgitta seemed to feel the weight of Bonnie's stare and opened her eyes.

'Hildegarde,' she said but there was no real sound of pleasure in her voice. It was as though she knew it could not be Hildegarde.

'It's Bonnie, Birgitta. How are you?' Bonnie whispered and then was furious with herself. Stupid question to ask! She tried again.

'I hope you're beginning to feel better.'

'That is not possible,' Birgitta said, and her voice was louder now, and Bonnie looked over her shoulder apprehensively. Maybe the nurse would come and tell them off, because of making too much noise? But no one had noticed, and she realized then that the noise coming from beyond the screen was considerable; a clatter of cups and saucers and voices and footsteps and from further away the rattle of lift gates and the insistent shrieking of unanswered telephones.

'I'm sure it will be,' she said heartily then. 'Honestly, Birgitta, they're awfully clever these days, they'll make you right as rain in no time.' I sound like Auntie Fido, she thought. It's ridiculous how hospitals make you feel and behave.

'It does not matter,' Birgitta said and closed her eyes again.

Bonnie sat and looked at her doubtfully for a while and then said brightly, 'I was very surprised to hear you were ill, Birgitta. And that you wanted me to come. I mean, I'm glad you did, it's a pleasure to – well, you know what I mean. But I was surprised. Was it – is there anything you want me to do?'

Birgitta opened her eyes again and stared at her, unwinking. She looks like a newly-boiled kitten, Bonnie thought. Drooping and clean with most of the colour lost in the wash.

'I am going to die,' she said, and it was like an announcement on a radio. Polite, informative and quite unemotional.

'Oh, not at all, not at all!' Bonnie said, embarrassment washing over her in a great wave. If Birgitta had pulled off her clothes and danced nude on her bed she couldn't have made her feel worse.

'It is so,' Birgitta said. 'I know it. I wish it.'

'You wish it? Oh, come, Birgitta, you're just depressed – being ill makes people think the stupidest things, honestly it does. I remember, I had flu once and –'

'I have not flu. I injure myself with cutting. With scissors. Big ones.'

'Oh.' Bonnie put one of her gloves on, and took it off again. There seemed no answer to be made.

'I ask you to come because no one else will,' Birgitta said after a moment, and now her voice was quieter and Bonnie looked at her and could see for the first time just how ill she was. She was much thinner as well as looking much older and her colour was awful, a putty tinge that looked dead under the faint film of sweat.

'I'll tell Hildegarde – she'll come. She'll be very upset when she knows,' Bonnie said eagerly. 'Was that why you asked them to phone me? Because they couldn't get hold of Hildegarde? She's away, I expect – she's always away, you know how she is –'

'No.' Birgitta moved her head on the pillow for the first time, turning away from Bonnie and then back, and there was a dampness on the pillow where she had been. 'You must not call her. It is because of Hildegarde I am here. She did this to me.'

'What did you say?' Bonnie leaned forwards. She's getting delirious. Should I call the nurse? What will she do if I do call her?

'Hildegarde. She does not love me, she treats me as dirt, so I am dirt. I die for her, like a piece of dirt,' Birgitta said, and fixed her gaze on Bonnie's face. 'You will remember this, Bonnie. I die for her. You must remind her many times, afterwards.'

'Of course,' Bonnie said weakly and sat back, not knowing what else to do. She's out of her mind, she thought again. She's like one of those foreign films where people jabber and jabber and the sub-titles come up in silly stilted phrases no one would ever use talking to real people, not ever, and then the critics say how artistic it all is. It's all so silly, me being here listening to it.

'You understand, Bonnie?' Birgitta said. 'You understand what I tell you? I am dying here, and it is all because of Hildegarde –'

The nurse came then, to Bonnie's huge relief, and there was a bustle as she checked a tube that was running out of the side of the bed under the bedclothes down to a bottle on the floor and Bonnie averted her eyes and moved outside the screen and stood there fixing her gaze on a bunch of chrysanthemums that was on a table in the middle of the ward. She counted them; it was a good way to prevent herself from looking anywhere else.

The nurse came out after a while and Bonnie said softly, 'She's a bit delirious, isn't she?'

The nurse looked surprised. 'I don't think so.'

'She's saying she's dying.'

The nurse's brow smoothed, became blank. 'Oh, you'll have to talk to Sister. She's in the office. I can't give any information, I'm afraid. Do you want to talk to Sister? I'll see if she's got a moment to spare –'

'Yes, please,' Bonnie said. Anything rather than go behind those screens again.

Sister was small and fat and wispy, her hair sticking out on each side of her cap in a startled fashion.

'Miss Olaf? Oh, yes, poor Miss Olaf, she's poorly, you know, she's very poorly – are you a relation? We had to have next of kin, you know, and there was no one, she said, so we said, well, what about a friend, and she gave us a number but that was no good, it was an office, some dress firm, they said they knew nothing, and you know how it is with foreigners, though I grant you she seems to speak good enough English, and then she gave us your name and of course we called you. I'm glad you could come. Related, are you?'

Bonnie blinked at the tide of words, and shook her head. 'Just a friend – well not even that, actually – just someone I've known for many years –'

'Oh, dear, she needs her family at this time, but there, poor thing, no relations, what can you do?' There was a lilt in her voice and Bonnie thought, she's Welsh. That's what it is. She's Welsh. I wish I could go home.

'Anyway, Mrs Marsden – oh, sorry, Maddern, you say? – well, Mrs Maddern, she's poorly as I say, and I can't really say much more, what with one thing and another –'

'What happened to her?' Bonnie said. 'She said something about – she was on about scissors.'

'Oh, indeed, yes, it must have been dreadful, dreadful. As I got it from the Casualty staff she was brought in by one of our doctors who'd been in France and been called on the case – you know how these things are – and Miss Olaf is a dressmaker – is that right? – and she injured herself with these scissors, fell on them, I imagine – but I thought you would know, and so did doctor, but of course if you don't – well, anyway, I'm glad she's got someone, poor soul. Visiting times – they're here on this card, and if you need to come at a special time you can just ring up and I'll see what I can do if I'm not too busy –' she looked very stern for a moment, as though Bonnie were clamouring for the right to telephone every half hour '– and no children, of course, there's some that say it doesn't hurt them, but not on my ward, no children to visit no matter what, though dying is a bit different of course. Well, come and see me if you're worried about her – did you say you were a relation? – and we'll do all we can. I'm glad she's got someone to visit her, anyway –'

After that Bonnie felt she had to continue to visit, and so she did. She would bring flowers and chocolates, knowing quite well that Birgitta never looked at the former nor ate the latter but it seemed indecent to arrive empty-handed, and the nurses probably enjoyed them. And she would sit and listen to Birgitta talking. Not a lot. Just odd words, about designs that were put away, drawings that Hildegarde had kept, about the journeys to Florence and Oslo, and then again about Hildegarde.

Bonnie thought about trying to call Hildegarde but somehow she couldn't. It wasn't as though they were close any more. They hardly ever saw each other these days, and anyway, Bonnie was embarrassed. The whole situation was so peculiar, so uncomfortable, she couldn't decide what to do about it, and just let the days drift by.

And then Birgitta died. She did it one Sunday afternoon, suddenly. Bonnie had come to see her and was waiting outside with the other visitors, wondering how soon she could get away this time, because Stanley had gone with the children to his mother's, and wanted her there by four, and it was quite a run to Finchley from here, when there was a bustle, with nurses flying about and Sister rushing into the ward from her office, breathless and wispier than ever.

They let the other visitors in and then told her in suitably lowered tones that Miss Olaf had passed away, they were very sorry, she'd just seemed to slip downhill steadily. Did Mrs Maddern want to see her? Bonnie had hurriedly declined and felt guilty about that, too, but what was the point? It wasn't as though they had been friends, specially. It had been Hildegarde, not her, who had been her friend.

Once it was all over she pushed the whole business to the back of her mind and never thought about it again. Why it had all been so embarrassing she wasn't quite sure, but it had been, painfully so. It was a red-faced shrinking awkwardness that had filled her every time she had gone to the hospital and the most embarrassing thing of all had been her immediate sense of relief when poor Birgitta had at last died. That had been an awful way to feel – so awful that she never let herself think about it again. Until she had to.

The silence that was in the court filled her ears, drowning the echo of her own voice and she blinked and looked down at the bent be-wigged head below her. All the time she had been speaking, answering his questions, she had kept her eyes fixed on her own gloved hands clasped in front of her on the edge of the witness box, but now the silence forced her to look away from them and at the court.

Faces, faces, faces, faces. Rows of them, swindling away behind the man in the silly wig, all upturned, all looking at her. Horrible. She swallowed.

'Let me understand you clearly, Mrs Maddern,' Wooderson said, carefully. 'You are telling the court that Miss Olaf *told* you that she had deliberately injured herself and caused her own death?'

'I told you,' Bonnie said, and was very, very weary, suddenly.

How much longer would this wretched nagging have to go on? 'She said she'd injured herself with cutting. She said she was going to die. So I suppose – yes, that's what she said.'

'And she said that Miss Maurice – Miss Hildegarde Maurice had been the cause of her action?'

Bonnie closed her eyes for a moment and then opened them and looked down at Wooderson almost sternly. 'I *told* you,' she said, irritably, as though he were one of the children. 'Why do I have to keep on and on?'

'It is vital that the court fully understand this matter, Mrs Maddern,' Wooderson said smoothly. 'I am sure you understand the importance of your evidence at this juncture of this case. It is most essential that there should be no – ambiguities left in anyone's mind about what Miss Olaf actually did say.'

'Important?' she said. 'I suppose so.' But she didn't really understand, though she was trying to. So much had happened these last few days, this eternity of change and confusion. How could she understand?

'We will not keep you much longer, Mrs Maddern,' Wooderson was saying. 'Just a little more – ah – you say that there were times during those days leading up to her death when Miss Olaf told you that designs of hers had been taken by Miss Maurice?'

Bonnie looked at him and her face creased with puzzlement. 'Did I say that?'

'Indeed you did, Mrs Maddern. You said that she talked on several of your visits about – let me see now, I think the words you used were – "designs that were put away – drawings that Hildegarde had kept" –'

Her face cleared. 'Oh, yes. She said that. A few times. But she was ill, you know, and dying. I thought – I didn't pay a great deal of attention to it. She was so ill, you see.'

'Yes. Of course. Most understandable. One does not wish to – ah – distress a dying person. So you did not question her about what she meant?'

'Of course not!'

'No, of course not. But that is what she said?'

'Yes!' And she almost shouted it.

Wooderson smiled at her suddenly, a warm friendly smile, and sat down in a flurry of silk and she turned to go, but then the other one was on his feet, and it started all over again, the

330

questions, the yeses and noes, the tedious explaining, repeating and re-repeating the same dreary story. Poor Birgitta. Why did they have to drag her out of her grave like this? Horrible, horrible –

But even though she was trying to concentrate on what the man was asking her, and was trying to make sense of it all as best she could, she realised that the mood of the court had changed. They weren't listening with that pointed concentration with which they had been filled before. It was as though they had really heard all they wanted to hear, as though it was all over.

She caught sight of Hildegarde's face and then Hester's as she at last was allowed to come down out of the little witness box. Neither was looking at her. They just sat there with their faces blank, but Hester's eyes seemed to glitter a little. Just a little.

What have I said? Bonnie thought suddenly, as she made her way back to the rows of benches at the back. What have I said? I wish it all made sense. It's so long since I even thought about Birgitta. I can't even work out what it all means, all this that I've told them. What have I said?

I'm tired. I really am very tired. It's been a dreadful day.

33

The whole atmosphere was different this morning. Even the weather had changed, the pouring rain of the past few days giving way to a blustery freshness that sent scraps of paper whipping round people's ankles as they went hurrying along the pavements, leaning on the wind.

And it was not just the weather outside; the atmosphere in the court was different too. The gawpers were back, for a start. After the first day most of them had disappeared, but now the rain had gone and somehow they seemed to have found out that today would be the last day and full of drama, for there they were. Rows and rows of them, elderly women in floppy, rusty coats and round straw hats and depressed-looking men in stained ties and girls nudging each other with their shoulders and giggling behind their hands as they stared at the gowns and wigs coming and going, the solicitors, the plaintiff and the defendant.

The plaintiff and the defendant. Funny to think of them like that, and not as Hildegarde and Hester, Bonnie told herself. They aren't people any more; they're play pieces in the chess game of the court with different labels and different functions. Plaintiffs move like pawns, straight ahead, forging through the opposition, making all the front running. But defendants are like knights and can twist and turn around and jump over other's heads – she shook her head. Stupid! This was more important than a chess game.

Last night had been awful. She had gone home, of course. All afternoon, while the opposing counsel made their speeches to the jury she had known that she would have to, had chased the thought round and round in her head and found no escape. And there had been no comfort from anywhere, for Sammy had had to go to the hospital.

A message had reached him in the lunch break about a patient, and he'd told her in a distracted sort of way that he'd tried to get out of it, tried to insist his registrar coped, just this once, because normally he never delegated such cases but this one was different, but it couldn't be done, and would she be all right?

She had sent him away with some anger because his protectiveness, much as she valued it for what it told her about his feelings for her, was beginning to irk a good deal. What was it about her that made people want to look after her all the time? Was she so wet, so droopy, so dingy, that the only way people could love her was to shelter her from living? That was how Stanley had always seen her and she had colluded with him in that, God help her. She had been as guilty as he was, for she had played the helpless poor-me to perfection. But she wasn't going to let it happen again, not now she knew, not now she had the answer to the whys of her life.

Why am I so unhappy? Because of being married to Stanley. Why did I marry him? Because I was too frightened not to. Why am I angry with Sammy? Because he wants to protect me. And because he isn't here to do it.

Oh hell, she thought, and tried to push it all away, the memory of last night, the thinking about today, the impossible guessing about tomorrow. But it was no use. Last night had happened, was still hanging over her like a great thick cloud, and it couldn't be ignored.

They had been married for more than twenty years. More than twenty years of what they both would have called normal ups and downs. Twenty years of irritations and suppressed feelings on her side, twenty years of God knows what on his. They had flared up sometimes, bickered, sulked, but never had they argued the way they had last night.

He had been there, waiting, when she arrived. To find him at home at half past six had been threatening enough, but to find him sitting there just waiting for her, not doing something he wanted to do like reading the paper or sitting at his Louis-Quinze-style desk in the den with a pile of paper in front of him; that had been terrifying.

She had known there would be trouble, but she had not expected it to be quite so troubling. She had visualized herself standing there bending before the battering of his words and his blustering, had imagined he would be noisy, but no more than that.

Certainly she had not seen herself remonstrating with him

333

because of what had happened with Hester. How could she, feeling as she now did about Sammy? The fault now was hers for staying away all night at Fido's. That would be what caused the trouble. She had expected that.

What she had not expected was the storm. He had not shouted; he had shrieked. He had not been threatening, but had actually struck her.

That had been the most incredible part of all. He had come loping across the cream carpet as she came into the room, past the smoked-glass tables with his hands thrust out in front of him, and had swung his arm and hit her. It had been a glancing blow, barely connecting with her shoulder, but the effect on both of them had been stunning. Her amazement had boiled up into a vast rage, a helpless fury she could not contain and she had leapt at him and beat him with her fists, banging at his chest until her arms ached, and he had tried to hit her back, and she knew he was crying and was glad of it. Her amazement at that had been the greatest of all; to inflict pain, and not care? What had happened to her?

And then the children had been there, standing at the door at first and staring, and then pulling them apart; Daniel, his face wooden with the shock of it all, and Warren, crying like his father, and the girls had run, both of them, cool Sharon and sleepy Tracy, they had come and looked and shouted too and then run to their rooms and stayed there. Even the au pair had appeared, her face scared and agog with interest and then gone away, taking her coat and running to the house next door where her friend lived; and somewhere deep in the remnants of her housewife's mind Bonnie had thought drearily, great, now all the bloody neighbourhood will know, and won't they love it, every last bitch of them –

A dreadful, dreadful time. Even when they had cooled down and been left stranded breathlessly on the shores of their rage, trying to recover, it had been dreadful. Stanley sitting very straight and rigid in the armchair, with his face puffed and purplish and looking much, much older; herself sitting on the sofa, her coat still on, her head back against the creamy suede, trying to find words to pull them out of the hole, and totally failing, and the boys sitting there staring at them, embarrassed and frightened.

334

They'd talked at last, of course, but very little. She'd started it, telling the boys awkwardly that she was sorry, but things had changed, that she had decided the time had come to let them know that she could not live with them any more.

'Not you,' she'd said, hearing the dreariness of exhaustion in her own voice and hoping they could hear the concern for them that was there too. 'It isn't you, it isn't your father. He hasn't changed. It's me. I'm different. I can't stay here because I'm different. I love you both. I love all four of you, but I can't stay here with you. You have your own lives, your own needs, you'll have to choose, I suppose. Oh, God, I'm sorry, but there's nothing else I can do, I can't live here any more, it can't be –'

'No child of mine is ever going to be kept by that bastard Stermont,' Stanley had said thickly, and she knew she should be angry, but she couldn't.

'It's nothing to do with Sammy. This case, meeting him again – they happened at the time when I had changed. Coincidence, just coincidence. They made me think more, maybe, but it's nothing to do with Sammy. I'm not going to Sammy.'

'Don't tell lies, you stupid bitch!' he'd shrieked and then it had started again, because Daniel had shouted at his father, told him not to talk to his mother that way, and then they were all shouting. But again they'd quietened and she'd tried again, tried to help them see. That she had to go, that the time had come.

And all the while, underneath, she couldn't believe it. Couldn't believe that this was her, that this was Bonnie, that all the years of children and house and Stanley had petered out in this stupid, brawling pointlessness. Because it was all pointless. They couldn't understand what was happening any more than she could. All she knew was that the children were not children any more, except perhaps Tracy, and she had always been a separate sort of a child, more involved with Stanley and school than with her mother. None of them needed her any more, and it was all over. It had to be for them, because it was for her. She knew herself to be selfish, knew herself to be wrong, knew she was treating them abominably and that they were bewildered and unhappy, and she couldn't do anything about it. Because she was as bewildered as they were.

She had slept in Sharon's room, because the girls had decided to sleep together, after they had been called down and told what was happening, and this morning when she had woken after sleeping extraordinarily well (and that had made her ashamed of herself too) she had found they had all gone. Stanley to work, the children to school. Only the au pair was there in the kitchen to look at her sideways with a knowing, half-frightened look on her face. No notes, nothing from any of them. It was as though it were the most normal thing in the world for her to tell them all she was leaving, for the house seemed as it always did, smelling of furniture cream and Sharon's perfume and Stanley's cigars and food.

There had been nothing else to do but come to court. It had been true, everything she had said last night about the case and Sammy's reappearance being coincidental. She had been coming slowly to the boil anyway; the case had been at most another bit of coal on the fire under the pot. But coincidence or not, the case was important to her. It had revealed new facts to her about herself as well as about her sisters and her husband and somehow she had to see it through, right to the end.

So she dressed as carefully as ever, and took her car out of the garage and drove sedately to town and parked in the Brewer Street garage and went to court.

Sitting there now, she watched them all, watched the brisker movements of the court officials, listened to the buzz of excitement that was building, watched the people coming in, pushing along the spectators' benches. After a moment she put her bag down firmly beside her, to hold a place for Sammy, in case he came. She didn't want to be protected, in future she wouldn't be. No one was ever again going to steal her life from her that way. But she wanted him to be there, all the same. So she told herself, and sat there quietly composed, waiting.

He came just in time. The court was abuzz with expectation, and she pushed down her disappointment and stiffened her muscles to stand up as the judge came in, and then there he was, Sammy, beside her, as crumpled as he usually was, but looking different now.

She gave him a quick sideways look as they sat down, and whispered, 'All right?'

'He died,' he whispered back. 'I should have gone sooner – he died.'

'I'm sorry.'

'Don't apologize. It wasn't your fault –'

'That was commiseration –'

'Then I'm sorry, I thought –'

The court usher threw disapproving looks at them, and they subsided, and she moved closer to him. To hell with whether or not he thought she sought protection. That could be explained later. Right now she wanted physical contact, and as the sleeve of her coat moved against the sleeve of his, her skin crept with need for him. She moved away again, embarrassed at herself. Not now. Now was the time for judgements of past deeds, not thoughts of future ones. She must push her mind outwards, away from her own body, her own needs, out to the court. On one side sat her sister Hildegarde, the plaintiff. On the other her sister Hester, the defendant. Concentrate, concentrate on them, on what the judge was saying about them. That is what matters today. That is all you dare think about today.

The judge had already launched himself upon his summing-up, sitting back in his great chair, his body turned a little so that he could look down on the two rows of blank-faced people on the jury benches. They looked back at him, polite and glazed, and showed no sign of reaction to anything he said.

'– a confusing and difficult case for you, but you must not feel this to be particularly confusing and difficult. Cases involving defamation often are complex, not least because matters that do not appear at first to be germane to the matter in hand so often become part of the evidence set before the jury. It has been so in this case.

'There has been much talk not only of a television programme in which the words and actions complained of were said to have been uttered, but of loans and repayments, of the alleged thefts of designs of clothes, of an alleged case of suicide.

'It cannot have been easy for you to have picked out of the mass of evidence placed before you the salient points, to have selected those matters which were relevant, and those which were not. It is, therefore, now my task to help you to reach your verdict by pointing out to you those aspects of the evidence which appeared to me to be the most significant, those which you may prefer to discount, and those upon which you may choose to place extra credence. It is also my task to explain the

337

law to you, in a case such as this not an easy task, but which must be performed.

'It may have seemed to you, ladies and gentlemen of the jury, that there was at times a good deal of spleen being vented between the parties. That perhaps is inevitably so in a court in which defamation of character has been alleged. But you may have felt that there was more spleen than might be accounted for by the events related to you here. You may feel that although the persons who here confront each other are most closely related, there is long-standing animosity between them that has been expressed in unnecessarily strong words about the alleged defamation.

'You may indeed feel that the parties in this case have used this court to discharge years of resentment over matters other than those before you. I cannot direct you as to that – you as sensible men and women must decide for yourselves whether the court has been used in such a disagreeable manner.

'It may help you to so decide if you consider the matter of the lapse of time between the television programme that was complained of – 1972 – and the case before you. It has taken the plaintiff some considerable period to come to the conclusion that she has been defamed. Close on four years elapsed before she issued her writ, and the wheels of justice were put in motion, culminating in this case before you today, fully six years after the alleged defamation. But, I must remind you that this aspect of the matter was dealt with in some depth in the evidence. Miss Maurice told the court that at first, distressed as she was, she hoped the defamation would be ignored and that all could be forgotten, if not forgiven. But, she said, over the succeeding years, she noticed a diminution in her success, noticed that some of her sales had decreased and decided that the cause of this diminution was the defamation uttered by her sister. Hence the bringing before you of this case.

'However, as the defence counsel has pointed out, this belief of Miss Hildegarde Maurice's must be considered against the background of the economic situation that has prevailed in these islands during recent years. Did Miss Hildegarde Maurice experience a diminution of her business success because everyone around her did – because the whole of industry was in recession – or because of one television programme shown in

338

1972? That is her contention, and it must be considered by you very carefully.

'Your deliberations may be further aided when you consider the matter of Miss Hester Morrissey's loan to her sister, and the manner in which it was later repaid by Miss Maurice's agent, Mr Bremner. You may feel that there were aspects of this transaction that were unedifying, but you are not here to consider either that or the moral behaviour of the parties involved. You are here to consider the allegation of defamation of character and here the evidence of Mrs Bonnie Maddern must be considered most carefully.

'The question you must ask yourselves, ladies and gentlemen of the jury, is whether that evidence in fact added anything to your grasp of the events that took place.

'You may feel you have no cause to doubt Mrs Maddern's word. You may feel she appeared to be a most creditable witness and one who displayed no – ah – hint of any moral turpitude. What she told you, you might think, can be accepted as an accurate account of what Miss Olaf said and did at the time of her death. However, we cannot know whether Miss Olaf herself spoke or acted misleadingly to Mrs Maddern. It is often said that a person's dying statement must be accepted as being totally truthful, but there is no basis in fact for such a statement. A person may not be aware of impending death when speaking. Alternatively, even when such knowledge is there, a person may be activated by malice, or mistaken in her assumptions or her perception of the truth, particularly when strong emotions are involved.

'Altogether, ladies and gentlemen of the jury, I feel it is my duty to advise you to scrutinize the evidence given by Mrs Maddern very cautiously indeed, taking into account the character of Miss Olaf, as far as you can assess it from what you have heard here in this court about her.

'Of course, the question of the alleged appropriation by Miss Maurice of Miss Olaf's designs, while highly germane to the question of the alleged defamation, is not the only matter that has been brought before this court. As I have already said, your deliberations may be further aided when you consider the matter of Miss Hester Morrissey's loan to her sister. You must ask yourselves whether the fact that Miss Morrissey was being paid

339

sizeable sums from Miss Maurice's business spurred the latter's memory of the television programme of 1972 and so suggested to her a way of ridding herself of an unwanted financial burden. This was the suggestion made by Miss Hester Morrissey and one that you must therefore consider seriously.

'Members of the jury, all the issues of fact are for you to decide, but you must take the law from me and I will now direct you as to that law as it applies in this case . . . .'

The voice went on and now she lost it. She listened, watched his lips move, felt the words he was uttering go into her ears, but she heard nothing. Words, words, words, but no sense. It was as though she had heard enough, as though somewhere in her brain a switch had been thrown to protect her from any more. She was insulated now, shut away cosily from all that was happening around her, and could sit in drowsy comfort and let it just happen.

It lasted a long time, that sensation. It seemed like weeks, like a lifetime, but was in fact little more than an hour. And then she was in touch again. The switch was thrown the other way and she could hear sense in the words, could feel the tension around her, was no longer drowsy.

'Come on,' Sammy said, a little impatiently. 'They won't be back for hours. This won't be one of your snap decisions. Do come *on*, Bonnie –'

'What?' she said, a little sleepily, looking up at him, for he was standing up, and was holding out one hand towards her.

'The jury are out. I doubt if they'll be back much before this afternoon, if then. We'll go and have some coffee, talk, plan – there's a lot for us to plan, isn't there?'

'Yes,' she said, and stood up. 'A lot.'

34

Outside in the big hallway David Spero watched them go, the gawpers and the counsel, the ushers and the clerks and then at last they came. Hester and that damned fat man who was with her all the time the first day; who was he? Why was he here?

The hell with him. Today she must stop and talk to him, surely today she must remember him. He'd let her get away from him before, but not this time.

She looked different now. That first day she'd seemed relaxed and nonchalant, but now her face seemed hard and even a bit lined. Looking at her it wasn't so easy to see the girl who had stood there with him in the dusty dressing room behind the stage of the Hackney Settlement. He'd seen her clearly the first day, but now she was shadowy, different, and he felt a stab of uncertainty.

That, of course, was his undoing. He told himself that lots of times afterwards, whenever he thought of her, in fact. That it hadn't been due to malice on her part. It had been his own fault for standing there and wavering, instead of being incisive. How could she remember him when he seemed to be just like all the other gawpers, the hangers-on, the starers at famous faces?

He moved forwards and then took a step back again as she came level with him and he said quickly, 'Hester,' and she looked up at him briefly, her eyes flicking blankly over his face.

'Hester – I tried to talk to you the first day – it's great to see you – it really is –'

'Christ!' she said, and whirled away from him, dodging behind the fat man so that he stood between David and herself. 'These bloody ghouls – can't they ever leave me alone? Get rid of him, Willy, for Christ's sake, get rid of him.'

'Go on,' the fat man said officiously, and pushed against David. 'You heard the lady. She wants no nagging now. Unless you make yourself scarce, then I get that policeman there to do it for you, understand? Come on, Hester – we'll find somewhere well away from these ghastly people.'

'Hester,' David said again, almost despairingly, but it was no use. She was gone, walking away swiftly down the hall, leaving him there staring after her, knowing the only chance he'd ever had of getting her back again had gone. He'd lost her for ever, the one and only real love of his life. He'd lost her.

He had lunch alone, staring into his plate and remembering the many times he'd spent with her, the way she had said she loved him, all those years ago. Somewhere deep in his mind a part of him admitted it wasn't true, that there had never been anything there at all, that he was remembering only his hopeful fantasies. But he ignored that. Without his memories what else would he have? So he spent the lunch hour assiduously remembering.

Sylvia and Fido decided to lunch at the same place they had used every other day the case had been on. It was a rather dingy hamburger bar, but they did a nice omelette, and the tea was good and strong, the way Fido liked it. They ate carefully, taking their time, ignoring the little queue of resentful office-workers staring at them, waiting for tables.

'How long, do you think?' Fido said after a while. 'Will it be a lot longer, Sylvia? I don't think I can stand it much longer, really I don't. My hands are aching something dreadful, really dreadful. Honestly, 'f I'd 'a known it was going to take so long I'd never have come in the first place. I'd 'a had nothing to do with it, I'd 'a made you come on your own, honestly I would. I mean, I know you needed me, dear. I know I had to be here for you to give you strength for giving evidence, but I'm not a well woman, Sylvia, really I'm not. I can't stand much more. What with all this, and then Bonnie coming the other night – it's a lot to ask of a sick woman. A lot to ask.'

Sylvia felt her jaw tighten, and said nothing. There was nothing to be said to Fido, ever. She saw the world and its events through her own distorting mirror, so that even her own attempts to get her to understand truth were twisted, turned back on themselves. That she could forget her eagerness to come to this case as soon as she had heard of it; that she could forget the bright-eyed lasciviousness with which she had listened to them all, Stanley and Mel and Hester – but there; Fido always did remember only what suited her. It was the only way she could live.

'Who do you want to win?' Fido said after a while, and looked up at her, her eyes sharp and knowing, and Sylvia looked back, her face as blank as she could make it.

'Whichever is in the right,' she said, and bent her head and stirred her tea.

Fido tittered suddenly, a silly little sound against the rattle of dishes and the hissing of steam from the counter where the coffee machines were. 'Go on with you,' she said. 'They're both in the wrong as much as they're in the right. There isn't a ha'penny to choose between 'em.'

Sometimes, Sylvia thought, looking up at the gaunt old woman and then away again, sometimes she lets the truth get out after all. Which is more than I ever do. Because if I ever allowed myself to think about the truth about Hildegarde, and about me, I don't think I could go on. I won't think about it, I won't. I never have, and I won't now.

'Will you have some more tea, Fido? No? I think perhaps we ought to go, dear. Those girls over there have been waiting ages for a table, poor things –'

'So sue me,' Hildegarde said, and laughed. 'I like that. So sue me. You've got a bit of experience now, haven't you? Sue me, and see where it'll get you. About as far as this case will get her.'

'You're so damned sure you'll win, aren't you?' Mel said, his face white with fear and anger. 'So fucking sure – so what'll you do if you lose, eh? What'll you do?'

She leaned back in her chair and took a long, slow sip from her glass, staring at him over the edge. Around them the pub rattled with noise and the pop music from the juke box in the corner ground the air to an almost painful beating rhythm.

'I won't lose,' she said confidently. 'I can't. Matter of simple law. They defamed me, they lose. *You* get away with it, of course, as far as the court's concerned. You're the bastard who made the whole thing happen, you're the bastard who set me up, and you're the bastard who screwed me for all that money and gave it to Hester. That ought to get you fifty years hard, as far as I'm concerned. Well, maybe the court can't do what ought to be done, but I can. You're out, ducks. Out on your thick ear. Go starve baby. You're on your own now. From here on in, Hildegarde Maurice is a one-man business. *Me*.'

'You can't do it to me,' he said again, as he'd been saying for the past hour. 'You can't do it to me. Not after all these years.'

'Just watch me,' she said with a high good humour, and finished her drink. 'You'll see what I can do. And enjoy doing, what's more.'

'But –'

'Oh, go away, will you? You're boring me –' She looked up and, across on the other side of the pub, Ken and the rest of the TV team caught her eye at last and Ken waved a hand. 'Pay for the drinks, Mel. It's the last time you ever will so make the most of it.' And she went sauntering through the lunch-time crowds, leaving him staring at her back. He felt very cold.

'Where will you go if you don't come to me?' Sammy said.

'A hotel for a while. I thought the coast, Bournemouth, maybe. I need time, Sammy. Over twenty years – it takes a lot of sorting-out. And I can't think of anything about the future while there's so much to be thought about the children – about Stanley.'

'I see.' He sat on the bench beside her with his legs stuck out in front of him and contemplated his feet. His shoes needed cleaning. He really ought to learn to look a bit more like Professor Sampson Stermont, a little less like a scruffy East End kid. 'I see.'

'I hope you do. I need you to see what I mean,' she said.

They sat in silence then, watching the pigeons strutting after each other, the hens scuttling, pretending unawareness, the cocks ruffling their feathers self-importantly as they trailed their ardour in the dust. Around them the Temple Gardens lay chilly in the thin March sunshine, the buildings lifted themselves complacently above the still-naked trees. He looked up at them, at the windows, blank and dull like dead men's eyes.

'Barristers,' he said. 'Every one of those bloody windows hides a barrister, you know that? I hate the law. All those people dressing up to make money out of other people's miseries. It's sick.'

344

'It isn't the law that's sick,' she said. 'It's the people who need it.'

She got to her feet then, and stood looking down at him. 'I'm not coming back to court, Sammy. I imagine the verdict will be published. I'll hear about it, won't I? I don't think I could be there watching them actually hearing it. I'm going to go now.'

He looked up at her, standing there in her neat Hildegarde suit with her Gucci shoes and the good leather bag and the brown silk scarf. Sumptuous, he thought. That's how she looks. Sump-tuous.

'You're sure?'

'I'm sure.'

'When will I see you again?'

'I don't know. How can I know? I told you – there's so much to sort out. The –'

'Yes, I know. The children, Stanley.'

'Yes.'

She stood for another moment, wavering a little, wanting so much to stay with him, to go home with him, to crawl inside him and be safe again, to be cared for properly this time, to be protected.

'I must go,' she said, a little more loudly. 'I really must –'

'I'm not stopping you.'

'I know. I just want you to understand.'

'I'm trying to.'

'Will you be all right?'

He lifted his eyebrows at that, sitting there looking up at her over his arms crossed in front of him, with his raincoat bundled untidily over them. 'All right? Of course I will.'

'All right then – I'll see you –'

'Bonnie – will you write? Tell me where you are? I can write letters to you, can't I?'

'Oh, yes,' she said fervently. 'Oh, yes. Please do. I'll wait for them, honestly I will.'

And then she really did go, walking away along the pavement with little swift steps, her shoes clacking against the stones.

And then, as she reached the corner where the road crossed Temple Gardens, she hesitated and then turned and came back.

'Sammy,' she said a little breathlessly, as soon as she was in earshot again. 'Sammy, when you write, will you remember to use my proper name?'

'Your proper name?'

'Yes. I'm Bertha Morris. Not Bonnie, Bertha. Don't forget.'

He smiled then, for the first time that day. 'I won't forget.'

MARCH 1978

'I can see clearly now the rain has gone,
I can see all life's problems slip away . . . .'

'Good evening. This is the nine o'clock news brought to you by City Television. In the Law Courts today the defamation case brought by Miss Hildegarde Maurice, the international dress designer against her sister Miss Hester Morrissey of City Television, following the broadcast of a programme in the *Spectrum* series in 1972, ended after a five-hour absence by the jury to consider their verdict. The jury found for Miss Maurice, but said they could award her only one penny damages. The judge said that he felt it would be appropriate to make no order as to costs, expected to be in the region of eight thousand pounds. This, of course, means that neither side won. To comment on the case we have in our news studio this evening Miss Hester Morrissey to give us her reactions to the verdict. But first, Ken Adams, our roving reporter, spoke to Miss Hildegarde Maurice earlier today. Here is his filmed report –'

Acknowledgements

The publishers would like to thank the following for their kind permission to reproduce quotations from their songs:

Page   9 *When You Wish Upon A Star*, from the film of *Pinocchio*, music by Leigh Harline, words by Ned Washington, © Irving Berlin Inc (now Bourne Inc) Chappell Morris Ltd.

20 Big Three Music Ltd.

27 *Lovesick Blues* by Cliff Friend and Irving Mills © 1922 Lawrence Wright Music Co Ltd.

42 *Do You Love Me* by Harry Ruby, © 1946 Gregman, Vocco & Conn Inc. reproduced by permission of Chappell Morris Ltd.

51 © 1951 Francis Day & Hunter Ltd. Reproduced by permission of EMI Music Publishing Ltd, 138–140 Charing Cross Road, London WC2H 0LD.

63 *Don't Laugh At Me* by June Tremaine and Norman Wisdom © 1954 Northern Songs Ltd.

72 *My Heart Cries For You* Music and words Percy Faith and Carl Sigman © 1950 Massey Music Co. Inc. & Bedford Music Co, Chappell Morris Ltd.

83 The administrators of Carlin Music Corporation.

92 © 1951 Francis Day & Hunter Ltd, reproduced by permission of EMI Music Publishing Ltd.

101 © 1937 Francis Day & Hunter Ltd, reproduced by permission of EMI Music Publishing Ltd.

112 *Don't Let the Stars Get In Your Eyes* Music and words by Slim Willet © 1952 Four Stars Sales Co., Chappell Morris Ltd.

347